Catching Cassidy

HARBORSIDE NIGHTS
Book One

"Catching Cassidy was laugh out loud funny,
heartwarming, sexy, and hands down one of my
favorite reads so far this year!"
—#1 NYT Bestselling Author of *The Bet*,
Rachel Van Dyken

MELISSA FOSTER

ISBN-13: 978-1-941480-07-6
ISBN-10: 1-941480-07-1

CATCHING CASSIDY

Cover Design: Elizabeth Mackey

WORLD LITERARY PRESS
PRINTED IN THE UNITED STATES OF AMERICA

A Note to Readers

When I met the characters of Harborside Nights, I couldn't wait to write their stories and bring them to you. This group of friends has known one another for years as "summer" friends, and they've come together after college to build their lives. They're sexy, hot, and evocatively real, and you'll read about all of their experiences—the heart-wrenching moments, the celebrations, and everything in between. I hope you fall in love with this group of friends, too.

Catching Cassidy is the first book in the Harborside Nights series. If you enjoy this series, you might enjoy my sizzling-hot contemporary romance series, Love in Bloom, featuring the Snow Sisters, The Bradens, The Remingtons, and the Seaside Summers group of friends. While each of my series books may be read as stand-alone novels, for even more enjoyment, you may want to read them in series order.

Melissa Foster

Harborside Nights is dedicated to my mother
For raising me to be open-minded

Chapter One

~Wyatt~

"HEY, ARMY! GET the hell over here!" my buddy Carter Young yells from the corner, where he's filling his plastic cup with beer. Some girl's running her fingers through his blond hair with a fuck-me look in her eyes.

I push from the couch and look at my watch, wondering where the hell Cassidy is. It's Saturday night at eight o'clock, and my buddy Carter's graduation party is in full swing. I can hardly believe I'm finally out of college. Four years felt like forever when I was going to classes, playing football, and trying to keep my head above water with my grades so my parents would stay off my ass. Looking back, even now, on the day we graduated, it seems like four years went by really fast. Strange how that happens.

Carter widens his glassy blue eyes and hollers again. "Army! Come on, man. It's our last party. Get your ass over here and toast with me."

I've known Carter since we were freshmen, when we were eyeing the same girl in one of our classes. I can't even remember which class it was, but I remember what he said to me on the way out the door that morning. *I'll flip you for her.* The son of a bitch won the coin toss, and we've been each other's wingmen ever since. Carter calls me Army because he says Wyatt Armstrong is a pussy name. Girls hear *Army* and they're all over me. Well, except Cassidy. She calls me Wyatt, always has. I pick up a plastic cup and hold it under the nozzle, then check my watch again while he pumps the keg. *Come on, Cass. Get here already.*

"To freedom!" He crashes his cup into mine, and our beers splash everywhere before we tip our heads back and drain them. "Dude, stop looking at your phone. I've watched you pine over Cassidy for four years. She'll get here when she gets here."

"*Pine,* my ass. She's just a friend and you know it. I swear, if that fucker screws Cassidy over again and she misses this party, I'm going to kick the shit out of him." My best friend, Cassidy Lowell, has been dating a douche bag for two years. Kyle Warner. Even his name is douchey. He graduated a year ago and works at a furniture store. Loser.

"Dude, fess up. You've banged her, right?" Carter flashes one of his come-on-dude-you-can-trust-me smiles.

"No, man. I told you. You don't bone a girl you've known since you were five." Cassidy's too good of a friend to sleep with. I've known her since we were kids, when she moved into my neighborhood in

Connecticut. Her sucky parents are never home, so over the years she's stayed at our house probably more than her own. Hell, the truth is, we've slept together many times. The key word being *slept*, as in not fooled around.

"That's fucked up." Carter stumbles backward and bumps into a hot blonde. "Hey, babe. Lemme ask you something," he says with his face so close to hers he might as well kiss her. He lifts his cup and points his index finger at me. Carter's blond hair is a shade lighter than the girl's. He played football for two years, until he blew out his knee. But he's still ripped, and the way the girl's eyeing him, she loves it.

He wraps his arm around her neck and I check my watch again. *Goddamn it, Cassidy.* I know Kyle's screwing her over again. He's always forgetting to pick her up or showing up late, but Cass is a girl, and they can be really stupid when it comes to guys. She forgives him and forgets, until the next time he treats her like she doesn't matter. I'd like to punch his lights out, but Cass gets pissed when I tell her that.

"If you were him"—Carter points to me again— "and you had a hot best friend, would you do her?"

The blonde smiles as she drags her eyes down my body. Yeah, I'm ripped, too. What twenty-two-year-old guy who likes getting laid isn't?

She nods. "Oh, yeah, and I'm sure your BFF is dying for it. I know I would be."

She steps closer to me as I pull out my phone and text Cassidy.

Where are you?

The blonde nuzzles against my neck and presses

her tits to my chest as Cassidy's response comes through. Blondie has no idea that there's no competition between the girl who wants to get laid and the one being stood up by an asshole.

He's late.

"No shit," I grumble, then text her back. *I'll come get you.*

The blonde pushes the phone down to my side and presses her lips to mine. I'm right there with her, sucking the beer from her tongue as she grinds her hips against mine, getting me hard as a rock.

My phone vibrates again. I tear my lips away and read Cassidy's text.

He'll get pissed.

No shit he'll get pissed. The douche hates me, as he should, because when you treat my best friend like shit, you're in my sights, and when it comes to Cassidy, my trigger finger is itchy. I text her back. *I'll send Delilah.* Delilah's my twin sister. She's standing by the back door with her fake boyfriend, Frank, looking bored to tears. Our parents are so conservative they've freaked her out about coming out, so she pretends to be straight, and Frank is her beard. I told her a hundred times that college is the time to let it all out and explore. Experiment. But she's convinced they'll somehow get wind of whatever she does, so she's never taken the chance. There's no arguing with Delilah when she's set her mind on something, and it pisses me off that our parents have this hold over her. Like it's any of their business who she wants to be with. I know they would never accept the lifestyle she wants. Delilah's decision to hide her sexual preferences may not be what *I* think is best for her, but I'll support her no matter what. The truth is, sometimes parents suck.

Blondie pushes the phone down again and kisses my neck as the phone vibrates.

"Are you going to keep texting?" she snaps.

"Yeah. Are you going to keep sucking my neck like a vampire?" I don't have time for this shit. Girls are a dime a dozen, but Cassidy's been screwed over for too long, and I'm getting more pissed by the second.

I read her text. *Thinking...*

What the fuck? *Thinking?* I grab the blonde's arm and turn her toward Carter. She wraps her arms around his neck. No one ever said college girls were discriminatory.

"Carter, take care of her, would ya?"

Two sheets to the wind, Carter sways as he asks, "Where you goin'?"

"Picking up Cass. I'll catch you later. Make sure you get a ride home. I don't want to read about your ass splattered all over the road." *See, Dad? I do listen.* I shove my hand in my pocket and whip out my keys. Cassidy can't miss this graduation party. This is supposed to be our big celebration, the end to four years of studying and all the bullshit that goes along with it. We made it. We graduated! We even made it through the boring ceremony. She's earned it. My parents made me and Delilah go to the ceremony. I didn't want to walk the stage, but they paid for college, so...They made a big deal out of graduation and even invited Uncle Tim, my father's best friend, who handles the bookkeeping for the Taproom, the bar my parents own in Harborside, Massachusetts. Even though he's not a blood relative, we've always called him *Uncle* Tim. I guess it's fitting that he'd be at our graduation. He's known us since we were born, and he went to our high school graduations. And if that wasn't bad enough, they brought Aunt Lara and made her suffer through it, too.

After the ceremony my father reiterated the same twenty-minute diatribe about driving drunk that he's given us a million times before, only this time it was complete with statistics about the number of kids who die after graduation parties. Give me a break. I was so relieved when they finally left to drive back to Connecticut an hour ago. I've got all night to celebrate with no driving in sight until tomorrow. My shit's already packed, and tomorrow morning, after I nurse a hangover for a few hours, Delilah and I will head home safe and sound.

I text Cassidy again. *Stay put. We're coming to get you.*

~Cassidy~

I'M SO MAD by the time Wyatt picks me up, I can barely see straight. I slide into the backseat and growl. Yes, growl.

"Thanks, you guys," I manage. I reach for my seat belt, trying to avoid Wyatt's gorgeous green eyes, which are currently filled with venom. He hates Kyle, and right this very second, I don't blame him.

"What's his excuse this time?" Wyatt asks as I click my seat belt into place.

I shrug. "Working late. He has my apartment key.

Would you mind if we swing by to pick it up?"

Delilah turns around, tucks her blond hair behind her ear, and looks at me like she feels sorry for me. Her green eyes are almost as pretty as Wyatt's, only his are a shade darker, and when I look at him, there's always mischief playing behind his eyes. Delilah's are...I don't know...more innocent, I guess.

"Why does he have your key?" Delilah asks. "I thought he had his own." She's tall and thin and so naturally pretty I'm sure girls want to hate her when they first meet her, but the minute she speaks, you just can't. She's too sweet and genuinely caring to hate.

"He lost it, so I gave him mine. He was supposed to come get me, remember?" It's a lie, and I hate lying to them. He took my key because he's crazy jealous. Hopefully, I can just run inside and Kyle won't ask about how I got there, but I need my key. Kyle thinks if I don't have my key, I won't leave the apartment because I won't be able to get back in. He's taken my key before, and I usually just roll my eyes at his stupidity. I mean, I get it. His dad cheated on his mom, so he has trust issues, but come on. I'd never cheat. I've never cheated on a boyfriend in my life, not that I've had many boyfriends to cheat on.

Ten minutes later Wyatt parks behind the furniture store where Kyle works. "Cass, you sure he's working? The lights are off."

When he says my name, it's softer, buffered from the tension I see in the bunching of his shoulder muscles.

"Yeah, they closed at eight, and his car is right there, so he's probably just clocking out." I unhook my seat belt and stare at the dark building, glad Wyatt is with me because for some reason, it looks dark and eerie.

"I'll go with you." Wyatt opens his door. "I'll be right back, Dee."

I get out of the car thinking about how much I love when he calls Delilah *Dee*. They are really close, and given their strict parents, I have no idea how they both turned out so awesome. Their parents love them so much, they do *too* much for them, whereas I think my parents love me, but I've always felt kind of like a third wheel. Wyatt's parents called and checked on them before practically every test and afterward to check on their grades. It drove Wyatt and Delilah nuts, and while I get it, it sure did magnify how hands-off my parents are. They make sure I have what I need, but that's about it. Who wouldn't feel like an imposition or an afterthought with parents who went to Europe for the summer and missed their only daughter's college graduation? I guess I'm used to it, so it doesn't really bother me as much as it did when I was younger. They're also not openly affectionate toward me, which might be why, after two years, I still haven't told Kyle that I love him, even though he tells me all the time. Or maybe it's because I'm not really sure what being in love feels like. I know it's different from just loving someone, but I've never felt the kind of passion I see in movies—or the love I see my parents lavish on each other. It's like my parents use up their love on each other and there's not much left for me.

We walk across the dark lot, and I notice Wyatt doing that thing he does, where he scans the area like he's Chuck Norris readying for a battle. He's always done it. Even as a kid. Actually, maybe that's a throwback from his parents always telling him and Delilah to be careful of...well, of everything under the sun.

"We should use the delivery door. He always tells me to go to that one." I knock on the heavy metal door, and we stand there in the dark listening to each other breathe for what feels like half an hour. I knock again and stuff my hands into the pockets of my hoodie.

"Sure he's here?" Wyatt asks again.

I nod toward his car at the other end of the parking lot.

"Why do you let him get away with this shit?"

The muscles in Wyatt's jaw bunch as he clenches his teeth. I know how much he hates Kyle. It's not like he tries to hide it, but Kyle has redeeming qualities. When he's with me and it's just the two of us, he's affectionate and caring. He can be funny and he's really smart, which I admire. When we go out together, he's attentive and fun, even if mildly possessive. I know he loves me. He just gets jealous, especially of Wyatt because we're so close. Thinking about it makes my stomach hurt. When Kyle sees me with Wyatt, he'll bitch a blue streak. Not in front of Wyatt, of course, but I'll hear about it later for sure.

Wyatt shifts his eyes to Kyle's car, then pulls on the metal door, which swings open and surprises us both. The inside of the building is dark. Wyatt shrugs and waves a hand in front of him, like I should go on in.

"Will you wait for me here?" I wish I knew where

the lights were.

"I'm coming with you, Cass."

He steps inside, and I press my hand against his chest, feeling the wall of muscles beneath my palm. Wyatt's built like one of those models you see in Abercrombie ads, six foot two of sculpted, tanned perfection. As we're having our little stare-off in the doorway of the furniture store, it occurs to me for the hundredth time that it's no wonder Kyle is jealous of him. Wyatt is totally hot. But he's also my best friend, and we've never crossed any lines between friendship and something more. I've never really gotten that flirty vibe from Wyatt before, at least not the same vibes he gives off to the girls he sleeps with—those vibes that heat up a whole room and steal my breath just thinking about how lucky those girls are.

"Please wait here." I don't feel like dealing with Kyle's jealousy.

He pushes past me with a *yeah, right* narrow-eyed stare. "Let you go into a dark building by yourself? I don't think so. Come on. Let's find him and get the hell out of here. We have a party to go to."

I roll my eyes, because as much as I want to spend my last night with Wyatt and Delilah before I take off with Kyle to spend the summer with his parents on Martha's Vineyard, I'm not really in the mood for a party. And as we walk down the dark hallway, I get more irritated by the second. I hate that Wyatt has to rescue me again after Kyle left me hanging. Wyatt never seems to mind, but still.

"Where is he?" Wyatt snaps. "And where are the lights in this place?"

"I don't know. Maybe he's in the office." I point down a hall and hear a loud bang. I gasp and grab Wyatt, who does what he always does when I'm startled, or when I'm sad, or when I want to talk about something important. He drapes an arm over my shoulder.

"Really, Cass? It's a furniture store. They're probably moving furniture." He leads me down the hall and slows as the noises become clearer.

My stomach clenches tight. "Is that...?" Moaning and sex sounds? I stand there for a second, my jaw hanging open and my heart slamming against my chest.

"Stay here." Wyatt stalks ahead of me with his hands fisting at his sides, and all I can think about is that Kyle will get pissed if employees are fooling around in the store. He's so careful about making sure everything is perfect, staying late for inventory when other employees don't show up and setting up the displays by himself in the evenings so no one else has to miss out on studying or late classes. I guess he won't have to worry about that now that school is over.

Wyatt stops in front of the stockroom door and holds a hand up for me to stay put. As Wyatt pushes the door open, it dawns on me that Kyle hasn't returned my last text. I pull out my phone and scroll through my texts. I must not have felt the text come through.

Hey, babe. Gonna be late. Shipment just came in.

That's when I recognize the sounds and realize who's behind that closed door. With my heart in my

11

throat, I reach for Wyatt as he steps into the room and flips on a light.

"What the fuck?" Kyle yells.

Wyatt turns and grabs me by the shoulders before I can get into the room.

"Go out to the car, Cassidy." Wyatt's face ices over and just as quickly turns threatening, which I know is not meant for me but for Kyle.

"No. What's he doing?" I push against Wyatt, but he's too strong, and he pushes me backward.

"Fucking Wyatt." Kyle sounds pissed and out of breath.

"You don't need to see this. Go to Delilah." Wyatt pushes me out of the doorway and into Delilah's arms. I didn't even know she'd come into the building. I can't stop the tears from escaping or my limbs from fighting as I try to get into the room. "Kyle!"

"Fuck. It's not what it looks like," Kyle hollers.

Delilah peers around Wyatt's shoulders. "Oh my God."

"Take her out, Dee. Now." Wyatt's eyes narrow. His tone leaves no room for negotiation.

I twist out of her arms and burst past Wyatt into the stockroom. Oh my God. I can't breathe. Kyle and some whore are scrambling to put on their clothes.

"Who are these people?" the girl screeches in an annoyingly high voice as she wiggles into a skirt. *Bitch.*

I'm frozen in place, shaking all over, trying to process what I'm seeing. Somewhere deep in my head a spear is tearing into the knowledge that the guy I gave my virginity to, the guy I trusted with my heart, the guy I spent the last two years of my life with, is *fucking* some other girl like I don't exist.

"Dee, take her outside. Now." As Wyatt grabs my shoulders and guides me back into Delilah's arms, my eyes lock on Kyle. His face is beet-red, but it isn't his face that makes me feel like I might puke. It's his limp dick, sheathed in a condom.

"You fucker! You asshole! How could you—" I can barely hear myself scream past the rush of blood in my ears. Everything seems like it's in slow motion. Kyle's mouth is moving, but I can't hear a word. Wyatt is in front of me, holding me back. Kyle spreads his arms out like he can somehow explain it all away. My legs turn to rubber, and I feel Delilah dragging me backward. How can this be happening? After two years, how? Why?

Wyatt turns on Kyle. I've never seen him so angry—fists flexing, muscles burgeoning, ready to attack. The last thing I see as Delilah drags me out of the room is Wyatt's massive arm coiling back and the shocked expression on Kyle's face. I hear a bunch of noises as we hurry down the hallway. The bitch is screaming, the guys are shouting, but it is all a blur, and when Delilah opens the door and the night air hits me, I collapse into her arms, yelling against her chest.

"He's an asshole!"

Delilah rubs my back, trying to soothe me. It doesn't help.

"Forget him. He's a jerk. Wyatt will take care of him."

Why do I feel bad that Wyatt is probably beating the shit out of him? My chest feels like it's going to explode, and my limbs feel weak as Delilah leads me to the car, like I'm the one who's been through a battle.

"My key," I manage.

"Wyatt will get it. I'm sorry, Cassidy. I'm so sorry." Delilah stands beside me as I lean against the car.

She's been there for me as often as Wyatt has. The one thought that fights its way past the chaos in my head is how lucky I am to have them with me now and to have them in my life altogether. I can't stop shaking. I take one gulp of air after another, trying to regain control.

The door to the building flies open and slams against the brick wall. Wyatt looks like the Hulk, dragging Kyle by the back of his shirt as he closes the distance between us. I spin around and face the car. I don't want to look at Kyle. I can't. I'm too hurt, too angry. And too humiliated to face Wyatt.

"Tell her." Wyatt's guttural command slices through the night.

"Jesus, Wyatt," Delilah says just above a whisper.

Kyle doesn't say anything.

"Tell. Her." I can tell by Wyatt's voice that he's straining to rein in his anger.

I turn, more out of morbid curiosity than anything else, like when you can't look away from a car accident. Kyle's eye is swollen shut, and his lower lip is torn and bleeding. Wyatt squeezes Kyle's jaw between his fingers and thumb. The skin beneath his hand is white from the pressure.

"Wyatt." It comes out as a shaky whisper. I've seen fights before, but knowing *Wyatt* did that to Kyle and that it was because of me makes me scared, embarrassed, and sad all at once.

Wyatt ignores my plea.

"Fucking tell her. Now, you asshole," Wyatt says through gritted teeth.

Kyle's eyes lock on mine, and I think I see remorse beneath the fear. "It's not what it—"

Wyatt silences him with a punch to the jaw, sending Kyle stumbling backward. Wyatt grabs him by the collar again and pulls his fist back. Kyle's hands fly up in surrender.

I realize that it isn't remorse I see in Kyle's eyes, and I hate him even more than I did a minute ago.

"I'll tell her!" Kyle spits, probably a mouthful of blood, and looks sheepishly at me.

I'm shaking so hard that when Delilah reaches for my hand, I can't hold on to it. How many times have I looked into his eyes and believed he loved me? How many lies has he told me? I have to look away again.

"Now," Wyatt demands.

"I've been sleeping with her for six months," Kyle admits, and my breath leaves me in a rush of hot air. "But it didn't mean anything. I swear it."

Wyatt shoves him hard, and Kyle tumbles to the pavement. Wyatt looms over him, his chest heaving with anger. "Didn't fucking mean anything? It meant something to Cassidy, you asshole. If I ever find you near her again, I. Will. Kill. You. Now give me your fucking keys."

"I'm not—" Kyle holds up his hands to ward off another blow from Wyatt. Then he digs his keys out of his pocket and tosses them to him.

"Here's what's gonna happen," Wyatt says in a dead calm voice that stills my heart. "We're going to get Cassidy's shit out of your apartment, and you will not show up there for at least two hours. We'll leave your keys inside, and you sure as shit better not show up, or I swear to you I'll finish the job." Wyatt starts to walk away, then turns back and crouches beside Kyle, pinning him to the ground with a dark stare.

"You were *never* good enough for her."

Chapter Two

~Wyatt~

AFTER WE GET Cassidy's stuff from the douche bag's apartment, she's too shaken up to go to the party, and I have no interest in going back there, either. All I want to do is make sure she's okay. I can't believe that asshole cheated on her. Cassidy is smart, funny, and too damn trusting. He's been cheating on her for six months. How could she not have known? Seeing her fall apart at the sight of that limp-dicked asshole made me want to kill him. My body is still buzzing with anger as I drive home.

"You're staying with us tonight, Cass." I glance in the rearview mirror at her red-rimmed, puffy eyes. I hate that that asshole has the power to ruin them, because she has the coolest hazel eyes I've ever seen. They're green and yellow in the middle and brown around the edges. For some reason they remind me of a cat—mysterious. Our hair is the same light brown color. Hers hangs to her waist. She's playing with the ends of it, so I know she's really shaken up. She plays with her hair only when she's nervous or upset.

She nods. "It's not like I have anywhere else to go."

"Well, at least you were smart enough to send most of your stuff home before your parents left for Europe, and we have the rest of your bags, so that's one less thing you have to worry about." Cassidy had packed to leave for the summer with Kyle, which I'd been trying to talk her out of for the past three weeks. But as vulnerable as she looks right now, she's equally as bullheaded.

I pull into our apartment complex and cut the engine. Delilah and I share an apartment. My parents basically demanded it. Controlling much? Actually, for all the strict parenting we endure—keeping tabs on every grade, making us live in the same place, watching over us like hawks when we're home—I can't really complain. I know they're strict because they love us. Our parents paid for college and gave us a stipend of blow money each month. So there's good with the bad.

I hop out of the car, and Cassidy drags herself out of the backseat. I grab two of her duffels and hang them over my shoulder.

"Don't worry, Cass. We'll get through this. Dee and I are here for you." I grab her other two duffels and toss them over my free shoulder.

Delilah pops the trunk and grabs Cassidy's favorite tote bag, which I know without looking contains her photography stuff. Cassidy's been taking pictures for years, and while her parents disregard her *little hobby*, she's an amazing photographer. She even won two awards while we were in school.

"I'll carry one of those bags if you want, Wy," Delilah offers, as if her feminine, long, lean arms are stronger than mine.

"Nah. I've got them." I sling an arm over Cassidy's shoulder and the duffel moves across my back. "It's gonna be okay. I promise. You deserve someone a thousand times better than him." I drape my other arm over Delilah's shoulder and feel the duffel bags collide. "Luckiest guy on earth. I get to spend Saturday night with my two favorite people."

"A loser and your sister. Real lucky." Cassidy bumps me with her hip and rests her head on my shoulder. "Thanks, Wyatt." She peers around me. "Thanks, Delilah. I didn't mean to make you guys miss the party."

We head up to the second floor arm in arm, squished together like sardines.

"Oh my gosh, Cassidy, do you *really* think I wanted to be there?" Delilah rolls her eyes. It's not that she hates parties, but it seems like the closer we got to graduation, the more she hated pretending to be something she wasn't.

I unlock the door and follow the girls inside. Delilah flicks on the lights, and Cassidy goes directly to the wine rack.

"Oh no. You've been robbed."

She looks like someone's popped her balloon, exactly how she did when we were in sixth grade, sledding down a big hill by our house. The three of us piled onto one sled, Delilah in the front, then Cassidy, then me behind them. I didn't have time to hold on to Cassidy before one of our friends shoved us from behind, sending us speeding down the hill. Cassidy fell off as we went over the first ramp we'd built in the snow. She sat on her butt in the snow with the same pouty expression on her face as she has now.

Delilah laughs as I stow Cassidy's bags in my room.

"Mom and Dad took our stuff with them, so we ditched the alcohol before they got here. All we have are our clothes and..." Delilah opens the fridge and pulls out three bottles of beer. "Wy always has beer on hand."

I grab the bottle of wine I stowed in my bedroom for Cassidy. I saved it to give to her for graduation, but now a graduation gift seems unimportant. I bring it into the living room, holding it up in the air. "Who's the man?"

Cassidy runs over and hugs me. "This is why I love you."

"'Course you do. Now release me, woman, and let's drink to your freedom." I open the wine and fall between Delilah and Cassidy on the couch with a loud sigh. I take a swig and then hand the bottle to Cassidy. "Here's to being a college grad."

Cassidy smiles and takes a drink, then hands the bottle to Delilah. I wipe a drip from Cassidy's chin and lick it off my finger. She looks at me funny, like I've never done that before, even though I have about a million times, but it's been a messed-up night, so I ignore it.

"What would I do without you guys?" Cassidy

asks.

Before we can answer, Cassidy's head pops up and her eyes open wide. "Oh no."

"What?" Delilah and I ask at the same time.

"I have nowhere to go. I was supposed to spend the summer with Kyle, and my parents are in Europe for three months. I can't go home. They signed up with that house-swap vacation program I told you about. The family they swapped with is staying in our house." She reaches for the bottle and chugs it.

Delilah and I exchange a glance, and I know by the way her brows are drawn together that she's thinking the same thing I am. We don't have that twin ESP thing that people talk about, but we're close enough to sometimes know what the other is thinking. That's how I figured out that Delilah's into girls, not guys. She was sitting with this dude that all the girls were gushing over, and he was totally into her, but she looked almost sad and definitely not interested. I asked her about it, and it had taken some coaxing, but finally she told me that she thought she was a lesbian because she didn't ever get excited to kiss guys. We were fifteen, and to this day, I swear that look still hovers in her eyes. I don't care if she's not into dudes. She's my sister. I wish my parents would be as open-minded as we are. I'll never understand them. I've always found it odd that my parents bought a summer house in Harborside, Massachusetts, in a community that is very diverse, when they make comments about how wrong same-sex relationships are. I swear, I can't wait for every state to make a determination, because I'm so sick of hearing about same-sex marriages on the news. I don't get why anyone should have the right to tell anyone else who to marry, and if I hear my parents make reference to it one more time, I might explode—at them.

I shrug off my thought and focus on Cassidy.

"Come home with us, Cass. You're still waiting to hear about that job in New York, and you have a dozen applications still out. Even if you get hired somewhere, you don't have to start until the fall, so we'll hang out this summer." Cassidy's degree is in accounting, and she's hoping to land a job with a big accounting firm in New York City.

I, on the other hand, have a degree in business with a minor in hot babes who like to go down on me. Delilah's degree is in business with a minor in marketing. My father forced us in the direction he felt would be best for us to take over the bar one day. Suits me just fine. I figure I'll want to run it when he retires, which won't be for about twenty years. There's great surfing at Harborside, and we have a kick-ass house and tons of friends there. Of course, I have no idea what I'm doing beyond this summer. Our father's hooking me and Dee up with his colleagues after we get home, and then I guess we'll start interviewing for jobs. I gotta give him credit. He does help us, *if* it's in the direction he deems appropriate.

"I don't know. Your parents might not be too thrilled to have me around for three months." She leans across my lap and hands the bottle to Delilah.

Delilah takes a quick drink. She's not much of a drinker. I think she likes to feel in control, and it's probably all wrapped up in not wanting to come out.

I've never asked about this, but I've wondered if she's afraid that if she drinks too much she won't be able to keep from acting on her impulses. I push that thought away and focus on Cassidy.

"It'll be fun, Cass. We'll hang out. Just the three of us."

I reach for the bottle. "Or even better, I know you can't turn down a summer at Harborside."

After I take a drink, Cassidy grabs the bottle again. "I do love the beach."

I put my arm over her shoulder and pull her close. "Don't fool yourself. You love me and Dee, too. So it's set. We have a plan."

They both roll their eyes.

"What?"

"You? *Plan?*" Cassidy laughs and leans forward again. "He's got a plan, Delilah. He doesn't even know how to spell *plan*."

I tickle her ribs, and she falls across my lap, laughing. It's good to hear her laugh. I reach for Delilah next and they're both in stitches when Delilah's phone rings.

"Wait, wait, wait." Delilah reaches into her back pocket and tries to stop laughing.

"It's Uncle Tim's number." Delilah answers the call, half laughing, half talking.

I can't imagine why he'd call Delilah so late.

Cassidy turns onto her back across my lap, still laughing. She reaches up and touches the scruff on my chin.

"When you get a real job, you'll have to shave more than once a week."

She's smiling, but I can feel the sadness behind it, like the minute she's alone she's going to cry again. That bastard really hurt her. I've been in a handful of fights, but I've never felt rage like I did tonight. The minute I saw Kyle lying naked on top of that bitch, all I could think about was how Cassidy was going to be crushed. I can't imagine anything worse than the ache I had when I turned around and saw the look in her eyes. It's seared into my memory. I know I'll see it when I close my eyes to go to sleep. That's the one thing I don't like about knowing Cassidy so well and being so close to her. Like with Delilah, I feel Cassidy's pain as if it were my own.

I touch my scruffy jaw, thinking about what she said. "We'll see about that. I can't see myself behind a desk. But I'm a kick-ass bartender." We've owned the bar at Harborside since I was a kid, and I basically hung out there and learned how to make every drink under the sun. I can still hear my father's voice telling me that if I learned to respect alcohol, I wouldn't abuse it later. That's one lesson Dad screwed up with, but it made me popular at parties.

I hear Delilah's breath catch and turn as she grips my hand. She's trembling, and tears are streaming down her cheeks. I rip the phone from her hands.

"Uncle Tim?"

"Wyatt." He sounds like he's being strangled.

Delilah stares straight ahead, her jaw hanging open, tears flooding down her cheeks, and she's barely breathing.

Cassidy sits up and crawls over me. "What happened?" She hugs Delilah, while sitting across mine and Delilah's laps. "Delilah? What is it?"

"What happened?" I yell into the phone.

"Your parents. We...They...There's been an accident."

His voice sounds a million miles away. A cold sensation pulses through my body. My hands clench into fists, and my throat closes. I can't focus, can catch only some of what he's saying. *Eighteen-wheeler. Crossed double line.* I feel like I'm in a time warp, and he's getting farther and farther away. *Four-car accident.* I pull Delilah into my arms. She's shaking so badly I hear her teeth chattering—and I know I can't fix this. Cassidy says something, but I can't hear past the rush of blood in my ears. Uncle Tim's voice pierces through.

They didn't make it.

Chapter Three

~Wyatt~

THE LAST FEW days have been a blur. Uncle Tim's been making arrangements for Mom and Dad's funerals, dealing with insurance companies and my parents' attorney, while Delilah has been vacillating between bawling her eyes out and shutting everyone out of her life, and me...Well, I feel like a robot on steroids half the time, trying to make sure Delilah and Cassidy are okay, and the other half of the time I feel like I want to kill someone. I'm worried about Delilah. She's shutting me out entirely. She's already hidden so much of herself for so long that I worry she'll shut herself away forever. She's been so afraid of our parents finding out about her sexuality that she's even hidden it from our friends. Now that our parents are gone, I worry she's going to be lost, or maybe she's relieved. *That's a fucked-up thought*—but maybe? Could I blame her? She's lived forever under a veil of secrecy. Now she's free to live her own life. I want so badly to talk this through with her, but everything makes her cry, and I want to fix it all, and I can't.

After the funeral everyone came to our house to pay their respects. Aunt Lara is a mess, because she was in the car with my parents on the way back to Connecticut when they were killed. She was in the backseat, and she has cuts and bruises and a few broken ribs, but I can tell she feels guilty for surviving. I guess when the police asked her who to call, she gave them Uncle Tim's number, which is why he was the one to call us. Uncle Tim said she was barely coherent for several days after the accident, and I believe it, because it's like she's still in shock. She's either crying or walking around like a zombie. Uncle Tim's been great, taking care of things around the house, answering the never-ending stream of phone calls, and trying to buffer me and Delilah from the onslaught of people who want to help us but in reality just magnify the loss of our parents. There are still a handful of people inside, and I swear if I have to see a look of pity on one more person's face, I'm going to lose it. That's why I escaped outside to the back deck.

Cassidy is running back and forth between me and Dee, doing all she can to be there for us. She didn't ask to be thrown into this mess when she's dealing with her own heartbreak. She's known my parents forever...*She knew...Fuck.* Thinking of my parents in past tense makes me feel like all the air has been sucked from my lungs. Cass *knew* my parents since she was five, when she moved around the corner from us. She *was* like their other daughter, coming and going without knocking on the door. That's why she was so worried about staying for three months. She's like that. She worries that she's taking advantage because she is *so* comfortable around my family. *Was.* She was so comfortable around them. But the truth is, my parents loved Cass. They wouldn't have cared.

Tears burn my eyes every time I think of my parents, which is just about every second. I press my thumb and index fingers to my closed lids, trying to stop the tears from falling, but it just makes my chest burn even worse, and the goddamn tears fall anyway. I swipe at them with my palm and look around our fenced backyard. Dad taught me how to play football here. He never cared if it was raining or cold or almost dark. Every time I asked him to toss the pigskin, he did. Now that I think of it, it's weird that he did, since he's Mr. Shirt-and-Tie conservative.

I mean, *he was. Fuck.*

My brain stops functioning for a minute, like someone turned it off, and I just sit there staring out at the grass. When the glass door slides open behind me, I close my eyes for a second, hoping it's not someone *checking* on me. If one more person asks if I'm okay, I swear I'll punch them.

I feel her hand on my back and intuitively know it's Cassidy before I see her. She sits beside me and puts her hand on my thigh. I'm so thankful it's her that I want to hug her. She's wearing a black dress that looks strange on her. She almost never wears black. She's one of those girls who looks like she belongs in California, not Connecticut. Her olive skin makes her look like she's always tan, and she wears colorful clothing that's loose and trendy, not conservative or dull. Delilah says she has a sunny personality. She's right. Cassidy pretty much lights up every room she walks into.

"This sucks." She squeezes my leg and rests her head on my shoulder.

I drape my arm around her because it's what I always do, and hell if I don't feel like a needy bitch right now. I need her comfort more than I need to breathe. She smells like flowers—familiar and safe—and...*Goddamn it.* I feel like I'm gonna cry again.

"Yeah, it sucks." I clear my throat to get rid of the gravelly, sad sound of my voice and look away. I don't want her to see my eyes all wet. The tears stopped, but I know they're not gone for long. "Where's Dee?"

"She's in her room. She doesn't want to see anyone. I think after today it'll be easier, but right now she's overwhelmed."

I nod, knowing the feeling.

"Your uncle said he's going back home tonight and that he'll take care of anything else you guys need him to."

I nod. He told me that, too. Aunt Lara is also leaving. She has two dogs, a cat, and two birds that her neighbor was watching, but her dogs are like kids—the oldest dog misses her when she goes away and stops eating. She lives less than an hour away, which is close enough for her to come back if we need her. I wonder if Uncle Tim or Aunt Lara told Cassidy that my parents left everything to us. The bar, the house...their money. None of it feels real. I mean, I know kids who can't wait to inherit their parents' money, and I feel like I want to tell them how much it sucks to have things handed to me instead of having my parents around. I'd trade everything to have them back in our lives. They might have been tight asses, but I love them.

Loved them.

Damn it.

I can't even think about all that stuff right now, and since Cassidy isn't saying anything more, I doubt they told her. Uncle Tim has been really great, taking care of everything and making sure we have whatever we need. Unfortunately, what we need is buried six feet under the ground.

"I heard Uncle Tim break down last night," I say to get my mind on something other than my parents. "It's gotta suck for him, too, having lost his best friend."

"Yeah, I know. He's been so strong. He said he told you and Delilah that you can go stay with him for as long as you want, and I guess your aunt offered, too, although she doesn't seem in any shape to take care of her pets—much less anyone else."

They both offered, but seeing everyone this week was enough. I feel like I'm boxed in and need space to breathe.

Cassidy reaches up and pulls my chin toward her so I have no choice but to look at her. "You're allowed to fall apart, you know."

I half smile.

"I don't mean like crawl into a fetal position and sob your eyes out, although if you want to do that, I'll be right there with you. I mean like get really trashed so you can't feel a thing, or break something."

I nod again, because she knows me so well. "Right now I gotta be mentally present for Dee, but when I'm ready to break something, it's good to know you'll be there." She squeezes my thigh again, and I hold her compassionate gaze, unable to look away. She brushes my hair out of my eyes and shifts her gaze away.

Her brows draw together. I never really noticed before, but when she does that, the edges of her lips curve up. It's cute.

"I hope when you get a real job, they don't make you cut your hair. I love your hair long."

I shake my head to the side, and my bangs fall away from my eyes. My hair isn't super long, but it touches my collar and hangs pretty straight to my eyes. Every time I ever went to a barber, they hacked my hair, so it was easier for Mom to just take a little off the ends. I wonder for a minute who's going to cut it now. I hate barbers. I drop my eyes, feeling stupid for worrying about something so lame when Mom's dead. *Dead.* I can't wrap my head around it. I expect her and Dad to walk out the door and tell me that I shouldn't leave my shit all over my room or something.

"I guess you'll be at the mercy of me and Delilah to cut your hair from now on."

I pull her closer, thankful she's here. "Trust you guys wielding scissors? Not on your life."

"Come on. You can trust us. Why would we want to make your hair look bad?" She's smiling, and I start to feel shitty again. Selfish. My brain is jumping from my parents to Cassidy, to Delilah, to that asshole I hit the other night.

"Cass, about the fight..."

She swats the air like it's no big deal. "I'm over it, Wy."

"No, you're not." I hold her gaze and have to pull her into a hug. I feel tears threatening again, and it pisses me off. I know she'll understand, but still. I'm not this fucking weak, and I need to be strong for her and Dee.

"I'm sorry he hurt you so badly, and I'm sorry all of this overshadowed it." I wish I could fix everything. For her, for me, for Dee. Actually, if I could fix one freaking thing, I'd be happy, but my father was the fixer. I just showed up and did shit.

It dawns on me that I thought *was* and *did* and somehow, with Cassidy in my arms, it didn't feel as bad. I ease my grip, but she squeezes me tighter.

"Aw, Cass." I feel her body shaking and hear her sniffle, and I know she's crying again.

"He's an asshole, and I'm glad you hit him. Does that make me a bad person?"

"No. It makes you normal."

She pulls back, and I reach over and wipe her tears with my thumb. I hate to see her sad. It does strange things to me and makes me want to beat the shit out of Kyle again, but it also tugs at me and makes me sad for her and want to take care of her and protect her from other assholes like him.

She reaches for my hand and rubs her thumb over the scabs on my knuckles. Then she brings my hand to her lips and kisses my knuckles while she's looking into my eyes. Cassidy has held my hand thousands of times, but she's never kissed me like this before. Or looked at me like she wanted more of me, like she is

33

now. It's not a look of just wanting to get laid, but I'm definitely sensing a desire for something *more*. If she were any other girl, I'd pay attention to the heat searing through my body, breaking through the sadness, which I would never have believed was possible. But Cass is my best friend. I know I shouldn't feel like I want her incredible lips on mine, especially now, when our lives are such a mess, but I can't stop myself.

I force myself to look away, and even as I do that, I feel the heat of her stare, and it's confusing the shit out of me.

~Cassidy~

WELL, THAT WAS about the most awful day ever, following the shittiest week ever. I wonder what life could possibly have in store for me and my friends next. A plague? I spoke to my parents earlier, and while they seemed shocked and saddened by the death of Wyatt's parents, they never offered to come home. Even though they know how close I was with his parents. And when I told them that Kyle and I broke up, they never even asked why. My father said something about more fish in the sea and finding a real *catch* when I work in New York, which I've heard a million times before, so I didn't try to discuss it any further. My mom said she was sorry about Kyle but that it just meant he wasn't the right guy for me, and that it's probably for the best, because New York will offer all sorts of opportunities. She followed that up with a ten-minute lecture about not wallowing in sadness because it makes women weak and pathetic to cry over men. She said I'm strong and bright and that I've got too big of a future waiting for me in New York to be held back by some guy. Then, as if she remembered that she's supposed to say something at least a little sweet and supportive, she said that when the right guy comes along, I'll feel like I can't breathe without him.

Whatever.

I've never felt that and can't even begin to imagine what it feels like. Sometimes I wish I had different parents, but then something happens—like knowing Wyatt and Delilah are left with *no* parents—and I realize I'm lucky to have any parents at all.

Wyatt's aunt and uncle left a few hours ago, and Delilah and I are sitting on the couch while Wyatt stalks around the house like he's looking for something. I've asked him a dozen times what he's looking for, but he just shakes his head and goes from room to room. He's just agitated and upset, and I'm sure at any moment he's going to break out the alcohol and bury his sadness in liquor. I'm surprised twenty minutes later when he returns to the living room and he's still not drinking.

My phone vibrates with a text, and I snag it quickly to delete the text before Wyatt sees it. I feel like I've honed stealth ninja skills over the past few days, trying to keep Kyle's texts from Wyatt. Kyle has texted me so many times that I want to change my number, but that would mean contacting my parents again and it's not worth the hassle. My emotions are all over the place. I know if Wyatt finds out Kyle's trying to reach me, he'll go ballistic, so I keep deleting his texts. I have this fantasy of seeing Kyle somewhere and popping him one in the nose, but I really don't want to see him again. Not even to hit him. I don't want to give him any of my thoughts, either, but every night when darkness hits and Delilah and Wyatt go into their rooms, I can't stop myself from crying. Two years is a long time, and when I'm alone in the guest room, I feel hollow and swamped with sadness. My best friends in the world just lost their parents, my boyfriend cheated on me, and my parents are in Europe. It's no wonder my head goes to this strange place. I start comparing Kyle to Wyatt. It's not a fair comparison, considering Wyatt's known me my whole life and Kyle hasn't, but still, I can't help it. Kyle even forgot my birthday this year, and Wyatt left me three hidden cards. It should be my boyfriend doing that, not my best friend. Or maybe *as well as* my best friend, because Wyatt's cards made me happier than Kyle's ever did.

The first night we were back, after we found out that Wyatt and Delilah's parents had been killed...Oh my God, that hurts to think about. I swallow against the lump in my throat. They were like parents to me. I miss them so much it hurts like an ever-present toothache, and when it's combined with the hurt of breaking up with Kyle, it's all I can do to make it through each day, let alone the nights. But I know it's so much worse for Wy and Delilah.

That first night I must have been crying really loudly. Either that, or Wyatt and Delilah needed company as much as I did, because Wyatt came into my room and sat on the edge of my bed. He didn't say anything, just leaned his elbows on his thighs for a second, and then he climbed in bed beside me, facing me, and wrapped me in his arms. I'm not sure if he knew that I knew he was crying, but my head was pressed to his chest, and I could hear the hitching of his breath. Delilah came in a few minutes later and climbed into bed behind me. She held me, too, and Wyatt reached an arm around her. He's always been my rock, and right now I know he needs me as much as I need him.

Wyatt comes out of his dad's office with a grave look in his eyes and crosses his arms over his chest.

"I can't stay here." His eyes shift to Delilah.

Delilah drops her gaze and traces the seam of her shorts with her finger.

"Dee. They're everywhere. I keep waiting for them to come through the front door. Don't you feel that way?"

Delilah raises her eyes, which immediately go damp. Wyatt's eyes soften, and he kneels beside her, takes her hand in his. "We're going to get through this, Dee. I promise you we will. But we can't stay here."

She nods as tears fall down her cheeks, and she sort of falls against him. I swallow back tears. I love the two of them so much, and I'm glad I'm here with them, because I wouldn't want them to go through this alone. I don't want to go through this alone.

Wyatt strokes the back of Delilah's head, following the slope of her long blond hair. His biceps flex, and his jaw clenches. I know he's holding back tears. He's big and broad, and Delilah looks small and innocent in his strong, capable arms. Wyatt's got an edge about him. He can slay a man or seduce a woman with a single glance.

It's embarrassing how many times I've fantasized about being that woman. Through high school and college my feelings toward Wyatt were usually just under the surface. I haven't ever known what to make of them, and I'd never act on them. But there have definitely been times when I've longed to catch his eye in *that* way.

I really need to distract myself from thinking about Wyatt that way. I glance at them, and think, not for the first time, about how different they are. Even though I've known them forever, sometimes I have to remind myself they're twins. Delilah always does the right thing. When we were in school, she studied every day, even if she didn't have a test coming up, and she sketched in her free time, more than she did anything else. She went to parties, but I could tell she was only there because Wyatt and I pretty much pressured her into it. Wy worries about her a lot, and I love that he does. But she's never going to be like him. He has no insecurities, at least not that I've ever seen. I've never seen him tentative about anything. He can handle whatever comes his way, and the way he takes care of me and Delilah proves time and time again that he's a natural protector.

I watch him closer now and see Delilah's pain mirrored in his eyes. His brows draw together like he's thinking, and a second later, as if he's inhaled strength and exhaled the pain, his voice is confident again as he takes control.

"I promise you, Dee, we'll be fine. We'll go to

Harborside and figure things out. The change of scenery will be good for us."

Delilah squeezes him tighter, then pushes back and wipes her eyes. "I'm sorry I'm crying and so...useless."

"You're not useless, and you should cry. A lot. They're our parents, Dee." Wyatt's voice is empathetic and confident, as if he's been through this before and knows how to guide her. He amazes me.

Delilah sucks in a deep breath. "But what about the house?"

"What about it? I'll have the neighbors watch it until we figure things out. I think staying at the beach house will be better for now. Staying here feels...dark."

I wonder what will happen to their house. I have no idea what happens after someone dies. I want to ask, but it's not exactly something I can just blurt out. *What happens now? Does someone read their wills?* It's all so morbid and sad.

Wyatt moves around Delilah's legs, presses his hands to my thighs, and squeezes. My whole body tingles at the way he's looking at me and the position he's in, which is weird, because he's knelt before me plenty of times, but the hopeful look in his eyes feels different this time.

"Cass, will you come with us? Please? I won't go if you don't want to." He's holding my stare as though his whole life depends on my answer. I would never turn him away, especially not now. Not that I'd want to. I just never realized how *much* I didn't want to until this very second. I feel like my next thought depends on the answer as much as his does, and the feeling takes me by surprise. I chalk it up to the last week of hell we've both been going through.

I manage a nod. "I'll go. Of course I'll go."

A smile breaks across his lips, and he pulls me into his arms. "Thank you." He hugs me, and somehow his arms feel stronger than they did earlier in the day. He tightens his embrace for a few seconds longer, and then he gently pushes back and keeps hold of my shoulders. He gives me a serious look again. His green eyes go all dark and smoky. God, I love that look.

Oh my gosh. It's *that* look.

That look that's usually aimed at the girls he's hooked up with.

A thrill thrums through me, and I glance quickly at Delilah, because if I look at him any longer, I'm going to do or say something stupid. I know I must be reading him wrong.

Delilah smiles and squeezes my hand. "I'm so glad you're coming with us."

Okay, so she doesn't see it. It's definitely my messed-up head.

"Me too," I say, trying to ignore my racing heart. I feel Wyatt's eyes on me as he reaches behind him and grabs my phone. I can tell by his steady, and slightly disappointed, stare that he knows about Kyle's texts, and I can't think of a single thing to say. It's not like Wyatt's my boyfriend, but he did come to my defense, so I kind of owe him honesty about Kyle.

"I know he's texting you. I've seen you deleting his messages."

I guess I'm not so ninja-like after all.

"This is your life, Cass, and if you want that

asshole in your life, it's up to you."

He holds my gaze, and conflicting emotions wash over his face—anger, concern, and something warm that makes my insides go soft. And just as quickly as he sucked me in, that look goes right out the door, replaced with a cold stare.

"All I can say is that I'm really not interested in pounding the shit out of him multiple times. If he comes to Harborside, I will hit him again, but it'll be the last time I have to. The son of a bitch won't be able to walk away, much less come back again."

"I don't want anything to do with him." The words come fast and hard. "I don't even read the texts. I just delete them. I didn't want to upset you."

He narrows his eyes, and it makes me worry that he doesn't believe me.

"I would have hidden the texts from you, too, Wy," Delilah says.

He looks at her and his eyes soften. "Why?"

I'm not sure which one of us he's asking, but I let Delilah answer because I don't have any idea what to say. *Because you protect me like I'm yours?* The thought races through my mind, and I don't say anything because I'm not sure I can.

"Because you'd beat the snot out of him again, and even if he deserves it, it's really hard to watch." Delilah's never afraid to tell him the truth, and right now I'm thankful that she's found her voice again. "She dated him for two years, Wyatt. That means something."

His eyes drift back to me, and I see the question in them.

"I didn't want to upset you." It turns out I can answer. Then again, talking to Wyatt usually isn't difficult.

He doesn't say anything, just runs his eyes between me and Delilah like we're a team or something. I think I see hurt in his eyes, but it could be confusion. Wyatt's never had a long-term girlfriend. He probably doesn't realize how much it hurts to spend two years with someone and realize too late that you never really knew him. Or to have someone you trust lie to you. He's been lied to, but the girl who cheated on him wasn't really cheating. He never hooks up with girls more than a few times before moving on to the *next-best thing*. His words, not mine. He's never been hurt by a girl who said she loved him. I've been trying not to think about that. It wasn't that I thought I was in love with Kyle. I didn't, or at least I don't think I was. I never thought of him as my happily-ever-after guy even though he told me he loved me a million times. Now I'm glad that I never said it back. That would probably hurt even more.

He sighs and takes his hands off my thighs. *Whoa.* Unexpected longing sweeps through me, and I swallow hard, trying to conceal the confusion it causes.

His jaw clenches as he rises and sits on the coffee table across from me and clasps his hands together. "Listen, Cass, if you're going to stay with us, then no hiding that type of shit. I'm your friend. I care. The last thing we need is him coming around and getting his face smashed in because I didn't know you invited him down there." He fists his hands. "And he's not staying with us. Ever."

I roll my eyes. "Really, Wyatt? Why not?" I can't help doling out sarcasm. He looks cute and angry, and things have been so stressful that I feel like shaking him and saying, *Wake the hell up! I don't want him around.*

His face blanches, and then his eyes go dark and sexy again. I steal a glance at Delilah to see if she notices, but she's laughing behind her hand. I think she feels the same way I do, that we needed a little teasing in our shitty week.

"You two will be the death of me." Wyatt rises to his feet and stretches. The bottom of his tank inches up, flashing his washboard abs. I don't even try to look away, but it takes all my willpower not to poke him in the stomach like I normally do. We tease like that all the time, but the way my mind and body have been reacting so strongly to him lately, I worry that poking him is the *last thing* I'll end up doing. I imagine the feel of his stomach against my palms and pressing my lips to each perfect muscle.

Holy mother of stupidity. What am I thinking?

I grip my thighs and tear my eyes away to try to squelch the desire simmering low in my belly.

I wonder if staying with Delilah and Wyatt for three months is a smart thing to do, but when Wyatt reaches for my hand and pulls me up so hard I crash against him, my hand accidentally on purpose slips down, and I cop a feel of that stomach I've thought about kissing more times than I care to admit, even to myself. And I know there's nowhere else on earth I'd rather be.

Chapter Four

~Wyatt~

DRIVING UNDER THE arched sign above the road that reads *Harborside, Where Heaven Meets Earth* is the best feeling in the world. It's a lame slogan, but if heaven is like Harborside, then I know my parents are in a good place. We've owned the house in Harborside since Delilah and I were little, and we've always spent summers and most school breaks here with our parents. It really is our home away from home. I glance at Delilah. She's been quiet the whole trip. I know she's totally freaked out about our parents. We all are, but she's been so withdrawn these last few days that I'm really worried about her. She's gotten so used to hiding her sexual identity from everyone that I don't think even she realizes how it's affecting the rest of her life. I hope that being back among our closest friends, in a more accepting community than our repressed Connecticut neighborhood, will help.

Cassidy leans forward from the backseat and touches my shoulder. She's probably done it a thousand times before, but now I feel myself hoping she leaves it there. She does, and as stupid as it sounds, I'm really glad.

"Can we go to the beach before going to the house? I want to take some pictures." She squeezes my shoulder as she asks.

That little squeeze stirs something it shouldn't. I glance in the rearview at her. Her eyes are wide with excitement, gazing out the window. I try really hard to suppress the desires brewing inside me, reminding myself she's my best friend, but all I can think is how much I want her to squeeze my shoulder again. I squeeze the steering wheel tighter, trying to get a grip on my thoughts, because they're fantasizing way beyond squeezing a shoulder.

"Dee?" I want to be sure Delilah is comfortable. Her sketch pad is poking out of the top of the bag at her feet. She's a really talented artist. She's always sketching something, but this week she hasn't picked up her drawing pad even once. I hope she'll begin sketching again while we're here.

"Sure. Sounds good." Delilah looks out her window as she answers.

I look at Cassidy in the rearview again, and she narrows her eyes in a way that says she feels really bad but doesn't know what to do to help Delilah any more than I do. She touches Delilah's shoulder with her other hand. Delilah reaches up and places her hand on Cassidy's, but she's still looking out the window.

Harborside is a midsized town, and during the summers it gets loads of tourist traffic. It's still early in the season, so I'm able to drive at a pretty good clip into town. The closer we get, the more tension eases off of me like a snake sheds its skin. I roll my window down and inhale. Harborside smells like someone took the ocean and sprinkled it into the air, then tossed in some coconuts, which is totally bizarre, since there are no coconuts in Massachusetts. Except the kind you buy at the store.

The main road into Harborside has two lanes, and it's lined with farms and little ranch-style homes. I imagine it feels a lot like a farm town. But just when you think you'll be bored as hell in the place, the road widens to four lanes and the next few miles are littered with beach houses. The farms give way to grass and sand, and finally, the ocean comes into view off to the left.

"There it is!" Cassidy's face is practically smashed against her window as she looks at the ocean. Her grip on my shoulder tightens.

She opens her window and sticks her head out. I glance at her in the side-view mirror. Her long brown hair whips around, smacking her cheeks. She laughs and then falls back against the seat as I turn down the road toward the pier, passing GiGi's Diner on the corner, with its bright yellow sign hanging above the door and big potted plants under the front window. Colorful storefronts line the road. I smile as we pass Pepe's Pizza, with its tables and big red umbrellas out front, the only twenty-four-hour pizzeria in town. We've sat beneath those umbrellas pondering surfing conditions and shooting the shit more times than I can count. Our friend Brandon Owens worked there one summer and brought us free pizzas almost every day. Brandon graduated from Harborside University with a double major in computer science and mathematics but refuses to work in an office—his form of rebellion against his straitlaced family who doesn't *get* him.

We pass Endless Summer Surf Shop, owned by our friends Jesse and Brent Steele, with brightly colored surfboards lined up out front and sale racks of T-shirts and wet suits. It feels good to be back.

I pull up to a red light and look down the road to my left, where I see the restaurant Jesse and Brent recently purchased and are currently renovating. Scaffolding blocks half of the brick paver walkway. Before buying the restaurant, Jesse ran the Taproom in the off seasons. Two months ago, the summer manager of the Taproom quit, and Jesse agreed to stay on until my parents arrived, which, of course now, they never will. I'm glad he's around because I know absolutely nothing about running a bar and grill. It's almost like our parents foresaw their futures when they guided us toward our degrees.

Ugh. That's a messed-up thought.

I pull through the light and my chest tightens as our parents' bar—well, *our* bar now—comes into view at the end of Harborside Pier. The pier runs high above the water like a bridge to another land and forms a T at the end, where the bar is located. My throat thickens as memories come flooding in. *Counting the slats on the pier with my father, eating ice cream as our feet dangled off the side.* How many times have Delilah and I raced down the pier while our parents strolled hand in hand behind us?

My dad will never again point out the constellations from a table outside the bar. He'll never stand with one hand on his hip, the other shading his eyes as he points to a boat in the distance and asks me what type it is, as if I were a midshipman and knew the answers. He will never jingle the keys to the bar and say, *One day this will be yours and Dee's, son.* One day is here. The bar is *our* responsibility.

Holy shit. We've inherited the Taproom. We have to *run* the bar.

I can't even think about all the stuff my parents left us without feeling sick. I glance at Delilah and she's smiling, looking out at the water. If her smile is any indication, I made the right decision by coming here. She'll do better now, but I know that if she's got any hope of getting through this, I need to suck it up and appear better now, too.

"I'm glad we're here," she says, kind of to herself.

I bury the memories threatening to pull me under, reach for her hand, and give it a gentle squeeze. "Me too."

Uncle Tim and Aunt Lara told Delilah and me about our parents' will, but we haven't talked about it yet. I'm waiting for her to bring it up so that I don't push any invisible buttons and upset her again.

"I wonder if everyone's here." Delilah glances out at the bar.

"Brandon said everyone's around. Jesse's managing the bar, and Tristan is bartending. Charley's working part-time this summer. She's also working part-time for the Brave Foundation, and Brandon said there are a handful of college kids working for the summer." When I spoke to Brandon the other night, it sounded as if not much had changed since last summer, which is good. Stability is probably the best thing for us right now.

As I park, another memory forces its way in, and I try not to linger on the sound of my father's long sigh, which always accompanied our first trip to the pier each summer. He'd stretch his long arm across the back of the seat and stroke my mom's neck. She'd turn and smile at my father, and then she'd look at me and Dee in the backseat and say, *Who's ready for sand between their toes?*

"What about Brooke? Is she around?"

Dee's voice breaks me free from the memory, and I cut the engine, hoping to distract myself.

Brooke Baker is a few years older than us and owns Brooke's Bytes, a café on the boardwalk. Like our other friends here in Harborside, we've known her for several years. I wonder if Delilah's thinking about all the mornings she and my mom used to walk down to the café and have breakfast with Brooke.

"Yeah. He said everyone's still around." Brandon told me that they're all really shaken up over our parents dying, but I don't want to tell Delilah that. I asked him to tell the others to keep it light when they see Delilah. Too much stewing over our parents might send her hiding in her room again, like she was doing in Connecticut. At some point she'll need to move forward and function normally. Although she's hidden her sexual identity from everyone for so long, I'm not sure what *normal* would be to her. Hiding who she is, is definitely *not* what normal *should* be. I feel myself getting angry at my parents again and swallow back the anger as I park the car.

Cassidy jumps out, grabs her camera, and then runs around to Delilah's door and tugs it open. "Come on." She pulls Delilah out of the car and takes a picture of the ocean. Then she turns to me and flashes a wide smile. "Just one picture? Please?"

I groan and stand next to Delilah. I don't mind Cassidy taking my picture, but I'm sure Dee isn't into it. Her eyes look flat, and I'm not sure if Cassidy thinks this will cheer her up or if she wants to add today to her collection of scrapbooks. In any case, as Cass takes the picture, she looks like she's just found a fountain of chocolate and clicks away. She's always happy when she's looking through the lens of a camera.

"Okay, thank you. I promise not to torture you anymore." She puts her camera back in the car and reminds me to lock it before grabbing Delilah and walking toward the beach.

I follow them, and when their feet hit the sand, Cassidy bends to pick up her flip-flops. I realize I'm staring at her ass in her sexy little cutoffs. There's a flowery patch right across her pocket, and when she stands up again, her tight gray T-shirt hitches on the waist of her shorts. Her legs are long and lean, and as she swings her arm over Delilah's shoulder, several silver bracelets slide down Cassidy's forearm. I feel like I'm seeing her for the first time in the seventeen years I've known her, and I stare at her like she's one hot piece of ass. I feel my dick stir in my pants again, and I shift my eyes away.

Shit. Shit, shit, shit. Whatever is going on with my body better stop, or I won't be able to hide that I'm lusting after her.

It's too early in the season for the beach to be crowded, but there are still bikini babes lying in the sun. They *should* hold my attention, but my eyes keep shifting back to Cassidy. She whispers something to Delilah, and then they both sprint toward me, laughing, and they grab my hands. I can't help but laugh along as they tug me across the sand.

"Come on, Wy," Cassidy says. "We want to put our feet in the water and then maybe walk on the boardwalk."

I'm glad to see Delilah smiling again, and I'm ready to pull my head out of the dark place it's been in since the fight with Kyle. I try to ignore the guilt I feel for thinking all sorts of inappropriate things about Cassidy—like wondering what it might feel like to touch that fine ass of hers. It's a strange thing to suddenly want to touch every inch of your best friend.

The three of us walk hand in hand along the surf for a while, and then we head up to the boardwalk. Cassidy's phone buzzes a few times, and she finally powers it off. My gut wrenches, knowing it's probably Kyle.

"I don't really want to go to the Taproom tonight," Delilah says.

"We don't need to, Dee. Do you want to go to the house? Or go see Brooke?" She and Brooke are really close, and I hope that Brooke might help her get through this. I've decided to try to talk to Delilah about

Mom and Dad next time we're alone again. I feel like I'm not doing anything to help her, and the problem is, I don't know how to help. We're usually so close that I instinctively know what to do, but this isn't like anything I've ever had to deal with before.

"Yeah. Let's go see Brooke. I'd love a latte anyway." Delilah drops my hand as she steps onto the boardwalk.

Cassidy bends to put her flip-flops back on, and I make a concerted effort not to stare at the curve of her butt peeking out the bottom of her shorts, but it's nearly impossible. I wonder if she can feel me looking at her. She glances up, still holding my hand, and I don't see anything different in her eyes. I tell myself to turn the goddamn horny thoughts off, but it turns out that it's not that easy. I'm stuck walking around with my dick at half-mast, and it's not a good feeling. Not just the discomfort, but this is Cassidy, and I love her as my best friend. The last thing either of us needs is to mess that up with some misplaced desire that's probably fed by everything we're going through.

It feels good to see the boardwalk shops and hear the sounds of people laughing and talking, with the ocean breeze sweeping off the beach. But at the same time, it's strange to see all these carefree people carrying on like nothing has changed, when our entire lives have changed forever. It's uncomfortably uplifting, but I think we all needed this, and I'm glad we came.

The boardwalk shops are built to resemble a small town rather than typical brightly colored boardwalk shops. They have cedar siding, like most of the houses in the area, and while there are two or three souvenir shops, they don't sell cheap plastic souvenirs. They sell artwork and crafts made by local artists. The restaurants sell things like lobster rolls and fish tacos, and there are no hotels rising high above the boardwalk, only two-story motels with wide balconies, built with the same New England facade as the houses.

The smell of popcorn and the *ping*ing and buzzer sounds drift out of the open arcade doors as we pass. The arcade is tucked between Hidden Treasures and Sally's Saltwater Taffy & Fudge. I remember my dad giving me and Dee a handful of quarters when we were little and waiting with Mom in Hidden Treasures while we played arcade games. The sadness that I keep pushing away presses back in.

Memories and sadness come in waves. Over the past week there have been times when I could function like nothing happened, and then something stirs a memory. It could be the smell of my father's cologne when I walk by his bedroom, or seeing my mom's car in the driveway. Sometimes I don't know what stirs the memories, but then again, the people who loved me most and were always in my life are gone. I'm sure they left invisible fingerprints everywhere.

Brooke's Bytes is on the other side of Sally's. It's the only Internet café around, and there are always people sitting out front at the round tables and against the wall of the café beneath the blue awning that boasts BROOKE'S BYTES in fancy white letters. Their eyes are trained on their laptops, and they don't even glance up as we walk toward the open door.

Delilah grabs my arm and stops walking. "Wy, I can't go see Brooke."

Her hand is trembling, and her eyes are wide, like she's seen a ghost. I realize she probably has. She's probably feeling the weight behind those invisible fingerprints, too. I put my arm around her to reassure her.

"No worries, Dee. Do you want to go to the house? You tell me where you want to go and we'll go. I have no plans."

She nods with a spaced-out look in her eyes that worries me. "I'm not sure I can handle the house, either." Her eyes get all watery, and I let go of Cassidy's hand to pull Delilah into a hug.

"Dee, it's okay. There's no pressure to handle this in one way or another."

She's sobbing now, and Cassidy is standing beside her, rubbing her back with so much empathy in her eyes I want to thank her.

"I just..." Delilah sobs. "How do you get past losing your parents? Wyatt, what are we going to do?" Her voice trails off as she cries.

I don't care that we're standing in the middle of the boardwalk and people are slowing down to look at us and then giving us a wide berth as they walk by. I don't care that my own heart is aching because seeing Delilah so sad on top of my own sadness nearly drowns me. My only thought is that I should take her home and my parents will know what to do, but that's totally messed up. Not only would they not know what to do, but they didn't even know who Delilah really was, and that pisses me off. My gut gets achy and tight, and I realize it's all on my shoulders now. I need to help her.

"Come on." I take Delilah's hand, then reach for Cassidy's, and I lead them off the boardwalk and across the road.

Delilah's hair curtains her face, but I can hear her breath hitching and know she's trying to stop crying. By the time we've crossed the main drag, she's sniffling less. I'm thankful that Cassidy is with us. I think girls have radar for helping each other more than guys do, even though I'm pretty in tune with both of them. As we walk, I think of my parents. My father and I stood eye-to-eye at six foot two. He had light brown hair like me, cut super short the way adults do. My mom was blond like Delilah and thin like her, too. The day they dropped us off at college, my father pulled me aside and said, *Your focus needs to be on your grades. I know you'll be into girls, but, son, they're going to come and go, and each time they go, you're going to learn something about women.* I still remember thinking that he was trying to tell me something, but I had no idea what. Then he turned his piercing green eyes back to me and said, *And when you graduate and get a job and find the one woman who finally stays—who you want to stay—she won't care that there's not a chance in hell you'll ever figure her out.*

I look down at our hands, then up at Delilah and Cassidy. Delilah glances at me and presses her lips into a line, like she is holding something back. I smile to let her know everything is going to be okay. Cassidy squeezes my hand, and I realize that while all the other girls I'd been with had come and gone and never meant anything to me, Cass has always been right there with me. With us.

Another reason not to let my mind wander in the wrong direction with her. Delilah and I can't afford for me to screw up our friendship with Cass.

Chapter Five

~Cassidy~

EVERY SUMMER I spend at least a week at Harborside with Delilah and Wyatt, and a couple of summers ago Wyatt took me to the creek when he wanted to get out from under his dad's thumb. I have no idea if there's more than one creek here, but Wyatt explained that this creek was his go-to place to be alone. It was his escape from the boardwalk and tourists, from his parents, from all the shop owners and friends who had known them since they were knee high.

We spent the afternoon sitting on the bank and talking about what life would be like after we graduated from college. I remember thinking that I had my life mapped out. I was going to get my degree in accounting, which I have now accomplished. Yay for me! And then I was going to work in New York. That's been a dream of mine ever since I visited the city with my parents. My parents are always jetting off somewhere, and seeing them so happy makes me want to live in the fast lane, too. They've made it pretty clear that if I lived in someplace like New York, where they visit often, we'd spend more time together.

At home, our lives are anything but fast, but maybe that's just my life, not theirs. When I was younger, they didn't travel quite as much as they did when I was in high school and college, but it was still often enough that I learned how to cook and do my own laundry by the time I was eight. Even when they were home, they were always rushing out to parties in the evening, or business dinners. I stayed with the Armstrongs so often that I used to wonder if Wyatt's parents felt like they had three kids instead of two. His mother always offered to watch me instead of my parents hiring babysitters. One thing about Mrs. Armstrong, she was always there for her kids.

Once I began college, between working, spending a week or two down here, and hanging out with friends, I wasn't home much during the summers, so my interaction with my parents has been limited anyway. My dad's an investor, so he's always breezing through the door late in the evenings and talking to Mom about his latest deal. I never paid much attention to what it all meant, or what he really did. Now that Wyatt's parents are gone, I miss my parents even more. I shouldn't, because they haven't called to check up on me, so obviously they don't miss me. But I can't help thinking...What if they get into an accident and I never see them again?

I was thinking about my parents when Delilah broke down on the boardwalk and Wyatt took control and led us here to the creek. I knew it was the one place Delilah *wouldn't* have memories of her parents.

The creek is about ten or twelve feet wide, buffered by trees along the far bank and nestled against a shore of grass and rocks on our side. It's peaceful, listening to the water move swiftly by, and it smells different from the seashore, like a grassy lawn after a downpour. It's strange to think that just across the road is the ocean.

Wyatt's standing with one foot on a big rock, the other on the grass, throwing rocks into the water. I allow my eyes to linger on him, which I haven't wanted to do the last few days because of the way my body has been reacting to him lately. His legs are strong and thick where they disappear beneath his cargo shorts, which ride dangerously low on his hips. His tank hugs his broad chest. I feel my cheeks heat up as I drink him in. He keeps glancing at Delilah, who's sitting next to me shredding pieces of grass. His eyes are filled with worry, but I have faith in him. He'll pull Delilah through this. He has such natural caretaking instincts, and yet Wyatt goes out of his way to remain single. I know he does, because one time we were at a party and he pulled this girl I knew he didn't like into a really hot kiss. I asked him about it afterward, and he pointed to the girl across the room he had gone out with the night before and said, *She's a clinger. I wouldn't want her to get her hopes up for anything long-term.*

A clinger.

I remember that night like it was yesterday. It was during our freshman year at college, when my feelings for Wyatt felt very real. I wanted to be the girl he'd kissed so badly I almost volunteered to be the hope killer at all future parties, but like I've done so many times that I usually don't even realize I'm doing it, I'd swallowed that offer and walked away.

I feel funny for thinking about Wyatt in that way, but the good thing is that I'm not thinking about Kyle.

Until now. I wonder if Kyle saw me as a clinger.

"You okay, Delilah?" As much as I am trying to distract myself from thinking about Kyle and Wyatt, I also really care about Delilah, and I want to make sure she's okay.

"I'm just thinking about stuff." She lifts her eyes and stares out at the creek. "I wished they weren't around."

Wyatt turns toward Delilah.

Before either of us can respond, Delilah says, "I thought if our parents weren't around, things might be different. I might be different. I mean, I am different, but maybe I would have acted differently in college." She shrugs, as if she hadn't just bared her soul.

"We all wish our parents weren't around at some point. I know I have, tons of times," I reassure her, hoping she really hears what I'm saying. I can't tell if she's listening. She's shredding blades of grass again. "You can't feel guilty over it. It's not like you caused their accident."

Wyatt sits beside her and rests his arms over his knees, but he doesn't say anything, and I wonder what he's thinking. I know he's wished his parents weren't around before, when they were calling too often, making him feel like he might fail if they didn't harass him about his grades, which he wouldn't have, but it's not like either of them wished they'd die.

"I know I didn't cause their...accident," Delilah says.

Wyatt and I share a glance, and I see tension in his jaw.

"What *do* you think, Dee?" he finally asks.

There's an edge to his voice that causes Delilah to turn toward him.

"That now I'll never know if Mom and Dad would have accepted who I am or not."

Wyatt rips a hunk of grass from the ground and shreds the blades, like Delilah is doing.

"I'm serious, Wyatt. I'm not like you. Dad loved who you were, even if he—"

"Bullshit." Wyatt's jaw clenches.

I shift my eyes away, wanting to give them privacy.

"Oh, come on." Delilah raises her voice. "You played football and you got good grades, and you never even had to try. I was always a disappointment. I had to work my butt off to get good grades—"

"But you did." Every word he says is laden with love and support. "Dee, they were so proud of you, but not me. I was the frigging disappointment. Dad hated that I went from girl to girl, and he hated that I drank and partied. Mom thought I was too unfocused and that I'd never be able to hold down a real job."

I swallow the sting of hearing Wyatt's inner turmoil, but I remain quiet. It's not my place to tell him how wrong his father was about him.

Delilah scoffs. "*Please.* You were his golden boy,

Wy. He was going to lead you to a great job, and he bragged about you all the time, while I was their dirty little secret."

I hear her voice trembling and almost reach for her hand, but I'm afraid to interrupt. She told me that she was into girls a few days after Wyatt had guessed it. I know Delilah never told her parents or her friends in school, and if she had told her parents, I'm fairly certain they would have reacted like she *was* their dirty little secret. She and Wyatt are staring at each other like their anger is directed toward each other, and it worries me. I'm not sure what to do.

"Bullshit, Dee. They never knew about...all that."

All that. I have no idea if that's an okay way to refer to his sister's sexuality, and I guess it isn't, because tears tumble down Delilah's cheeks.

"Yes, they did." She holds Wyatt's stare as his jaw drops open.

I know mine's doing the same, and I make an effort to close my mouth.

"You told them?" he finally asks.

"Before the graduation ceremony," Delilah says softly.

Wyatt reaches for her hand, and his eyes soften again. "Dee. Why didn't you tell me?"

She shrugs. "I was going to, but everything happened so fast. Right after I told Mom, they called us to line up." Her lower lip trembles as she continues. "Mom didn't say anything. I watched her as I walked away and could see her telling Dad."

"And?" Wyatt urges.

She shrugs again. "He held her hand and looked at

me with that disappointed look. You know that one that makes your stomach fall to your feet?"

"Yeah," Wyatt says as he folds her into his arms again. "I know that fucking look."

He rubs her back and looks at me over her shoulder. I know my eyes are damp, but I keep the tears from falling.

"They didn't expect it, Dee, but it didn't change their love for you." Wyatt says this like it's a fact, and I don't know how he can be sure. If I were Delilah, I think I'd call him on it, but I hear her sniffling and I know she's crying again.

"I know they loved me," Delilah finally says. "But you know...loving and accepting are two different things. I wanted them to accept me, and I knew from the look in their eyes that there was no way that was going to happen."

Chapter Six

~Wyatt~

AFTER DELILAH DROPPED her bomb, she clammed up. Cassidy and I tried to talk to her more about what happened, but she eventually got up and walked away. I didn't follow her. I know Delilah, and when she needs time alone, she *needs* time alone. Cassidy and I talked by the creek for a long time about what we could say to help Delilah, but no matter how many things we came up with, I knew they were all just words and that nothing would take away the sting of the look my parents gave her. That stupid look that cut my sister to her core and had done the same to me more times than I care to remember.

Delilah comes back about an hour later and apologizes for walking off, but she doesn't need to. I get it, and I know Cass does, too. Her eyes are clearer, and she seems to be in a better mood. I'm not about to try to talk to her about our parents again, but I will when I think she's ready. I could really use a *How to Help Your Sister Come Out of the Closet and Get over the Death of Your Parents* guide.

I thought Cassidy's life was going to be so messed up after we caught Kyle cheating on her, but the death of our parents made me realize that breakups aren't the end of the world. And now I realize that even our parents dying isn't the end of the world. But the mess of emotions that Delilah is left dealing with? That's pretty damn bad. She's going to be dealing with that for a long time. I just hope it doesn't mess her up forever. I mean, I know our parents loved her, but I also know they were too conservative to probably ever have accepted the lifestyle she wants and needs. It's who she is, and they would have tried to change that. I'm sure of it. I have no idea how such smart businesspeople could be clueless when it came to their own daughter. Right now I kind of hate my parents, and I'm not going to feel guilty for that. If they were alive I'd call my father and give him hell. I wish I'd been there when she told them. I wish she hadn't tried to handle it on her own, but I know Dee, and she probably had about thirty seconds of courage and thought she'd blast through it. She doesn't always need me by her side, but this time I wish I'd been there. I wouldn't have cared about lining up for graduation. I would have confronted my parents and tried to make them see that Delilah's an amazing person and her sexuality doesn't change a thing.

Who am I kidding? There would have been no changing their minds. They were stubborn pricks when they wanted to be.

After a while we go into town and buy groceries. Then we drive around talking about what we want to do this week and wondering what our friends are up to. Basically, we avoid talking about anything relating to our parents. As we pass the pier, I know we have to face the bar at some point. Maybe tomorrow. Delilah doesn't need to deal with this stuff, and I have no idea what *this stuff* might be. I don't even know what it means that we own the bar. I mean, my parents ran it during the summers and Jesse takes care of it the rest of the time, or at least he did until he bought his restaurant. I doubt he'll want to take over this fall. I guess I'll figure it out at some point. The staff has to know what to do, right? I imagine there isn't much to owning it, but then again, what do I know?

I hear Cassidy power up her phone as we pull down the street toward our house, and my mind careens to a halt, revisiting the reason she'd turned it off in the first place. I hear *ping* after *ping* of text messages coming through and glance in my rearview, fighting the urge to ask about them. She's staring at her phone with an angry look in her eyes, so I know Kyle has texted, and I tighten my hands on the steering wheel. I don't say anything as I drive down our street. Our beach house is built at the end of a private road, so we don't have neighbors on either side of us. The neighbors pretty much keep to themselves, even Mr. Mahoney. He's a curmudgeonly old man whose house is closest to ours. He's practically deaf, and a glance in our direction is all he ever offers.

There are only five other houses on the street, and they're all a good distance from ours. Three of them have been flipped in recent years and renovated, with second stories added to the ones that were only one story. Most of the houses, like ours, have cedar shingles that have aged to varying shades of gray. Two of the recently renovated homes have a different type of siding that's beige, and I think they look out of place. All of the houses have gardens that look like someone dumped a bucket of mixed-up seeds in the dirt and then forgot about them. Colorful flowers and tall grasses billow out over the garden edging.

"I always forget how much I love the gardens here. They're so different from back home," Delilah says as she tucks her hair behind her ear.

I park in front of our house and watch Delilah for signs of sadness, even though she sounds fine at the moment. I'm also waiting for my own discomfort to set in. We sit out front for a few minutes, staring at the two-story, seven-bedroom house. It was a bed-and-breakfast before my parents bought it, and they never changed the setup, so each bedroom has a full bath with a shower, which is pretty cool. The house has an open floor plan, with a great room, a large, open kitchen, and three bedrooms on the first floor. There's a loft with a pool table, as well as four more bedrooms upstairs. It's way more than we ever needed, and I remember telling my father that when I was finally old enough to see that it was. As a kid you never think of those things. It's just a house. But by the time I was in high school, it struck me how enormous the house was compared to our friends' houses. My father had said, *If you work hard and get good grades, you'll be able to afford homes this big, too.* He had a way of skirting my questions and needling me at the same time.

Even though I'd take a little needling over my parents being gone, I'm astonished when I get out of the car and don't feel anything weird. I thought I'd feel a punch to the gut, but there's nothing strange going on inside me.

The girls get out of the car, and we grab our stuff from the trunk and head inside.

"You okay, Dee?" I ask, eyeing Cassidy as she sends a text. I've never cared who she texted before, but now I want to ask. I try to push the thought away. But the annoyance doesn't disappear. It just sort of festers, burning a hole in my gut.

Maybe there's no room for a gut punch about my parents because the idea of Kyle and Cassidy talking is taking up all the space.

"Surprisingly, yeah. I am okay." Delilah manages a smile as we walk up the slate path toward the front door.

The front of the house has a large deck that wraps around the side. There's a slate patio out front with deck furniture, and we have the same type of overgrown garden as everyone else does, only ours has mostly yellow flowers because our mom was a freak for yellow. We have yellow towels, yellow blankets in the guest bedrooms, and back in Connecticut we had so many yellow knickknacks they probably could have lit up the house enough that we wouldn't have needed lightbulbs. Strange how I didn't even think about that when we were home.

The flowers are knee high and brush against my legs as I walk down the stone path toward the deck. I fish for the right key and unlock the door, then push the door open. We all stand there, staring inside. The afternoon sunlight floods the first floor. That was one of the things my mother liked most about being in Harborside. She used to sit on the deck and drink coffee, listening to the ocean and smiling. I often wonder about my parents' decision to buy the bar. They weren't drinkers, and even now I can't really put the pieces of that purchase together with them in my mind, but there's no doubt they loved owning it and they loved Harborside.

My dad was a keen businessman, though. Throughout the years he'd bought and sold many businesses. I don't know why the Taproom is the one he chose not to sell, but he'd guided me and Delilah toward taking it over for the last four years, so I know his plans were to keep it.

I push thoughts of my parents to the side and take in the rest of the room. There are no curtains on the two sets of French doors on either side of the open kitchen. The enormous bay window behind the kitchen table is also void of any curtains, as is the window over the sink. We have a clear view of our private beach. I drop my duffel bags in the center of the room.

"Looks like home." Feels like it, too, familiar and comfortable. I don't have the feeling that my parents are going to come through the door like I did back in Connecticut, where I felt like the walls were confining and my lungs were constricted. I inhale deeply, relieved that I can. My parents were with us every time we stayed here, but unlike home, there were no grades to ask after, no pushing us toward our future. Even though they owned the bar, it was like this was where they could let their hair down, kick their feet up, and be a little less controlling.

Cassidy closes the screen door behind her, leaving the front door open. I cross the well-worn path in the hardwood to the back doors and pull them open. Salty sea air mixes with the scents of sand and seaweed and wafts through the screens. I love everything about being here, from the smells to the sights, but there are two things that make Harborside my favorite place on earth. There's nothing better than hanging out with good friends and falling asleep to the sound of the waves breaking. Even though we see our friends here for only a few weeks out of the year, we talk about deeper stuff, and I trust them more than any friends I met at college.

I shrug off the dissection of our friendship and point up at the ceiling. "I'm taking my stuff up." I shrug the straps of my duffel over my shoulder, then reach for Delilah's. "You taking your regular bedroom, or staying downstairs?"

"Regular bedroom," she says, and hands me her bag.

"Cass? Pick a room." I reach for her bag, and she rolls her eyes.

"I always stay down the hall from your room. Why would I change?" She shoves her phone in her pocket.

I slide the strap of Cassidy's bags over my other shoulder and carry all of our bags upstairs. Mine and Delilah's bedrooms are in the back of the house, overlooking the water. I toss my stuff on my bed and pull open the doors to the second-story deck, drop the girls' bags by their beds, and walk out onto the deck. The deck wraps around the second floor. Each of the bedrooms has access to it, and as I look out over the water, I think about how many times Delilah, Cassidy, and I snuck out over the summers when we were growing up. Our parents were more relaxed here than at home, and their rules were somewhat less stringent. With no grades to ask after, they were happy to let us wander the boardwalk with our friends during the day as long as we checked in with them often. Once the sun went down, however, strict rules came back into play. We had earlier curfews than our friends, and sneaking out was the only way we ever saw any nightlife. Every single time we snuck out, Cassidy would cling to my arm like she was afraid of the dark.

My thoughts linger on Cassidy for a minute, and I realize there's another reason it feels so right being here. She's here with me.

"Wyatt?"

Speak of the devil. "Out here!" I holler.

"Hey." She's got her camera strap around her neck when she joins me and leans on the railing. "It's so beautiful."

"Yeah. Thanks for coming with us." I purposely lean over the deck beside her so my eyes don't betray me and look at her sweet ass again.

"I can't think of anywhere I'd rather be."

What are her alternatives? Cassidy has a strange family life, which is why she stays with us a lot. Her parents are always going somewhere and leaving her behind. My parents might have been conservative and strict, but our vacations were always taken as a family. I've always felt like Cassidy's parents' loss was our gain. I love having Cassidy around, and I can't imagine my life without her in it.

"Delilah and I were thinking that a bonfire might be fun tonight. Are you up for it?" She shields her eyes from the sun and looks up at me.

"Always. Does she want to invite everyone?"

Cassidy shakes her head. "She didn't say so. She just said she wants to eat hot dogs over the fire for dinner."

I groan and Cassidy laughs. Hot dogs are about the grossest food on the planet, but they're Delilah's go-to meal when she's coming out of anything distressing.

"I know." She smiles. "But that's a good sign, right?"

"Grossly, yes. It's a good sign. Did she ever contact Frank about our parents?" I'm even worried about Delilah's fake boyfriend? I roll my eyes at myself.

"Yeah, she called him. He was really sweet to her. I feel bad for him. He really likes her." Cassidy turns around and leans her back against the railing. She aims her camera at me, and I turn away.

"Please, Wy?"

Why does she have this hold over me? I've never been able to turn her away. When I turn and look out over the water, I hear her take a picture. "One," I say.

"Two?"

I hear the shutter clicking and turn to face her, and she takes another of me looking directly at her. As she puts the lens cap back on, she smiles up at me again. I love her smile way too much.

She hooks her finger in my pocket and her eyes turn solemn. "I know you don't want me to ask how you're doing, so I won't. Just know that I'm here if you want to talk, okay?"

When I don't answer, she hooks another finger in my other pocket. She's done that a million times and never once have I ever felt anything sexual, but she's looking up at me with her lips slightly parted, a sweet smile on her face, and her eyes dark and warm, and hell, I feel myself getting hard. This is becoming a problem, and I don't like it one bit. I like being comfortable with Cass. This is totally messed up.

"Thanks, Cass." I try to turn away, but she hooks her fingers deeper into my pockets and uses them for leverage to pull her body against mine. I stifle a groan.

"Look at me, Army."

She narrows her eyes, and I laugh, because she looks adorable, which I know is not at all how she wants to look. She calls me by my nickname only when she's trying to get my attention about something important, but her lips are pursed and she looks like she's ready to kiss me. Epic fail on her part. She looks sexy as hell.

"Don't laugh. I'm being serious." She tugs on my pockets like that's going to help.

I wonder what she'd do if she knew that the friction was making me harder. I draw my brows together and press my lips into a firm line, trying to concentrate. "Sorry. Go ahead. What did you want to say?"

"Just that, you know, your parents dying is a huge deal. *Huge.* It's not like they're away for a while and they're coming back."

I grit my teeth against the truth.

"And I know you're tough and all, but I also know you loved them very much, and at some point you might want to talk about it."

Her fingers are still in my pockets, but she is no longer holding me against her. She's looking at me like she always does, like she cares. Like she's my best friend. And I think I have a new companion, called Guilt, for being aroused when she's only trying to be sweet.

"I'm fine." I'm pretty far from *fine*, but that's not something I want to lay on Cassidy, especially since my body is throwing me off-balance and reacting to her as if she were some random hot girl. I feel like a jealous boyfriend about Kyle texting her, and I've got no business feeling that way. All of it makes it difficult for me to act normal around her.

"Yeah, I know you are." She rolls her eyes and moves away. "Just like I'm fine about Kyle."

Chapter Seven

~Cassidy~

AFTER GRILLING HOT dogs and burgers we go to the liquor store and pick up just about everything under the sun. I think Wyatt's planning on drinking himself into oblivion, and I guess I don't blame him. At least Delilah is talking more now. I'm not used to her being this silent, but I can understand that, too.

The three of us sit on the deck drinking. Delilah and I are sharing a bottle of wine, and Wyatt's drinking beer. The sky is eerily dark, without a star in sight, and the moon has a fuzzy bluish glow around it, the kind you see in werewolf movies. It's kind of fitting, given the darkness of what's happened lately. I pick up my camera and take a few pictures, then set it back on the table.

I watch Wyatt finish his beer and open another. He's not a mean drunk, like some guys. He gets more introspective when he drinks, but before he gets to that point, he gets really fun. I'm waiting for the fun Wyatt to kick in, which is probably selfish, but I think he needs the distraction as much as I do. I left my phone inside because I know the constant texts bug Wyatt as much as they bug me. I'm still trying to decide how to handle Kyle. I don't know why he keeps texting me and I don't care. I'm never going back to him. I deserve a guy who at the very least likes me enough not to cheat on me. Every time I think of him and that girl, it makes me wonder how many others I didn't know about. That just sends my mind spiraling into a really dark place, where I blame myself for not noticing. I know it's crazy, but it's hard to remember that when my head feels like it's going to explode.

"Hey, Army, you around?"

We all turn at the sound of Brandon's voice coming around the side of the house. I know Wyatt's friends pretty well from spending time here with them each summer, and I like them all a lot. It's my fault that they call Wyatt *Army*. The summer after our freshman year, I was making fun of the nickname, trying to get him to stop using it because I love his real name so much, and Brandon clung to it like it was honey and he was a bee. He and Tristan have been calling Wyatt *Army* ever since.

"Dude!" Wyatt leaps from his chair and embraces Brandon. Brandon's our age, and he's a really cool graphic designer and an amazing guitarist.

Delilah and I both stand to greet him, and then I see Tristan Brewer, Jesse Steele, and a really pretty girl I don't know come around the corner of the house. I hate the way my eyes shift to Wyatt to see if he notices her. His smile tells me he does. I shouldn't care if he thinks she's pretty. She *is* pretty. I remind myself that Wyatt's not my boyfriend. I didn't realize until this very second that this has become a familiar mantra over the last four years. I've stifled my attraction to him at least that long. And it's crazy because he will never be my boyfriend, so I need to get over him. *I'm not his type. He doesn't commit. He doesn't want me in that way.* I have more reasons why we'll never be a couple than I care to rattle off at the moment, the least of which is that Wyatt doesn't even know what the word *couple* means. In an effort to distract myself, I hug tall, dark, and handsome Tristan.

I feel like I'm living on distractions lately.

"Cass. I should have known you'd be here." Tristan pulls back, holding me by the shoulders, and rolls his soft brown eyes down my minidress. "Wow, you look gorgeous, hon."

I hear Brandon telling Wyatt and Delilah he's sorry about their loss, and my heart aches a little more.

"Thanks. So do you." I squeeze Tristan's biceps. "Have you been working out?" Out of the corner of my eyes I notice Brandon introducing Delilah and Wyatt to the girl. She's got blond hair, blonder than Delilah's and longer. It hangs in long golden streams to the curve of her butt.

"Have to," Tristan says. "Guys around here aren't into fleshy bodies, if you know what I mean." He winks, and I tousle his dark hair. Tristan is about Wyatt's height with a body built for hard work and a heart big enough to save the world. I'm convinced that if he ever tried to do something other than bartending, he could do any number of things to help others. He's a great listener, and he always puts others before himself. He could take part in a Big Brother program, go to school for social work, or become a police officer. There are so many things he could do, but he seems content with bartending.

"Brooke, you made it." Jesse waves to her as she climbs the stairs to the deck. Brooke's long dark hair hangs loosely over one shoulder. She's carrying two Pepe's Pizza boxes, which Tristan takes from her and sets on the table.

"Hi. Sorry I'm so late." She hugs Delilah. "Hi, babe. Are you doing okay?"

"Yeah. Pretty much, anyway." Delilah steps aside as Wyatt leans in to hug Brooke.

"Hey, Brooke. Good to see you." Wyatt kisses her cheek.

"How are you holding up, Wyatt? I'm so sorry about your parents."

"We're doing as well as can be expected." Wyatt shoves his hand in his pocket, and I know he's putting on a brave face. I can tell by the way his eyes are darting around the deck.

"I'm here if you guys need me, so don't be afraid to ask. Delilah, if you want to talk, you've got my number." Brooke touches Wyatt's arm. "You too, Wyatt. Whatever you guys need, I'm here."

She turns to talk to Delilah, and Jesse sets down the paper bag he's carrying and hugs me tight.

"Cassidy, I knew you'd come with Wyatt." Jesse's the epitome of what I always thought a biker would look like, because he is one. He has three motorcycles, lots of tattoos, and his brown hair almost reaches his shoulders. He has a mustache and keeps a short, well-groomed beard. But he doesn't look like a greasy biker. His hair is always brushed back away from his face, and he's got the warmest eyes that totally conflict with his rough, hard-bodied image.

"Of course I'm here. Where's Brent?" Jesse's twin brother, Brent, plays in Brandon's band. I know Jesse is running the Taproom since the summer manager quit, but with his recent purchase of his own restaurant, I wonder how long Jesse plans to help out now that Wyatt's father is gone.

"He's on a date. Where else?" He hugs me again, glances at Wyatt, then reaches for Delilah. "Delly, come over here."

"Jesse, I've missed you." Delilah remains in his strong arms for a long time, like she needed his comfort really badly. I noticed last year how close she was with Jesse and Brooke. She spent a lot of time hanging out at Brooke's café, and whenever Jesse was around, they'd talk privately for long periods of time.

I hear Jesse asking how she's doing and telling her he's there if she needs him. The tenderness in his voice tells me how sincere he is. I walk away to give them privacy.

Wyatt, Brandon, Tristan, and the girl are sitting on the steps that lead to the beach. I take my wine and contemplate where to sit. The four of them are sitting shoulder to shoulder. Normally, I'd push through them and sit in front of Wyatt, but I don't like the jealousy pooling in my stomach about him and that girl. I hate this feeling. I was never jealous of Kyle and other girls, and now I know I should have been. Leave it to my stupid heart to be confused. I stand behind them on the top step and tighten my grip on the wineglass.

"Get down here, girlfriend." Tristan scoots over and pats the step in front of him. I hate that I wish it were Wyatt doing it.

I sit sideways on the step in front of Tristan so I can see Wyatt and the girl. Tristan rests his hand on my shoulder. They're talking about college, and it sounds like she knows Brandon from school. I realize I didn't actually say hello to Brandon yet and tap his knee.

"I was wondering when you'd get around to giving me my hug." Brandon reaches for me and squeezes me tight in his long, sinewy arms. He's as tall as Tristan and Wyatt, but much leaner. He reminds me of a starving artist. He actually could be one, I realize, because other than playing in Brent's band and doing some graphic design work on the side, I don't think he works.

"How long are you here for?" Brandon asks.

Wyatt glances at me as I sit back down in front of Tristan. "I'm not sure. I guess however long Wyatt wants me to stay." It's a barb, and I feel guilty after I say it, because I said it with an infliction that any girl would read as there being something between me and Wyatt, when there's not.

The girl looks at me and smiles. Wow. Her smile lights up her whole face, and she's even prettier.

"Hi. I'm Ashley."

"Hi. I'm Cassidy."

"Oh, you have wine?" she gushes. "I'd rather have wine. Do you mind if I have some?"

She says this without so much as a hint of faking a damsel in distress wanting Wyatt to cater to her.

"I'll get you a glass," I say in an effort to rein in my bitchy jealous claws. I step between Tristan and Brandon as Jesse, Brooke, and Delilah join us. Jesse takes my hand and pulls me up the last step, and then the three of them walk down to a lower step. I go inside and fill a glass with wine, trying not to peek outside. *Ugh!* I hate this feeling.

When I bring her the glass, she smiles that gorgeous smile again. "Thanks so much, Cassidy." She moves toward Brandon and allows me to step between her and Wyatt. Wyatt grabs my calf, nearly sending me tumbling down the steps. He catches me by my hips, eases me down to sit on the step in front of him, and rests his hand on my shoulder.

I like his touch way too much to try to decipher why he did it. It's not like he gets jealous, especially of guys around *me.* He's protective, but he's never been jealous.

Tristan slips off his flip-flops and puts his toes over mine. He's such a lovable dork. His dark hair is short on the sides and spiky on top.

I feel Wyatt's hand tighten on my shoulder, which is weird, considering Tristan is gay. The truth is, Tristan is anything *but* a dork. He's six two, solid muscle, and handsome as the ocean is blue, but I have no idea why Wyatt is acting possessive of me tonight.

Tristan's lips quirk up in a coy smile, and he leans across Brandon's lap to get closer to me. "How am I going to catch up with you sitting over there?"

"While you're down there," Brandon says to Tristan. He lifts his eyebrows in quick succession, and I turn away.

"You're a pig." Ashley smacks Brandon on the back.

Brandon puts his arm around her. "Aw, babe, did I make you jealous?" He points to his crotch. "Have at it."

Delilah and I share an eye roll. Brandon sleeps with everyone and anyone. Guys, girls, both at the same time. I don't really care who he sleeps with, but I worry that he'll be one of those forty-year-old guys who hang out in bars trying to pick up twenty-somethings and will end up alone and lonely.

Tristan moves to the step I'm sitting on and puts his feet between mine, then reaches for my free hand. "Are you still dating Kyle?"

I cringe inside, and the smile I was sporting falls flat. I see Tristan's eyes shoot to Wyatt, and I glance up. Wyatt's shaking his head and giving Tristan a dark look that clearly tells him not to go there.

Tristan returns his attention to me. "Aw, I'm sorry. Guys can be real dicks."

"No kidding." I down my wine.

"I took care of him," Wyatt says as he runs his hand through my hair, which makes my entire body tingle in a way it shouldn't. "Now it's up to Cassidy to get him to stop texting her." Wyatt moves his hand away, and I miss it instantly. I hate that I miss it, but I tell myself that he's my best friend, so it's okay to miss it.

Maybe just not so much.

"Sorry about your breakup," Ashley says.

"Thanks." Does she have to be so nice?

"Hey, why don't we hit the Taproom tomorrow night and we'll find you a new guy. Or even better, I'll take a hit for the team," Brandon offers with a coy smile.

"Dude, back off. She just broke up a week ago." Wyatt presses his knee against my arm, and I'm pretty sure it's by accident, but my whole body warms.

I roll my eyes at Brandon and feel like I should move away from Wyatt until I can figure out why I'm suddenly analyzing everything he does. It bothers me that I'm analyzing him. *Ugh.* I push to my feet, and suddenly I want to be very, very drunk and forget *how* to think.

"The best way to get over a guy is to get under a new one," Brandon quips.

Wyatt punches his arm.

"There might be some truth to that statement," I joke, but the look in Wyatt's eyes tell me he doesn't think it's funny. "Anyone up for shots?" I push my way past Brandon and escape toward the kitchen.

"Shots?" Wyatt follows me up to the deck and into the kitchen, ahead of the others, who are making comments about who's going to go down first.

"Shots?" Wyatt asks again.

I shrug. I reach into the cabinet and grab a few shot glasses, and when I turn to go outside, he grabs my arm and searches my eyes. My heart stops at the way he's staring at me, like I've done something wrong.

87

"What?" I ask.

"You okay?" He eyes the glasses.

Okay, so I'm not a big drinker, and for me to suggest we do shots is a little out of the ordinary, but if ever there was a time that I needed to drink, it's now. And I need to drink a lot, because my heart started racing again from being so close to Wyatt, and heat's running through my veins.

"Yeah, fine." I take a step toward the door, and he holds me too tight to move forward. "Wyatt, are *you* okay?" I feel my eyes widen, wondering what's up his butt at this point.

He narrows his eyes, and I know he wants to say something about the joke I made to Brandon. I can see it in his eyes and in the way he's clenching his teeth like he's deciding if he should. Then the look in his eyes turns smoldering hot and my entire body warms from my head to my toes and all the best places in between. I can't tear my eyes from his. Delilah and Ashley come inside and reach for a few of the glasses to help me carry them. Wyatt's still holding my arm, and I can't look away from his steamy gaze.

"I have to warn you guys, I'm a total lightweight," Ashley says.

"Me too," Delilah admits. "We'll hold each other's hair back when we puke."

"Hey," Jesse says as he comes inside. "No puking tonight, girls. Let's try to be a little responsible." He's the oldest in the group and is always looking out for Wyatt and his friends.

"Buzzkill." Brandon grabs a bottle of rum and carries it outside.

"Army, can you grab the Tabasco and cinnamon schnapps?" Tristan calls from the doorway.

Wyatt finally releases my arm, but he holds my gaze. I'm relieved, because if he held me much longer I might have given in to the urge to press my lips to his and taste what I've dreamed about for so long—the heat of his touch.

"I'm on it," Wyatt answers, his eyes still pinning me to the floor.

Delilah takes my arm and drags me out to the deck. I should thank her for getting me outside, where fresh air fills my lungs and starts to kick my brain into gear again, but my body is still humming with lust for her smoking-hot brother.

Brandon turns on the stereo, and we gather around the table on the deck. Brooke puts a hand on Delilah's shoulder and leans in close.

"Don't let these guys make you drink too much, Dee."

"Don't worry. I learned my lesson when I was fifteen. Drank way too much beer and puked all night. Wyatt told Mom I ate bad seafood at our friend's house."

"Yeah, I don't drink much either," Brooke says. "And I'm not drinking at all tonight. I have to work early tomorrow morning. You should stop by when you have time."

"I will, thanks," Delilah says.

Jesse leans on the table and slides a narrow-eyed stare over each of us, bringing all chatter to an abrupt halt. He looks ominous when his eyebrows do that dip-down thing, and when he taps his index finger on the table he looks even more threatening. I know Jesse would never hurt any one of us. On the contrary, he's like an older brother to everyone. But this particular stare still rattles me.

"Keys. Now." Jesse eyes Tristan, who tosses his keys onto the table, and then he stares at Brandon.

"Come on, man." Brandon crosses his arms.

Jesse lowers his voice. "If you're going to do shots, you're going to give me your keys, Brandon. Otherwise, you can be damn sure that not an ounce of that alcohol is touching your lips."

Brandon holds up his beer bottle and takes a sip, and then he shoves his hand in his pocket and tosses his keys on the table, holding Jesse's stare the whole time. "You'll let me drink beer and drive but not do shots? That's some strange thinking, dude."

Jesse swipes the keys from the table and smiles. "Who says I would have let you drive after drinking beer? I just didn't feel the need to swipe your keys because of one beer, but at two, you're damn right I'd have taken them. I'm not letting any of you take chances with your lives."

Brandon scoffs. "You're not at the bar, Jesse."

"No shit, Sherlock. But you're my friends." Jesse pats him on the back, and Brandon tries to suppress a smile. It's obvious this feather ruffling is common between them, because neither seems upset.

"What about Ashley's keys?" Delilah asks.

"Oh, Brandon drove me over." Ashley glances at Wyatt, then at Delilah. "He talks about you guys all the time, so I wanted to meet you. I hope you don't mind."

Delilah smiles. "Thanks, Brandon. I'm glad you

brought her along."

"We girls tend to be outnumbered—don't we, Delilah?" Brooke winks at her.

"Yes, but we're catching up," Delilah answers.

Tristan rubs his hands together and begins mixing shots with the precision of the practiced bartender he is. "Who's ready for a fireball?"

I'm standing across from Wyatt, who is standing between Ashley and Delilah. Jesse, standing on Ashley's other side, puts his arm around her shoulder. "Ash, don't overdo it. You don't have to keep up with Brandon."

"She can hold her own," Brandon says, which makes me wonder if Ashley is with him, as in really *with* him tonight.

"I'll be fine," Ashley says.

We all reach for our shot glasses.

"To my parents." Wyatt holds up his glass.

I'm not sure why this surprises me, but it does. It makes me realize he's thinking about them even though he doesn't want to talk about it, and I wish he would talk to me about it. I'm not sure why his shutting me out bothers me more now than it did earlier in the day, but it does.

We down our drinks. My mouth is all tingly, and the shot burns all the way down my throat and tastes like cinnamon. It's a wonderful mix of pleasure and pain and is exactly the escape I need. *Ah, cinnaburn.*

"Nice," Wyatt says as he sets his glass back down. "Another five or six and I'll be feeling just fine."

"Sometimes it's weird to watch you guys drink. I feel like I should tell you not to drink too much, but I also don't want to ruin your fun." Brooke looks at Jesse. They're the closest in age, and I know she wonders if he feels the same way.

"All we can do is keep them safe," Jesse assures her. "We were their age once." He winks at her, and it makes me wonder if they've ever hooked up.

None of my business.

Tristan makes another round. "Remember when I was first learning to be a bartender?"

"Yup. You used us as guinea pigs. *That* was fun." Brandon scoffs, shakes his head.

"Yeah, well..." Tristan hands out the next round. "We all remember when you were learning to play the guitar." He laughs.

"I remember a few eardrum-cracking notes," Jesse teases.

"We all gotta start somewhere." Brandon picks up his shot glass and holds it up.

We follow suit, and I have no idea I'm going to say anything, but words spill from my mouth like a leaky faucet. "To new beginnings."

"To new beginnings," they all say in unison, and we down the shots.

The cinnaburn feels so good I close my eyes and revel in it for a minute. *New beginnings.* I meant it about me, breaking up with Kyle, but I realize that it's a very apropos toast for Delilah and Wyatt, too. Delilah reaches for my hand and squeezes it. I know she has figured that out, too.

Tristan fills our glasses again, and this time Jesse holds his glass up high. "To good friends and a safe summer." He gives us all another earnest stare. "Y'all know, wherever you are, you call me or you call a cab, but don't ever get behind the wheel when you're drinking."

Tristan, Wyatt, and Brandon all groan. Brooke flashes an approving smile.

"What is up with you this weekend?" Brandon asks.

Jesse glances at Wyatt, and I know exactly what's up. Wyatt hasn't talked about it, but at the funeral I heard his uncle tell him that the driver who caused his parents' accident had been drinking. Now I feel really stupid *and* guilty. *That* must have been why Wyatt was looking at me funny when I suggested that we do shots. I really want to apologize to him, but I don't trust myself right now. I promise myself I'll apologize as soon as I gain some control over the lust steaming up my girlie parts every time I'm near him.

Sometime between my fourth and fifth shot, I make my way around the table and stand next to Wyatt. I'm a little unsteady, and I lean against him to keep from falling. His hand naturally drapes around my shoulder.

"I'm sorry, Wy." My voice sounds too loud, and I want to cry because I feel guilty about suggesting the shots.

"About what?" His eyes are glassy and serious.

"Because I suggested shots, and after what happened with your parents..."

He pulls me tight against his side, and it feels way too good to have all his muscles pressed against me. "No worries." He downs another shot and leans in real close to my face.

On some cognitive level I know I should ignore the way my pulse speeds up and my mind records everything in an instant—the feel of his body against mine, the sweet smell of cinnamon on his breath, his fingers pressing against my hip. But it has the opposite effect. I want his full, sexy lips on mine. I want to taste *his* cinnaburn.

"You should stop drinking," he whispers.

I don't know why that makes me angry. Maybe it's because Kyle used to tell me what to do when we were together, and right now I don't want to think about Kyle. In fact, I don't want to think about Wyatt, either. It feels like I've had to think my way through life since I was little. Wyatt and Delilah's parents planned things for them. Wyatt didn't have to interview for jobs during the last three months of school, hoping and praying that someone would find him worthy of an offer, like I did. I don't begrudge him for it. I know his father was well connected and Wyatt is brilliant and savvy, and besides, I'm used to looking out for myself.

I look around the table at everyone laughing and talking. Ashley's moving to the music, and for the first time since we left Connecticut, Delilah looks happy, dancing with Ashley, Brooke, and Tristan. Jesse and Brandon are talking about the band and the bar, and here I am, overthinking myself into a corner.

Just this once, I want to not think, not feel, and just be.

I push my glass over to Tristan again.

"Cass?" Wyatt says in a worried tone.

I wave him off. "I'm fine."

I have no idea how many more drinks I have, or

how I end up on the beach, sitting in the sand near the water. A breeze makes me shiver, but I feel hot inside. The music from the house sounds very far away, and I wonder if I've wandered too far. I turn and look behind me, and everything is blurry. I make out a few fuzzy lights. I guess I had too many fireballs, but I sure do feel good. I can barely feel at all, and that's wonderful. Now I know why people drink a lot. I usually stop when I feel buzzed, but this is so much better.

I sit for what feels like a long time, but it could have only been minutes. I can't tell. The sand is cool beneath my bare legs, and I pull my knees up to my chest and bury my toes in the sand, wondering if I can stay in this drunken state for a while. A year would be good. Then I wouldn't have to worry about why I feel funny around Wyatt, or why Kyle won't stop texting me, or if Delilah is ever going to be okay again.

It's so quiet out here. I listen to the waves breaking against the shore. Something presses against my leg and I push it away. I turn and everything spins. Oh no. I feel sick.

Whoa. This is not a good feeling at all.

Oh yeah, this is why I don't drink a lot.

The thing next to me presses against my leg again, and I turn and try to focus. It's a person. For a split second I think it's a stranger and I think I've wandered onto another private beach. Instincts bring my voice before I can stop it.

"Wyatt?" I call into the darkness, knowing that if he can hear me, he'll come.

A hand grabs my shoulder, and I swat it away. It's

too dark to see who it is. Where's Wyatt? Oh no. Did I piss him off? I scramble onto my hands and knees, and big hands grab my arms. I struggle to get free, but they're holding too tightly, and suddenly I'm on my feet and pressed against a wall of muscles. I close my eyes, and his scent finds some fraction of my mind that still seems to be grounded in sobriety.

Wyatt.

"Will you please stop fighting me?"

He's cocooned me in his arms. I couldn't break free if I wanted to, and I'm too drunk to know if I want to or not. My body revels in the feel of his firm thighs against mine and the breadth of his chest, which feels so good against my cheek. I close my eyes and give in to the comfort, listening to the fast beating of his heart. I wonder if he can feel mine, too. And then, out of nowhere, my body floods with anger.

I shouldn't be cataloging how good he feels, or the fact that something hard is pressing against my belly, when it totally shouldn't be. Oh my gosh! That means he feels this intense connection between us too. Why does that surprise me? I swear, since we've arrived, it's like sparks fly every single time we're near each other. Wait...What if he's just looking for sex from anyone? It's been a while since he's been with a girl.

Oh no. That's even worse.

I try to push away from him again, and he eases his grip but doesn't release me. It's a good thing, because my legs have forgotten how to work. My knees are weak, and I'm not sure if it's from being so close to Wyatt or from the alcohol, but it doesn't matter. I'm fairly certain that if he wasn't holding me up, I'd fall.

I don't look up at him. I'm afraid if I do he'll see what I'm thinking. Then I think of his hard-on, and I wonder if I just felt his zipper. I want to know for sure, but I can't look *there*, and I can't exactly press my body against his again.

Oh, this sucks.

I stumble backward. Wyatt catches me as I almost face-plant in the sand.

"Whoa." I cling to his arm. "Thanks."

"I'm not going to tell you that I told you so, but..."

"Shut up." It comes out with a girly giggle that shocks me. I cover my mouth with my hand, and his eyes are holding my gaze with that prickly heat again. "I'm okay." I force myself to stand up tall and try to get my legs to work again. My knees collapse, and he scoops me into his arms.

Oh...

I like this.

Way, way, way too much.

"I've got you," he says against my cheek.

He smells like warmth and strength and hot cinnamon. I wonder what it would be like to taste that cinnamon from his lips. I think I'm staring at his lips, but I can't stop, and we're moving. Well, he's moving. Carrying me toward the fuzzy lights. I close my eyes and rest my cheek against his chest, wrapped in warm thoughts of kissing the one guy I shouldn't want to and memorizing the feel of being in his arms. Because somewhere in my drunk mind I realize that I'll probably never be here again.

The thought makes me sad.

"You okay?" he asks, like he can read my mind.

"Mm-hm."

"You moaned, like I hurt you." He's climbing the outside stairs up toward the second floor and stops midstep to look at me.

I moaned? Holy crap. That's embarrassing. "Um, no. I'm fine." It dawns on me as he starts walking up the stairs again that I'm probably heavy, but he doesn't act like I'm heavy. He carries me across the deck to his bedroom, and some part of my brain registers that we're not going into my bedroom. I'm both excited and worried about this. I trust Wyatt. I've slept in a bed with him a million times before, but never when my body was begging me to get naked with him.

"My room?" I manage.

"Can't, Cass. Apparently, Tristan thought it was a good idea to take the only bed that had sheets on it. Brandon and Jesse are on the couches downstairs. Ashley's with Delilah, sleeping on her futon, and we never made up the other beds downstairs." He lays me on his bed, and the whole room spins.

"Whoa." I try to sit up, and he must have gone into the bathroom, because he comes out a minute later with a cup of water and hands it to me.

"Ibuprofen." He hands me two pills. "Take it and drink the water. It'll help in the morning." He sees me struggling to sit up and sits on the bed beside me, then pulls me up against his chest and lifts my hand with the cup in it. "Take them, Cass."

"Why aren't you taking any?"

"Don't worry about me."

I take the pills and drink the water, and my

stomach rebels for a minute. I squeeze his thigh as I swallow back the bile rising in my throat. He wraps his arms around my chest and rests his cheek on mine. Gosh, I love that. I could turn a little and our lips would touch.

"You okay?" he asks softly.

No, I'm not okay. I want to make out with my best friend in the whole world really, really badly. I nod, or at least I think I do. My heart is racing and my stomach did not like that water, but I'm also warm and feel wonderful pressed up against him and I have no desire to move away.

Except...

"I might be sick," I warn him.

"I know, but if I get up and get a bucket, I'm afraid you'll fall over and really be sick. It's better to sit up."

I don't think about this for very long before my body relaxes against him as it's done a million times before. A few minutes later I hear him talking in a quiet, thoughtful voice.

"I miss them, Cass."

I want to turn and see his face, but I'm afraid I'll puke, so I wrap my arms over his and hold them tight. I feel tears burning my eyes and know it has nothing to do with the alcohol. Hearing the longing in Wyatt's voice is sobering.

"I know," I whisper.

I feel a hot tear on my shoulder and realize it's not mine. I want to see him through my camera's lens, where everything else disappears and I have one singular focus. I want to be in that lens with him and hold him until his sadness goes away. I've never seen

Wyatt cry, and I want to turn around and hug him, but I hesitate. Will he be embarrassed if I see him crying? Will he pretend he's okay? Will I puke on him? I can't make heads or tails of my thoughts. I just know that I want to make him feel better, so I push all the confusion away and turn in his arms, which leaves us face-to-face. His eyes are wet and full of sadness. There's no embarrassment. He doesn't try to hide his tears, and that's when I realize how much of an idiot I am. Wyatt trusts me. He trusts me enough to cry in front of me. This big, strong, alpha male isn't worried about looking weak, and here I am, thinking about doing all sorts of dirty things with him.

I'm both embarrassed and disgusted with myself. I feel unworthy of his friendship, but I'm so glad for it that I wrap my arms around his neck and hold him closer, offering him the same comfort he readily gives me. I listen to his quiet breaths and I don't say anything, because I know that Wyatt doesn't need my words. He needs my love.

I will never, ever think those thoughts about you again.

I repeat this silent promise over and over. One of his hands slides up my back and presses my chest to his, and his other covers the entirety of my lower back, keeping my whole torso close, and I know I've just lied.

Chapter Eight

~Wyatt~

I LIE IN bed watching the sun rise and enjoying the feel of Cassidy sprawled across me. She's wearing my T-shirt, and it barely covers her butt. Her arm is lying across my chest, and her cheek is resting on my arm, which is numb, but I don't want to wake her by moving it. Last night I wanted Cassidy all to myself. Not to fool around, although my body was craving her in the most torturous way. I just needed Cassidy. I should have walked away or asked someone else to take care of her, but despite my intense longing for all the things I can't have, I needed to be with her. Sadness slipped out of the darkness and conquered me last night, and I knew the only way to survive it was with Cassidy.

Last night after everyone went inside, I was sitting on the deck watching her out there in the sand by herself, trying to make sense of all the feelings I've been having. I felt too far away from her. She'd told us that she wanted to think down by the water, because she said the breakup had messed with her head. I get that. I mean, the breakup should have messed with her. They dated for a long time. So I let her have her space. But I couldn't be away from her for long. And when I was carrying her inside, I wanted to be even closer to her. I didn't care that she was drunk, or that she might puke on me, which she did. That's what friends are for, having each other's backs, and even though I've been thinking of all the things I'd like to do with her while she's *on* her back, friendship trumps desire.

I brush her hair off her cheek and I get that warm sensation in my chest again. I want her so badly that I can barely see straight, but I have no idea why I want her now, after all these years. I chew on the thought awhile and realize I'm stroking her hair and it feels really good. Soft and familiar. I think my feelings for her began to change the second I realized that Kyle had cheated on her. I had more than a visceral reaction to the hurt in her eyes. I wanted to be the man in her life. I wanted to protect her, to show her how she deserved to be loved. To make up for the hurt Kyle laid on her.

But that's not a good thing.

I'm not good at relationships.

Cassidy is very good at relationships.

I would end up doing something stupid and hurting her and then I'd lose my best friend. I can't chance that.

She breathes in deeply and stretches. Her breasts

press against my chest, and her hips put enough pressure on mine to get me hard again. I shift on the bed, and she gazes up at me, blinking the sleep out of her gorgeous eyes.

"Hey," she says sleepily, then presses her hand to her forehead. "Ouch."

"The morning after kind of sucks." I regretfully move out from under her, trying to cool the heat racing through my body.

She looks around the room, and her brow wrinkles in confusion. She looks down at what she's wearing and her hand slips down and covers her eyes.

"Did I puke?"

"Yup." I lean back against the dresser and cross my ankles, hoping my jeans camouflage my hard-on.

"Oh Lord." Her eyes are still covered. "Did we...?" She spreads her fingers and peeks out from between them.

She's so cute it makes me laugh.

She cringes. "Really?"

I laugh again, because why on earth would she jump to that conclusion? I have to tease her a little bit. "I spent the night fending off your advances."

She falls onto her back and lays her arm over her eyes. "Oh no. Dragon breath and all? That must have been attractive."

I smell coffee and realize that the others must be awake. I debate torturing her a little more, but then I decide that it would just be cruel, so I sit on the edge of the bed and move her arm from her eyes.

She closes her eyes tight. "Don't look at me."

"I like to look at you." I steal a glance and

immediately regret it. My T-shirt is hiked up above her panties, sending a bolt of lightning straight to my dick. I get up and go into the bathroom without a word, turn on the cold water, and spend the next five minutes freezing the image of Cassidy Lowell lying in my bed in her pink panties out of my head.

Five icy minutes later, when that doesn't help, I take five more minutes to jerk off so I can function again.

Make that ten minutes.

When I come out of the bathroom Cassidy is gone. I assume she's gone to her bedroom. I have a towel around my waist and I am pulling a pair of boxers and shorts from my drawer when I hear Ashley and Delilah laughing. I peer into the hallway.

They're hanging on to each other's arms, whispering and laughing.

"Mornin', girls."

Ashley turns around and her eyes hang on my chest.

Delilah bumps her with her elbow. "He's my brother."

Ashley shakes her head. "I wasn't staring because I like him, although he is hot. I told you that I paint. I was thinking about how great it would be to paint him."

"That's a new one," I say jokingly as I walk back into my bedroom and close the door. I'm glad Delilah has a friend, and as I dress it dawns on me that normally I'd be all over a girl like Ashley—cute as hell, hot body—but last night I couldn't take my eyes off of Cassidy. And even now my mind is drenched in thoughts of her.

I realize this is more of a problem than I'd thought it was, and I'd better get my shit together before I lose my parents and Cass during the summer from hell.

Downstairs Brandon and Jesse are drinking coffee at the kitchen table. Delilah and Ashley are sitting outside on the back deck, eating bowls of cereal.

"Where's Tristan?"

Jesse points upstairs. "He's still sleeping, I guess. He hasn't made it downstairs yet."

My brain immediately puts Cassidy wearing nothing but my T-shirt and pink panties in the room with Tristan, who might be gay but is still a dude. This borders on ridiculous, but claws of jealousy are scratching at me and I'm wondering if she's showering just a wall away from where he's sleeping. Or if she's lying on the bed talking to him.

I want to be lying on the bed with her, and the idea of her naked and showering with only four inches of wall between us makes me hard again. I'm screwed.

My legs want to carry me upstairs, but my brain won't let them move. I seriously need to get a grip. I fill a second cup with coffee, add cream and sugar, and bring them both to the table.

Jesse glances at the second cup. "Thirsty?"

"It's for Cass," I say, like he should know. He nods, like he does know. "Where's Brooke?"

"She went home last night. She had to open the café this morning. We should talk, Wyatt." Jesse looks outside at Delilah. "Is she okay?"

I shrug and sip my coffee. "As good as can be expected." That's when I remember that Cassidy saw me crying last night. My hand freezes midair as embarrassment drags on my skin like a spiny rake.

It's Cassidy. It's okay.

And just like that, it does seem okay.

"I don't want to push you too fast into all this stuff, but we should figure out what's happening with the Taproom. I'll stick around as long as you need me to, but I'm usually back at my own properties by next weekend, so I'd kind of like to make sure you have a handle on things, I'll help find someone else to step in if you need me to." Jesse fiddles with the thick leather band on his wrist.

"Oh. Right." I haven't spent any time thinking about the bar much past knowing I'd have to deal with it at some point. "There can't be that much to learn, right? I mean, you and the employees seem to have a good handle on things."

Jesse laughs as he lifts his coffee and takes a sip. "Sure we do, but *you* need to have a good handle on things, Wyatt. There's inventory, purchasing, accounting, all sorts of things that need to be handled. Your mom used to go over the books, but she was tied up the last few months, so the books haven't been reviewed for the past quarter."

"Oh, shit." I run my hand through my wet hair and hear footsteps coming down the stairs. Cassidy's hair is wet, I assume from the shower. She smiles, but it's not her usual light-up-the-room smile. It's a shy, embarrassed, half smile with downcast eyes. "Cass, come here for a sec."

She smells amazing.

"Where's Tristan?"

"Zonked," she says. "Did you know he sleeps in the buff?"

I grit my teeth against her comment.

"Maybe I should go upstairs and check it out," Brandon says with a devilish grin.

She laughs. "I'm kidding. He's fully dressed and out like a light." She points to the coffee. "Mine?"

She takes a drink and closes her eyes. "Thank you. Mm. This is heavenly." She opens her eyes again. "Ibuprofen would make it even better."

Brandon reaches into his pocket and tosses a square packet of ibuprofen across the table, the type of travel pack with two pills in it that you buy at a gas station.

"You're like Santa Claus. Thank you." She struggles to open the package, so I take it from her, tear it open with my teeth, turn her hand over, and shake the pills into her palm.

"You carry those with you?" I ask Brandon.

"A man's gotta always be prepared." He tosses a condom on the table.

Jesse shakes his head. "Boy, you have got to learn to control yourself."

"Hey, I didn't do anything. I slept alone on the couch, remember?" Brandon leans forward, and his straight black hair falls in front of his eyes. "Would you rather I walked around unprepared?"

"I'd rather you found some morals," Jesse says.

"Look who's talking. When's the last time you had a long-term girlfriend?" Brandon downs his coffee and gets up from the table to wash his cup.

Jesse ignores his jab. "Wyatt, when do you want to

come by and go over things?"

I look up at Cassidy. "Cass, can you help me go over the books for my parents'...for the Taproom?" That was weird. But not as painful as it was a few days ago.

"The books?" She looks between me and Jesse.

"My parents left the bar to me and Dee, so..."

She puts a hand on my shoulder, and I can see questions ticking off in her mind, probably about our inheriting the bar. She blinks several times, her brows knitting together. I can tell she's holding herself back from asking.

"You cleaned up my puke. It's the least I can do. I don't have that much experience, but I'm happy to try."

I'm wondering when she's going to bring up the fact that I had to take off her dress and her bra because they were both covered in puke. I'd be lying if I said I didn't look. I tried not to, but I'm only human.

"You did the bookkeeping for that coffee shop the last two years of school." I look at Jesse, hoping that her experience is enough for what we're facing.

"I think if it's just reconciliations and stuff, I can do it. And if it's too complicated, I can always call my old boss. She'll be happy to walk me through whatever we need, so I should be fine."

"Well, we won't know until we try. Want to meet me there this afternoon?" Jesse looks out at Delilah again. "What about Delilah?"

"I'll talk to her. We'll meet you there around three. Does that work?"

"Sure. You've got my cell if you get hung up." Jesse

carries his coffee cup into the kitchen, rinses it, and puts it in the dishwasher. "I'm glad you came down here, Wyatt. I know your dad would have wanted you to be around everyone."

I nod, because really, what am I supposed to say? I have no idea what my dad would have wanted, but I know that staying at home was impossible, and after being here for one day, I already feel better. I like that my friends aren't staring at me like I have three heads or tiptoeing around me because my parents were killed. Back in Connecticut, it felt like everyone was waiting for me and Delilah to fall apart, which made it even harder not to.

Jesse tosses everyone's keys on the table and waves as he heads out the door.

"Cass, your dress is hanging in my bathroom. I washed it in the tub last night. I wasn't sure if it could go in the washer."

Cassidy sits at the table, her cheeks flushed. I know she's thinking about me undressing her.

"Don't worry. I didn't grope you or sell tickets for everyone to see your boobs." I smile, and she covers her eyes as I push away from the table and walk toward the deck. "You probably owe me for that. I bet I could have made a lot of money."

"I don't owe you. You saw me without my shirt on," she hollers.

"No wonder you came downstairs smiling." Brandon follows me outside. "She puked?"

"Yeah, whatever." I sit beside Delilah at the table. She and Ashley are talking about drawing pencils. It's so good to see her smiling that I debate not talking to her about the Taproom, but I know I shouldn't keep it from her.

"Why are you looking at me like that?" Delilah asks.

"I'm trying to decide if I should talk to you about something or not." I clasp my hands behind my head and glance inside at Cassidy, who's talking to Tristan as he fills a coffee cup. I look out at the ocean, feeling more normal than I have for a week.

"Dee, we need to talk about the Taproom."

I see the moment the smile leaves her eyes. It's like they cloud over. She shifts in her seat, looks at Ashley, and then back at me. "Okay."

"Well, Mom and Dad left it to us, so we have to figure out what to do with it." I'm relieved when she doesn't immediately tear up at the mention of our parents.

"What do you mean, what to do with it? We're *not* selling it." She pushes her hair over her shoulder and sits up taller. "Neither of us has a job, so we can run it."

I nod, not really knowing how I feel about any of it at the moment. "Is that what you want?"

"Yes? No? Maybe? I don't know for sure, but right now, yes. Why not? Do you really want to work in an office somewhere?"

"Hell, no." That much I do know for sure. "I'd like to surf all day and hang out."

She rolls her eyes, and I reassure her. "I won't, but hey, you asked."

"I don't know what I want, Wyatt, but Mom and Dad wanted us to be involved with the bar. That's the whole reason Dad pushed you into getting a business degree."

"I know." All too well.

"Then why is there even a question?" She cocks her head and looks at me like I really do have three heads.

"It's not. I just wanted to talk to you about it. I'm going down at three to go over things with Jesse, and I think you should come. You're much better at these things than me. If we're keeping it, then we need to figure out who's going to do what."

She crosses her arms and smirks. "I have a feeling that this is going to be a lot like when we were little and pretended we worked at McDonald's. You'll make all the rules and tell me what to do."

"Would I do that?" I snag the back of Brandon's shirt when he walks by. "I've got a few hours. Want to go surfing?"

"Absofuckinglutely." Brandon raises his brows at Delilah and Ashley. "Wanna go?"

Ashley holds her hands up. "No, thanks. I have no idea how to surf."

"You don't?" Delilah asks.

Ashley shakes her head. "The whole idea of it scares me."

"I was afraid at first, too. Maybe I can show you how to surf sometime and you can show me how to paint." Delilah turns to us. "I'm going to skip surfing, too. I want to go down to visit Brooke at the café this morning. But I'll meet you here, and we can walk down to the Taproom together. Two thirty?"

"Sure." I head inside and find Cassidy and Tristan sitting on the couch together with their feet up on the coffee table. Cassidy's leaning against Tristan's shoulder, looking at something on his phone. I'm irritated with myself for being jealous over two of my best friends.

"You guys up for surfing?"

"Thanks, but I've got to meet Ian in a few minutes. He's not very pleased that I didn't come home last night." Tristan holds up his phone and shows me a picture of a good-looking, dark-haired guy. "That's Ian."

"You live with him?" I know they've been seeing each other since the end of last summer, but from what I've heard from Brandon, Ian's a bit of a douche bag who doesn't always treat Tristan very well. He makes plans and then stands him up a lot. I'm surprised Tristan moved in with him.

"My roommate moved out a few months ago, and Ian suggested I move in." Tristan shrugged. "Saves on rent."

"Yeah, for Ian," Brandon scoffs. "He's so self-centered. He treats you like shit."

"Says the guy who never thinks of anyone but himself," Tristan says with a smirk. Tristan's right about Brandon being self-centered, but his smirk tells me that he's also irritated, and that irritation tells me that Brandon may be right about Ian.

"Yeah, well, at least with me the people I hook up with know what they're getting into. Ian pretends to be into you and then talks shit behind your back."

Tristan looks away, which is all the confirmation I need. I didn't meet Ian last summer. They got together after Delilah and I went back to school. Tristan's my buddy, and I feel protective of him, like I would of any of our friends at Harborside. The idea of anyone treating him badly pisses me off. Not that Tristan can't handle himself. He definitely can. The dude's as big as I am, but when he cares for someone, he'd never hurt them. And if he's living with Ian, he's got to care. I want to judge this Ian guy for myself.

"Tristan, why don't we all go out for a drink at the Taproom tonight? I'm going to be there anyway, and I'd like to meet Ian."

Tristan shrugs. "Sure. Sounds good."

"Cass? Surfing?" As much as I want to spend time with her, the idea of seeing her in a bikini isn't something I can handle without sporting a woody, so I hope she doesn't want to go.

"Thanks, but I think I'll hang out here with the girls. Maybe I'll make up the other bedrooms, just in case anyone needs a place to crash." She puts her hand on Tristan's leg, and it's that small gesture, the compassion in her eyes, that gets my insides all tied up in knots this time.

Turns out I don't need to see her in a bikini to be knocked off-kilter by her.

"Sorry, hon." Tristan leans his shoulder into hers. "I won't take your bedroom anymore."

"I didn't mind." Cassidy lowers her chin and looks up at me through her long lashes. Her cheeks pink up, and her look says so much more than it ever has— flirtation, lust, desire, all wrapped up in a neat bow of hesitation. I realize she feels the electricity between us, too, and the way her eyes just darted away tells me that she knows we shouldn't be feeling this way.

I remind myself of what Brandon said to Cassidy. *The easiest way to get over a guy is to get under another.* I'm thinking that goes for guys, too. The easiest way to chase away these feelings for Cassidy is to hook up with another girl.

~Cassidy~

I FEEL LIKE I'm holding my breath until Wyatt leaves the house. All I could think about the whole morning was the fact that he'd taken my clothes off last night after I puked. He saw me naked. Well, almost naked, except for my underwear, but that's pretty darn naked. As close as Wyatt and I are, he's never seen my bare breasts before. I hate that just thinking about it stirs butterflies in my stomach, and when we locked eyes earlier, my nipples got hard and my whole body went hot. If I were a guy, I'd be sporting a hard-on.

This is so wrong. I try to imagine what went through his mind last night. Was he turned-on? Did he want to touch me? *Did* he touch me? No. I'm sure he'd never do that. What if he didn't even *want* to touch me?

I groan at the thought.

I try to conjure up the image of his eyes seeing me bare from the waist up. Did he look at me hungrily? Needful? Was he so lost in desire that he couldn't see straight? I need to stop this craziness. He's my friend, and despite the fact that every time we're together lately sparks nearly ignite the room, I have to believe he took it all in stride. Otherwise, how am I supposed to function? Or face him again?

After Delilah and Ashley leave to go see Brooke, I

whip through the house cleaning everything I can. I wash all the sheets, scrub the kitchen, and make up the guest bedrooms. I sweep the floors and the decks—upper and lower. Delilah and Ashley beg me to go out to lunch with them, but every time I look at Delilah, I feel like she thinks Wyatt and I fooled around last night. They saw me leave his room in *his* T-shirt. She hasn't said anything, but still. Now I feel uncomfortable around her, for an entirely different reason than I feel uncomfortable around Wyatt.

Maybe I should start calling Wyatt *Army*. Maybe if I call him Army I'll stop thinking about how much I love his real name. I remember when I first heard it. My mom told me we were going to meet the new family around the corner and that they had kids my age. I thought he and Delilah were so lucky to have such cool names, but *Wyatt Armstrong*? Just thinking about his name makes me feel all swoony. I don't think it used to, at least not like it is right now. My heart is fluttering like I am a schoolgirl with a crush. Over the years, *Wyatt* came to represent everything I respect and love about him. His strength, his generosity, his caring nature. Just thinking about him makes me hot all over.

I finish cleaning and take a cold shower. It's almost time to go down to the Taproom, and it sounded like we were all going to walk down together, so I make the water icy cold, hoping it'll stave off that flippin' heat that zaps me when Wyatt and I are together. I don't want to feel this way about him. I've been single for only a week, and I want things to stay the way they've always been with Wyatt. I want to be best friends forever. If there's one thing I've learned, it's that boyfriends come and go, but real friends, friends who will beat up the assholes and not let anyone see your boobs when you're too drunk to know? Those friends are rare. *That* friend is rare.

I've always been able to tuck my feelings for him away—so much so that I never realized I was doing it. But I know I won't be able to do that anymore, and that's scary. I don't know how to walk this tightrope.

Oh, Wyatt. What is happening to us this summer? Why are we looking at each other this way?

On the way to the Taproom Wyatt and I don't make eye contact. That's how I know he's just as confused and feels the same heat ricocheting off the pavement between us as I do. I wonder if he regrets taking care of me last night. His gaze zeroes in on a group of girls in bikinis as we cross the parking lot toward the pier, and I know that I need to *stop* thinking about him.

He's obviously figured out a way to push our attraction aside.

The pier is bustling with tourists. We walk toward the Taproom at the end of the pier and I try to pretend I don't see Wyatt looking everywhere except at me. I focus on the bar. I've always loved its rustic character. It's built of dark, wide planks of wood, and each side boasts a large driftwood sign with THE TAPROOM painted on it.

Brandon is talking with Wyatt about some girls they met on the beach, and I try not to eavesdrop. I wonder why Brandon is even coming with us. Aren't we here to talk about the business and go over the books? Doesn't he have to work at all? As in *ever*?

Why do I even care?

Another futile effort in my anti-Wyatt distraction plan.

Delilah's smiling, and I know it's because she found a new friend in Ashley. I can't help but steal another glance at Wyatt, drinking in his handsome, tanned face. His broad chest fills out his tank top, and the way his board shorts hang dangerously low on his hips makes me *want, want, want*. He's smiling, but his brows are knitted together. Brandon has captured his full attention. I wish I were Brandon. I want Wyatt's attention. I don't want a new friend, like Delilah has found in Ashley. I just want my best friend, Wyatt, back and our friendship to remain the same as it's always been.

Wyatt holds the door open, and we all head inside. The Taproom smells like the ocean, beer, and French fries. Jesse waves from behind the bar. He's got a white dishrag hanging over his shoulder, and there's a waitress and a waiter who look around nineteen or so, running from table to table. The bar runs the full length of the wall across from the door. There are two guys sitting in tanks and bathing suits on the barstools. Most of the booths around the room are taken, as are a few of the tables in the middle of the room. I glance out the window that faces the end of the pier and spot another waitress out there, taking an order. I'm surprised at how busy they are, given that it's only three o'clock.

We follow Wyatt over to the bar, but Brandon breaks off from the three of us and walks to the stage in the back of the room. He disappears behind the black curtain, and while Wyatt's talking with Jesse, he comes back out with his guitar, drags a stool to center stage, and begins playing. Now I know why he came along.

I love listening to Brandon play. His face changes when he's playing. All the tight lines that usually surround his dark eyes and the tension he's carried in his shoulders ever since the day I met him ease. I wish I had my camera and make a mental note to try to get some pics of him playing.

I focus on the tune, and it helps fill the crevices in my mind that Wyatt has been slowly seeping into.

"Cass?" Wyatt touches my arm.

"Huh? Sorry." I turn and realize that they're all waiting for me.

"Let's go into the office and we'll start to figure this out." Jesse leads us through swinging double doors into a back room. It's warmer back here, and it looks like a stockroom, with big metal shelves lined with cans and bottles. The kitchen is off to the right, separated from the inventory by an enormous stainless-steel counter. Dutch, the cook who has worked here for at least three years, wipes his hands on a towel at his waist and elbows two other guys, nodding to Wyatt.

I watch Delilah roll her lips into her mouth and reach for the ends of her hair. I know she's nervous. But it's Wyatt's behavior that surprises me. He's been open about his father wanting him and Delilah to one day take over the family business, but he's always sort of laughed it off. *Whatever. That's light-years away. I'll worry about it when it's time.* Now he's making jokes about the inventory and hiring big-boobed girls to wear shirts like they do at Hooters to work there. Jesse's brows are drawn together, and I can tell he's annoyed that Wyatt isn't taking this seriously. I thought Wyatt would snap out of his never-planning-a-thing stage and grow up overnight. I guess I was wrong.

Dutch comes around the counter and settles his hands on his wide hips. He's got a mop of curly brown hair and a beer belly. His sideburns are superlong, almost to the edge of his jaw, and curly like his hair. He has kind of an imposing presence, but that might just be his size. He's taller than Wyatt, and broader, too, but soft broad, not hard-bodied like Wyatt or Jesse. When he cocks his head to the side and presses his lips together, his green eyes fill with compassion, and when he opens his arms, Wyatt and Delilah walk right in. His arms engulf them. I think Wyatt and Delilah must be soaking in his comfort even more because he's older than us, around Jesse's age.

They don't have parents anymore.

The realization makes me feel even guiltier about how I've been thinking of Wyatt. Of course it's not heat that I feel coming from him. I've misinterpreted everything. It must be the need for comfort.

I stop myself from literally bonking my hand to my forehead.

Jesse leans in close to me and turns his back to the others, then speaks in a hushed tone. "He's in denial, Cass. He'll get through this. We're all here for him. Just don't take what seems like disregard for his parents as anything but what it is. Cold. Harsh. Denial."

I feel so stupid. Before I can stew on that thought for too long, Uncle Tim comes out of another office. I notice his name on a plaque beside the door and realize it's his office.

"Wyatt, Delilah." Uncle Tim opens his arms and Delilah falls into his comfort. As he soothes her, he holds Wyatt's gaze, then reaches out and pats him on the shoulder. "You holding up okay, Wy?"

Wyatt shrugs. "Thanks for taking care of everything, Uncle Tim."

Tim's eyes drop, and he scrubs his hand down his face. "Yeah, well, your dad..." He shakes his head, and his eyes go damp. "I'm sorry you lost them."

Dutch pulls me into his arms and squishes me against his stomach. He smells like grease and onions, and my stomach growls. I forgot I haven't eaten today.

"You okay, kid?" Dutch is talking to me, but he's eyeing Tim as he talks with Wyatt.

"Yeah. I'm good." Something about the way Dutch asks me makes me think of my breakup with Kyle, and I realize that I haven't thought about him at all today. Until now. I push the thought away as my stomach growls again.

Dutch touches my arm, eyes still locked on Tim. "I'll fix you something to eat."

"It's okay. I'm not that hungry." I hate to be an imposition, especially when it's obviously Wyatt and Delilah who should be getting extra attention at the moment.

"Your stomach says otherwise. You need to eat, sweetie." Dutch walks back to the kitchen, and I wonder why he's still watching Tim as he cooks whatever he's making me. My stomach growls again as we follow Tim into his office. I'm glad Dutch is making me food. I'm famished.

"How do you want to do this?" Jesse asks.

"I went over a few things that I thought of with Ashley earlier." Delilah pulls a piece of notebook paper from her pocket and unfolds it. She hands it to Jesse, who reads it and smiles as he looks up at her.

"Ashley worked as a manager for a restaurant when she was in school, so she has some idea of what we'll be doing. Obviously, it's not everything, but I figured Jesse would fill us in on the rest." Delilah pauses for a second. This is the Delilah I know. Her confidence is coming back, and even if it's here for only a few minutes, or long enough for her to deal with today, I'm warmed by it. It gives me hope that even if it's a long road to healing, she won't be lost forever.

"Impressive. You've hit most of the major things we need to go over." Jesse hands the list to Wyatt, and I glance over his shoulder and read it.

Inventory

Distributors

Employee schedules

Finances/payroll

Marketing

Difference between off-season and on-season (in all regards)

Emergency procedures (fire, etc.)

Now that Jesse pointed out that Wyatt's in denial, I feel myself looking at him differently. I guess that's what Delilah locking herself in her bedroom for a week was all about. I make a mental note to do a little research about grieving. If I understand it better, maybe I can help them, instead of feeling like I'm just floating around trying to put the pieces of this unfamiliar puzzle together.

"Divide and conquer." Wyatt hands the list back to Jesse.

"There's a lot to cover, and it's going to take a while, so why don't you and Cassidy start going over things with Tim, and I'll show Delilah the ropes of how we do inventory." Jesse nods to Tim, who agrees.

Tim is a tall, thin man with short brown hair that's parted on the side and perfectly combed. Even though I saw him a lot in the days around the funeral, things were so chaotic I didn't really *see* him. Now I study his beady brown eyes and thin lips. He's got dark circles under his eyes and looks like he hasn't slept in days. His face is very angular, and he reminds me of Taylor Schilling in *Orange Is the New Black*, even though she's a girl. He's the only one in the place wearing nice pants and a dress shirt, and for some reason he reminds me of Kyle. I try to hide how my whole body bristles.

"There's no rush," Jesse reminds us. "If it takes a week or three months, or six. It's all good. I'd never leave y'all hanging."

"Thanks, Jesse. Dee? You okay with this?" Wyatt asks.

Her eyes widen when she smiles, and I think she likes the idea of having a project. "Yeah, sure."

Wyatt still hasn't made eye contact with me, and in Tim's office I can't hear Brandon playing the guitar as well as I could out in the bar. I'm going to have to focus extra hard on the books to keep from focusing on Wyatt not paying any attention to me. This is doubly hard because for some reason I'm not as interested in working with numbers as I used to be. I'm not sure why I'm just realizing this, but wow, this is totally boring work. I could do it in my sleep. I wonder why I used to think it wasn't. How did I make it through four years of studying accounting? *Ugh.* Maybe when I found Kyle with that girl, it sparked a fire in my brain and short-circuited it or something, because right now I can't imagine spending eight hours a day looking at numbers. I could stare at Wyatt all day, though, and looking at Wyatt does make a certain double-digit number come to mind, a very dirty one that involves two numbers that look the same but one is flipped upside down.

I feel my cheeks burn and clear my throat to try to rid my mind of dirty thoughts.

"Wyatt, I know your parents would be proud of you, taking these steps. As always, if there's anything I can do for you and Delilah…" Tim points to the chairs on the opposite side of his desk. Wyatt and I sit down beside each other.

"Thanks, Uncle Tim. Dee and I appreciate that." Wyatt drops his eyes to the binders on the desk.

We spend the next three hours going over the processes that Tim uses for the bookkeeping. He shows us QuickBooks, which I used at my previous job, and the way he's describing his process is all fairly straightforward and simple. I'm sure Wyatt can handle this on his own, and the fact that he's not looking or talking to me makes me so uncomfortable that I contemplate asking if he minds if I leave. But then I think about what Jesse said. Maybe this new attitude toward me is part of his grieving process. I decide to give it a name, make it another stage of grieving to make myself feel better.

He's *pushing*. Wyatt's pushing me away.

I hate *pushing*.

The highlight of the afternoon is the steak-and-cheese sub that Dutch made for me. He even remembered pickles, my favorite part.

"Okay, so that's how it works." Tim leans back in his chair and folds his hands across his chest.

I'm not sure what we're supposed to accomplish today, but all we've really done is talked about the process. He's shown us where he records the assets and liabilities and the inventory binders. He spent a lot of time on those binders. But he hasn't shown us the actual system or the general ledgers.

"Shouldn't we go over the reports and ledgers so Wyatt understands how to read them?" I look at Wyatt, and he lifts his eyes—for a split second I think he's going to finally look at me, and my heart speeds up. I hate that it does, but at the same time, he is my best friend, and I'm feeling like I'm outside his circle of friends at the moment. So I allow myself the quickening of my pulse for purely friendship reasons.

But his eyes lift to Tim and his mouth quirks up in a slanty smile. "I trust Tim. It's not like *we'll* be doing the books. I think it's time for a cold one."

Just like that, my heart feels like it shatters in my chest. Being ignored by Wyatt is a worse feeling than catching Kyle with another girl. It's a worse feeling than when I get lonely for my parents, which isn't often, but it hits me pretty hard sometimes.

As I watch him walk away without as much as a glimpse in my direction, I wonder if his parents' deaths have changed him—and us—forever.

Chapter Nine

~Wyatt~

I'M PRETTY SURE that drinking myself into oblivion isn't the best way to deal with everything that's going on right now, but I don't care. There's not a single ounce of me that gives a shit about anything as I down my fifth drink. Well, that's not exactly true. I care a whole hell of a lot about drinking until I can't see straight. It's one of the advantages of living in walking distance to the bar. I know Jesse will watch over Delilah, and now that Tristan's here with his asshole boyfriend, Ian—and Brandon was right. He is an asshole. He's been ignoring Tristan and eyeing other guys all night—I know Tristan will watch out for Cassidy.

I slam my glass down on the bar and turn back toward the band. Brandon is onstage with Brent and the rest of their band. He's totally in the zone. His fingers move adeptly across his guitar strings, and every time they hit a hard note, he thrusts his head forward. There's a flock of fangirls checking them out. They've been playing since eight o'clock. I have no clue what time it is now, but I know it's time for another drink. I smack my hand on the bar. The hot, part-time bartender comes to mix my drink. I wish I could remember her name, but it totally eludes me. Krystal? Kerry? Shit. I can't remember. She's hot, though.

She leans over the bar, and her boobs practically fall out of her shirt.

"Haven't you had enough, big boy?" Her voice slides over my skin. I have no idea if it's the alcohol or her big boobs, but I finally feel a stirring of something resembling horniness for a woman other than Cassidy.

"Never enough," I say, and lift my glass again.

She arches a brow, and a smirky I'm-into-you smile curves her lips. She stands up slowly, doing that thing girls do, where they arch their backs and as they turn away they look over their shoulder, giving you a clear shot of their ass and their boobs. *Nice.*

Tristan sidles up beside me at the bar and elbows me. I turn and lean my back against the bar, like he is.

"Shouldn't you be careful with the staff, now that you own the joint and all?" He says this with a serious tone that makes me laugh. I have no idea why I'm laughing, but I go with it, because I have no idea why I'm doing anything lately.

"Ian's an ass." I nod at Ian, standing over by a booth and talking to a handful of guys and girls. He's been ignoring Tristan all night, and when Tristan approaches him, Ian still checks out other guys. I don't know why Tristan is putting up with that bullshit. He's too soft hearted.

Tristan sighs. "Whatever. I'm not talking to you about Ian when you're drunk. You can judge him when you're sober. You should be more concerned with the image you're presenting to your future staff."

"Shit." I turn around and grab the drink. "What time do you get off work Ke—"

"Lori." The bartender shakes her pretty little head and drags her eyes up and down my body. "I'm off in ten minutes. You think you'll still be *up*?"

"Baby, I'm always *up*." At least when Cassidy's around. Hell. The alcohol isn't stopping my thoughts of her at all.

Charley Hayes, one of my friends and a part-time bartender, sidles up to Lori, narrows her brown eyes, and sets a harsh stare on me. Her brown hair tumbles over her shoulders as she leans forward, grabs Lori's arm, and pulls her away. "I'll take care of him."

I return her stare until she scoffs and throws her dishrag on the bar.

"Really, Wyatt? You're *taking over* the bar." Charley looks at Tristan, who shrugs. "You can't hook up with the help. It's wrong on so many levels."

"Who are you to tell me what's wrong on any level?" I take my drink and push away from the bar, too drunk to care if I've annoyed Charley. Tonight is about getting Cassidy out of my mind, and there's only one way to do that. I need to get laid.

I spot Cassidy talking with some guy by the stage. She's tucking her hair behind her ear. That long, shiny hair that I ran my fingers through this morning. I rake my eyes down her slinky little shorts and tank top, and when she turns away from the guy, I swear for a split second her eyes are searching for me. I smile when they drift in my direction—then pass completely over me and land on Tristan. What the hell?

She turns back to the guy, and I hate how my insides burn at seeing the two of them standing so close. I take a step in her direction—for what, I have no idea. I just know that I want to come between them. I don't care who he is, but he's staring at her tits, and I don't like it. I spin around when a hand touches my arm.

K...Lori.

"We still on?" she asks as she loops her arm into mine.

I'm three steps from Cassidy. If I reach out, I can touch her shoulder, but I remind myself that the best way to get over whatever is going on with me and Cassidy is to get *into* Lori. Cassidy laughs and then turns toward me. Her eyes land on me and pin me to the floor. Disappointment simmers in her beautiful eyes as her smile fades, and she shifts her gaze away from me.

Fuck it.

I head for the door with Lori hanging on my arm and saying something I don't hear. Her hand slides up my arm, and she squeezes my muscle.

"Wyatt!" I turn toward the bar, and Tristan and Charley are both looking at me like I'm a total asshole, which is fine. Whatever. Maybe I am one, but right now I need to be. I down my drink, set the empty glass on a table, and head out the door. The minute the cold air hits us, I spin her around and pin her against the side of the building, crashing my lips over hers. I don't care who sees us, and I don't care that this feels wrong in about a hundred different ways, when two weeks ago it would have felt like the rightest fucking thing in the world. All I care about is that this girl who's smashing her tits against me and grinding her crotch against my leg is going to take the pain away. She'll breathe air back into my devastated lungs and make me forget my parents were stolen from my life and that I've somehow turned into one of those messed-up guys who wants to fuck his best friend when I know damn well it'll ruin our friendship.

Her hands are all over me. She's cupping my balls and stroking me through my shorts, and I'm so hard it hurts. I drag her down to the far end of the building with no endgame. I don't want to bring her back to my place, not with Cassidy staying there. That would be a dick move, even though we're not even dating, for Christ's sake. My car's at the house, which leaves sex on the beach. A little sand never hurt anyone.

In my periphery I hear the door to the bar slam and see Cassidy with her arms coiled around the waist of the asshole she was talking to inside, and it stops me cold.

Lori sucks on my neck and pulls at my shirt. I focus on her to get the image of Cassidy and that guy out of my head. She moves her mouth to my chest and licks a path lower, still stroking the hell out of my dick. I try to ignore the fact that I have zero emotions for this girl and that the fact that she's not Cassidy sickens me. Sickens me! I try to push the thought away. I know she'll blow me right here if I let her, but hell if my body isn't screaming for me to get away from her. I don't want her blowing me. I want Cass. My eyes seek Cassidy out and find her still standing by the door to the bar, pushing away from the guy. He grabs her hand and pulls her in to him again, shifting so his back is to us and I can't see what she's doing.

"Stop!" Cassidy yells.

I don't think about the fact that Lori's unbuttoned my pants or that I'm hard as a rock. I don't think about the fact that there's so much anger coursing through me that I might actually kill this guy as I close the distance between us and yank him off of Cassidy by the scruff of his neck.

"She said stop." I have no idea how I manage the words when my fist is hitting his jaw, then going back for his eye, his chest, and just about anything it can connect with.

He clocks me in the jaw, and I stumble back, for the first time realizing how formidable the guy is. He's got a good four inches on me. What the hell? Is there a basketball team in town?

"Don't! Wyatt!" Cassidy cries.

I turn, and while I'm turning to look at her, he connects with my jaw and sends me stumbling backward again. I hear the door to the bar slam against the building, but I'm blinded with rage. This asshole represents the tractor trailer that killed my parents. I connect with his gut and he doubles over. He represents the fact that I have to suddenly take over a business I have no clue how to run. A right hook clocks his jaw. My left jab and uppercut send him flat on his back and represent the bullshit that's got me tied in knots over Cassidy. The final blow that connects with his jaw again and makes his eyes roll back in his head is for *everything* else. For the way my parents fucked up Delilah, for them leaving us, and for the fuckers who are pulling me off of this asshole before I kill him.

So much happens over the next few minutes—or hours. I'm not sure how much time passes. The police come, and I have no clue why they don't arrest me, but they talk a lot and shake their heads and spend forever with Jesse. I know by the look in Jesse's eyes when he returns to where I'm sitting in the back of the bar that he's just saved my ass. I'm too drunk and angry to be grateful. I scrub my hand down my face and glance at the booth up front where Cassidy is tucked beneath Tristan's arm, sitting between him and Ian. Brandon starts playing his guitar again, I guess to ease the tension that's so thick I need a chainsaw to cut it, but he's got a bead on me that I can feel like a laser. So fucking what? *I'm a drunk, angry asshole tonight.* Some things can't be helped. My parents just died. Cassidy was being mauled by that jerk. I'm allowed to be an asshole. Deal with it.

I feel a hand on my shoulder and whip around, still seething. My jaw hurts, my hands hurt, and I'm ready for another fight. I must look like it, too, because Delilah steps back. My throat nearly closes up.

Aw hell. She looks terrified.

I reach for Delilah's hand, and she drops her eyes to my bloody knuckles. She runs for the door, tears slipping down her cheeks. I'm right behind her. I pull her into my arms as soon as my feet hit the pier, and she tears herself from me.

"I'm sorry, Dee." My voice cracks with my plea, but she's backing away, stumbling over her own feet. She's crying and shaking her head, and it's not just my heart that's cracking. I feel it tear apart. A searing, deep pain shoots across my chest.

"You're an asshole. An asshole," she says through her tears.

"Delilah, wait." I jog to catch up with her, and she turns and runs to the end of the pier, where I see Brooke standing by her car with the door open. Delilah must have called her. Can tonight get any worse? I sprint and throw by body against the door, banging on the window before they can pull away.

Delilah rolls it down an inch.

"I'm sorry! Delilah, I'm sorry!"

"I'm staying with Brooke for a few days."

"What?" I have no idea what to say or how to react. I feel like I need to keep her with me. My parents are already gone. Cassidy won't look at me. I can't lose Delilah, too. I cling to the window, trying to push it down. "Dee, please!"

"You want me to watch you fight?" Delilah cries. "We lost Mom and Dad. I'm not going to watch as I lose you, too." She starts to close the window, and I have to tear my fingers out of the crack before it closes on them.

Brooke pulls away, and I sink to the ground and bury my face in my hands. The gravel cuts into my knees, and I dig them harder into the sharp, pointed rocks. I need the pain. I need to feel something, because right now I feel like I've fallen into an abyss, and I have no idea how to climb back out.

Chapter Ten

~Wyatt~

THE NEXT MORNING I still feel like a dick, and all I did was try to protect Cassidy, so I'm not sure why. Cassidy and I aren't dating, so why do I feel like I cheated on her by making out with Lori? My head is so messed up that I stay in bed until nearly eleven o'clock, then finally shower and go downstairs. I wish I could just sleep until this whole mess passes me by. And by *this whole mess*, I mean my life.

I know I need to go down to the bar and face the music with Jesse, but it's the last thing I *want* to do. I look at the stairs and wonder when Cassidy is going to come down. Probably not until I leave. I stood outside her bedroom door for half an hour this morning, trying to figure out what to say to her, and for the first time ever—*ever*—I didn't have a clue. I feel like I'm standing in the eye of a hurricane with blood rushing through my ears and all the pieces of my life, and the people I love, whirring around over my head. I can't grasp any part of it. Now, on top of our parents dying and the guilt I have about my feelings for Cassidy, having to learn the business and decide if we're going to keep it, and the shit I really don't want to deal with, like figuring out what to do in the long-term with the houses, Mom's car, and our parents' stuff, Delilah's moved out. Even if it's only temporary, I feel like hell for scaring her last night. The look on her face was equally as painful as the look on Cassidy's when they dragged me off of the guy who was pushing himself on her.

Tristan walks out of one of the first-floor bedrooms in his boxers. "Hey, Army," he mumbles as he shuffles into the kitchen and pours a cup of coffee.

"Hey. You spent the night?" We all walked home in a group last night. One big, silent group. Cassidy wouldn't even look at me.

"Figured you guys needed someone to play interference." He sips his coffee. "You see Cassidy yet this morning?"

I shake my head, not wanting to talk about last night.

Tristan leans his hip against the counter and scratches his chest. "Dude, she was a mess."

"I know."

"Delilah, too."

"Yup." I feel like he's turning a screw in my chest, but I know he's just working through shit in his own head.

"What's your plan?" He moves to the table and sits down.

I sit on the edge of the couch and shrug.

"Delilah will get over this. She's dealing with everything as best she can."

"Yeah." I nod, because there isn't much to say. It kills me to think that Delilah had to run to Brooke's to get away from me.

"What's up with you and Cassidy?" Tristan holds my gaze, and I know he can tell there's more to my feelings for Cassidy than there used to be.

"Don't know what you mean." The lie tastes like acid.

Tristan sets his coffee cup down and turns to look out the back doors at the ocean. It's a sunny day, and the sounds of the waves breaking slice through the silence between us.

"He means that you two look at each other like you want to rip each other's clothes off, and you didn't used to." Brandon says as he saunters out of a bedroom. His hair is askew. He's wearing a black T-shirt and a pair of black jeans that hang off his hips.

"You spent the night again, too?" Not that I care. I actually like having my buddies around. It helps take the focus away from my parents *not* being there.

Brandon stretches and pulls a mug from the cabinet. "You mind?"

"No. 'Course not. Where are you living these days, anyway?"

Brandon shrugs. "I've got a place with a few roommates over on South. They're a drag, though."

"Should I expect anyone else to come out of that bedroom?" Brandon collects lovers like kids collect frogs. He feeds his needs for a day or two, then releases them back into the world, sexually satiated.

Brandon's mouth curves into a smile. "Nah. Too much craziness going on last night. Figured Tristan might need backup."

Tristan yawns. "Now that we know there are no more people in the bedrooms down here, care to answer my question? What's going on with you and Cassidy?"

I finish my coffee, take one last look toward the stairs, and try to ignore the ache of missing Cassidy. How is it possible to miss someone when you just saw them a few hours ago?

"Nothing." I head for the front door. "Not a fucking thing."

Thirty minutes later I walk into the Taproom. I don't know if it's my imagination or not, but I feel like all the customers are looking at me like they know I was an ass last night. The strange thing is, in my head I don't think they're looking at me like that for getting into a fight. I think they're looking at me like that for making out with Lori.

What the hell is *that* about?

"Hey, it's Rocky." Charley elbows me as she walks toward the kitchen. Charley's worked at the Taproom for the last few summers. She's got long brown hair and she's a tiny girl, only about five foot two or so. Today her hair is pulled up in a ponytail.

"Sorry about last night, Charley. I thought you were working evenings because of your internship."

"Lori quit, thanks to you." She presses her lips together, but I can see the smile behind it.

"She quit?" Shit. Jesse's going to be more than

pissed.

"Yup. Left a message last night. Jesse needed the help, so..." She shrugs. "Thank goodness my boss at the Brave Foundation is all about loyalty. He knows I've known y'all forever, and well..."

She doesn't need to say that once she told him about my parents dying, he was happy to let her help out. I can tell by the way her brown eyes have warmed. I've known her boss, Dane Braden, the founder of the Brave Foundation, for years. Dane's brother Treat is married to my cousin Max. I'd reached out to Dane to help her get the job with his foundation in the spring.

I sigh loudly, chalking up two more people's lives I've messed up. "Sorry about that, Charley. Tell Dane I said thanks." Charley's working on her master's in marine biology, and the Brave Foundation is a marine-research company that uses education and innovative advocacy programs to protect sharks, and in a broader sense, the world's oceans. I would hate myself if I messed up that opportunity for her after helping her get it in the first place.

"Dane's the best boss ever, and I love his fiancée, Lacy. They understand. Besides, Jesse called one of our summer waitresses. Livi should be here by the afternoon rush to help out."

I nod, feeling more like a jerk than before.

"Delilah's here." Charley nods toward the doors to the back room.

"Good. I'm glad. Thanks." I head into the back to face my first grovel of the day.

"There's the man," Dutch hollers from behind the

stove. "Way to protect Cassidy, man. That guy's a douche."

"Hey, Dutch." I can't force myself to say thanks, because I feel like crap knowing Lori quit and Charley had to come in, not to mention the summer help.

I see Delilah crouched with a clipboard by a box on the other side of the room. She doesn't look up when I stand in front of her, so I crouch beside her.

"Hey, Dee."

"Hey." She doesn't make eye contact. Her brows are pinched together so tightly I know she's feigning concentration so she doesn't have to face me.

"I'm sorry about last night. When I saw that guy forcing himself on Cassidy, I had to do something."

"Mm-hm." She checks something off on her clipboard.

"And I'm sorry I scared you, Dee. I wasn't thinking. I just..."

She lifts her eyes and stares at me. When she speaks, it's just above a whisper. "I know."

I shake my head. "That's good, because I don't."

She sits on the floor and crosses her legs Indian style. In my head I hear *crisscross applesauce*, which is freaky, because we haven't said that since we were kids. And it's our mom's voice I hear saying it, just like she did every time we sat cross-legged as kids. I wonder if Delilah hears it, too.

"I don't know how to do this." She looks down at the clipboard.

"Jesse will teach us what we need to know." I sit beside her and reach for the clipboard. She pulls it out of my reach.

"Not *this*." Her eyes well with tears, and I realize she's talking about losing our parents.

I do what I've had to do to survive these last two weeks and bury that hurt as deep as I can shove it. I push it past the bile in my throat, past the burning in my gut, until it's so deep that I can no longer feel its claws. Only then do I put my arm around Delilah and pull her against me.

"Me either, Dee. But one thing I know is that Mom and Dad would want us to keep living. They'd want us to figure out our lives and move forward." I'm not sure of this at all, but it feels like the right thing to say.

"We never got to say goodbye."

"I know."

Tears slip down her cheeks, and I fight to keep mine from springing free.

"I miss them so much. It's not like we talked all the time, but, Wy, knowing they were there was..." Her tears steal her voice.

I pull her into a hug and kiss the top of her head. "I know, Dee. We'll get through this. We'll figure it out."

"What are we gonna do with their stuff? And the house? Do we keep the bar? I want to keep the bar. Dad wanted us to keep the bar." She's talking fast, like she can't stop her words from flowing.

I tuck her blond hair behind her ear and gaze into her sad green eyes. "Then we'll keep the bar."

She nods. "I'm so scared." She hugs me so tight that it reminds me of when we were in sixth grade and our dog, Mackadoodle, got hit by a car. She crawled into my bed for a week straight because she had dreams about him trying to cross the street and getting hit time and time again.

"Are you dreaming about Mom and Dad?" The words come before I can stop them.

She shakes her head. "No."

She wipes her eyes, and I'm not sure if I believe her or not.

"We're alone, Wyatt."

I push her gently away and search her eyes. I can tell she believes this, that we're really alone. "Dee, we are not alone. You will never be alone. We have Cass, and Brooke, and Jesse." I hope I still have Cassidy. "We have Tristan and Brandon, and Charley. We have *all* of our friends and Aunt Lara and Uncle Tim."

She wipes her eyes and nods. "I know. It just feels different."

We both settle back against the wall. "I know, and it should. But try to think of it this way. We're adults now, Dee. We would have relied on them less, and even if they were alive, we'd both find jobs and work full-time, and we wouldn't have seen them that much." None of this makes up for losing our parents. I'm grasping at straws to help her, when the biggest truth of the situation comes to me. "And at least you don't have to hide who you are anymore."

She nods, but I can see she doesn't want to talk about that, either.

"How was it with Brooke last night?" I'm hoping Brooke is talking to her about Mom and Dad. They're so close. I have to think it would help.

"Brooke is great. We stayed up and talked for hours. It reminded me of when Mom and I used to go see her at the café for breakfast or lunch." Her eyes glaze over. "I...Do you mind if I stay there for a while? Not because I'm mad at you, but because I need to?"

"No, Dee. Whatever you need. But just know that I'm here. You're never going to be alone, and I promise I won't fight anymore. I wasn't thinking."

"I know." She lowers her eyes again. "Have you talked to Cass? She texted me last night. She was pretty upset."

I shake my head. I have a feeling that talking with Cassidy will be much harder than talking to Delilah.

"Wyatt, you didn't hook up with her, did you? Because I'm not sure that would be a good idea."

She lifts her eyes to mine, and in that second, any thoughts I might have been entertaining about me and Cassidy go out the door. If we hooked up, it could only end in disaster, and then Delilah would lose Cassidy, too.

The final nail in the proverbial coffin.

Chapter Eleven

~Cassidy~

I LIE ON the bed staring up at the ceiling and wondering how many more days I can stay in bed. I got out of bed yesterday and heard Wyatt, Brandon, and Tristan talking downstairs, so I eavesdropped. I didn't mean to, but...Yeah, I did mean to. When Tristan asked Wyatt what was up with us, his response sent me to my knees. *Not a fucking thing.* It wasn't the words he used. It was the inflection in his voice, like he was disgusted by the idea. That means I've been totally misreading him, and that tells me one thing. One very big thing.

My judgment sucks.

I haven't moved much from my bed since I heard him say that. I'm on day two, and I wonder if anyone would notice if I stayed in bed even longer. A week? A month? Until they find my body shriveled up from sadness?

There's a knock at my door. I glance at the clock. It's four o'clock. It's been three days since the fight at the Taproom, and I have yet to come face-to-face with Wyatt. I've got this avoidance thing down pat. I know he went to the bar, so I don't even hope it's him.

"Yeah?"

The door pushes open and Tristan peeks his handsome face in. "It's that time."

I worry I've forgotten something important and shoot up to a sitting position in my pajamas.

"What time?"

"Shower time." He comes into the room and sits on the edge of the bed in his board shorts. His brown eyes are full of worry, and I wonder if he spent the night again and knows that I've been hiding up here this whole time.

I fall back down and cover my head with the blankets. "I don't wanna shower."

Tristan tugs the blanket down. "Well, tough shnookies, hon. Just because you make out with a loser doesn't mean you're a tramp."

"How do you know that's why I'm in here?" I won't dare tell him the truth.

"I'm human. You feel like a slut, which you're not. And you don't know how to act around Wyatt, which is okay, because none of us do right now."

I sit up and fidget with the seam of the blanket. "I didn't feel like a slut until you said that."

He rolls his eyes. "We all feel like sluts sometimes." He stands up and pulls me from the bed. "We're supposed to feel like sluts. God gave us *lust*, right? Well, we're only human, so we take that word and we mix up the letters." He shrugs and I laugh.

"You're so weird."

"Maybe so." He goes to my dresser and picks out a bikini and a pair of shorts and then leads me into the bathroom. "Shower. And be sure to shave those hairy legs of yours."

He closes the door behind him and I stare at it, and then I look in the mirror. Holy crap. I can't believe how bad I look. My eyes are puffy from crying on and off over the last forty-eight hours, and my skin looks gross, which I'm sure is from dehydration. I turn on the shower and stand beneath the warm spray for a long, long time, thinking about my life.

I wonder why I don't feel like an orphan, too. I should, given the way my parents ignore me. They've checked on me only once since Wyatt's parents died, and they spent that time telling me how they hoped I'd get the job in New York so that I could make a name for myself and build a strong career. They talked about making money and climbing corporate ladders. They didn't seem concerned about how Wyatt and Delilah are holding up. Kyle cheating on me after two years should make me feel even worse, and it does make me feel like shit, but I know that was his issue, not mine. You can't love someone *and* cheat on them.

I think about the fight at the Taproom and the look in Wyatt's eyes when he was defending me. And the look in Tristan's eyes when he just came in and dragged me out of my bed. I think about the concern on Brandon's face two nights ago when he was watching Wyatt as we walked home after the fight. Those are the looks that matter. They were filled with compassion and drawn from the heart, not born of insecurities. And Wyatt. Sweet, wonderful, protective Wyatt. He saved me when that guy was forcing himself on me. I could have really been hurt. But on the way home, Wyatt had so much anger in his eyes that he scared the shit out of me, and I wonder how much of it, if any, was because he thought I deserved it or was asking for it. Or if he's angry because he's felt the energy between us shifting, or worse, because he's felt it shifting and then I had my arms around that guy. I'm not sure if it's anger toward me or not, but based on what I overheard yesterday, I can only assume it is. While he and I were busy *not* looking at each other, I was stealing glances at him. I saw a wide range of emotions, including an overpowering amount of regret that overtook all the others. I just wish I knew how to navigate this unfamiliar territory we've found ourselves in.

I shave my legs, then turn off the water and dry off. While I get dressed I think about Wyatt taking care of me when I was too drunk to walk, and then I think about the end of summer, which feels like it's fast approaching even if it's not. An icy feeling of loneliness seizes my chest. I open the bathroom window to clear out the steam and listen to the sounds of the ocean waves breaking and faint voices in the distance. I inhale the sea air, smiling as it fills my lungs. I don't feel lonely because I feel like I fit in here, and I realize that just like when we were at college, when I'm with Wyatt, I always feel like I fit in.

Except now that fit feels off, like it's forced and unnatural for the first time ever.

I gaze out the window, thinking about school and how it was a given that we'd all attend the same college. The three of us never questioned it. One day we were having lunch at Wyatt's house and he looked at us and asked if we wanted to do college apps that evening to get it out of the way. We didn't even discuss what schools we liked or anything. His parents had given them the names of three colleges and we filled out our applications. My parents hadn't even offered to help. I told them I'd applied to schools and they said that was *good*. Like they'd expected nothing less.

My thoughts turn to New York and how badly I wanted to work there. I've only been there once to visit, though I did take a quick trip for my interview. When I visited with my parents, they showed me the entire city. We saw a Broadway show, ate at strange and unique restaurants, shopped, and it was like the days and nights blended together. I felt like I had their attention for the first—and only—time in my life. I was thrilled when my interview with the accounting firm in Manhattan went so well. It's weird to think that in a few weeks my whole life could change and I could be living in Manhattan.

On my own.

In a strange city.

Without Wyatt.

I lean against the windowsill and try to imagine my life without Wyatt. He hasn't texted me at all since his parents died, and he used to text me. Never a lot, but sometimes. He's more of a face-to-face guy, and it's one of the things I love about him. He doesn't skimp on seeing me.

Until now.

"Cass?"

Tristan's voice pulls me from my self-imposed torture of dissecting my future.

"Yeah, I'm coming." I pull the door open and run a comb through my hair as Tristan leans against the doorframe. "Where are we going, anyway?"

"Everywhere. You needed to get out of bed. We're going to the library to make sure my brain doesn't turn to mush, and then we'll have lunch at Brooke's, and then...if you're a really good girl, we'll go hang out on the beach and get that hot bod of yours a nice golden tan."

I set down my comb and fall against his chest. "Thank you, Tristan." If I do get that job in New York, I wish I could pack everyone up and bring them with me.

"Come on, slut girl. Grab your camera and let's go."

I know Tristan is kidding, but my mind goes directly to Wyatt, and I wonder if *he* thinks I'm a slut for real.

Chapter Twelve

~Wyatt~

I'VE MANAGED TO avoid a run-in with Cassidy, and while I thought it would make me feel better, now, several nights later, I still feel like shit. And I miss the hell out of her. I stay after work with Jesse to have a few beers and talk about the bar. He wasn't pissed at me for the fight, but he's definitely still tense. Even though it's dark out, I can see his jaw clenching even more than usual, and he's glanced at me only out of his peripheral vision, not head-on, like he usually does. I don't like knowing I caused this rift between us.

"Everything go okay when Tim showed you the books?" Jesse asks.

I shrug. "He showed us his procedures, but we haven't really gone over the books yet."

"But you're looking for someone to audit them for the last quarter, right?" Jesse shifts his eyes to me, and I know he's concerned. "You can't let that slip, Wyatt."

151

"I know. My plan was to have Cassidy help me do it, but..."

Jesse runs his hand through his long hair and narrows his eyes. "Don't tell me you're still not talking to her. Dude, that's so uncool."

I down my beer, not wanting to talk about Cassidy. Just thinking about her makes my body react in ways that it's not supposed to. I don't know how to control that without either being a dick or acting on it. I feel her slipping away. Last night when I came home she was out on the deck with Brandon and Tristan. Brandon was playing his guitar and she was singing with Tristan on the steps of the deck. When she sings, it's like every word is seeping with emotion. Just like the photographs she takes. Everything Cassidy does comes from her heart.

She didn't even look at me, and I knew she must still be pissed. I worry that it's more than that. That she knows what I'm feeling, and maybe that upsets her more than me hitting that guy. So instead of hanging out with everyone, I went upstairs and shot a round of pool and nearly sent a ball across the room because I was so angry at myself.

"What's the deal between you two?" Jesse sets his beer down and stares at me until I look away. "What happened? Did you two sleep together?"

"No, we didn't fucking sleep together. Nothing happened. It's just...all this shit, that's all." I get up, feeling torn between wanting to punch something and wanting to spill my guts to Jesse about how I feel about Cassidy. I don't know if I'm angry that he thinks I'd sleep with Cassidy and then not talk to her, or if I'm mad that I *want* to sleep with her. I can't think clearly, and I just want all the tension to disappear.

"I'm getting another beer. You want one?" He hasn't finished his first, but I figure it'll save another trip inside.

Jesse shakes his head, and I feel his eyes follow me into the bar. I grab another beer and sink onto a barstool for a minute. I hate everything right now. I hate the bar, I hate my parents, and I sure as hell hate this shit between me and Cassidy. When I go back out to the pier, Jesse's on his cell phone with a pinched look on his face.

"You all right?" I sit down and he nods, then shakes his head.

He ends the call, shoves his phone in his pocket, and runs a frustrated hand through his long dark hair. "Do you think you can handle the bar for a week?"

"Sure. Of course. What's up?"

"Nothing. I've just got to take care of some business." He rubs his hands down the thighs of his jeans and exhales loudly, like whatever business he's taking care of is pissing him off. Better the business than me.

"No problem. I can handle it." I wonder why he's not telling me what he's got to take care of, but knowing Jesse, he probably feels like I already have enough shit on my plate. He's not one to share his burdens with others.

"We're short staffed, Wyatt. I was going to hire another two full-time employees, but I haven't had time, and we have a party of fifteen booked for Wednesday."

I didn't think his eyes could get more serious, but they do. "Jesse, I can handle it. I'll make sure we're staffed." I have no idea if I really can handle it or not, but since the fight, I feel like a noose around the guy's neck. Time to lessen his burden and figure stuff out on my own.

"We have a delivery coming in in two days. Delilah has a handle on the inventory and how to handle deliveries. I've gone over it with her."

"Yeah, she told me. I've got it—no worries."

He nods. "I hate to leave you hanging when things are so up in the air."

"No problem, man." I can't imagine that it's going to be as difficult as he acts like it will be. It's a week of running the bar, something my dad made look easy. I'm sure we can handle it.

"You've got to keep a clear head, Wyatt. That means no drinking. Not on the job, not with the employees when they're off and you're in charge."

"Yes, father dearest. I think I can handle myself. I'm not an idiot."

Jesse leans forward and sighs. "I didn't mean it like that. But this business of coming in at eleven won't cut it."

He may be right, but he's starting to piss me off. "I've got it. I said no problem. The fight the other night was a mistake. I've got my head on straighter. I'll be fine." I hope he's buying this. The last thing I want is to let Jesse down after he saved my ass.

"Hey, guys."

I turn at the sound of Brooke's voice. She's smiling, but her eyes are filled with worry. Jesse pulls a chair out for her, and she tosses her dark hair over her shoulder and sits between us.

"Hey, Brooke. Where's Delilah?" I don't like the idea of her being alone when she's going through such a hard time.

"She's with Ashley. They went to a movie. That's kind of what I wanted to talk to you about." She reaches for Jesse's beer and he smiles and nods. She takes a sip and then turns her attention back to me.

"I got your text earlier. She's okay, Wyatt. This will take some time for her. Delilah is so sensitive, and I know that guys can sort of muscle through these things a little better than girls can in general, but I wanted you to know that I'm your friend, too. If you need me, I'm here."

"Thanks, Brooke. I know that. I'm good, though. Really." I sound so confident that I almost believe it.

She touches my hand. "We haven't had much time to talk. Are you really okay?"

"Yes. I'm fine." I finish my beer, knowing full well I won't be fine until I clear things up with Cassidy.

"We had a nice talk about your mom, but I think it's all hitting her now that she's here. You know, waking up and smelling coffee brewing and expecting to see her mom even though she knows she's gone. Those types of unexpected things are hard for her. Do you mind that Delilah's staying with me?" Brooke takes another sip of Jesse's beer. "I think she needs the quiet, and the guys said they've been staying at your place."

"I don't mind. I just wish I could be the one helping her through all of this."

Brooke places her hand on mine and softens her voice. "I know, Wyatt, but sometimes girls need to be around other women."

I nod. "Whatever she needs. I just want her to be okay, Brooke, and if that means staying with you for a while, then that's what it means."

"Wyatt, I know the guys usually spend a lot of time at your place, but given your situation, if you don't want them around, you can tell them," Jesse suggests.

"It's really fine." The truth is, I've pretty much come to the conclusion that I need them around right now. I need the company, and I've been worried about Cass keeping to herself so much. I'm glad she has them, too.

"I saw Tristan and Cassidy," Brooke says. "They had lunch at the café. Cassidy's going to work with me a few hours each week."

"She is?"

Brooke reaches for Jesse's beer again. "I'll buy you another one. I promise."

"Yeah, right." Jesse laughs. "You've been drinking my beer for years and you have yet to replenish my stock."

I feel like I'm waiting on pins and needles to see if she says anything else about Cassidy. I want to know how she is. Did she mention me?

Brooke crinkles her nose. "Sorry, Jesse. Wyatt, Cassidy said she wanted to work a few hours here and there, and I have a big event coming up that I could really use her help with. She also said that if she gets that job in New York, she'll be leaving in a few weeks."

My chest constricts. How did I forget that? How

has the month gone by so fast? "Uh, yeah. If she gets a job in New York, I guess she will be leaving."

"That's what she said. She's applied for junior accounting positions, and it sounds like she felt confident about getting one of them. She seemed nervous, though. She said she's been to New York only once, with her parents."

"Well, she only visited once with her parents, but she also went for the interview. Even though it was a quick trip, she was excited about the possibility of moving there." The thought of Cassidy leaving makes me edgy. I knew she wanted to move to New York, but back then I didn't feel about her the way I do now. *Or at least I didn't realize it if I did.*

The way I shouldn't.

I get up to get another beer. Drowning my thoughts seems to be the only way I can deal with this. Jesse grabs my arm. I stare at his leather wristband, then lift my eyes to his. He says a hundred things with that one look. He reiterates that he needs me to be sober when I take over the bar for the week. He wonders if I'm falling down a rabbit hole, and I want to tell him I'm not that stupid, but right now I don't have any words to give him. I need to fall down that hole. It's the only way I'll survive losing my parents and Cassidy in this effed-up summer.

Chapter Thirteen

~Cassidy~

I NEVER THOUGHT I'd be so thankful for a summer job, but helping Brooke is about the only thing that's keeping me from going insane with the way Wyatt's doing everything he can to avoid me. I keep waiting for him to say something, anything, but he doesn't even look me in the eye. When he comes down in the mornings, it's like he's gone all vacant stare on me. It's been days since the fight, and I still can't shake the guilt of knowing that he fought that guy because of me. And the only reason I even kissed the guy was that I was pissed that Wyatt was leaving with that bartender. She was all over all the guys that night, and he had to pick her? Of all the girls in there?

I hated thinking, *Why not me?*

That's why I did what I never do, and left with that guy.

It was easier to fill that void than to suffer alone

and wonder what it felt like to be the woman in Wyatt's arms.

Thankfully, the guy was on probation, so he didn't press charges, and I have no idea what Jesse did to get the police off Wyatt's back, but he said he knew the officers and they owed him one.

Lucky Wyatt.

Lucky me.

Wyatt really did save me from him. I told him no, hit him, tried to get away from him. I can't even begin to imagine what might have happened if Wyatt hadn't come to my rescue.

Wyatt, I miss you so freaking much.

I have to stop thinking about him. At least tonight I'm helping Brooke with a wedding, which should keep my mind plenty busy. Talk about being thrown straight into a fire. Oh my gosh, I know absolutely zero about weddings, but one of the girls who was scheduled to help Brooke backed out at the last minute, so here I am beneath a star-filled sky, making sure the tables are in order while about fifty people gather around in beautiful dresses and the bride and groom—who apparently don't care if they see each other before they say their vows—gaze into each other's eyes off to the side. The florist brought in a gazebo and twined flowers around the railings. There's a path of candles creating an aisle for the bride to walk down, and it's just about the most beautiful, romantic setting I've ever seen.

Brooke is serving drinks, and there's no one around the buffet table because the ceremony hasn't taken place yet, so I sneak my camera bag from under the table and snap off a few shots of the bride and groom when they're completely unaware. The handsome groom has one hand on the bride's hip, and he is whispering in her ear. The glow of the moon behind them makes a perfect silhouette. The way he's touching his bride reminds me of the way Wyatt leans in close and shares inside jokes—*or used to before I started wanting to become our own secret.*

Stop thinking about him!

I walk around the table and focus on the wedding guests, taking a few candid shots, including the cutest little flower girl with golden hair and a halo of pretty white flowers. She's barefoot, and I get a shot of her and the ring bearer, an adorable little towheaded boy, holding hands.

I can't help but get a little closer and try a few new angles. I'm crouched beside the gazebo, taking pictures angled up at the bridesmaids, when I feel a hand on my shoulder and hear Brooke's harsh whisper.

"Cassidy!"

"I'm sorry. I'm so sorry, but no one is eating yet. I'll get right back to the table."

Brooke pulls me behind the gazebo. "No. It's not that. The photographer canceled. She had a family emergency. She's already forty minutes late. Of course this happens the one time I try to help out a friend. I should have just catered the wedding, but *no.* I have to offer to do it all—hire the photographer, book the venue. What was I thinking? Naomi's going to kill me. Can you take her pictures?"

I feel like my eyes are bugging out of my head.

"I'm not a professional photographer, Brooke. I've just taken a few classes and I take pictures for fun."

"But you're all I've got, and didn't you tell me that you won a few photography awards?" Brooke's brows are knitted together. She's wearing a pretty blue dress, and her long dark hair is pinned up in a bun with a few tendrils hanging down, framing her face.

"Yeah, but that was in college. Not like *real* awards." I'm proud of those achievements, but they're not *wedding photography* big, even if they were pretty big deals to me. Brooke told me that she'd gone out on a limb coordinating this event because her friend seemed overwhelmed putting it together. I know how important it is that she pulls this off professionally and seamlessly, and that's what worries me the most. What if I mess up?

"Please? I'll pay you what I was going to pay the photog. You can't leave me hanging."

The bride heads in our direction and holds up her palms, which I can easily read as *What's going on? Where's our photographer?* I can't turn Brooke down.

"Okay, but you don't have to pay me. And, Brooke, you have to tell her that I'm not a pro. It's important that she knows these could be subpar, okay? I don't want her to hate me."

"She never would, and if she hates you, she has to hate me, too, so we'll suffer together." Brooke takes my hand and walks quickly to the bride.

"Naomi, this is Cassidy Lowell. Cassidy, Naomi."

"Hi. This is a beautiful wedding." I'm not sure what else to say, and I'm too nervous to make small talk.

"It will be if we ever get started. Brookie, what's

happening? Where's our photog?"

"She had an emergency, Naomi, and I'm really sorry, but it's okay. I promise. Cassidy's going to take your pictures." Brooke pushes me forward, and Naomi's face fills with confusion.

"Didn't I see you at the buffet?" she asks.

"Yes. I also take pictures. For fun." Uh-oh, not exactly the right way to calm a nervous bride. "But I've won a few awards. Here, look." I pick up my camera and scroll through the pictures I've just taken, hoping they look good. Naomi looks over my shoulder, so I have no time to hide them if they suck.

"Oh my gosh. Brookie, these are amazing!" Naomi smiles and pulls Brooke over to see the pictures.

They're excited, pointing at the pictures and whispering. The fact that they think they're great makes me even more nervous.

"Cass, these are fantastic," Brooke says.

I tell myself I can do this, mentally prepare for my first real photography assignment. I want to grab Brooke and scream, *Can you believe it? I'm the photographer!* But I want to hide beneath the table, wrapped up in the tablecloth, and let someone else be the photographer, carry the weight of knowing that if they mess up the pictures, the bride and groom won't have any shots to reminisce over and show to their grandchildren.

Nothing like pressure to make your hands shake and your head spin.

Several hours later, after what was the most romantic wedding I've ever seen—which isn't saying much since I've only been to one other wedding in my life—after cleaning up with Brooke and after going home to a Wyattless house, I pull out my laptop and load the pictures onto it. I sit in the middle of my bed, scrolling through more than five hundred pictures. Some of them are clearly awful. The lighting is off or the angle is funky. But others take my breath away. The candid shots are the best, and some of the candid shots of the bride and groom bring tears to my eyes. Or maybe it's because seeing these two people so much in love makes me think of Wyatt, and thinking of Wyatt these last few days steals my breath in another way.

I miss him so much, and I can't keep it bottled up any longer. With my laptop scrolling through one romantic shot after another, I let my tears flow like a river. An hour later, my tears have dried and I've finished looking at the wedding pictures. Instead, I start to scroll through old pictures of Wyatt.

I smile at pictures of him as a teenager, recognizing how his face has turned from boy to man. His eyes are more reflective now, his features more striking, a little harder, and his body—*good Lord, his body*. He was always hot, but looking at these older photographs, and then the more recent ones, it's easy to see how his body has thickened and become broader. How he became a man right before my eyes.

When I close my laptop and lay my head on the pillow, I think about how, in seventeen years, this is our first real falling-out. This is the first time I've been staying in the same house as Wyatt when we haven't been as close as two peas in a pod, and it hurts. Boy, does it ever hurt.

I hear footsteps on the stairs and I know it's him. I hear him walk to my door and stop, and for a minute I freeze. I can't move. A minute later his footsteps trail down the hall, and I hear his bedroom door open, then close, and a tear slips down my cheek.

Chapter Fourteen

~Cassidy~

IT'S BEEN SIX days since Wyatt and I have spoken more than a grunt or a nod to each other, and Delilah is still staying at Brooke's. Delilah said she needs to be able to work through everything without facing so many reminders of her parents. I guess I understand that. Meanwhile, Brandon has stayed at Wyatt's house every night since we arrived, and Tristan has basically taken over one of the downstairs bedrooms, staying four of the last six nights. I don't think Wyatt minds, but it's hard to tell. He's cordoned himself off from me, and I hate it. He spends the mornings surfing and works long hours at the bar, but he hasn't asked me to help him with the books again. I've been working a few hours at the café with Brooke, and I really like working with the customers. Brooke's friend Naomi loved the pictures I took for her wedding, which is a big plus, and I should be elated, but it's hard to be elated when I miss Wyatt so much.

Brooke and I talk about everything—except how I really feel about Wyatt. I'm afraid to say it out loud, given his current stay-away-from-me attitude. I hate that things have gone so awry between us, but more than that, I wish I understood why they have. I'm not sure what to do or how to handle things.

I can't go home, and I can't live like this.

I eye my vibrating phone and scroll through to the incoming text. My heart speeds up, hoping it's Wyatt.

Kyle. Darn it. I've been thinking about Kyle a lot lately, trying to figure out how I missed his cheating. I'm pissed at him, and I'm pissed at myself. I don't know how I could have had such bad judgment.

I toss the phone onto my pillow just as Tristan appears in my doorway. I don't know how he always seems so casually comfortable, even when I know he and Ian are having trouble. Even though he doesn't talk about how Ian treats him, anyone can read it in his eyes. That's the thing about Tristan—he wears his emotions on his sleeve, so even when he's trying to cover them up, they find a way out. As he sits on the edge of the bed, I recognize worry in his soft gaze, and I hate that I've caused it.

"Hi, hon." Tristan eyes the phone. "Kyle again?"

I nod, feeling like a total loser because while I don't miss Kyle, the guy I dated for two years and gave my virginity to, I miss Wyatt. It feels like I lost a piece of me, and I miss everything about him. His slanty smile, his mischievous eyes. I miss the way he grabs my hand, the weight of his arm over my shoulder. I miss the smell of him, which is stupid, because he just smells like a *guy*. A really hot guy. No. He smells better than every other guy on earth. He smells uniquely like Wyatt, and I want to hug him and smell him and hear his voice so badly it hurts. Each night while I lie in bed listening for his heavy footsteps to make their way down the hall, I wonder if he misses me, too, and I worry about him. I know he misses Delilah, and I know he blames himself for her leaving, which maybe he should, but still. I know Wyatt well enough to know he feels like he's failed her. And then there's the biggest, most gigantic, most painful worry of all, which is also a really selfish one...*Is he burying me right along with his parents?*

Tristan picks up my phone. "Do you want me to talk to Kyle and tell him to stop bothering you?"

Tristan has been so good to me this past week. So has Brandon. I feel like we've become even closer friends. I care about them deeply, and in getting to know them better, I worry more about Brandon. When I see him come and go with different lovers, I want to reach out and talk to him about what makes him jump from one person's bed into the next. And *Tristan*. When I think of Tristan and Ian, I get angry. Ian doesn't deserve him.

I clutch my pillow against my stomach and shake my head. "I'm going to. It's time. I thought he'd stop texting, but apparently he thinks cheating on someone means you still deserve to be tied to them."

Tristan hands me my phone, then pulls his knee up onto the bed and leans back on his palm. His voice goes soft. "Maybe you should take care of the Kyle thing now. One thing off your plate and all that?"

I look at the phone. "Yeah. I just...What do I say to him? I haven't wanted to text him, because I feel like he doesn't deserve to take up a single second of my time. I'm definitely not calling him, either."

"Text him and tell him everything you just told me." Tristan settles his hand over mine with a gentle, reassuring touch. "You can't move on until you put him behind you. And I have a feeling that you need to move on with Kyle before you can move on with...the rest of your life."

His dark eyes roll over mine, and I know he's searching for an affirmation. I know he's right, and I also know he's referencing Wyatt. "What if it just makes Kyle text me more? I don't want him to show up here and for Wyatt to beat him up again. Wyatt doesn't need that kind of stress, and I know he won't let Kyle hurt me anymore."

"Listen, Cass. Wyatt's a big boy. He can handle himself. I think you two are just working through a really tough time. He doesn't want to fight. That's not Wyatt. You know that better than anyone. His feelings for you are pouring out of him like sweat. He can't stop them, but this is Wyatt. He doesn't know how to deal with them either. And let's not forget what Wyatt doesn't want to talk about—the loss of his parents, the bar, and Delilah. I think we both know he'll figure everything out, and I think we also both know that he feels horrible for fighting." Tristan pauses, like he's giving me time to think about what he's said.

It doesn't surprise me to hear Tristan talk about Wyatt's feelings for me. Tristan is an emotional guy, so this conversation feels natural coming from him, and my whole heart wants to believe he's right, that Wyatt's just dealing with these new emotions while he's drowning in the wake of his parents' deaths. But I'm so afraid I'm going to lose him forever.

"What if...? What if the only way he can deal with everything else on his plate is to push me away? I feel him doing it, Tristan. He can't even look at me right now." Tears stream down my cheeks, and I don't try to hide them or wipe them away, because in this house, with these friends, I know it's okay to be me. And as Tristan wraps me in his arms, I'm so very thankful for him, for everyone here, that it brings more tears.

"One step at a time, Cass. We're all so messed up this summer, but we'll get through it. Wyatt might be putting distance between you two right now, but he'll come back around."

I pull back and swallow my hurt, clinging to the hope that Tristan is right.

"Thank you, Tristan. You're so good at this."

Tristan laughs. "Only with other people's relationships, as you've seen." He hands me the phone.

I'm more than ready to erase Kyle from my life, and I pray that I haven't lost Wyatt forever. The room goes silent, and I feel like there's a void around me, even though Tristan is right here. I think I miss my mother. I never miss my mother. I mull over that entirely strange feeling and realize it's not my mother I miss. It's *Wyatt's* mother. She might have been strict with Wyatt and Delilah, but she was there for them. For all of us. She was *present*. So present that we never questioned it. We knew she'd have breakfast ready for us, she'd ask about our school day and make sure we had warm jackets in winter. Even me. And she'd done it for so many years in my parents' absence that I grew to accept it without guilt. And now she'll never be present again, which makes my stomach sink.

I feel empty.

I stare at the phone, and anger fills my chest as I realize how much time I've wasted thinking about Kyle.

Tristan doesn't hurry me along. He doesn't pressure me to talk or make a decision, and it makes me hate Ian even more. Brandon is right when he says Ian treats Tristan like he's expendable, but it didn't hit me with such a hard impact until just now. Tristan is *not* expendable. He's good and loyal, and sweet, and I realize I'm being selfish again. Tristan's spent several nights here, and I never even asked him if *he* was okay. What kind of friend have I become?

"Tristan, why have you been sleeping here?"

His eyes fill with sadness as he shrugs. "Ian's going through something."

"Why do you stay with him?" I think about how I stayed with Kyle despite how possessive he was.

"I stay because hearts aren't as smart as heads." Tristan nods toward the phone.

Hearts aren't as smart as heads. Ain't that the truth?

I stare at my phone for a long time before figuring out what I want to say to Kyle. Then I type it in and stare at it for an even longer time.

Stop texting. It's over. I think about texting more, telling him he doesn't deserve me. But he's not the one who needs to hear the rest—I am. I deserve a man who will always be there. A man who will love me for my faults and my good points. I deserve a guy who loves me with his heart *and* his head. I deserve a man who will stand up for me, not a man who will do all he can to hurt me. *I deserve a man like Wyatt.*

"Army *will* get past this, Cassidy."

I smile at the nickname. "I know. Jesse said he moved right past denial and into anger. Did you know there are five stages of grieving? I Googled it. Bargaining, depression, and acceptance are the next three stages. I'm not sure what bargaining means, but it doesn't really matter. Wyatt doesn't like to play by the rules."

"No, he doesn't. But he sure has a handle on the anger part. Cass..." Tristan runs a hand through his hair, like he's weighing his next words, and when he finally speaks, his tone is stronger, heated. "He was jealous when he hit that guy."

He holds my gaze for a long time. I don't say anything, because it feels strange to hear him validate Wyatt's feelings. It feels good, but it also feels like something I shouldn't hold on to. If there's one thing I've learned from Wyatt's radio silence, it's that hope is a hurtful thing.

"I think he's working past the anger, though." Tristan's voice is soft again, like he's offering this up to tell me that I should hope, that he's trying.

My phone vibrates, and we both look at it sitting in my palm like a ticking grenade.

"Do you know how to block a number?"

He reaches for the phone, reads the text, and starts pressing buttons, then hands it back a few minutes later.

"What did you do?"

"Blocked Kyle's number." He rises to his feet.

"Thank you, but as far as Wyatt goes, he wasn't jealous, Tristan. You guys weren't there. The guy was forcing himself on me. Wyatt was protecting me."

Tristan nods. "I know he was, but trust me. I know guys. Or at least sometimes I think I do. Right now I'm questioning my own knowledge in that department." Sadness passes over his face again, then he shakes his head and the sadness becomes compassion. "I've seen you guys together. It's different from the way it was last summer. In this case, jealousy and protectiveness kind of go hand in hand. Listen, Wyatt's down at the Taproom working with Jesse. Want to go down and get a drink?"

I shake my head. I'm not ready to try to break the ice. What if Tristan is wrong about Wyatt? What if Wyatt doesn't want what I want, and this is the only way he knows to turn me away?

"Okay. Hang in there, hon. This will all be water under the bridge in no time."

I watch Tristan leave, then turn away from the door and look out the window, wishing I could figure out what to do about Wyatt. When my phone vibrates again, a pain sears through my stomach. Tristan must not have blocked Kyle's number right. I pick up the phone, ready to type a nastier message, like, *Fuck off Kyle. I'm done*, when I see Wyatt's picture appear on the screen.

My heart skips a beat. I'm afraid to look at the text. What if he tells me that he made a mistake and he needs me to move out? What if he's pissed because he got in another fight because of me? With shaky fingers, I open the first text and read it.

It's been weeks since my parents died and it still hurts like hell. It's been 6 days since Delilah moved out, and even though we've made up, that hurts like hell, too. But the last 144 hours have been the worst of my life because you and I have grown so far apart.

The worst in his life? He cares. I read the text again, and another comes through before I'm done.

I get it if you want to go someplace else. I've been an asshole and I'm sorry. If you want to get a short-term apartment or fly to see your parents, I'll pay for whatever you need. We have money from our parents, so it's not a problem. But

But? The text bubble must have run out of characters, and I think I'm going to die if the next one doesn't come through fast. My phone vibrates again with another text, and I scroll to it with my heart in my throat. I pull it up and devour the words as fast as I can.

But I wish you would stay.

I read the message at least twenty times. I read it until the words blur together from the tears in my eyes. I read it again and again, until I can feel his presence, smell his scent. I read it until it's memorized and there's nothing left to do but try to remember how to breathe.

I read the text again, because it brings his whisper to my ears, and I've missed hearing him so much that I want to soak it in. Every breathy sound, the way the *S*'s slide off his tongue like a secret. I read it again, hoping and praying I can hear his voice again. When it doesn't come, I close my eyes and clutch my phone to my chest. I swear I can feel him right here with me. I open my eyes and turn toward my bedroom door— and my heart stills. Wyatt's standing beside my bed, reaching a hand out toward me. I blink several times and I look at the phone, sure I've conjured him up in my confused head. Then his warm hand is on mine, and his green eyes are reaching for me, too, and my body is moving without my head telling it what to do. I stand on the bed and leap into his arms, knocking him backward into the wall. My arms and legs wrap around him like an octopus, and I kiss his forehead, his cheeks, his chin, everywhere except his lips, because something in my head *is* working. I somehow understand that my *friend* is back. *My friend.* My very best friend in the whole wide world, and he filled my emptiness in the space of a second.

~Wyatt~

CASSIDY'S IN MY arms, pressing her body to mine. She's here. Really here with me. Those are the things that are going through my mind. I can't believe we're finally together again, and all the angst of the last week falls away. She smells like heaven, and her lips feel so good, pressing against every inch of my face, except the one place I desperately want them to land. She's holding me so tightly that every part of me aches for her. I never want her soft lips to stop touching my skin or for her grip on me to ease. She's kissing me fast and hard, and my hands are roaming up her back, into her hair, down to her ass, and I can't stop them. I want so much more of her. I want all of her—her heart, her words, her thoughts, her love. I feel her heart beating fast and crazy against mine, and I close my eyes and revel in the feel of her in my arms. How did I survive six days without her? Without holding her hand or seeing her smile. My mind goes foggy as her lips touch the corner of mine. That tiny touch, that tiny taste, sends a bolt of heat through me, and I close my eyes against it, but my hand is already fisting in her hair and tilting her head back. I bring my lips to her neck, and I can feel her frantic pulse with my tongue. Damn, she tastes good. Her skin is warm and salty, and...I can't stop myself. I kiss her neck and feel her fingers digging into my back, her hips pressing against my abs as she tightens her legs around my waist.

Every muscle in my body flexes as I strain to refrain from doing more of what I want to do so badly. I tug her head back and search her dark, hungry eyes. They're too seductive for me to turn away from. I'm pushing her lips toward mine, but I can't control myself.

"Cass?" A whisper. A plea.

She doesn't answer, just looks into my eyes and tightens her grip on my back again. Her lips part, and I don't know if it's an invitation or a warning. Although every ounce of me wants her, the rational side of my brain is waving red flags like there's a bomb coming. But when Cassidy whispers, "Kiss me," I'm powerless to resist her.

Our lips crash together like we've broken free from a lifetime behind bars. Her lips are soft, but the pressure of our mouths coming together for the first time is rough and needful. I want to lay her down beneath me and tear her clothes off, feel her passion while buried deep inside her. But this is Cassidy, and while our mouths are claiming each other, my mind slowly comes back into focus and my grip on the back of her head eases. Cassidy's eyes are still closed as our lips part. She's breathing hard, and for a split second I drink in her swollen, pink lips, the beautiful bow of them, and the fluttering of her long lashes as she opens her eyes and meets my gaze for the first time since we've crossed this invisible line.

Her lips curve up a little more, and I know, I just *know*, that what I'm about to do is exactly what we both want. I loosen my fist in her hair and bring her lips to mine, brushing them lightly together. I run my tongue along her lower lip, then memorize the swell of the top. Finally, I press my lips to her gently, savoring the sensation of our tongues exploring each other's mouths. We fit together perfectly. The gentle pressure of our mouths lingering, tasting, savoring is the most incredible sensation I've ever experienced. I take her lower lip between my teeth. She stills, and her breathing becomes shallow as I love her mouth with the attention it deserves. Her eager tongue meets mine stroke for stroke, and I feel her body melt into me. The tension in her hands eases, and a sexy little noise leaves her lungs and fills mine, pulling a heady moan of desire in return. Our lips part, lingering a breath apart, then come together again, like we need each other to survive.

Cassidy's hands slip to the back of my neck, then slide into my hair. She moans again, and I kick the

CATCHING CASSIDY

door closed behind us. Our lips part with the slam of
the door, hesitate against each other, then they come
together again and it's nowhere near enough. I need
more of her. I trap her lower lip between my teeth
again and give it a gentle tug. Her lips curve up with
the tease, and I drag my tongue across the tender spot
I'm sure I've left. She arches her neck, and my teeth
graze her jaw, her cheek. She's panting, her eyes
pleading for more. I settle my mouth over her neck
and suck gently, feeling her body shudder against
mine. Somewhere in my head thoughts are ping-
ponging, telling me not to lower her to the bed and
follow her down even as I'm doing it. I know I should
back away, but I don't. I can't. I push the unwanted
thoughts away.

Our hands and mouths take the feel of the
mattress as a green light, and we paw and grope,
fervently tasting as much of each other's exposed flesh
as we can. I'm hard as a rock, and when she presses
her hips against mine and makes a sound of
appreciation in her chest, my entire body thrums with
desire. One hand grips her hip while the other slides
beneath her shirt. Her nipple rises to a taut peak
beneath my fingers and I need to taste it. I need to
taste her. I tear her shirt up over her chest and pull
her bra strap down her arm, freeing one beautiful, full
breast. *Christ.* I've seen plenty of boobs in my life, but
nothing compares to seeing Cassidy's. My chest feels
full, and an emotion I've never felt before washes over
me. I pause to really look at her, but I don't just see her
bare breast. Her eyes are still closed, and as I take in
the upturned edges of her slightly parted lips, the feel

179

of her body trembling against me, I realize the unfamiliar emotion is honor. I'm honored that she trusts me to be this close to her.

I hesitate long enough for her to stop me if she wants to. She presses my head down, and I take her rosy nipple into my mouth, licking circles around the peak, teasing it with my teeth, earning me a heated moan that spears more heat through me. I move to her other breast, groping the first with my hand while devouring the other. My hips are grinding against her hot center, and she's returning each move thrust for thrust. We're totally in sync, and nothing has ever felt so right. I manage to quiet the voices in my head, hoping they're gone for good.

My hand trembles with need as I reach for the button of her shorts. I hear something in the distance, but I'm too lost in finally coming together with Cassidy to know or care what it is. I take her breast in my mouth again as I unzip her pants and slide my hand beneath her panties. *Christ*, her skin is so smooth. She's shaved bare, and she's wet. So fucking wet. She arches against my hand, and our mouths come together as my fingers dip inside her. She rides my hand like she's been craving it forever. Neither of us hears the doorknob, but it must have turned, because the door swings open, and we both startle.

"Oh, shit." Tristan backs out of the room fast, closing the door behind him. "I'm sorry. I'm so sorry," he says through the door.

I touch my forehead to hers and close my eyes, trying to reel in my desires.

"Cassidy," I whisper. "I'm sorry." I withdraw my

hand from her pants and gently pull down her shirt.

She doesn't respond, but her hands press against the back of my head, keeping me near.

"God, Cass. Where'd this come from?"

"Don't know," she says breathlessly. "Don't care."

There's a knock on the door, and her eyes widen.

"Uh, guys. I'm sorry. So sorry." It's Tristan again.

Feeling protective of Cassidy, I roll to my side, blocking her from the door, even though it's closed. Guilt swamps me. She trusted me. She's the one person I don't want to lose from my life, and what do I do? I let my feelings overtake what I know is right. The look in Delilah's eyes when she asked me if I hooked up with Cassidy comes rushing back. The concern in Jesse's eyes when he asked if I'd slept with her bowls me over. They both know the kind of guy I've always been, and it makes me feel low and unworthy of Cassidy's trust. Of her emotions. Jesus, what was I thinking?

"But, um..." Tristan's voice is hesitant. "I thought you'd want to know that Brandon's band is here, and they're setting up out on the deck."

We listen as his footsteps descend the stairs.

I reach down and button Cassidy's shorts, zip her zipper, knowing that if I'm really going to protect Cassidy, then I need to protect our friendship, too. Despite the way my heart feels full for the first time in my entire life and the way our kisses were like nothing I've ever experienced before, I know what we're both dealing with this summer. And I know I can't survive the loss of my parents without her friendship.

This was a mistake, and one I can't afford, and

neither can she. I feel like my heart's breaking into a million little pieces, and I'm afraid I might not ever be able to put it back together.

Cassidy's looking up at me with trusting eyes, and I desperately want to disappear into her with another incredible kiss. I want to forget what I have to say, and I know that's not an option. I went six days without my best friend. I can't...I'm not willing to risk that again.

"I'm sorry, Cass. I don't know what came over me. We shouldn't have..."

She turns away as I sit up.

"We can't do this. We can't risk our friendship. It was a mistake."

"A..." She folds her arms over her stomach, and her shoulders round forward.

I feel her disappointment like a knife to my gut.

"Right," she whispers.

"Cass, I'm sorry. It's all this stuff that's going on, and..." *And I want you more than I've ever wanted another woman in my life.* I want her to hear those words so badly, but we can't be together, and they would only push the knife deeper into both of our hearts.

Her cheeks are flushed, and her lips are still pink. She swings her legs over the other side of the bed and lets her hair fall around her face like a shield. I have to say something. I want to say something, but what I *want* to say and *have* to say are two different things, and I have trouble forcing the words from my lungs. Every time I open my mouth to speak, no words come. There's a war going on in my head. I want to take her in my arms and bury myself deep inside her, forgetting what's right or wrong, and do what we both want. Take us both to that intimate, erotic place that I know will feel so damn good it'll be worth everything I'm feeling right now. As these thoughts careen through my mind, cording my muscles tight, I know I shouldn't do it. I don't know how to be the man Cassidy deserves, and I can't lose what we have.

"Cass, I'm sorry. I don't want things to be weird between us." I'm a fucking idiot. How can they not be weird? Jesus, I really am a prick. Right now I hate my parents, and I hate Tristan for interrupting us. I know I shouldn't hate any of them, but maybe if my parents hadn't died, I wouldn't have known how I really feel about Cassidy. Or if Tristan hadn't come in...I don't even let my thoughts go there, because it makes me more of an ass. I would have made love to her until we both forgot how to speak, and that would have been worse than trying to get over a little heavy petting and a kiss. Even the best kiss of my life.

"They won't be." She fixes her bra and shirt and crosses her arms over her chest. A barrier between us.

I add that to the list of things I hate.

"You sure?" I close my eyes, not wanting to hear her cuss me out for letting us go too far. Jesus, my fingers were inside her. I know how she tastes. I know how she feels. How can anything ever be the same again? Anger swells within me. It's a goddamn *good* thing Tristan interrupted us. Otherwise I'd know what it felt like to really love her, to be buried deep inside her, and then what? We would have been stuck trying to navigate through *that* in our friendship.

She gets up and goes into the bathroom without

saying a word, closing the door softly behind her. I sit on her bed for a few minutes, knowing I've fucked up. What's worse is that after kissing her, after touching her, I realize that all these feelings I have for her aren't sudden at all. They're filling my body, my mind, and I know they're just surfacing after years of repressing them.

I get up and stand by the closed bathroom door, wondering if she's regretting what we did. She's the only woman I want and the one woman I can't have.

By doing what I think is right for both of us, I feel like she's being ripped from my life, just like my parents were. Only it hurts so much worse.

Chapter Fifteen

~Cassidy~

I DON'T KNOW what's worse, wanting to be with Wyatt or knowing Wyatt thinks being with me was a mistake. Or, of course, the most embarrassing of all, having Tristan walk in when Wyatt's hand was down my pants. I look up at the deck from where I'm standing on the beach, among a sea of people I don't know, and I feel like I took one giant leap forward and was kicked in the face and thrown a hundred steps back. It hurts like hell. When I came out of the bathroom, Wyatt was gone. I heard him in his shower, and I came downstairs before I could run into him again. It was easy to get lost in the crowd. Apparently, Brandon and his bandmates know every person who lives in Harborside, because by the time Brandon and the others finished setting up their equipment on the deck, the house and the beach are packed.

Brandon's band is playing one of their songs that I

recognize from last summer, though I don't know the words.

"Hey, Cassidy." Jesse startles me when he puts a hand on my lower back. I didn't hear him approaching. He's dressed in his usual jeans and T-shirt with a chain running from his belt loop to his wallet in his back pocket. I don't have to look to know he's wearing his boots. He always wears boots, despite the fact that it's summer. "How are you?"

"Hi, Jesse. I'm good, and you?" I'm getting really good at lying. I'm glad *I'm good* sounded believable. What I'd really like to say is, *Totally sucky right now, thank you very much. Tristan just caught Wyatt with his hand down my pants, Wyatt says it was a mistake, and I want to make that mistake over and over and over.*

"Okay. I'm going to be taking off for a few days. Did Wyatt ask you about going over the books?" He runs a hand through his long hair and shakes it out, scanning the crowd as if he's looking for Wyatt.

"Uh. Wyatt and I haven't really talked much." *Unless you count moaning into each other's mouths.*

"Oh?" Jesse draws his brows together.

"I was just about to ask her." Wyatt drapes an arm over my shoulder and one around Jesse's, and I wonder if he and Tristan attended the same sneak-up-on-others class. "Cassidy, can you show me how to reconcile the bar books tomorrow?"

"Sure." *Really? You're going to act like nothing happened between us? This is what we're going to discuss after what happened earlier?*

"Well, then, I'll leave you two alone to discuss it." Jesse disappears into the crowd.

Wyatt leaves his arm around my shoulder, and for a minute we just stand there in a bubble of discomfort among the music blaring and the waves crashing and people laughing and carrying on. I'm surprised that the urge to push him away isn't stronger than it is, but my heart is so full of him that even the hurt he causes me isn't enough to make me want to push him away. His kisses consumed me. His touch made me feel ripe with desire and sexy in a way no man ever has, and I want more of it all. I want more of Wyatt.

He starts walking, and I'm moving alongside him, pressed to his side like old times, only my heart is hammering and my pulse is racing, and I'm not sure if I'm mad about earlier or if I'm hopeful for what this moment might bring.

We walk down the beach until the music becomes faint, and then we sink down to the sand. I'm still tucked beneath his arm, and it seems our bubble of discomfort has morphed into a bubble of silence, because neither of us says a word. It used to be that we could sit in silence all afternoon and never feel funny. Now every second that ticks by feels like an hour. I don't like this new us. I wish I had magic shoes that could transport me back in time with a click of my heels.

I wish. I wish. I wish.

But I don't have any magic shoes, and when Wyatt turns his dark green eyes on me and looks at me like he wants to kiss me again, there's no place in the world I'd rather be.

Part of me hates that I'm a weak girl right now, falling under his spell and not wanting to break free.

But another part of me feels his warmth, knows his kindness and generosity, and there's no denying that he long ago claimed a piece of my heart that I know no one will ever be able to touch. I tell myself that it's okay to be a swooning, weak girl when I'm with him.

"Are you okay?" His jaw isn't clenched and his hands aren't fisted, but his eyes are filled with what looks like regret. I don't want it to be regret, so I hope I'm reading him wrong. He's not really looking at me. His eyes are partially occluded by his hair, so I convince myself that maybe I'm misinterpreting it altogether.

It's a simple question, one he's asked me often. But the answer will be so telling that I hesitate. *Am* I okay? No, not really. But this very second, sitting with Wyatt like we used to, being in his world again? Yes. I'm okay right now. I love Wyatt's world. I don't respond, because if I tell him I'm okay, he'll think I really am, and if I tell him I'm not, then he'll feel worse than I think he already does.

"Cass?" He runs his finger through my hair, and it reminds me of his big hands tangled in it when we were making out.

I like that too much and fall deeper into him. My body sinks into his side. "Yeah?"

"We left things sort of hanging before, and I thought we should talk. I really missed you this week."

He hasn't shaved in at least a few days, and I find myself staring at the spot where the scruff on his cheeks meets his mustache. I reach up and touch my upper lip, remembering the way it tickled when we kissed, and I feel myself smile.

"I missed you, too." I can't drag my eyes away. I remember the feel of his tongue dragging across my lower lip, and wish I could feel it again. Nothing will ever come close to the feel and taste of his delicious kisses or the way his weight on top of me felt perfect and right.

He pulls me closer against him. Our knees are bent and our legs are pressed together from hip to calf. I feel the familiar rush of anticipation that vibrated through my body right before our lips met for the first time. I don't ever want that feeling to go away, and I know it's going to. I know he's going to tell me we can't be together, because didn't he already tell me that once? But I'm not ready to hear it yet, so I stay in my bubble of bliss and hope he doesn't pop it too soon.

Wyatt wraps his other arm around me and hugs me close. He presses his lips to my forehead, and I hear him breathe me in. I love the sound of it, like he's memorizing my scent.

"Cass, kissing you was like nothing I've ever felt before."

Thank you, thank you, thank you, God!

"Was it like that for you?" he asks.

This is one of the things I love about Wyatt. He talks and shares his emotions with me in a way that most guys don't, and I know he doesn't share them with other girls. It might have taken him six days to come back to me, but he did. Boy, did he ever.

I drop my eyes and nod. "Yeah." I don't spill my heart to him, because I still don't trust where we're headed. I'm afraid I'll scare him off. I heard him loud and clear in my bedroom, and he wasn't spewing an invitation for more. He was telling me that it was a mistake. A *risk*. I've never been very risky, but boy do I ever want to take this risk with him.

He touches my cheek and tilts my face up, so we're looking into each other's eyes. He's so handsome and his eyes are so serious that it takes all of my concentration to remember to breathe in, exhale, then repeat it again and again.

"I want to kiss you again." His voice is tender, but his eyes are dark and his stare feels urgent. His thumb slowly strokes my cheek as his fingers draw me closer to his lips.

"Cass."

His breath whispers across my skin.

"I don't know why it's happening now, after all these years. It's the totally wrong thing for us to do," he says against my lips. I want to press our mouths together, to silence his words until they don't exist.

"Why?" The word escapes before I can stop it. I don't want to hear the answer. I'm afraid it's going to make sense, and I don't want that. I wish I could take it back. His fingers tighten against the back of my neck. His thumb presses against my jaw, making me even more aware of how close our mouths are.

"It's tricky." His other hand finds my thigh and holds me tight, like he's afraid I'll run away.

If only he knew that I don't have control over any of my muscles at the moment.

"Why?" I manage.

"What if we...don't make it? What if we do *this*...?" The word lingers between us, begging to be defined. "And it doesn't work between us? I can't lose you,

Cass. It's too much. I need you."

"You need me." I don't know why I'm repeating him. Maybe to reiterate it to myself, but my brain isn't working right. All I hear inside my head is *kiss me, kiss me, kiss me.*

His lips curve up at the ends. "More than you'll ever know."

"Then show me."

His eyes darken like a lion about to claim his prey, and in the next second our lips touch, my eyes close, and the smell of the sea, the sound of the waves, and the cold sand beneath my feet fall away. There's only Wyatt's talented tongue, his luscious lips, and his strong hands touching me, sweeping my body beneath his. He settles over me with such ease, it's like we've been together forever. He laces our fingers together and pins them beside my head as we kiss until my head spins. He's hard. Rock-hard, and oh my Lord does he feel good. And big. *Huge.* I want to touch his body, to feel his strength inside me, but he's got my hands pinned as he stares into my eyes with a look that says he wants to take me right here and now. I rock my hips, letting him know I'm right there with him. His eyes narrow, and he presses my hands deeper into the sand.

"Cassidy." My name sounds like a warning as he grinds his hard cock against me, leaving no room for misinterpretation of his desires.

"I want you, Wyatt. I want this." I've never said those words before. With Kyle I had sex because it was what was expected of me after dating for so long, but I never wanted him like I want Wyatt. I'm wet between my legs, swollen with need. My heart is beating like a battering ram against my chest, like it's going to break through just to reach him.

He releases one of my hands, and I run my fingers down the back of his arm. I love the feel of him. He scoops his hand beneath my back and presses me to him.

"Cass." It's a guttural whisper against my cheek. "I want to be inside you. I want to feel you take every inch of me in and I want to love you until you can't remember a time we weren't together. I want to make you mine in every sense of the word."

"Yes." I realize it's all I've ever wanted.

"Risky." He draws back and searches my eyes, and I wonder why he doesn't see the remedy.

"Then we'll go inside."

"Us. We're risky."

I feel like I've been punched in the gut. I've completely misunderstood. I thought he meant being there on the beach, out in the open. I hear myself suck in air and I try to turn away, but my eyes betray me. They're frozen on his, and anger bubbles out of my mouth like someone turned on a faucet.

"*We're* risky, Wyatt? You fuck half the girls at school and *we're* risky?" I can't believe how bitchy I'm being, but I can't stop myself as I struggle to get out from beneath him. His eyes widen, and his jaw falls open. I've taken him as much by surprise as I've taken myself.

Good. Let him hurt.

"Cassidy, that's not what I meant."

I flail my arms until my hands break free from his

grasp, and I push him off of me.

"I can't do this, Wyatt." I stand and brush the sand from my clothes.

"Cassidy, wait." He reaches for me, and I turn away and stomp back toward the house. He's beside me in two seconds flat.

"You're my best friend. You're *Delilah's* friend."

"Big shit." I can't help it. It just comes out.

"Big shit? Is that what our friendship means to you? Cassidy, I can't lose you. I can't make out with you, make love to you, and then realize we don't work and lose my best friend in the whole world."

I stop walking, feeling like steam is coming out of my ears. My hands fist at my sides, and I force myself to face him.

"That's what life is, Wyatt. One fucking risk after another. We won't know if we work without trying. That's the reality of life. We might work, or we might not, and if we don't, then we don't, but at least we would have tried."

He clenches his jaw and steps in close. Then his eyes soften, and he tilts his head just a fraction of an inch. I wouldn't even notice if I weren't so in love with everything about him that I have every one of his mannerisms memorized. A flutter of hope floats in my chest. He reaches for my hand and drops his eyes to my lips, making my body hum all over again. How can he do that with just a look? For a split second I think he's going to kiss me and tell me I'm right. When he lifts his eyes to mine again, the desire I saw before is tethered, as if he'd thrown a lasso and pulled it back in. He squeezes my hand.

"Nothing is worth the risk of losing your friendship, or losing you in my life forever."

"Well, you're doing a hell of a job of pushing me away." I turn around, worried about the same thing he is, glad it's just as important to him as it is to me, but I want him so desperately that I can't control my emotions. He grabs my arm and pulls, and I stumble and fall against his chest. He takes me in a deep, passionate kiss that steals any chance I have at rational thought. I feel the rigidity of my muscles melting against him and hear the music filter back into my ears. What am I doing? He just told me we're not worth the risk.

But this feels so good.

He feels so good.

He tastes so—stopstopstop!

My body stiffens, and I push away as my brain begins to fire again. We stare at each other for a long moment. He's lightly holding my wrists, like he expects that I'm going to come right back into his arms.

I want to. Lord, how I want to.

But I made a really bad judgment call with Kyle, and I'm not going there. I know Wyatt. I trust Wyatt. I trust him with my life, and I trust him with my friendship, but he's a one-night-stand guy, and I have no idea why after all this time this is just coming to the forefront of my mind. But it is. And it's staring back at me like a marquee. I can trust him with so much of myself, and I'm ready to hand over my heart, even after he told me not to. He must know he can't be trusted with it.

I should probably thank him for knowing himself well enough to protect us both, but all I can do is wonder how he can do this to me and try to remember I'm strong enough to get through this. I'm strong enough to survive without him. I'm not a weak girl! I'm smart and strong, and I survived being left behind for years, being forgotten, being cheated on. I can survive loving Wyatt Armstrong and losing him.

I pull my arms free and narrow my eyes in an effort to keep my angry tears from falling. I don't have the words to say what I feel. How can I tell my best friend that he's just broken my heart worse than the guy I dated for two years? How can I tell him that he's drawn the line, and I'm not going to be foolish and force myself on him? I can't afford to make another bad decision.

Walking away from Wyatt is the hardest thing I've ever done in my entire life, but somehow I know it's the only choice I have.

Chapter Sixteen

~Wyatt~

THE MUSIC IS blaring as I watch Cassidy storm off and disappear into the crowd. My chest feels like it's compressing, like it's too small to hold everything in and my body's going to shatter into pieces right here in the sand. I need to go after her. I need to tell her all the things racing through my head, but I'm frozen in place. I've hurt her twice in one day, and I feel like shit. I stand at the edge of the crowd and watch her make her way across the deck, pushing her way through the people who are dancing. Tristan's on her heels, and when she runs inside, he turns and scans the crowd. The scowl on his face is nothing compared to the knife I'm twisting in my own gut. He stalks down the steps and I wait, because I deserve whatever he's going to dole out.

Tristan grabs my arm and drags me down by the water. His grip is tight, and if I didn't feel like I deserved it, I'd knock him away, but I need the pain.

Down by the water the breeze is stronger, and it cools the sweat that's formed on my brow. Tristan drops my arm and paces in front of me. He stops and puts his hands on his hips.

"What the hell?" His nostrils flare with anger. I expected him to slug me or to give me shit like I'd give anyone who hurt Cassidy. Instead, I'm staring at more than six feet and about two hundred pounds of muscle that could give me a fairly matched fight, and he doesn't say another word. He doesn't have to, because Tristan has these eyes that say a hundred things at once, and his message is loud and clear: *I'm a dick.*

"I love her, man. But she's all we've got left besides you guys. She's..." I cross my arms and turn away, realizing I've just admitted that I love Cassidy. I hadn't even realized it myself, but hell if it isn't the absolute truth.

Tristan scrubs his hand down his face, rubs the scruff on his chin. "Shit, Army. Then what the hell are you doing?"

I scoff, although what I really want to do is find myself in a back alley and beat the shit out of me. Since *that* can't happen, I have no clue what to do but be pissed at myself.

"You love her? You've never been in love with a woman. You've never dated a woman for longer than a week." Tristan lowers his chin and sets an assessing gaze on me.

"No shit."

"So how do you know you love her?"

It's a simple question. I bet a thousand guys could

give you a million reasons how they know they love their girlfriends. I've got nothing. Not a single thing. I know what I love *about* Cassidy, which is every fucking thing, but how do I know I love *her*? All I can do is tell him the truth, no matter how lame it sounds.

"I don't see fucking fireworks, if that's what you're looking for. She's it for me, man. I feel it, okay? She's always been the one for me and I've never let myself feel it. Hell, *I* didn't even realize it until just now."

His eyes soften, but he doesn't say a word. It's like he's trying to figure out if I'm full of shit, which, okay, yeah, sometimes I am, but not now. Never about Cassidy.

"I know it's fucked up. You're not supposed to fall for your best friend, especially when she's your fucking twin sister's good friend, too. And that's why I'm letting her go, Tristan. I was a business major. I know all about assessing risk, and Cassidy? She deserves more than a risk. More than *this* risk. She needs me and Delilah as much as we need her, and I can't screw that up for all of us."

"Sit." Tristan rarely gives commands, but the seriousness of his voice sends me to the sand. I'm relieved, actually, because what I feel like doing is taking off for a ten-mile run.

"You've got to tell her how you feel, all of it. To us you're Army, the guy who parties hard and takes whomever he pleases. But to Cassidy, man, she sees all the things you don't show us but we know are inside you. I've seen it in the way she looks at you, man. She loves you."

I press my fingers and thumb to my temples and

exhale loudly.

"She can't love me, Tristan. If she gets that job in New York she'll be leaving soon, and I've got all this crap to deal with. What are we going to do? Fall for each other and break up when she leaves? Because that's worse, and you know me. I might not have had many girlfriends, but you've seen me with Cassidy. I'm possessive and protective of her, always have been. And that's when we were just friends. Once I really let my feelings out, how long do you think I'd last with a long-distance relationship? You know damn well I'll want her with me every second, and that's not fair to her." I pause, because the words vying to be released are more painful than any realization yet. But one look at Tristan's expectant gaze and they fall free.

"And how long would it take for Cassidy to be swept off her feet by some rich city guy?"

"She doesn't care about that bullshit, and you know it. That's called *jealousy*, my friend. You're just not used to it. You're used to being possessive as a friend, but not jealous, like a boyfriend. It's your own insecurities poking their ugly head out, and that's okay. But Cassidy isn't a cheater any more than you are." Tristan pats me on the back. "Wyatt, what do you want with her? Because this crap you're doing, making out one minute and walking away the next, it's going to make you lose her faster than lightning."

I look at him out of the corner of my eye. "Dude, you don't date chicks. How do you know all this shit?"

"Emotions are emotions. It doesn't matter if we're talking about a guy or a girl. Love is the same, man. After all this time, don't you know that?" Tristan shakes his head like I'm an idiot. "No, I guess you wouldn't. You've never been in love. This is new territory for you."

"Yeah, I need an ATV to figure out this stuff."

Tristan laughs. "No kidding. We all do." He glances back up at the house. "You gotta fix this, Wyatt. One way or another, you need to go up there and make Cassidy stop hurting. She's fresh off a breakup, and even if she says she's fine, she's not. She's sensitive and she's vulnerable. And let me tell you, that girl up there worries about you and thinks about you nonstop. We went to Brooke's for lunch the other day and every conversation circled back to you. She's afraid you're not dealing with the death of your parents. That you're sweeping it under the rug."

"I'm not—"

His stare stops me cold.

"Fine. Whatever. I'm dealing the best way I can. I need to be strong for Dee."

Tristan leans forward and places his hand on my shoulder. He lowers his voice, and his eyes soften again. "And what about for Wyatt?"

"I'm fine, Tristan."

"Right." He pushes to his feet. "Because guys who are fine let the woman they love walk away crying."

I don't know how long I sit out on the beach, but it's long enough for about six girls to hit on me and for me to blow them all off. Before I realized how I felt about Cassidy, I'd have hooked up with any one of them without a thought. *Out for a good time*, that's what I've always been. I've always watched out for Delilah and Cassidy, but at the end of the day, any girl would do to ease the tension, help me forget about an impending test, or blow off steam for a hundred other reasons. Now the idea of putting my lips on another woman isn't even an option. I looked long and hard at the last one who approached me. She squatted beside me in her miniskirt, giving me a clear view of her pussy, because who wears panties to a beach party? Whatever. She tried all the stuff girls do to let me know she was free and easy. She whispered, brushed her tits against my arm, touched my face, even ran her fingers through my hair, and it fucking repulsed me. When Cassidy's hands were in my hair, all I wanted was for them to stay there, or even better, to touch me all over. But that nobody? That girl who would let me blow my load in her and be happy with what I had to give for the night, knowing I'd never see her again? I wanted to smack her hands away.

I stay on the beach until the music stops and the people clear out. I wait until the house is dark, and then I push to my feet and go up to the deck, still thinking about Cassidy. I hear noises inside the dark living room and close my eyes for a beat before going inside, where I find Brandon sitting on the couch with a girl straddling his lap and a guy kneeling beside him with his tongue shoved down Brandon's throat.

I smack Brandon on the back of the head.

"Dude?" the guy who's sucking Brandon's face snaps.

"Take it into the bedroom." I point my thumb over my shoulder and head for the stairs. Brandon has his own shit to deal with, and I have mine. We all handle things in different ways.

"Sorry, man," Brandon says.

I hear three sets of feet shuffling toward his bedroom. The girl giggles and then the door closes. Upstairs I head for my bedroom, then turn back toward Cassidy's. I stand outside her bedroom door, trying to figure out what to do. It takes only a few seconds to decide. I hate the idea of hurting Cassidy. Of all the people in the world, she's the one person who doesn't deserve it.

I knock on her door and listen to the silence. She's probably sleeping. I open her door as quietly as I can and see her sleeping in my T-shirt, the one I put on her the first night we were here. She must have gone into my bedroom to get it, because I washed it the other day and put it away in my dresser. The idea that she wanted to sleep in it makes me feel even worse, and I stand with one hand on the doorknob and one foot in her room.

Cassidy sighs in her sleep, and I turn to leave.

"Wyatt?" she says sleepily.

"Sorry, Cass. I didn't mean to wake you."

She pulls herself up to a sitting position. My shirt hangs off her bare shoulder. The blankets are in a pile at the end of the bed, and the shirt is bunched around the tops of her thighs. She looks sexy as hell, and way too tempting. I know I should leave, but something in the way her eyes catch mine makes me powerless to walk away. She looks sad and hopeful, and I know I have to clear the air.

She pats the bed beside her. "You didn't wake me. I was just lying here."

We both know she's lying as I sit on the edge of

the bed. She smells fresh and citrusy, like she's just showered. She brings her knees up to her chest and wraps her arms around them. I want them wrapped around me.

I shift my eyes away and press my hands to my thighs in an effort to distract myself.

"You okay?" Her voice is just above a whisper.

I turned her away twice, hurt her so bad I can't imagine how she's not punching me in the stomach, and she's asking if I'm okay? That's Cassidy. She couldn't hold a grudge if someone strapped it to her arms, which makes my thoughts shift to Kyle. I see her phone on the nightstand and the message light is blinking. I want to reach over and check to see if it's him, but I don't. That's not what I'm here for.

"Listen, Cass. We should talk."

Her face blanches, and I feel, more than see, tension in her entire body. This is why we need to talk. I can't do this to her.

"Okay." She sounds like she's just lost a battle.

I meet her worried gaze and can't help myself. I reach out and touch her cheek, run the back of my hand down it. The feel of her soft skin and the trusting look in her eyes fills me with desire again. I drop my hand and she takes it in hers. She turns it over and runs her index finger across my palm.

"Remember when we were little and we used to read each other's palms?" She smiles, and the memory makes me smile, too.

"Yeah."

She traces the lines on my hand. "I've always loved your hands, Wyatt. They're big and strong." She lifts her eyes and meets mine. "Like you." Our eyes linger on each other's for a minute, maybe more. The bedroom grows ten degrees hotter, and she drops her eyes to my hand again.

"I told you that you were going to live a long life, remember?" She doesn't wait for me to answer. "And you said that I would live a long life with you."

I had forgotten about that, and it does something funky to my heart, like it's squeezing really tight. "Yeah, and I meant it."

Her finger traces a vein up my wrist to my forearm. "I think I was twelve when you said it, and I think I fell in love with you a little that night, but I didn't realize it until just now."

"Cass." My heart is racing, and every instinct draws me closer to her. I want to fold her into my arms and kiss her. I want to lower her to her back and learn the curves of her body, bring pleasure to every ounce of her until she's begging me to stop because she can't take any more. I want to love her until I feel her crawl under my skin and know she'll always be there.

But we can't always get what we want.

I wanted my parents to be there for us after graduation.

I wanted to watch my parents' eyes light up when Delilah got married.

I wanted to look at my dad when I had already made my way in this world and was ready to take over where he left off as he put the keys to the Taproom in my hand.

And in every scenario that I imagined, Cassidy was

always there. At our house when we got home from graduation. At Delilah's wedding as a maid of honor. Sitting on the side watching as I took those keys from my dad. But I never thought about what *Cassidy* wants. I never even thought to play out *her* life. I've lived in the selfish head of a college student for so fucking long. And now, thanks to my parents' untimely deaths, the mind of an adult—the conscience I always thought I'd grow when I was good and ready—has started to take hold of me. And the last thing I want to be is that selfish college kid. Especially with Cassidy.

I never knew that death could change a person so much.

"It's okay, Wyatt. I'm sure you think I'm ridiculous, or on the rebound from Kyle, and maybe I am. Ridiculous, I mean, because I'm totally over Kyle."

"I don't think you're ridiculous."

She shifts her eyes, and I realize I'm fiddling with the ends of her hair. I don't stop. I can't. This may be the last time she ever lets me do it.

She smiles and presses her hand to my cheek. Her eyes narrow, just slightly, as she brushes her thumb close to my lips. I can feel the tension in her hand, like she's being careful not to touch them.

"I loved kissing you. It was just like I've always thought it would be. Only about a million times better."

I take her hand in mine and press a kiss to the back of it. "I have never told a woman that I love her in that way." I look her in the eyes, and the love I feel for her swells and swoops inside me. It feels too big, too real to deny, and I don't *want* to deny it. I'm done denying what I'm feeling for her. I hope she sees, hears, feels, *believes* that what I'm about to say is true.

"I love you, Cassidy."

"Like a friend," she says with a smile that never reaches her eyes.

I shake my head and shrug. "I have no frame of reference, but what I feel for you is so much bigger today than it was before we..." I almost say before we kissed, but I realize that I must have felt this way before we even came to Harborside, because that's when I began noticing the way she was looking at me and how things felt different between us.

"Before we made out?" This time her smile is real.

I smile, too, because she's trying so hard to be the Cassidy she's always been, and I love her even more for it.

"No, actually." This causes her smile to fade real fast. "Before I saw Kyle with that other girl."

"Wyatt..." she says just above a whisper. Her brows pull together as if she's trying to make sense of what I'm saying.

"I'm serious, Cass. The minute I saw him cheating on you, something inside me snapped and all these feelings came storming out. I've been trying to ignore them, but..." I shake my head, and when I reach for her hand, instead of holding it, I press it to her thigh with mine on top. I'm afraid to hold her hand, afraid I'll pull her into a kiss, because I want to kiss her so badly I can already taste her sweetness on my tongue.

"But...then...why?"

"Why do I keep pulling away?"

She nods.

I look away for a beat, and when I look at her again, that selfish part of my brain is pushed aside by the part of me that recognizes the need to grow up.

"Because, Cassidy." I release her hand. "Because you've wanted to move to New York since you were a senior in high school, and I'm not going to take that away from you. Because if I let myself love you and it doesn't work out, I lose you forever, and that's more than I can take. Because if I don't push away these feelings, I can hurt you, me, and Delilah, and she needs to lose you about as much as she needs a hole in the head."

"But I'm not sure about New York." Her words come fast and determined.

"You say that now because of us, but, Cass, it's all you talked about when you went for the interview. You've been counting on that job at the accounting firm. I can't be the cause of you giving up that dream."

She pulls her shoulders back and narrows her eyes. I know this look. She's about to rip me a new one. I'm ready, and I'm sure I deserve it, so I don't look away, but when she speaks, it's with an even, sensible tone that takes me by surprise.

"So you think it's better if we don't act on our feelings?"

I nod, unable to answer.

Her eyes go damp, and it just about kills me.

"Can I ask you one question?"

"Anything."

"What makes you so sure we wouldn't work out? How can you know that we won't last forever?" She presses her lips together, and I know it's to keep from crying.

All I can do is give her the truth. "I don't."

"So...What then, Wy? You calculated the risk of us and it was too high? Or are you basing this on your history with women? Because shouldn't I be the one afraid of that?" Her voice escalates, and a tear slips down her cheek.

"Are you willing to risk everything, Cassidy? Think about it. Let's say we have a great relationship and then you get the job and you decide not to go to New York. What if you give that up and three months later you think I'm a douche?"

"You're not."

"I'm not exactly stable, though, am I?"

"You're the most stable and honest man I know."

I frown, because I know she's talking herself into this.

"Okay," she relents. "So you're not stable relationship-wise, but you've always been nothing but honest with me. You're as stable as they come when it comes to me and Delilah and all your other friends."

"Cassidy, I beat the shit out of two guys, and I'm not sure I wouldn't have kept going with that guy down at the bar."

She grabs my hand, and I feel hers trembling. "You did it because you were protecting me, Wy! Doesn't that tell you something?"

"Yeah, it tells me that where you're concerned, I am less stable, or maybe not stable at all. Cassidy, I want more than anything to take this risk, but I can't do it. I can't imagine my life without you in it, and if that means that we have to be friends." I shrug to buy myself a minute to get my emotions under control. My throat is closing, and this feels like the stupidest thing I've ever done in my entire life.

I try to lighten the mood. "We're really good at being friends, Cassidy."

She crosses her arms and nods, blinking away the tears in her eyes. "Okay, so how do we do this? We ignore the sparks flying between us all the time? Like right now? Your body is coiled so tight. I know it's because you feel it, too, Wyatt. I know you want to kiss me as much as I want to kiss you. I know you want to feel your body pressed to mine. That's why your muscles are flexed. It's why you keep looking away." She presses her hand over my heart, then takes my hand and puts it over hers. "It's why your heart is beating as hard as mine."

I feel the frantic rhythm of her heart against my palm and know everything she said is true. So stinking true it pisses me off. I grab her shoulders and bring my face so close to hers it takes all of my focus not to kiss her. She's shaking, and she's right—my muscles are coiled tight—but that's nothing compared to what my heart is feeling right now. Really feeling, not lusting, not the rate at which it's beating. The love that is spreading through my body for this woman who knows me better than I know myself.

"You're right. I want all of those things and so much more." I pause as the weight of my words sinks in for us both. "But do you really want to if you know that in a few weeks it'll be over? Because, Cassidy, I'll lay you down beneath me right now and bury myself deep inside you until you can feel everything I feel for

210

you. Until you know what it feels like to love someone with your whole soul, because I know you never have. I know you, Cassidy. Your parents never showed you enough love to really feel it. And if they did, you'd have to magnify it by about a thousand times to feel what I feel for you."

"You're right. They didn't. But you've shown me love every day of our lives."

Her words stop me cold. *I've shown you?*

"Don't you see it, Wyatt? You've loved me forever. You've just never let yourself see or feel it." Her lower lip is trembling so hard I can feel the pulses in the air between us. She clutches my arms so tight it makes me want to do crazy things, like follow through with my feelings regardless of the risk.

"You're right, Wyatt. My parents have shown me what it's like to feel like a third wheel. An afterthought. But you never have."

"And I won't now, either." I force myself to move away from her to the other side of the bed, and I lean my elbows on my knees and hold my face in my hands, trying to make sense of everything. Our friendship. My feelings. The lust driving through me like a bullet train.

"Cassidy, I just need to do this right. I need to do something right, right now. I'm sorry that I hurt you."

"You didn't."

I turn and look at her with disbelief.

"Okay, so you hurt my heart, but I understand. This is you protecting me again, Wyatt."

"Why can't you see me for who I am? You'll go to New York and realize I'm a loser who never plans for anything. I'm taking over a bar with zero experience, flying by the seat of my pants, and I could fail. Badly. You deserve a lot more than that, Cassidy. And chances are, when you go to New York, you'll find some guy who's as focused and determined as you are, and you'll wonder how you ever thought you loved me."

"One day you'll realize that you are focused and determined. I don't want some other guy, and I don't want you to change, Wyatt. I believe in you. I trust you to find your way. You're always watching out for me and Delilah. One day you'll realize it's your turn to have the things you want, and I hope it's me and that I'm there when you do." She grabs my forearm before I can even process what she's said. "I'll respect your decision because I have to, but not because I want to. Just tell me what to do. How am I supposed to act for the next few weeks? What do you want from me?"

What I want from you and what I'm going to tell you are two different things.

"Act like my friend. Act like we always have. We'll work through the finances at the bar, hang out, have fun like always." Even as I say it, I know nothing can ever be the same, because I'll live every second of every day wanting more of her.

"Okay. I'll help you at the bar. We'll try to be normal, whatever that is, but certain things have to change. There are some things we can't go back to."

I wait for her to say more, knowing she's right and hating it so much I rebel against asking what things she's talking about.

"You can't hold my hand or put your arm around me without me feeling like I do right now." She shrugs.

"It's just impossible. Every time I see you my body gets all..." She blushes and turns away.

"So you're telling me that I've already messed up our friendship?" I feel like I'm falling into a dark hole, grasping for a frayed rope that becomes more threadbare every time I touch it.

"You're used to making out with girls and it not meaning anything."

"That's hardly fair. You mean everything to me, Cass." Right this second I truly hate my past.

"I'm not used to it. You know that about me. I don't usually make out with a guy who's never taken me on a single date, much less let him touch me...there."

Jesus. How could I not have seen this coming? She's right. I'm a dick. A total dick. I never should have let myself touch her.

"I'm sorry, Cassidy. You're not just some girl. You've never been just some girl."

She shrugs as if nothing I'm saying really makes a difference, or she's accepted it without any more heartache. She's compartmentalized it. I know Cassidy. It's how she deals with her parents. It sucks knowing I fit into the same type of slot in her head as they do.

"I know. I'm your friend, and you love me, but still, if I'm going to remain sane, things have to change."

"Cass, if I thought it wasn't risky—the two of us— I'd try. But you can see that I can barely handle myself right now. Do you understand? How can I expect to handle us?" I let those words sink in to my head as much as hers. "What you're telling me is that I've already ruined things between us? By doing the right thing I've made things worse?"

"Being friends, drawing that line between us right now, Wyatt. That's *your* right thing. Not mine. I'm just trying to figure out a way to move forward without losing my mind."

The thought of moving forward without one arm securely around Cassidy? I've clearly already lost my mind.

Chapter Seventeen

~Cassidy~

I CLAIMED TO be sick yesterday and begged off helping Wyatt with the books. I know it's a chickenshit move, and it probably makes me a bitch on some level, but all morning I've felt sick to my stomach. Heartsick. The idea of working closely with Wyatt is too much for me to take. So I hide. From him. From everything we said. From what we did. From myself.

Wyatt texts and calls and checks on me a hundred times, and by this morning I feel wildly guilty and give in to the promise to help him with the books. We work closely in Tim's office. Tim is out for the afternoon and Jesse is gone for the week, taking care of his own business. It feels funny working with Wyatt in this new ocean of discontent.

Delilah comes to the doorway and leans against the doorframe. "Hey."

"Hey, Dee. What's up?" Wyatt asks. He sounds too

upbeat, and I know Delilah can tell something is going on. Her eyes are darting between the two of us.

"Did something happen that I should know about?"

I'm not sure if she means between us or just in general, and I'm not sure if Wyatt knows either, because he doesn't look at me, so I can't see his eyes.

We both mumble a negative response, and Delilah sighs, then leaves the room and goes back to work.

Hours later we're still poring over the books side by side. Our legs keep brushing against each other, and every time they do, my heart skips a beat.

Wyatt is smart, and he picks up on the process of reconciliation easily. It turns out that it's not just the last few months that aren't reconciled. It's a time-consuming process to tie the canceled checks to the invoices, and it becomes apparent that Tim isn't as organized as he seems, which makes the job that much more difficult. I'm so bored with these reconciliations already, I can't imagine how I'll work with numbers all day long. I want to be taking pictures, or helping Brooke in the café, or...Even better...I want to be making out with Wyatt.

I'm losing my mind, because that is definitely not on the agenda.

I push that thought aside and turn back to the books. Tim has invoices on his computer and some printed out, but nothing is where it should be, and I can't concentrate on numbers when Wyatt's sitting so close to me. I fight the constant urge to try to talk him into giving us a chance and settle for a few stolen glances. I can tell Wyatt's trying not to look at me. The veins in his neck are thick, and his fingers grip the pencil so tightly that they're turning white.

As the day rolls on, I feel the heat of his eyes on me, like he couldn't resist the temptation, and by late afternoon, my insides are going a little crazy and the air is pulsing with heat again.

He leaves the room, and two seconds later my phone vibrates with a text. I grab it, glad for the distraction.

It's from Wyatt, and I wonder if he's going to tell me that he can't work with me after all. I open the text and pray for the best, only I don't have a clue what *the best* means.

Can you handle things for about thirty minutes?

I wonder why he needs me to and why he's even asking. It's not like the bar is relying on us to make it function properly. I text him back, *Sure.*

A minute later he returns my text. *Good. Heading home for a cold shower.*

I'm glad no one is around to see the big, cheesy grin on my face.

Chapter Eighteen

~Wyatt~

AFTER ONLY ONE day of working together, I can no longer trust myself to work in the same room as Cassidy. Every time we're together, the room feels like it's closing in on me. I'm drawn to everything about her, and when she gets close to show me things on the ledger, it takes all of my energy not to take her in my arms and devour her. Luckily, Tristan took the day off to go somewhere with Ian, leaving me on bartender duty. I'm happy for the change of pace. I'm pretty sure having blue balls all the time isn't good for a guy.

Delilah took the afternoon off to go meet a therapist with Brooke, which I'm all for. I think Dee has too many things to worry about to focus on the bar, and now I have an excuse to work on something other than finances with Cassidy. One of our part-timers called in sick, which leaves us shorthanded.

The bar is getting busy, as it does most afternoons,

and Dutch is in the back cooking up a storm. Livi and Charley are waiting on tables. My phone vibrates with a text from Jesse.

Did you hire anyone?

Shit. I totally forgot. I text him back. *Sorry, man. Totally forgot. Been busy.*

I serve up two drinks and then read another text from Jesse.

You staffed for the party tonight?

I put the glass that I'm drying down too hard on the bar, and three customers look over. I totally forgot about the party, but I can't tell Jesse that I'm not prepared for it. I don't want him to worry. Instead I reassure him.

I've got it covered.

I lean on the bar, watching Charley and Livi wait tables. This is Livi's first summer with the Taproom, but she seems responsible. When they're finished, I come around the bar to catch them before they walk into the back room.

"Hey, guys, we're a little shorthanded. Any chance you can stick around tonight?"

Charley's hands immediately go up in surrender. "I can't, Wyatt. Sorry. I promised Dane I wouldn't miss the group lab assignment we're working on tonight, and we leave tomorrow for a three-day project, so I won't have time to make it up." She glances at her watch. "Shoot. I have to leave in ten minutes. I'm so sorry. You know I'll help any time I can, though."

"I know. No sweat, Charley. Tell Dane I said hello."

I worked with Livi the other day. She's sweet as the day is long, way too mature for whatever age she is, which I imagine can't be more than twenty, and she takes a minute to think about her answer.

"I really don't want to turn you down, Wyatt. I need this job. But this weekend is the anniversary of my mother's death, and I need to drive home tonight to be with Holly and Jack."

I open my mouth, but no words come. The anniversary of her mother's death. Next year, and every year after that, we'll have to revisit the anniversary of our parents' deaths. The thought makes my gut feel like there's lead in it.

She tilts her head and looks at me expectantly, reminding me that I should say something.

"Oh gosh. I had no idea. Sorry, Livi. Are Holly and Jack your siblings?"

"No. They raised me after my mom passed away when I was fourteen. It's complicated." She smiles, and I can tell she doesn't want to talk about her family situation. "I heard about your parents, and I'm really sorry. If you ever want to talk." She shrugs. "I've been there, and I'm a good listener."

"Thanks, but I'm good, and don't worry about the job. It's here for you. Drive safely this weekend."

"I can probably stick around until about eight or so. I'm only driving to the Cape, so..."

"That would be awesome, if you're sure."

She nods. "Absolutely. I can use the extra money."

I thank her again and then go back into the bar, wondering what it must have been like to lose her mother at such a young age. Delilah and I are having a hell of a time dealing with it at twenty-two. Then I realize she said Jack and Holly, whoever they are, raised her after her mother died, and I wonder what happened to her father. I don't have time to decipher her life when I can hardly navigate my own. I force the thought away and focus on work.

I try to reach Delilah to find out where she's put the schedules, but she's not answering her texts or her calls. Instead, I spend the next two hours riffling through files, trying to find the other employees' phone numbers before I realize that there are no *other* employees. I head back out to the bar to figure this out. I call Brandon to see if he can help out, but he's got a gig tonight. I call Brooke, but she's not answering either. Brandon calls back a minute later and says he asked Ashley to help, and she'll be here in half an hour.

Gotta love my friends.

Over the next hour the bar gets progressively more crowded. Cassidy left before Jesse reminded me about the party, and I don't really want to bother her with this, but I have no choice. The bar is busier than hell, and Livi and I are doing all we can to keep up. The party that was booked has tripled in size, as the original fifteen people are joined by two more groups that come through the door hollering orders for drinks. I pull out my phone and see that I've missed a text from Cass.

The accounting firm in NY checked my references. That has to be a good sign, right?

Good? Good? No, it's not good—not for me, anyway—but yeah, it's a great sign for her.

"Hey, can I get two Jack and Cokes and a gin and tonic?"

I look up at the gray-haired guy and nod, thankful

that I don't have to card a kid. I hate that shit. I shove my phone in my pocket, fix his drinks, and after he pays, I give him his change. He leaves me a dollar tip, and I wonder why Delilah wants to keep the bar. I can't imagine doing this all day and night. Then again, I'm too distracted to think of doing much. Cassidy's text is weighing heavily on my mind, and I still need more staff. Pronto.

I pull out my phone and text her.

A great sign for sure. I'm stuck down here with no staff and a big party. Any chance you can help me out?

Ashley walks in and comes straight over to me. Her long blond hair is pinned up in a ponytail, swaying with each determined step.

"Hey, Wyatt. Tell me where you need me."

I'm so relieved, I hug her. "Thanks, Ash. Livi needs to take off. Can you take over for her?"

"No prob." She smiles as she crosses the floor and says something to Livi, who hands her the order pad and a pen, then another pen that she has tucked behind her ear.

Livi goes into the back, I assume to clock out, then comes back through the doors and heads directly to me. "Is it okay if I take off?"

"Of course. Thanks, Livi. You saved my butt tonight."

"Hardly," she says with a smile. "I'm always happy to pull an extra shift if I have the time." Livi takes a step away and then comes back and leans across the bar.

I lean down closer to hear her.

"I know it's none of my business, but...I've seen

Delilah crying in the ladies' room."

Delilah cries in the ladies' room?

"Please tell her I'm here if she needs someone to talk to. You know how they say time heals all wounds?" she asks.

It's all I can do to nod. I'm still thinking about Delilah, and now I'm even happier that Brooke's taking her to see a therapist, because I'm obviously not equipped to help her through this alone.

Livi narrows her eyes and smiles. "They're right. Time does. It just sort of kicks the daylights out of you first."

As I watch her walk out the door, I'm not sure if she's serious or kidding, but I understand about the daylights being kicked out of me. I've got that part down solid.

My phone vibrates again, and I read the message from Cassidy.

Yeah. Can I drive your car? I don't want to walk down alone.

This makes me happier than it should. She's asking me for something. It's such a small thing, but it's huge in the realm of finding some modicum of normalcy between us. I text her back. *You bet. Keys are on my dresser.*

When Cassidy shows up, the bar is busier than it's been all summer. I'm dying to talk to her about the job in New York, to see what else the company said to her, but I'm doing all I can to keep up with the drink orders while she and Ashley wait on the tables. Customers are drinking and hollering to one another. A wave of people file out the door, but it barely makes a dent in the crowd.

"Two shots of tequila and a gin and tonic," Ashley says as she leans over the bar.

I fill two shot glasses and mix the gin and tonic. "Here you go. You holding up okay?"

"Yeah. I waitressed through college. I'm cool." She disappears behind a broad-shouldered man.

I see Cassidy come out of the back with a tray of food. She's tied her hair back in a ponytail, and her eyes are serious as she weaves through the crowd and delivers the food to a table in the back.

"Three screaming orgasms." A petite brunette slides onto a barstool and pushes money across the bar.

"Sure thing." I mix the shots and give her the change.

"Keep it." She winks as she walks away.

I shake my head, and my eyes lock on Cassidy as she approaches the bar.

"Screaming orgasms, huh? You dole them out to just anyone, or do I have to be someone special?" Her voice is seductive, and her eyes are playful.

I lean across the bar and lower my voice. "Depends. You want the kind that come in a glass?" I have no business taking the bait, but I can't resist her.

Her cheeks flush pink as a guy comes up behind her and places his hand on her shoulder. She spins around and smiles at him.

"Hey there, Cassidy. Sorry to bother you, but do you think we could get another tray of fries?"

I narrow my eyes at the tall guy who's way too old to be looking at her like he is, and she's drinking it all in.

"Sure thing, Tom. I'll bring it right over." She watches him walk away, turns back to me, and rolls her eyes.

"Do all the customers tell the waitresses their names?" I sound, and feel, like a jealous boyfriend, which pisses me off.

"Better tips this way. Livi clued me in." She brushes her fingertips over mine. "Besides, you and I are just friends. Why do you care?"

"I don't. Just curious." I spend the rest of the night watching Tom eye Cassidy and getting angrier. Correction. I know the difference now. I hate it, but I can't deny the truth. What I'm feeling are the ugly claws of jealousy, and I'm getting more jealous by the second.

~Cassidy~

BY THE TIME we're done cleaning up, it's after one o'clock in the morning, and my feet are killing me. Wyatt's been in a pissy mood ever since he made the comment about telling the customers my name, which has made for a very tense evening. But really, what does he expect? If he doesn't want to cross that line with me, then he can't be mad if I act like I'm not his girlfriend.

Which I'm not.

Even though I want to be.

It sucked flirting with all those guys tonight when there's really only one guy I want to flirt with. Wyatt, Ashley, and I walk outside, and Wyatt locks the Taproom doors. His ass looks amazing, and I feel myself staring like I've never seen it before, even though I've taken many eyefuls recently.

"Stop staring at my ass," he says without turning around.

"Jesus, you have eyes everywhere," I say, and Ashley and I laugh.

"That and I saw you in the reflection of the glass." He looks from me to Ashley as we walk through the parking lot. "Thanks for helping tonight, you guys. We made a great team, and you both saved my ass."

"Anytime. I'll see you guys later." Ashley waves as she opens her car door.

Wyatt swings an arm over my shoulder, and for a second my insides get all hot and tingly, and then I remember we're *just friends*. I move out from under his arm, because as Tristan said, hearts aren't as smart as heads, and there's no way I'm giving this heart of mine a chance to screw with my head again.

"Hey," Wyatt complains.

I glare at him. I already put myself out there with the screaming orgasm tease, and I have no idea where it came from. Wyatt's response surprised me, and when the customer ordered his drink, I was relieved for the diversion, because I'm not certain that I wouldn't have scrambled right over that bar and thrown myself at Wyatt.

He opens the car door for me, and my stomach gets nervous after I settle into the seat and he crouches beside me.

"Cass, thank you for coming out tonight. I really appreciate your help, given this whole thing between us."

I swallow hard and stare straight ahead to keep from chickening out of giving him the answer I want to.

"Don't you mean the whole thing that's *not* between us?" I steal a glance at him. He nods and rises to his feet before closing the door. I watch him walk around the front of the car, run his hand through his hair, and pace for a minute. I try to imagine what he's thinking and hope it has something to do with the look in his eyes when he asked if I wanted the kind of screaming orgasms that came in a glass. He looked like he wanted me again, like if I had said that I wanted the kind that only he could provide, he might have considered lifting the getting-too-close ban.

The truth is, I've never had a screaming orgasm, or a quiet orgasm for that matter, and just the idea of anything like that with Wyatt makes my whole body ripe with desire. When he slides into the driver's seat, he stares straight ahead as he starts the car, then pulls out onto the main drag. We drive home in silence—that is, if you don't count the grinding of Wyatt's teeth.

He parks in front of the house, and I notice Tristan's car isn't there, but Brandon's motorcycle is. I have no idea how many vehicles Brandon has, but so far he's driven a van, a motorcycle, and a beat-up old car. At least we won't be alone in the house. I don't know why that makes me feel better, but it does. It's like having a chaperone on a date. If I know there are other people in the house, I know I won't get out of my bed and climb into Wyatt's, which, embarrassingly, I've contemplated for the last few nights.

We sit in front of the house in silence, and before I

can stop them, words fly from my lips.

"Why can't we be like normal twenty-two-year-olds and just go upstairs and sleep together and worry about the ramifications later?" Holy shit. I can't believe I said that. I curl my hands into fists and tuck them under my thighs.

Wyatt stares straight ahead, his jaw working double time. "Is that what you want?"

His voice is calm and cold. I'm not sure I've ever heard him sound so cold when he wasn't pissed off. I turn to look at him, and his hands are splayed flat on his thighs.

"Sort of," I admit.

He turns to look at me, and his face is a blank slate. "You don't fuck someone because you *sort of* want to."

The way he says *fuck someone* feels like a slap. Now I'm clenching my teeth together. I want to say, *Why not? You did. More times than you probably remember.* But I rein in that anger and respond from my heart.

"I don't want to *fuck* you, Wyatt."

"Well, that's what you're talking about, Cassidy. Do you think I cared about any of those girls I slept with? Do you think I cared if we remained friends or not? Do you think I was even friends with them? I was a stupid kid. I didn't give a shit about any of them."

"That was only a month ago, Wyatt, not ten years ago."

"That's where you're wrong. The last time I fucked a girl was three months ago. And if you think I'm the same kid I was before my parents died, you're wrong."

MELISSA FOSTER

He opens his door and steps out of the car. I scramble out and grab his arm.

"You can't tell me that part of you doesn't want to do this."

"Do what?" He doesn't even look at me. His eyes drift around the yard like he's bored, and it pisses me off. I have no idea why he's acting this way.

I step closer to him. Our thighs touch, and his eyes darken. I steel myself against the feel of him and force myself to speak with as much confidence as I can muster, which isn't much at all. "Sleep together and see where we end up."

He backs me up until my butt hits the car. Then he leans over me, pressing his hips to mine, and buries his hands in my hair. I'm turned-on and a little frightened, because he's looking at me like he's angry.

"Is this what you really want, Cassidy? To be one of the girls I fuck? You want me to take you and not care if it ruins our friendship? Because I've had a hell of a night, and if that's what you want, who am I to turn you away?"

My body trembles, and I hate myself for wanting to tell him yes. Yes, I want this. Yes, I want to be close to him, because I fully believe that once we're in each other's arms with nothing between us, everything else will fall into place. I open my mouth, but no words come.

"Tell me, Cassidy." He presses his hard cock against me. "You know I want you. Come on. Give me permission."

He tugs my hair and brings his lips so close they brush against my cheek. His warm breath slithers over me, making me shudder with need. He settles a hot, openmouthed kiss on my neck, then sucks my skin into his mouth and strokes it with his tongue. My lower belly tightens, spreading heat through my body like wildfire. I close my eyes and feel his hand between my legs, rubbing me through my jeans until I'm wet and my knees go weak. I shouldn't be turned-on when he's acting cold and hot at the same time, but I can't think straight. And as quickly as he pinned me to the car, he releases me, breathing as heavily as I am.

"Tell me if that's what you want, Cassidy. 'Cause I can fuck you better than any other guy can, and if that's all you're looking for..."

I push him away, angry at him for being such an ass and furious with myself for getting so turned-on.

"You think this is easy?" His eyes are dark, his words scathing. "You think I don't think about what it would be like to be inside you? To have your hands all over me? To wake up to you tomorrow, and the next day, and the next?" He searches my eyes, and I feel stupid for challenging him in the first place.

"God!" I'm shaking all over, and when he steps impossibly closer, I somehow convince myself to speak. "Grow up, Wyatt." I regret the words as soon as they leave my lips.

A slow grin spreads across his face. "Maybe that's the problem. I am growing up. Faster than I ever wanted to. I don't have a choice, Cassidy. My life is fucked. It's sink-or-swim time for me and Delilah, and maybe that's too hard for you to handle." He takes a step back. "If I'd known you wanted to be a notch on my belt, I would have fucked you years ago. Stupid me.

My parents died and I see things differently now. I thought I was doing the right thing. I thought there was a difference between making love to someone you love and fucking a girl. Funny how life changes us, isn't it?"

I wish I had something to throw at him as he saunters inside.

The minute the door closes I realize it's not him I want to throw something at. It's myself.

Chapter Nineteen

~Wyatt~

I'M UP BEFORE dawn the next morning after an agitated night's sleep. I take a cold shower to try to freeze some energy into my exhausted body, throw on a pair of running shorts, grab my sneakers, and then head downstairs. Tristan is lying on the couch asleep, fully dressed. There's a leather duffel bag beside the couch. I wonder what's going on with him and Ian, and part of me hopes he's finally left him for good. The house is silent, and the sun is pushing its way into the morning. I open the back door as quietly as I can and walk out onto the deck. Inhaling a lungful of chilly air, I sit on the steps and put on my sneakers.

I walk down to the water's edge, trying to leave thoughts of last night behind. I haven't gone for a run in weeks, and I know that no matter how much I need this, it's gonna suck. I head down the beach at a steady pace, hoping it's going to clear my head. I felt guilty all night about how I handled things with Cassidy, but I have no idea how else to handle any of this. For once in my life I'm paying attention to what comes next. I'm growing up like I'm supposed to. Aren't I? Isn't that what you're supposed to do when your parents die? I feel like it is. I mean, if not now, then when? I'm not going to be one of those losers who sits around drinking their life away and working at a shitty-ass job. I don't know if I want to work at the Taproom, but Delilah feels bound to it, so I'll figure out how to run it and make it work for her. She deserves that after the way my parents messed with her mind. I know that once she gets past all of this, she'll be able to run the bar and hire the right people. I just need to get to the point of understanding it all so Jesse can take care of his own business. The last thing I want is to be a burden to the guy after all he's done for my family. No one wants to be the reason someone else isn't doing what they want. I imagine Jesse telling people he's helping out at the Taproom because our parents died, and it leaves me with a sour taste in my mouth.

Like last night when I threw my parents' deaths at Cassidy like a weapon. It was a crappy thing to do, but she freaked me out. Most guys would sleep with her the minute she showed interest. But what I said is true. When I was in the thick of partying and dorm life, then later, apartment life, surrounded by girls who wanted nothing more than a few hours of pleasure, I took full advantage and had a lot of meaningless sex and never thought anything of it. I had Cassidy to talk with about things that mattered, like what we wanted to do after college or when I was worried about

Delilah. I know she never talked to Kyle about her parents. She told me that. It was like we had other people to fill those physical voids in our lives, but we had each other for the real stuff. I don't want to have meaningless sex with Cassidy. Now I want her to fill all of my voids, to share my life. I want to be the one loving her at night *and* talking about everything that matters.

I run past a couple heading in the opposite direction and wave. There are more houses at this end of the beach. I look up as I jog past, wondering what the people inside are doing. Are their lives changing at breakneck speed like mine? Did they wake up this morning wanting to walk down the hall and climb into bed with their best friend? My mind drifts back to Cassidy.

Cassidy, Cassidy, Cassidy.

Who am I kidding? I've been consumed with thoughts of her for weeks. My mind doesn't have to drift far. She's always right there. She shocked me in the bar when she made the comment about screaming orgasms, but that was nothing compared to what she said about us sleeping together. I had to jerk off twice last night just to get past the urge to walk down the hall and give her what she wants—what I want. The problem is, I know she doesn't want to fuck and see where we end up. That's not Cassidy, which means she's as frustrated as I am.

I force those thoughts away and run for another mile, then turn back toward the house. The sun beats down on my shoulders. I love the heat of the sun. I want to touch Cassidy's skin when it's hot from being baked in the sun. We've been so busy with the bar that we've had almost no time to just hang out and chill. I keep thinking that we'll have time for that, but then my mind shifts down a dark path that splits like a fork. One side is Cassidy moving to New York, and the other is darker. The unknown. The possibility that our time will never come. That it'll be stolen from us, like my parents' lives were stolen from them.

I see a man walking hand in hand with a little boy down the steps of his deck. They sit on the beach and the little boy fills a bucket with sand. It makes me think of my father and the way we used to build dribble castles in the sand. He'd get wet sand and cup it between his big hands, then dribble it into pointy mounds, and together we'd create a world of dribble castles. Delilah would draw in the sand by the blanket where my mom was usually reading, and every once in a while we'd call each other over to see what we'd made.

I slow my pace and walk for a while, thinking of my parents. I can't help but wonder, if they had known they were going to die, what would they have said to me and Dee? Would they have told us what they expected us to do? How to live our lives? What to expect? Parents prepare you for your first day of school. They teach you how to drive and help you learn right from wrong. But no one ever sits you down and says, *Hey, son. One day I'm going to die, and when that happens, I want you to...*If my father ever had, I probably would have rolled my eyes and blown him off.

I'm starting to forget certain details about my

parents, and that scares me. I can no longer remember their voices. For the first week or so I was able to hear their voices by thinking about them. That was one reason I left Connecticut. It was too painful to walk into a room in our house and hear my father calling out to my mother about when dinner would be ready or some other mundane thing I'd heard a million times. I wonder if one day I'll forget the way they looked or the way they smelled. It's a strange thing to know your parents your whole lives and then suddenly the people who loved you unconditionally are buried six feet under.

A memory.

A fading memory.

I think of Delilah and I remember that their love wasn't unconditional after all.

Our house comes into focus, and I see movement on the deck upstairs. *Cassidy.* I watch her walk sleepily along the deck. She's wearing my T-shirt again, which makes me smile. The railing of the deck blocks most of her from my view, but I can see her from the waist up. She shields her eyes and presses her face to the glass doors leading to my bedroom. When my parents were alive, Mom never knocked on my bedroom door, and it used to piss me off that she'd barge in. Watching Cassidy peer into my room reminds me of how she always thinks of me before herself. I never had to ask Cassidy not to wake me in the mornings. Delilah would knock on my door and holler, *Wy?* Even when Cassidy stayed at my place after parties, she never woke me up. Sometimes I'd wake up and find her reading at the foot of my bed. When I'd have a bad game, my father would tell me it didn't matter anyway. *At least you didn't fail a test,* he'd say. Cassidy knew how seriously I took football. She'd ask me what I thought went wrong and listen while I bitched. She'd smile and ask, *So what are you going to do different next time?* She knows me better than my parents did. I think they knew how to guide me toward what they thought was best, but Cassidy has always supported what *I* thought was best.

Until now.

She's going along with it, but I know it's killing her as much as it's killing me.

I walk up the stairs on the side of the house to the second level and around the corner of the house toward my bedroom. Cassidy's butt is sticking out from beneath the shirt, which is hitched on her panties, as she peeks into my room.

"Why don't you open the door?"

She jumps back and covers her mouth. "I'm sorry." Her face is beet-red. "I just wanted to talk to you, but I didn't want to wake you up."

I pull out a chair and sit down, enjoying the way her cheeks pink up. She looks so innocent standing there bare-legged, with the T-shirt hitched on her panties, and fidgeting with the edges of her shirt. God, I love her so much. I can't help but tease her.

"It's okay. I'm used to girls trying to sneak a peek. Not many girls can resist me."

She swats my arm, then fixes her T-shirt. *Damn.*

"Yeah, about that..." She sits across from me and puts her foot on my chair between my legs. She seems a lot more comfortable than she was when she was challenging me last night.

She sighs and rests her head back. Her hair falls behind the chair and nearly touches the deck. The shirt slides up her thighs and stops short of her panties. That's a dangerous shirt. Every time she wears it, I get myself in trouble.

"Do you know how much I love it here?" She's staring up at the sky as she asks.

Do you know how much I love you? "I know how much you love it here. That's why I was so surprised when you said you wanted to move to New York so badly."

She rights herself in her seat and tilts her head. "You *were* surprised, weren't you?"

I nod and watch her eyes slide south and linger on my mouth, then slip lower to my bare chest, where they remain. She licks her lips. I pick up her foot and rub my thumbs along her instep the way I know she likes when her feet are sore. I know I shouldn't do it, but I can't help it. I *want* to touch her. *Need* to touch her.

"You might want to lift your eyes." I smile when she blushes.

"See? Things have gotten really weird between us. I used to be able to ogle your chest without feeling funny about it."

The spark of mischief I see in her eyes cuts right to my heart. The sensuous sound of her voice strokes over my skin, stirring my desire to be inside her. I'm in way too deep, and there's no lifeboat in sight. I don't know exactly what's changed, but I can't fight the current running between us, and I have no desire to. I want to fall into it.

"And I used to be able to look at you without wanting to be inside you." Her jaw drops open, and I laugh. "What?" I've hit a wall. I was fooling myself, thinking I could resist Cassidy. We're too close. She means too much to me, and I want her like I've never wanted another woman in my life. There isn't a chance in hell that I can ignore what I feel anymore. Yes, it's risky. Yes, it's probably unfair, but it's only unfair if *she* determines it to be, too. This isn't a matter of trying to be with her. There is no trying. My emotions are bigger than me. Sometime between my run and climbing those stairs, my emotions took any control I had and shredded it.

"You can't say things like that." She says it all breathy and has no idea how hot she looks sitting there in my T-shirt, with no bra on, flashing an eyeful of pink panties.

She kicks me, and I shake myself out of my own stupor, but the need to be close to her, to continue stroking the fire is too strong.

"You may want to lift *your* eyes," she says, her voice laden with sarcasm.

"Why?" I hold her stare and tell myself that I'm playing a dangerous game, but I know this is no game. I'm completely powerless to resist her. I bring her foot to my mouth and press a kiss to the tips of her toes. The muscles in her leg flex. "Babe, the view of your eyes is just as hot as the view of your chest or those pink panties peeking out from under my T-shirt you've confiscated. I'll set my eyes wherever you want me to."

Cassidy pulls her foot from my hands and scoots

to the edge of her chair. Her knees fit perfectly between mine. She leans forward and places her palms on my thighs. "Why are you so hot?"

I grin. "Good genetics."

She rolls her eyes. "Your skin, dork."

Despite knowing I should keep my distance, I lean forward, pressing the insides of my thighs to the outside of hers. I put my hands on her waist and touch my forehead to hers. She smells familiar and fresh as the morning sun.

"Went for a run."

"Oh."

"Had to." I rub my nose against hers. "A little sexually frustrated lately."

"Oh," she whispers.

I brush my cheek against hers, then press a kiss to the sensitive skin beneath her ear. "How about you? Did you think about me last night?" I feel her inhale a sharp breath.

"Yes," she whispers.

"And?" I drag my lips along the shell of her ear, then take the lobe between my teeth and lave it with my tongue. I feel her body shudder beneath my hands, and I pull her toward the edge of the chair.

"And?" Her voice is shaky and thin.

"What did you do when you thought about me?" I rub my cheek up her neck, loving the way her fingers grip my thighs, and air leaves her lungs in a rush. Knowing I have this effect on her makes me harder. I know Cassidy well enough to understand that talking dirty isn't something she's used to, but I can't help myself. I want to know if she took things into her own hands last night, as I did. When she doesn't answer, I grip her hips and lift her onto my lap. Her legs naturally straddle my waist, and I guide her arms around my neck and press her back, so her chest rests against mine and our cheeks touch.

"Do you trust me?" I'm hard as steel, and I know she feels what she's doing to me.

"Yes." She doesn't hesitate. Her body melts against me.

"I love you, Cass. Do you know that?"

"Yes."

"As way more than a friend. Like I've never loved another woman. Like I never *want* to love another woman."

She doesn't respond, and I need her to know what I feel for her is real. Bigger than anything I've ever felt. I gather her hair in my hand and hold it over one shoulder, baring her other for me to kiss. We already share secrets. I want to share more. I want her to know that I'd bare my soul to her and protect her to the ends of the earth.

"You can trust me, just like I can trust you."

"I know," she whispers as her fingers slide up the back of my neck, making it hard for me to concentrate. The breeze from the ocean sweeps up the deck and across our heated skin. I feel goose bumps form on her thighs, and I rub my hands down them.

"I wish I was with you last night. I wish it was your hand stroking me when I came instead of just me and my fantasies of you."

Her breathing hitches. "Fantasies...I have fantasies."

242

"Tell me." I kiss her neck, hoping she trusts me enough to share her most intimate secrets, because if she doesn't, I can't make love to her until she does. She's too special, too precious.

"I...They're..." Even without seeing her face, I can feel her cheek heating up against mine. "They're about you."

I kiss her collarbone, and she closes her eyes as I slide my hands beneath her shirt and up her back.

"What are we doing in your fantasies?"

"We're..." Her voice is heady, lustful. "You and I, we're together. Naked..."

"Mm. Tell me, Cass, last night...How did you satisfy that need? How did you quell the ache between your legs? Did you feel your own wetness?"

"Yes." A whisper that sounds like it came from the depths of a secret place.

"Did you make yourself come while you thought of me?"

She opens her eyes and gazes into mine with so much trust and love I can feel it in every part of my body.

"I touched myself wishing it were you touching me. Wishing you were loving me. But I didn't...come. I want you to love me, Wyatt."

I cup her cheek, my heart swelling with love for her. I know how much courage it took for her to trust me with her innermost thoughts and desires, and I know in that second that I will never, ever turn her away again. I'll never breach her trust or risk losing her. Not any part of her.

"Baby, I do love you, and I know you didn't mean

what you said last night. You don't want me to just fuck you." I hold her, worried she'll retreat but needing her to hear me. When she nuzzles against my neck, I know she's embarrassed, and that's not what I wanted to accomplish either.

"I just want you to know that I get it, Cass. I get you."

She tightens her fingers on my neck and kisses my shoulder.

"And I can't resist you any longer." I can hardly believe this is happening after wanting her for so long, and as much I've tried to deny myself Cassidy, I can't do it any longer. She consumes my thoughts, and I know my body already belongs to her. I want her to feel my love for her and never, ever doubt how I feel or whether she can trust me again.

I don't think as my hands slip to the curve of her hips, and I hold her still as I rock my hips against her bottom. She makes the sexiest little sound against my neck. My hands travel beneath her shirt again and I grip her waist. She begins to move her hips against my hard length, driving me out of my ever-loving mind.

"Cass," I whisper. I need to see her eyes.

She pushes from my shoulder and looks at me from beneath heavy lids. Her eyes are dark and seductive, and I know we're on the same page.

"Don't resist me, Wyatt."

"I need to be sure we both understand what we're getting into so we can weather this together. The risk...It's still there. We have to know that going in."

She lowers her eyes. "I know, but it's you who sees a risk. I see the only man I want to be with. Ever."

I feel my world shift. All the pieces of my life fall into place like pieces of a puzzle, securely connected. I cup the nape of her neck and bring her lips to mine, hovering there for a long moment, thinking and not thinking at once. I'm being. Just being for the first time in my entire life I'm not rushing to get to the next thing, the next place, or worrying about what I'll miss. I'm here with Cassidy, in the moment, and nothing has ever felt so right. I want to always remember how this feels, the look in her eyes. I gaze into her eyes one more time before finally taking her in a deep, passionate kiss that breaks the dam of emotions that I've been holding back. We kiss and moan, nip and suck. My hands touch her back, her hips, her breasts, her stomach, anyplace I can reach. Holding her against me with one hand, I rise to my feet and pull the door open. Our mouths are still sealed over each other's as I carry her into my bedroom. I'm so hard, and she's so soft as I lay her beneath me. It's the most perfect feeling in the world.

"The door." She turns and looks at the open bedroom door.

I reluctantly get up and push it closed, then I come right back down on top of her, lift her shirt over her head, and toss it off the bed.

"Christ, you're beautiful."

I take her in another greedy kiss while my hands explore her body. Her breasts are full and soft. Perfect. I lower my mouth over her nipple and her hips rock off the mattress. She fists her hands in my hair, spurring me on to take more. I drag my tongue down the center of her body, feeling her shiver. I linger around her belly button, not wanting to rush through our first time together. I lick along the edge of her panties, then nip at her hip bone, earning myself another sexy gasp. She arches her hips, and I know what she wants, but she's too sweet to hurry. I kiss my way back to the center of her panties, hook my fingers beneath the edges and pull them partially down, leaving her sex covered, and I kiss her hips, running my hands up her thighs. My fingers graze the damp material between her legs as I lick the insides of her thighs. She clutches at the sheets, bucking her hips again. I move back up her body and take her in another needy kiss, tasting her, loving her, claiming her, as I slide my finger beneath her thin panties and feel her wetness. I can't stifle a groan at the feel of her, and it's not enough. I need more of her. So much more. I know I'll never get my fill. I touch my forehead to hers, needing to know she wants this as much as I do.

"You okay?" I whisper.

"More than." She smiles, eyes closed.

I kiss each of her eyelids, then her lips again, and she presses my shoulders, urging me south. I love that she's not shy with me in bed. I want to please her until she's so sated that her limbs turn to jelly.

Kissing a path straight down her stomach, I ease her panties off and toss them aside, nudging her thighs open with my knees. I steal a glance at her parted lips, at the flush of her skin. I never thought we'd find ourselves here together. She's my best friend. She knows all about my past, and I know how lucky I am that she trusts me. She's fucking incredible. I can't wait to feel her coming apart against my lips. I lift her hips off the mattress and slick my tongue across her velvety heat. She moans and drops her head back against the pillow. She's sweet and hot and tastes so good I have to remind myself to go slow. Cassidy meets every stroke of my tongue with a thrust of her hips. She's so sexy. I lift her knees, and they naturally fall open, giving me better access to pleasure her. I use my fingers and tease her sensitive bundle of nerves as I stroke her with my tongue. Within seconds she's panting, gritting her teeth.

"Wy...Wyatt..." She clenches her teeth and turns away. "Ohgodohgodohgod."

I slide two fingers into her, furtively seeking the spot that will take her over the edge while I devour her with my mouth. Her legs stiffen, and she cries out my name as her inner muscles pulse around my fingers. I slow my probing fingers, prolonging her orgasm, and loving the feel of her as she comes apart.

"Oh...God..." She shudders, fisting her hands in the mattress, and good Lord, she's sexy as she falls limply to the mattress. Her beautiful breasts rise and fall as she tries to recover.

I move up and seal my lips over hers, knowing she might push away at the taste of herself on my lips. When she doesn't push me away but kisses her own juice right off my tongue, it nearly pulls me over the edge. Our bodies tangle together, slick and needy.

"Condom," I murmur between kisses.

"Do...what you did...again." She opens her eyes and glances down between her legs.

"Baby, I'll take you over the edge as many times as you'd like."

I move between her legs and devour her, loving, licking, taking her clit between my teeth, and reveling in her writhing body as another orgasm sends her hips bucking and her body quaking. As she eases down from her climax, she moans, and I can't help but give her more pleasure, with my hands and mouth. She buries her hands in my hair, holding my mouth to her. As if there were anyplace I'd rather be? Not a chance in hell. Bringing her pleasure, knowing she trusts me, fills my heart to the brim, and hearing her call out my name again as she spirals over the edge nearly does me in.

"Ohmygod." She pulls on my arms, and I move up so we're face-to-face. "I've never...um..." She traps her lower lip between her teeth.

It takes my mind a minute to grasp what she's trying to say. At first I think she's telling me she hasn't had oral sex before, but then I realize what she means and I fold her into my arms and kiss her until we're dizzy with need. I want to tell her that I'll give her more orgasms than she can handle, but I don't want to embarrass her.

"I'm honored to be your first." In my head I'm hoping to be her last. The thought of her with another man isn't one I want to entertain. I brush her hair from her forehead and press my lips to it. "And your second." I kiss her again. "And third."

She presses on the back of my hips and arches up to meet me. "And my fourth?"

"You're too cute for your own good." I pull open the nightstand and grab a condom, then make quick work of taking off my shorts and rolling on the latex sheath.

Seeing Cassidy in my bed, her hair strewn across my pillow, and her gorgeous, naked body waiting for me, wanting me, is almost too much to take. I settle my knees between her legs and lower my chest to hers. Our lips come together, and I wonder how I got so lucky and how she knew we belonged together.

"Once I'm inside you, there's no going back. I'm yours, Cassidy, and I won't be able to walk away. So if you have any hesitation...Are you one hundred percent certain that you aren't going to wake up tomorrow and regret this? That you're willing to cross this final line and risk our friendship?" My heart feels like it's going to explode as I wait for her answer.

"More than I want to breathe." She wraps her hand around the back of my head as I lower my lips to hers and push inside her until I'm buried deep.

We both still, soaking in the newness of us, and reveling in how right it feels. Her body welcomes me like I've come home. She's tight and hot, and when she wraps her legs around my waist and I push in impossibly deeper, holding her close and gazing into her eyes, her lips curve up in a smile.

"Oh my God," she whispers. "You feel amazing."

"Careful. You'll give me a big head."

"You already have one." She glances down between us. "Two."

When she giggles, it vibrates through her body right down to my cock. I seal my lips over hers as we begin to move in slow, tentative strokes, finding our rhythm. Then she presses on the back of my hips again, giving me permission to thrust harder, take her more eagerly. I slide my hands beneath her hips and lift, angling them so she can take me deeper. She gasps and digs her fingernails into my lower back. I feel her body begin to quiver as I increase my pace.

"Wy..."

"Come on, baby." I settle my mouth over her neck the way she loves. Learning what she likes and feeling her body respond nearly pulls me over the edge.

"You're so beautiful, Cass."

She clutches my arms and presses her head into the mattress with her eyes slammed shut.

"Wy...Wyatt..."

I thrust into her harder, moving faster. Craving the sound of my name coming off her lips again, I bring my hand between us and stroke her, teasing her, drawing out her pleasure. Her inner muscles pulse in fast succession as she claws at my back, my arms, wherever she can find purchase, as her hips buck and her body shudders around me. My hands slide up her sides. She feels so fucking good.

"That's it, baby. Jesus, you feel so good."

She rocks her hips, and heat shoots down my spine. My balls tighten. I can't hold back any longer, and I give in to my own intense release. Every thrust draws more come, until I feel like I've been sucked dry, and we collapse, tangled together like we were always meant to be.

Chapter Twenty

~Cassidy~

THE NEXT MORNING, sun peeks through the curtains in Wyatt's bedroom, slicing across the foot of the bed. Nothing feels better than waking up in Wyatt's strong arms. Even sleeping he's strong. He's spooning me, with one arm beneath my head and the other draped around my body. Only it's not really draped. He's *holding* me. I don't dare move. I like it here, all bundled up against him with his heart beating against my back. The hair on his legs tickles the backs of my thighs, and his head is tucked against mine. I close my eyes and listen to the peaceful cadence of his breathing.

Over the past few weeks I must have thought about what it would be like to make love with Wyatt a million times, but never in my wildest dreams did I think it would be anything like yesterday. Wyatt was so loving, so giving...so *good*. I never realized how close I could feel to another person, and with Wyatt,

251

it's like we really did become one yesterday. Not just physically, but like our hearts were joining together as much as our bodies were. And I saw it in his eyes, too. I don't know what made the difference for him, or why he changed his mind about us, but lying here with him, I know he made the right choice.

His arms tighten around me, and it makes me smile as he breathes in through his nose and squeezes me again as he exhales.

"Please tell me you're not regretting yesterday," he says in a craggy voice.

I turn in his arms and face him. He's so beautiful. Seriously too beautiful for words. I know guys are supposed to be handsome and rugged and all things manly, and he is. Wyatt's a total alpha, but his forest-green eyes and sun-kissed skin and that luscious, talented mouth of his are so striking that he's also beautiful. What makes him truly beautiful is his heart, and somehow when he looks at me, I feel his heart all around me.

"I'm not regretting yesterday. I'm wondering if it would make me a slut to climb on top of you and get a rerun."

Wyatt sweeps me beneath him and settles his naked body over me. "Reruns are boring. Why not start fresh?"

He kisses my neck and trails feather-light kisses across my collarbone, swipes his tongue across the dip in the center, and my whole body shivers.

He laces his hands with mine and raises them above my head, holding them prisoner while he kisses my shoulders, my jaw, and moves his cheek against mine. I arch my hips, wanting him inside me.

"Oh, you like that, do you?" he teases.

I close my eyes and all my senses heighten. I feel his lips hovering over mine, the tip of his arousal pressing against my center. I feel his body heat infiltrating my skin. His lips meet mine, urging my mouth open with his tongue. My lips part and he kisses me slowly, like he's discovering my mouth for the first time. His tongue slides over my teeth and the roof of my mouth, and then he outlines my lips. It's the most erotic sensation I've ever felt, and when he shifts his hips so his cock is resting over my pubic bone and his balls are against the wetness between my legs, it sends prickling heat through me. I fight against his strength, wanting to touch him, needing to feel his muscles beneath my palms, but my hands are trapped beneath his. He takes my breast into his mouth, and I close my eyes tight, feeling my nipple harden against his tongue. I swear there's a nerve that goes straight from my nipple to between my legs, because the friction of his erection and his balls rubbing against me while he sucks my breast makes everything in my lower belly tighten. My sex swells with need. He shifts, holds both of my wrists in one of his hands, and squeezes my nipple between his finger and thumb while he sucks the other, and he presses his hips tighter to mine.

Ohgodohgodohgod.

"Wyatt..." I plead, already feeling the tease of an orgasm. I angle my hips, wanting to reach it and not knowing how. His hand slips between us, and he finds the spot that takes me right up to the edge. Then his mouth finds mine and—*good Lord*—I can't breathe. My body flashes cold, then hot and tingly, and I have no control over my bucking hips or the cries that escape my lips. He releases my hands, and I clutch at his body, urging him inside me, but he doesn't give in. He keeps up this exquisite torture until I'm writhing and begging and clinging to him as the orgasm goes on and on, pulsing through me. When it finally starts to ease, he slides his fingers inside me, and in seconds I'm riding another incredible orgasmic wave. I lie beneath him, unable to believe how good he makes me feel.

"Wow." I pant, trying to catch my breath. "I didn't know it was possible to come so many times in a row, or so hard, or…" I open my eyes, and Wyatt's smiling down at me with so much love in his eyes that I almost feel guilty. I was so wrapped up in what he was doing to me that it didn't even occur to me to reciprocate, and boy, do I want to reciprocate. I want him to feel all the things he made me feel.

"I didn't know it was possible to love someone this much." He presses his lips to mine, and it fills me with a second wind.

When I was with Kyle, he never, ever paid even one-tenth of the attention to my body or my needs as Wyatt has in the last twenty-four hours. He never cared if I was into it or not. Sex wasn't enjoyable and it was always standard, missionary position with no foreplay or even cuddling afterward. I had no idea sex could be this fun, and I definitely never felt the desire to reciprocate, because there wasn't much *to* reciprocate.

I touch Wyatt's cheek, playfully push him onto his back, and straddle him. His eager erection is between my legs, and I'm a little embarrassed by how wet I am, but the look in his eyes tells me not to be.

"I like where this is going," he says with a coy smile.

I place my hands on his biceps and touch my forehead to his. I like this position. I feel powerful being on top, and when our foreheads touch, it feels like *our thing*. He touches his forehead to mine a lot, and I always know that whatever he's thinking at the moment comes straight from his heart. I want him to know that this is coming from mine.

"Close your eyes." I'm not sure I can do what I want to if he's looking at me. I have butterflies in my stomach, and my heart is sprinting in my chest, but down low, sensuality is brewing in a way I've never felt before, and I want to explore it. With Wyatt I want to explore everything. I don't want to hold back.

He closes his eyes, and I stay where I am, drinking him in, learning the hard angles of his body. His biceps are firm even when they are relaxed, and I let my hands glide over them and across his chest. I close my eyes, too, letting my heart guide me. My hands travel over the dips and arcs of his torso. I decide that I must have a smart heart, because I'm with Wyatt and it feels so right. I trust my heart even though I screwed up with Kyle. This thought gives me pause, and my hands still on Wyatt's chest. I feel his heart beating hard beneath my palm. I try to push away thoughts of Kyle, but they're pressing in on me, and I allow myself to deal with it once and for all in the safety of this room with Wyatt. I think about how we met, at a parents' weekend function. He was talking with my father, and my father introduced us. I remember thinking he was cute, and I liked that my father liked him. I roll through the memories quickly. It feels like it takes an hour, but I know by Wyatt's breaths that it's only a few seconds, and it hits me like a brick. Kyle wasn't my choice for love. Kyle was my choice for trying to win my father's attention. But even that weekend, my father paid more attention to Kyle than he did to me.

Wyatt opens his eyes, and he must see something in mine, because he reaches up and touches my cheek, and his brows knit together.

"Babe?"

I blink away the harsh thoughts. "I'm okay." Looking into Wyatt's eyes, I know I am okay, and I know that I really do have a smart heart. It's exactly like Tristan said. My head wasn't as smart as my heart. What happened with Kyle was my way of trying to become something to my parents that I will probably never be. *Like going to New York.*

These thoughts bring a sense of freedom rather than sadness.

I take Wyatt's hand in mine and hold it to my chest. "What do you feel?"

"Your heartbeat." He lowers his hand and cups my breast, brushes my nipple with his thumb.

Lord, it feels good when he touches me. I force myself to move his hand away and concentrate.

"It's not just my heartbeat. It's a smart heartbeat."

His brows draw together, and rather than explain, I press my lips to his.

"I trusted you, so trust me."

He smiles against my lips. "Babe, I trust you more than you'll ever know."

"Good. Then close your eyes again. This is all kind of new to me, so if I hesitate, let me work through it, okay?" Surprisingly, I'm not embarrassed when I tell him this. I trust him explicitly, and I feel like I'm taking control of parts of my life I never realized had slipped from my grasp.

I lower my lips to his chest and let them lead me. My hands explore the plains of his muscles while I taste his heated flesh. I drag my tongue over his pecs, then over his nipple, and he sucks in air between gritted teeth. He likes that. I never would have imagined that a guy would like that. What else have I missed out on? What else don't I know? I lick his nipple again, and it pebbles against my tongue. He reaches for my hips and clutches them tight.

"Uh-uh. No fair." I push his hands off, even though I really want them there. I like feeling in control, and I love how his body reacts to my touch. He rocks his hips, trying to get inside me, but teasing him is way too exciting to stop. I take his lead from yesterday and slither down his body, then press my hands against his hips, stilling them.

He groans and fists his hands against the mattress. I kiss the ripple of his abs and trace the lines in between each muscle with my tongue. Oh, he likes that. His erection bobs up as I do it, like it's reaching for me. I move lower and wrap my fingers around his hard length. He's much bigger than Kyle was, much thicker, and way more talented. I smile at the thought and steal a glance at his closed eyes, his fisted hands, and I want to ease the clenching of his jaw. I drag my tongue up his rigid length from base to tip, lingering at the head and swirling my tongue around his sensitive flesh. I lick his shaft again and again, until he's slick and my hand slides easily up and down while I take him in my mouth.

"Fuck. Cass..."

His plea makes me want to pleasure him even more. I take all of him in my mouth, and moving on instinct, I cup his balls. His hips shoot off the bed, and now that I know what he likes, I don't want to stop. I suck and stroke and tease until he's practically growling. He grabs my head with both hands, but he doesn't guide me. He just holds on tight and lets me take him to the edge.

"Cassidy. Stop. I'm gonna come."

I don't stop. I never did this with Kyle, but I want to do *everything* with Wyatt, and for some strange reason the idea of him coming in my mouth doesn't gross me out. It totally turns me on. He turns me on. I'm so wet and swollen between my legs that I can hardly believe touching him does this to me, and I like it. A lot. I love that when I love him, I feel it, too, and that when he loves me, he can barely hold back. I swallow him deep and suck for all I'm worth, working him with my hands and my mouth. I feel him swell impossibly larger against my tongue, and I squeeze tighter as he calls out my name and his hips buck as he comes. I swallow every hot drop he has to give and continue stroking him as his body quakes with a final shudder. When he pulls me up and kisses me without a care about the fact that I probably taste like him, I know he's right there with me, as deep in love as I am.

Chapter Twenty-One

~Wyatt~

IT'S ONLY EIGHT o'clock in the morning and I feel like I've lived a lifetime since yesterday. Cassidy and I are drinking coffee on the deck, and I think it's the first time I've slowed down enough to really relax since graduation. Cassidy's hand is warm and soft and fits in mine like we were made for each other. I feel more connected to her than I ever have.

"This has been a crazy time, babe. I'm sorry I fought what's between us for so long. At first I worried that what I was feeling was driven by my parents' deaths or your breakup with Kyle." I wonder why words come so easily to me when I'm talking to Cassidy. I've never felt much beyond being horny around the other girls I've been with, much less honesty one hundred percent of the time. "But I realized that you were right. I've loved you for a very long time."

She moves from her chair onto my lap and circles my neck with her arms. "I've been thinking about that. I'm glad you waited to get together with me. I'm glad our friendship was so important to you that you weren't willing to risk it. I know we haven't talked about it, and we don't need to, but I like that you set me apart from the other girls you've been with."

"Set you apart? Babe, you and I are on a planet all by ourselves. If I haven't made it clear, let me do it now." I press my hands to her cheeks and hold her gaze. "I have never loved another woman. I've never wanted to wake up with a woman in my arms. And with you, I never want to wake up alone again."

"Finally." We both turn at the sound of Tristan's voice. He's standing in the doorway shirtless, wearing a pair of faded jeans and a smile, and holding a coffee mug in one hand, rubbing the back of his neck with the other.

"Wow, you have a knack for walking in on the most private times, huh, buddy?"

Tristan lifts his chin with a coy grin.

"Everything okay with you?" I ask as he sits across from us.

"It will be. It has to be, right?" Tristan looks out over the water.

"I saw your duffel bag. I assume you're moving in?" I set my coffee down and wrap my arms tighter around Cassidy.

"I wasn't sure where else to go," Tristan answers.

"It's cool. Tristan, you can stay here for as long as you want. We love having you around, and it's not like we need seven bedrooms." As bad as I feel for him, I think he's better off without Ian.

"Thanks, Army." Tristan's eyes bounce between me and Cassidy. "At least you two have stopped the ridiculous dance you've been doing."

I know he means he's happy for us, but the way he says it stings, because as ridiculous as it probably looked to an outsider, coming together with Cassidy was the biggest risk I've ever taken in my life.

"It wasn't a dance. It was the hardest and most important decision that I've ever made."

Cassidy touches her head to mine.

"Hey, Tris. I'm sorry about Ian," Cassidy says. "Do you want to talk about it?"

Tristan runs his hand through his hair and shakes his head. "Thanks, hon, but some things are better left unsaid. I saw the writing on the wall weeks ago, but I wasn't ready to face it."

"It's that head and heart thing." Cassidy covers Tristan's hand with hers. "You have the biggest heart, Tristan, and the right guy is going to see that. He's not going to be able to resist falling in love with you."

She could easily be talking about herself.

"You know, I wish that were true, but things are different in the gay community." Tristan's eyes turn serious. "I mean, love is there, but you know that whole *next-best thing*, thing? It's a million times worse with gay men. Some are committed, but think about it. It's usually the girl who puts on the brakes, right?"

Cassidy and I share a confused glance.

"Okay, well, not with you two." Tristan rolls his eyes. "But in general, guys are like, *Wanna have sex? Done.* Girls are the ones who slow it down. With guys there's no one to slow it down, so we sometimes know each other physically before we even know each other's last names. And that can go on for who knows how long, whereas a girl would know everything there is to know about the guy they're dating in three seconds flat."

"Sounds like you need to be straight." I can see by his smile that he knows I'm kidding.

"Seriously, my life would be a lot easier if I were. Finding a guy who's not out to play is tough."

"Even so. Things can change. People can change, Tristan. You just haven't found the right guy yet." Cassidy gives me another one of her knowing looks, and I know she's talking about the way the loss of my parents changed me.

"Well, it is what it is." Tristan finishes his coffee. "Are you guys going to the Taproom?"

"Yeah. We have to get through those reconciliations." I check my watch. "We've got to go in a few minutes. Hey, if you need time off, just let me know."

"No way, man. I heard you were left shorthanded the other night. I'll be there from now on." Tristan kicked his feet up on the empty chair. "I'm glad you guys are together. So I guess you worked out the whole New York thing?"

Aw, hell. I haven't thought about that since we got together. I pat Cassidy's thigh, trying not to think about when it was last wrapped around me.

"We still have some things to talk about. I'm not going to stand in the way of Cassidy going to New York."

She fidgets with her shirt, and I know she's nervous. "What if I don't want to go?"

"Cass, it's all you talked about. If you get an offer, you can't stay around here for me."

Tristan rises to his feet. "I think I'll go take a walk." He pats each of our shoulders as he walks behind us. "I'm sure you guys will figure it out. Thanks for letting me hang for a while."

"Whatever you need, man." After he leaves I turn my attention back to Cassidy.

"Cass, I won't let you throw away a job in New York because of me. We can still see each other. We'll only be a few hours apart." The thought makes my gut ache, but I don't want to stand in her way.

"It's not that. I'm starting to wonder if I want to be in a big city."

"You've wanted to live in New York since you visited with your parents."

"Yeah, but I'm trying to figure out why." She drops her eyes, and I can see this has been weighing on her.

I lift her chin and kiss her softly. "Let's not worry about this until we have to. I think we deserve a few hours of just enjoying being us." I don't tell her that I don't want her to leave and just the idea of being without her makes me miss her.

She smiles, and I swear her smiles have a direct line to my heart, because my chest feels full and happiness spreads through me. Christ, I sound like a chick.

One more glance at Cassidy makes me not care what I sound like. I love her so much, and as we get up to go to work, I try to figure out how I'm going to tell

Delilah about us.

Delilah is already at the Taproom when we arrive. She's working through schedules at the desk near the back door.

"Hey, Dee."

"Hey."

She's wearing her favorite girlie combat boots, unlaced, with cutoffs and a pink tank top. I haven't seen her wear them since we left school, and it gives me hope that she's starting to find her way through the pain of losing our parents. But something in the way she's avoiding eye contact tells me something is wrong.

"How'd it go with the therapist?" I sit on the edge of the desk.

"It was okay. It wasn't a therapist. It was a group therapy session." Her eyes remain trained on the clipboard.

"And? Is that good or bad?"

She shrugs.

"Are you going to go back again?"

She shrugs again. "I heard you had some issues with schedules."

"No biggie. Part-timer called in sick. Charley's stuck on the boat for a few days, and Tristan was off. Livi stayed late, and Ashley and Cassidy came in to help."

She lifts her eyes and gives me a disapproving look that rubs me the wrong way. "Why did you give Tristan the night off?"

I shrug. "He asked."

"Wyatt, we have a business to run. You can't just

give someone the day off without checking schedules. What if Ash and Cassidy couldn't come in?"

The therapy must have helped in some way, because Delilah has been so placid since our parents died that as much as I don't want her giving me shit, I'm glad she's finally coming back into her own again.

"Sorry, Dee. But it's Tristan. I knew he was having trouble with Ian and I felt bad." I look at Tim's office. "Speaking of taking time off, have you heard from Uncle Tim? He's been out for a few days."

"I thought he told you he was taking time off."

"Just the first day. Cassidy has questions about invoices. I guess we'll have to just work our way through." I debate not telling her about me and Cassidy yet, but I know the minute she sees how we look at each other she'll figure it out. Luckily, Cassidy is out front with Livi, so I have a few minutes before she sees us together and calls me on it.

"Speaking of Cassidy, um…"

Delilah sets her pen down. "What? Did she get the job offer? Is she going to New York?"

"No offer yet, but, well, there's only one way to tell you this."

"You slept with her." Delilah's deadpan gaze worries me.

"It's not like that, Dee."

"Wyatt! What are you thinking?" She turns away and crosses her arms.

"I love her, Delilah. Jesus. Do you think I'm stupid? I tried to fight it because I didn't want to risk our friendship, but I couldn't. She couldn't. And I promise you, she's not just a fling for me. She's *everything*."

MELISSA FOSTER

I feel a hand on my shoulder and look up. Cassidy shifts her eyes to Delilah, and they both burst out laughing.

"So, I'm *everything*?" Cassidy blushes, comes around the side of the desk and stands between my legs. "Everything?"

"You told her." I grab her ribs and squeeze. Cassidy squeals and jumps back. I point at Delilah, who's grinning like a fool. "You're a pain."

"We're girls. I knew before you did." Delilah smiles. "I texted her this morning, and she told me that you two are a couple now. I'm happy for you guys. I wouldn't have been if you had jumped in bed with her without thinking, but I know you didn't." She points at me. "Just don't mess it up."

I pull Cassidy into an embrace, feeling a million times better knowing Delilah isn't mad. "I have no intention of messing up anything, and somehow I know that if I do mess up, you guys will whip me into shape before I know what's going on."

~Cassidy~

THREE HOURS INTO the reconciliations I realize that the invoices I'm looking for simply don't exist. I've checked every drawer, every computer file, and Tim isn't returning our calls. I am starting to believe Tim's doing something underhanded with the books, and I'm so sick of accounting I can hardly see straight. I swear it's a visceral reaction. I see the books and I want to turn away, but I don't. I know how important this is. But I can't help feeling like things between me and Wyatt opened new doors in my head.

268

It's like seeing Wyatt's walls come down allowed me to reassess my own walls. Walls I never knew existed. For the first time ever, instead of following the path my parents set out for me, I'm taking my concerns about New York and even my career choice seriously and *thinking* about them.

I stare at the ledgers. Numbers make sense to me. They always have. But they definitely don't excite me in any way. I keep thinking about going to New York, where I don't know anyone but one crazy aunt, and sitting at a job that is probably going to be boring. My parents' lectures about establishing a strong career and making a name for myself play over and over in my mind. Their voices go from strong to faint as my mind tries to wrap itself around and grab hold of their excitement, when really, all I want to do is go out to the beach at sunset and catch the beauty of the setting sun on film. I want to take more pictures of brides and grooms promising each other forever and catch the contemplative look in Wyatt's eyes on film when he's lost in thought. Even the thought of helping Brooke later today is more interesting than crunching numbers.

"What do you make of it?" Wyatt's voice pulls me from my thoughts. He's sitting next to me in Tim's office with one hand on my thigh and the other fisted on the desk.

"I don't want to assume, but..." I don't want to say the rest. I can tell by the way he's clenching his jaw that he knows what I'm thinking.

"But Uncle Tim's pulling some shit." He slams his palms on the desk. "*Uncle* Tim. Uncle fucking Tim."

I shrug. "I don't want to accuse him, but something's off. About twenty-thousand-dollars off."

Wyatt pulls out his phone and clenches it in his hand, then runs his other hand slowly over his mouth and down his jaw, as if he's biding his time.

"I'm calling Jesse." I listen as he explains the situation to Jesse. "We've got more than twenty thousand dollars' worth of invoices for Reiker Industries, paid out in a few thousand each month. Tim's got them listed as inventory, but we've scoured the back room and can't find anything from Reiker— no packing slips, no inventory, no boxes. We checked his computer files. No email contacts from Reiker, nothing." He pauses and nods, holds up a finger as if to tell me to hold on a second. Then he covers the mouthpiece. "Cass, can you go ask Dutch if he knows of Reiker?"

"Sure." I go to the kitchen and ask Dutch, who crosses his arms and stares at me. His hair sticks up in curly tufts, and he's got about three days' scruff that creeps down his neck, making his scowl look even more intense.

"Reiker? Yeah, I know all about Reiker."

"Oh, good. What is it? What do they provide for the Taproom?"

"They? Near as I can tell, Reiker's a fake company. I told Ed Armstrong about it a few times over the last few months before he...well, before he died. Far as I knew, he was looking into it."

"You told Wyatt's dad?" My stomach sinks.

"Yeah, and he said he was going to talk to Tim."

Livi comes through the double doors and slaps an

order on the wheel. "Double burger with fries, no onions. Thanks, Dutch." She smiles at me. "Hi, Cassidy."

"Hi, Livi." I wave and go back into the office, where I find Wyatt with his elbows on the desk, his hands fisted in front of him.

"What'd he say?" Wyatt asks.

"He thinks it's a fake company. He said he told your dad about it. What did Jesse say?"

"Same. He said Dutch told my dad and that he and my mom were too busy to go through the books, but he noticed that after Tim's divorce, Tim started disappearing for a few days at a time."

"Like now," I point out.

"Yeah." Wyatt shakes his head. "This isn't good. I want to be wrong about this in the worst way, but this trail"—he waves at the files—"and what Dutch and Jesse said don't leave much room for misinterpretation. How does a guy break the news of his best friend's death to his children and then go to his friend's funeral knowing he's screwed them all over? I need to find him and figure out what's going on."

"I'm sorry, Wy. Hopefully, it's all a misunderstanding."

"If it's not, I'm left firing the guy who's been like an uncle to me and Dee forever. The guy who helped my dad get this business up and running." His eyes cloud over, and I can't tell if it's anger or sadness hovering in them, or both. "He sat with me and explained what business courses and risk assessment were before I started college. Risk assessment. If he did this shit, he knew all the risks, least of which is being fired." He shakes his head. "I do not want to do this." He pushes away from the desk. "I didn't ask for any of this mess."

I don't say another word. I'm not sure how to make it easier for Wyatt, but as he contemplates the situation, his eyes fill with determination.

He nods, more to himself than to me, I think.

"Okay, so here's the plan. I'm going to drive over to Tim's and see if I can track him down. Delilah will hold down the fort. I know you have to get to Brooke's soon." He reaches for my hand. "If he's skimmed money off the business, I'll have no choice but to let him go, but if he can produce the inventory and the receipts, then it's a nonissue and we need better accounting practices."

I know he thinks the latter is a long shot. He was right the other day. He has grown up. He may have been forced into this situation, but he's facing it head-on, and I'm so very proud of him.

My cell phone rings, and I grab it off the desk. "It's a New York number."

He smiles, but I can tell it's forced. I answer the call, trying to ignore the nervous twist in my stomach.

"Hello?"

"Hi. Is this Cassidy Lowell?" The woman's voice is unfamiliar.

"Yes. This is she."

"Cassidy, this is Carol Barker from SNC Financial. We'd like to offer you the position of junior accountant that you interviewed for back in April."

"Thank you." It's a bittersweet moment. This is the job I wanted in the city I was dying to live in, but that was before getting together with Wyatt and before I let myself start to think about what I really want. I know it will please my parents. If I take it, I'll probably see more of them. I also know I can do the job well, but as I listen to the details of the position and Carol agrees to give me a week to think about it, I'm so conflicted I feel dizzy.

I end the call and lower myself into a chair, wondering what the hell I'm going to do.

Chapter Twenty-Two

~Wyatt~

I FIND DELILAH by the bar and ask her to come with me outside. She eyes me warily, but I just nod toward the door. Once we're outside, I guide her away from the building. I'm still trying to figure out how to tell her about Uncle Tim. I can tell she's heard something, because she looks like *she's* trying to figure out how to tell *me* something, too.

"What is going on?" she asks. "Dutch said he thinks Tim is embezzling money?"

"We don't know for sure, but it looks that way." We walk out to the edge of the pier, where we can talk in private.

"I don't understand. Why would he do that? Dad would have lent him money if he needed it. Why would he steal from us?"

I shake my head. "I don't know, but I'm going to try to track him down and find out."

Delilah crosses her arms. "I thought this was going to be like running a normal business, and now we're tracking down a thief?"

"Dee, this is part of running a business. Dutch said he told Dad about this and that Dad was supposed to talk to Tim."

"Uncle Tim. God!" She turns away.

"Yeah, well, if this is true, he doesn't deserve the *Uncle* part."

She covers her face and then turns back to me with anger in her eyes. "I'm coming with you."

"I don't think that's a good idea." I'm still reeling from the idea that Uncle Tim could have done this shit. *Uncle Tim*, the guy who took care of my parents' funeral, the guy we've known forever. My father's best friend. *What the hell?* I have no idea what will go down with Tim when I confront him, and I want to protect her from anything bad.

"I don't care if it's a good idea or a bad idea. I'm going."

"Who's going to run the Taproom? Cass has to go to Brooke's. Please stay here, Dee. I'll handle it and—"

"Fine, but if he stole from us, what do we do then?" Delilah crosses and uncrosses her arms as she paces.

"We fire him, but not before I find out why." I watch her pacing and pull her into a hug. "This all sucks, I know. If you change your mind and you don't want the bar, tell me. We'll sell it or something." As I say the words, I'm not sure what I will do if she changes her mind. I'm beginning to realize just what it takes to run a business, and with all this stuff coming up, I want to protect what our parents worked so hard to build. Delilah was right when she said Dad wanted us to take it over, and so what if it's sooner than he had thought? Than we'd all thought?

"I don't know what I want. I think I want to go back to bed and wake up on graduation morning and tell Mom and Dad not to drive home."

Her words hang between us like ghosts.

"I know, Dee. Do you want to talk about it?"

She shakes her head fast and hard.

I know I need to change the subject quickly, before she gets sucked into grief again. "Okay, well, how did you know I was stuck the other night?"

"Ash told me. We've been coming out to the beach in the evenings and sketching. She couldn't meet me that night."

Relief washes through me. "I'm glad you're sketching again."

"Yeah, me too. I don't do it much. Sometimes I just sit while Ashley draws, but I'm trying to be normal, whatever that is after your parents die."

I hug her again and watch her walk back inside, hoping her version of normal doesn't mean trying to hide her sexual identity, as she's done for so long. I head down the pier toward my car.

"Wyatt!"

I turn at the sound of Cassidy's voice. She's running toward me with a worried look in her eyes and a slight smile on her lips. In that instant I know two things for sure. She got the job offer, and the conflicting facial expressions probably only touch the surface of how conflicted she is inside. I ready myself to be the supportive boyfriend I'm supposed to be and not the selfish prick who wants to beg her to stay with me in Harborside, even though that's what I want to do.

"I got the job." She fiddles with the ends of her hair and drops her eyes.

She worked hard for this, and I'm proud of her. I want her to be happy, even if that means that we have a long-distance relationship until we figure things out. I have no idea what *things* might include, but with the new information about Uncle Tim, I have to prioritize. Right now, figuring out what the hell is going on with the business has to come first.

"Congrats, babe. I knew you would. They'd be crazy not to hire you."

"I don't know what I'm going to do yet. They're giving me a week to decide." Cassidy reaches for my hand and holds on tight.

I kiss her and try to reassure her. "You worked hard for this, and you wanted to be in the city." Afterward I wonder if she can see how hard it is for me to say these things without asking her to stay.

"My parents wanted me to be in the city."

"Maybe, but so did you. Don't let our relationship cloud your judgment. You have a week, babe. Just let it sit in your head for a while and see how you feel in a day or two." If I don't get out of here soon, I'm going to cave and beg her to stay. It's too hard to look in her eyes and *know* she wants to be here just as much as I do, then force myself to tell her not to follow her heart but to think it over.

"I've got to handle this stuff with Uncle...with *Tim*,

but we can talk it through tonight. How late do you work tonight?"

"Brooke needs me until ten." She puts her arms around my neck. "I'm sorry, Wyatt."

"Sorry? Why?" *Have you already made a decision?*

"The job offer came at a rotten time, and this stuff with Tim." She searches my eyes, and I try to mask my agreement.

"Don't be silly. I'm glad you got the offer, and I can handle this stuff with Tim. I'll call Jesse on my way to Tim's." By some miracle, I feel like I really can handle this situation with Tim, even if I have to fire him. But Cassidy leaving Harborside? I'm not nearly as certain.

"You okay?"

"Yeah. Thanks, Wy. I'll clean up this stuff before I go to Brooke's."

"Thanks, Cass. I'll text you when I know something." I kiss her again, burying my worries about her leaving as deep as I possibly can. "Don't worry about us. I'm not going anywhere, and New York isn't California. We'd only be a few hours apart. We'll figure it out if you decide to take the job. Just don't turn it down for us."

She nods. "I won't. I can't. This has to be my decision, otherwise I might resent you in the future, and I don't want that to happen."

"That's my girl. Always planning ahead."

"In this case, I kind of wish I hadn't."

No shit. So do I. I muster another supportive smile. "Don't be silly. This is a great opportunity. Focus on that." *While I try not to focus on the hole you'll leave behind.*

279

Chapter Twenty-Three

~Cassidy~

THE CAFÉ HAS been busy since I arrived, and I don't have much time to think about the job offer. I haven't heard from Wyatt in hours, and I wonder if he's tracked down Tim, and if so, what's going on. The bell above the door rings as a woman and two teenage girls walk in.

I smile from across the room and wave at the tables. "Hi. Find a seat, and I'll be with you in a sec."

The walls of the café are painted powder blue, and each table has fresh flowers in the center. Brooke has a deal with a local florist, who brings her fresh flowers every other morning for the vases. She is all about aesthetics. She says it's too easy to forget that things should be pretty as well as functional. The counter is set up like an old-fashioned diner, with round red vinyl stools that swivel and old-fashioned chunky napkin holders. There's a jukebox in the corner that doesn't take quarters and plays all day long. The valance above the picture window in the front is checked with red and white. Considering that it's an Internet café, the mix of the old and the new makes it feel like I've stumbled back in time to 1980 with a link to the future.

They sit at a table near the window, and I finish making sandwiches for my other customers, then I take an order from another table and refill sodas for a third group sitting at the counter working on their laptops. My phone vibrates with a call from my parents for the millionth time today. I wish I hadn't sent them the text about getting the job offer, but I had to, or maybe I didn't. Maybe some part of me is clinging to the hope of seeing them more.

God, I hate this. Why couldn't I have had normal parents who wanted to spend time with their daughter?

They've left at least four messages since. I'm relieved when the call finally goes to voicemail after the longest four rings of my life.

Brooke comes out of the back carrying a tray of soda bottles and refills the cooler in the front of the café. We've fallen into a pattern that works well. While I'm handling customers, she restocks, and when I need a break, we switch. I love working with the customers so much more than crunching numbers.

My phone vibrates with another call from my relentless parents as Brooke joins me behind the counter. Why weren't they this interested after Wyatt's parents' died? Or when I was walking at graduation? Or when I was playing fucking lacrosse as a kid?

"At some point you have to answer their calls." Brooke arches a brow. "Go take it. I'll be fine for a few minutes."

"Ugh. Can't you tell me I'm not allowed personal calls on business time or something?"

"I'm not that much of a bitchy boss. Besides, you're helping me out, and your parents have called more times in the past hour than mine call me in a month. If you don't answer it now, they'll keep calling. Just get it over with. You'll feel better."

I doubt that.

I let the call go to voicemail, set the pitcher on the counter with a sigh, and take the order of the woman and two teenage girls and serve their drinks before I walk outside and return the call. There's a group of teenagers sitting against the front wall using their laptops. They look up for half a second, then drop their eyes again as I cross to the far side of the boardwalk. I take a lungful of the night air and call my parents back.

"Hi," I say, already feeling like I wish I hadn't called. I know they're going to be overly excited, and I'm not sure I want to hear it.

"Hi, honey. It's Mom. Dad's here, too. We got your text. You must be over the moon! Are you making plans? Have you talked to Aunt Aggie about staying with her until you find a place of your own?"

"Mom, I *just* got the offer." I weave through the crowd on the boardwalk and sit on a bench across from the café. "I haven't even decided if I'm taking it yet."

"What? Oh, honey, what else would you do? This is

what you've worked so hard for. It's why we spent thousands of dollars on your schooling. You'll go to New York and make a name for yourself. You're so smart. You'll go right up the ranks, and before you know it you'll be CFO of a large corporation."

I watch a group of women and young children walk by and wonder if they'll pressure their kids and ignore their children while they're busy living their own lives, like my parents do to me. As if they've heard my thoughts, one of the women scoops a young boy into her arms and smothers him with kisses. I long for a relationship I know I'll never have.

"Honey?"

"Sorry, Mom. It's a junior accountant position, and honestly, I'm not even sure I love accounting anymore." Or that I ever did, for that matter.

"Oh, pish posh. Of course you do. You've always loved numbers. You're just spending too much time in that Podunk town, getting all caught up in the world of the unmotivated. I knew you shouldn't have gone with Wyatt and Delilah for the summer."

World of the unmotivated? I bite back the desire to set her straight. She knows Wyatt and Delilah like the ice cream man knows his customers: quick smiles and pleasantries, then she's off to someplace else. I wish she could have seen Wyatt this afternoon, taking complete control of the situation with Tim, or the other night when the schedules went awry. He may not have ever been a planner, but he has always been motivated as hell. He had to be in order to be so successful in school while also being a great football player and, if I'm honest with myself, having a social life, too. And the way he's always watched out for me and Delilah also takes motivation and dedication.

Ugh. It's not worth explaining, because by the time I get the words out she will have forgotten them.

"Honey? Are you there? I only have a minute."

Of course you do. "I'm here. That's not it at all, Mom. No one's unmotivated."

"Sure they are, honey. Summertime fun is hard to walk away from. But Harborside is no place for someone like you. You're better than that."

I lower the phone from my ear and close my eyes as she goes on about how smart I am and how she and my father are so proud of me. I want to tell her to get off her high horse and remind her that Harborside is the one place I have always fit in and that there's nothing to be *better than*. Our friends here are real, they're caring, and they'd drop everything to help any of us, not to mention that I love it here. And I'm in love with Wyatt. Thinking of Wyatt makes me want to remind her that both Wyatt and Delilah are now running their father's bar and grill, which is a huge, important job. But I don't. I let her go on, and I bite my tongue again, because I know it's not worth my energy.

"Besides, once you're in New York, you'll see us more often, Cassidy. We go there a lot, and it would be so fun to take you to dinner and to a show."

And there it is. The dangling carrot.

I hate the way my heart swells with hope with her promise of seeing me more and spending time with me. It shouldn't affect me the way it does. I know it's an empty promise. Why wouldn't it be? This is the same person who told me that if I took singing lessons she'd sing in the mother-daughter pageant with me when I was nine and then went off to Las Vegas instead. The same woman who buys me grapefruit oil and lotions when she knows I'm allergic. The same woman who told me that she and my father were going to take me to Japan after my lacrosse playoffs in high school, only to find out that they *accidentally* booked the wrong date and they had to leave before my playoffs even began. Thankfully, Wyatt's mother was willing to let me stay with them for the week *and* take me to playoffs.

"Wouldn't that be fun, honey?"

"Yes," I admit, because in my head those unattainable dreams of being enough to hold their attention still dance with hope—even though I know they're not just unattainable dreams. They're also unworthy of my thoughts. I should save my dreams for people who matter, like me and Wyatt.

"Then why haven't you taken that job yet? And don't tell me that you're dating someone from that little town and you can't leave him, because you know this is too big of a decision to base on a summertime fling. You are not one of those weak girls who coordinates her life around some man's needs."

Okay, I won't tell you. "Mom, I've got to get back to work. Thanks for calling."

"Okay, honey. Sorry to keep you so long, but take the job. We'll call Aunt Aggie and arrange for you to stay with her. We're so proud of you, Cassidy. We always knew you'd take life by the horns."

Funny. I feel like I'm being bucked off at every turn.

After we end the call, I return to the café, and the woman who came in with the teenage girls waves me over.

"Hi. Are you the girl who helped Naomi plan her beach wedding and took the pictures?" The woman looks to be in her midthirties, with short blond hair, big brown eyes, and a round, friendly face.

I point to Brooke. "Actually, Brooke planned the wedding. I just helped and took pictures."

"That's not what Sarah said," one of the teenagers says. "Sarah said that Brooke planned it first, then everything fell apart and you took over."

I glance back at Brooke, careful not to take credit for all of her hard work. "Well, I think your friend is mistaken. Brooke planned it all, top to bottom. All I did was help with some incidentals. Brooke is amazing if you're looking for a party planner."

"She is amazing at party planning. You're absolutely right," the woman says as she waves to Brooke. "I love Brooke. My sister wants to have a beach wedding and she loved the pictures from Naomi's wedding. I was wondering if we could put you in touch with her."

She loved the pictures!

For a few seconds my heart races with excitement, but when I open my mouth to tell her yes, I remember that if I take the job in New York, I won't be here anymore. My stomach sinks at the thought of sitting behind a desk pushing numbers all day when I could be doing all the things I love in a place I love, with Wyatt and friends I adore. I'm trying so hard not to put Wyatt into my decision-making equation. I love him so much I know I want to be with him, but as my parents pointed out, this decision is too big to make based on a relationship.

"I'm not sure if I'll be here or not for much longer, so why don't you put her in touch with Brooke. If I'm around, I'll work with her to coordinate your sister's function." Before she can tell me no, I wave Brooke over and leave her to discuss the event.

As I'm making their sandwiches, Brooke sidles up to me and turns her back so the customers can't hear her.

"You know, I just helped Naomi on a whim, but I think we could make a go of this." Brooke fills a pitcher with soda.

I finish making the sandwiches and force a smile through my indecision.

"We should talk about it," she urges.

I escape to deliver the sandwiches and get pulled over to another group of customers. By the time we have a break, my stomach is tied in knots. I have no idea what to do about the job, and I'm worried about Wyatt and Tim. Brooke and I sit at a table and she starts making a list.

"What are you doing?"

"Well, I thought we should give a party-planning business some serious consideration. I'm writing down what I did to coordinate Naomi's wedding." She stops writing and looks at me. "You'd be our resident photog, of course."

"Brooke, you know I might not be here long-term, right?" Even though I don't want to mislead her, I can't hold in my excitement over the prospect. "But, oh my gosh, Brooke, do you know how fun that would be? Party planning and taking pictures?"

"Why?" She continues writing, and I have a feeling she's avoiding eye contact on purpose.

"Because of the job in New York." Brooke knows about my offer, and she knows I haven't made a decision, but I am considering taking it. I told her when I first got into work today. "Don't pretend that I didn't tell you about it."

She still doesn't look at me.

"Brooke?"

"I'm not pretending."

"Then what *are* you doing?"

She sets down her pen and finally looks at me. "Well, you told me about the offer, but you also told me about you and Wyatt, so..."

"So?" I shrug like it's no big deal, when even hearing his name sets my mind reeling back to how good it felt to be in his arms.

"So...you're not going to leave Wyatt, are you?" She leans across the table. "I thought you really liked him."

My feelings burst free without any thought. "I do. I *love* him. I love him from his toes to the tippy-top of his head and every delicious spot in between." My body shivers with the memory of making love to him.

Brooke's eyes widen. "Wow, then you're *really* not leaving."

"Brooke, you of all people should know that I can't make such an important decision based on a guy. Not even on Wyatt." Brooke had followed a boyfriend to another state. A handful of lies and one broken heart later, she returned to Harborside and set down roots.

She sighs. "Just because my relationship didn't work out doesn't mean yours won't. Wyatt's a great guy, and you two have been close forever."

"I know that, and I'm not even sure I want the job in New York, but so much has happened these last few days that I need time to process it all. I can't just make a snap decision. I love what I'm doing here with you, and the idea of doing more of it and having time for photography is so exciting. But there are risks associated with staying here and turning down the job, too." My own words come back to me. *That's what life is, Wyatt. One fucking risk after another.*

"What does Wyatt want you to do?"

The bell above the door rings, and a group of teenagers come into the café before I can answer. I'm relieved, because I know that despite what Wyatt says, he wants me to stay as much as I want to.

"I'll take them." As I stand, Brooke grabs my arm and looks up at me.

"Wyatt's a good guy, Cassidy. And I'm pretty sure we can make a party-planning business work hand in hand with the café. I know it's not a posh career, but will you at least think about it?"

"Wyatt's better than a *good* guy, and I have a feeling this is all I'll be thinking about for the next week."

Chapter Twenty-Four

~Wyatt~

THE ADDRESS IN Tim's personnel file leads me to an apartment complex at the edge of town. I'm surprised that Tim would move to such a shabby-looking place. Not that there are bad neighborhoods in Harborside, but the complex looks run-down. There's no real landscaping, save for a few scraggly bushes, and the cars in the lot are mostly older and beat-up models. I've been to the house where Tim lived with his wife a dozen times with my parents. It was a beautiful house at the north end of town. I can't begin to imagine him living in this run-down area, but then again, I never imagined that Tim might do something like embezzle money from our family business.

Fuck. It doesn't even feel right to think about Tim doing this shit.

I pull around to his building and recognize his car in the parking lot. I head up to his apartment, talking myself out of being nervous. It's not every day I have to ask a family friend and employee if he's stealing from my family. I know my father's looking down on me, and I can't help but hope that Cassidy and I didn't miss something and misinterpret the entire situation.

The Harborside Apartments have sidelight windows by the doors, and after knocking several times, I peer inside. It's hard to make out much more than the entryway, where I see his keys on a table, and I realize the muffled noise I hear is coming from inside his apartment. It sounds like a television. I'm trying not to think about Cassidy's job offer, which has made my gut feel like lead ever since she got the call. Standing here, waiting for Tim to answer the door, brings it to the forefront of my mind. I'm getting more anxious by the second about Cass possibly leaving and about confronting Tim, and when I bang on the door again, my anxiety turns to anger.

"I know you're in there, Tim. You might as well open the door." I pound on the door again.

I pace the hallway, run my hand through my hair in frustration, and kick the floor. I didn't ask for this shit. I didn't ask for the bar, or the headaches, or the accounting nightmare with Tim Johnson.

As I head for the stairs, ready to leave Tim and his thievery behind, Tim's door swings open. He leaves it open and staggers back into the apartment. I follow him through the entryway to the small, messy living room, where he tumbles down to the couch. Tim's hair looks like it hasn't been washed in days. His clothes are rumpled, as if he'd slept in them, and his living room is littered with beer cans and pizza boxes.

Tim waves to the chair across from him, but I'm too frustrated to sit. I cross my arms and stare at him, biting back the urge to let him have it. He's supposed to be at work, not drinking like a college kid on a binge.

"Go ahead. Say it." Tim rests his head against the back of the couch and closes his eyes. "Tell me how I should know better. How I let your father down. How I fucked up everything good I've ever had in my life."

My father. I don't know if it's the way Tim referenced him, as if the words *your father* were curses, or the fact that I'm looking at a guy my father trusted with his business and Tim's disrespecting him as if he didn't matter. But something inside me snaps, and for the first time since my parents died, I realize the magnitude of my responsibilities and I don't feel them as a burden but as an honor. I stifle my anger, shove my fisting hands into my pockets, and think about how my even-tempered father would have handled this situation. After a minute of contemplation, I know it doesn't matter what my father would have done.

I'm not him.

I sink into a chair with the realization and lean my elbows on my knees. I'll never be Ed Armstrong. I'll never be as conservative or as even-keeled as he was. But I'll also never be a man who makes his daughter feel like who she is isn't good enough. I repress that thought because that's not something I can deal with on top of all of this. My mind shifts to the ways my father and I were similar. He was a provider, a caretaker. A leader. I'm all those things, and I'm proud of them. Although my father's love came with strict expectations, many of which I didn't believe in, I know he loved me and Dee, and I know my father loved and trusted Tim as if he were family, too. Hell, we all did.

I look at the disheveled man across the room and want to understand what went terribly wrong with him to end up like this.

"*You* tell *me* what's going on, Tim. Then I'll figure out if I need to tell you you've fucked up your whole life, because the only thing I know right now is that my father worked his ass off for years to build the Taproom into the best damn bar and grill in Harborside, and someone's siphoning money out of it."

Tim sits up and meets my stare.

"Start talking before I lose my patience." I watch his eyes narrow and his lips press into a thin line. He opens his mouth to speak but remains silent. I wait him out, losing my patience by the second.

I rise and pace, trying to keep it together as thoughts of my father race through my mind. He was big on giving people second chances—everyone except me and Delilah, that is. He expected us to always make top grades and prepare for the future.

The future.

I stop pacing with the weight of those words. The future is now. It's no longer a fictitious time years away. It's my here and now, and I'm not going to walk away from what my father built or let some guy steal my father's money. Not even the man I know as *Uncle* Tim.

I turn my attention back to Tim, who's sitting with his face buried in his hands.

"I'm going to ask you once and only once. Did you embezzle nearly twenty thousand dollars from the Taproom?"

Tim lowers his hands but doesn't meet my gaze.

"Tim?"

"I'm trying to figure out how to answer you. The short answer is yes, but the long answer..." He exhales and rubs his jaw. "I think you should sit down for the long answer."

"I think I'll stand." I'm too edgy to sit. My hands curl into fists as I process his admission. He stole money from my father's business, and it sets off a reaction akin to the way I felt when I saw that guy forcing himself on Cassidy. My blood boils, my hands fist, and I clench my teeth so hard it hurts. I can't settle this with a fight, and I don't want to. I know now that the beating I gave Kyle was driven by my feelings for Cassidy, and the fighting I did recently was driven by my feelings for Cassidy and on the heels of the death of my parents. Fighting isn't my go-to way to handle situations, and I know it won't be in the future, either. This is the real world, and I feel like I'm on the precipice of major change. This is my world now. My future. Delilah's future. This is our here and now, and we have to handle it like adults, not angry college kids.

Tim exhales loudly again and reaches for a beer on the coffee table.

"Don't." I pin him to the couch with a dark stare. "From the looks of things, you're already messed up enough. You don't need that shit."

The side of his mouth lifts to a smile. "When did you grow up?"

"When some fucker killed my parents. Start explaining. I've got a business to run." *My father's business.* The bar might not be a multimillion-dollar company, but it's my father's legacy, and right here, in the middle of Tim's pigsty of a living room, I vow to keep it going.

Tim rubs his fist with his other hand, and when he speaks, he stares at the floor. "At first I took just a few hundred dollars. I thought I'd pay it back with my next win. That's how it happens, you know. You think you'll win the next time, or the next." He looks up with sorrow in his eyes. "I spiraled into a black hole of debt, and I had no way out."

"Why didn't you ask my father for a loan?"

Tim shakes his head. "I did, and he gave it to me."

"And?" My chest fills with rage, because I know what's coming next. He continued to steal from him.

"Gambling isn't something I can just turn off. It isn't a choice. It's a disease." He buries his hands in the sides of his hair and his face contorts. "I couldn't stop. I kept thinking, *Just one more night. One more bet. One more fucking win.*"

"One more fucking win? You took my father's hard-earned money and you...What? Lost that, too? Then stole from him to gamble again?" I'm pacing, breathing hard, trying to figure out this messed-up situation. I cross my arms to restrain my anger. "Did he know you were embezzling?"

Tim meets my stare and doesn't say a word, just shakes his head.

"Goddamn it, Tim. When would you have stopped? After you ran him dry?"

"I tried to stop. What do you think ruined my marriage? Why do you think I'm in this shitty apartment?" He rises to his feet and staggers.

I reach a hand out to steady him, and Tim crumples back down on the couch, tears in his eyes, and covers his face with his hands. *Fuck. Fuck, fuck, fuck.* Part of me wants to tell him everything will be all right, but it won't. I have enough on my plate. I can't be expected to save his ass, too. I sink down to the couch. He was my father's close friend, and close enough to me and Delilah to be called *Uncle* Tim. How can I turn my back on him? I'm twenty-two years old and totally ill prepared for this shit. My instinct is to pick up a beer myself and drink until it doesn't feel like such a nightmare.

I cross the room to a bookshelf and freeze as my parents' smiling faces come into focus in a framed photograph. I pick it up with shaking hands and touch their image. I haven't seen their picture since we left Connecticut, and my throat instantly thickens. My eyes tear up as I drink them in. They're standing with me, Delilah, and Tim. We're in the Taproom, and my father's smiling with an arm over my shoulder. He used to do that a lot. No wonder Delilah wanted to get away from me. I do it, too. She must see our father in many of the things I do. I'd almost forgotten the way his eyes lit up when he smiled and the feel of his big, calloused hand on my shoulder. And my mother. *God, my mother.* She was so beautiful. I almost forgot how much Delilah looks like her. Memories come rushing back to me, and I grab the bookshelf for support. I remember sitting on the pier with my father and Tim when I was a boy and thinking about how big and strong my father was and how I thought he could figure out any problem. How I hoped one day to be as big and as smart as him. I remember the way he and Tim laughed, their deep voices filling the summer air. I remember laughing, too, even though I had no idea what they were laughing at. I was probably only eight, but I remember desperately wanting to stay in their coveted circle. I dreamed of being an adult with them, and now that dream will never come true.

Tim's voice filters into my ears. He must have been talking this whole time, apologizing, telling me that he needs to get help and explaining why he hasn't come back to the Taproom, but it's like listening to a Charlie Brown cartoon. His words are muffled by memories.

My hand shakes as I set the frame back on the bookshelf and close the distance between me and Tim, and his voice comes back into focus. He's talking about his friendship with my father, and I know what I have to do. What I want to do.

"Did my father try to get you into some kind of support group or addiction program? Gambling, they treat that like any other addiction, right?" I lost my father, and although Tim isn't my uncle, he's been in our lives for so long he feels like family. Despite what he did.

"Right before he died we talked about it. I told him I'd get help. For the drinking, too."

"So you've got a drinking problem, too? This isn't just a onetime thing?"

He nods and splays his hands out before him. "One

leads to the other."

"And what happened to getting help?"

He points to the small kitchen table, where I see a number of brochures. "I was supposed to go in the week your parents died."

I close my eyes for a beat, processing the magnitude of his statement. My parents' deaths must have knocked him completely off-balance, too. While I was getting drunk and beating up an asshole, he was falling down his own rabbit hole.

"I couldn't do it. It was all I could do to get my ass down to Connecticut and take care of the arrangements for...I want to do it, but your father...he was like a brother to me, Wyatt. I tried to go back to work and do things right, but I don't have control over any of this shit. I'm a fucking lost cause. That's why I haven't been back to work. I can't even look at myself in the mirror. I hurt your family. I lost my wife. I should have been the one who died, not your father. He was a good man." Tears stream down Tim's cheeks.

"Don't." It's all I can manage. I don't want to hear about how my father shouldn't have died. It won't change the fact that he's dead. It won't bring him and my mother back. It won't make this any easier.

I have to move forward, and I can't afford to be hung up on worthless wishes. I draw my shoulders back and hold Tim's gaze. Growing up sucks ass.

"You know I have to fire you."

Tim nods.

I pick up the brochures and find one with notes written on it. "But I can't leave you to hang yourself. Did you call this place?" I hold up the brochure.

He nods again. "They've got all my admission stuff. They keep leaving me messages."

"Go pack your shit."

Tim's eyes fill with confusion.

"Go pack your shit. One way or another I'm getting you the help you need. The rest of your life will be up to you, but my father...My father loved you, and I love him. So I'll take your sorry ass to rehab, and then you have no excuses."

"Wyatt..."

I hold up my hand to silence him. "Don't. I might change my mind."

"I'll pay you back. Every penny."

"No, you won't. When you get out of rehab, assuming they'll still take you, I want you to stay away from me and Delilah. I don't want you anywhere near the Taproom ever again. My father loved you. He trusted you, and you made awful, selfish choices in spite of that trust. I'm not my father. I need to protect his bar, and I need to protect what's left of my family. That means making tough choices. This is one of them."

Chapter Twenty-Five

~Wyatt~

AT TEN O'CLOCK I'm standing on the boardwalk outside of Brooke's Bytes, waiting for Cassidy and Brooke to close the café. There's a guy leaning against the wall staring at his tablet, but other than him, the Internet dwellers have left the premises. I watch Cass through the front window as she cleans the tables and swings her hips. I assume they have the radio on, and watching her dance without being able to hear the music is kind of erotic and sexy. She has the greatest hips. I love the way they fill my hands and the way she moves in sync to me no matter what position we're in.

She disappears into the back of the café, and I turn around and lean on the railing, looking out at the ocean. There are still people on the beach even though it's late. Teenagers in shorts and sweatshirts sit on blankets, and couples walk hand in hand. I've been coming to Harborside since I was little, and this afternoon, when I was dealing with getting Tim admitted into the rehab facility, I thought about all the time I've spent here. I'm not sure I ever want to go back to Connecticut, and I wonder whether I'd want to move to New York if Cassidy decides to take the job there. Or if she'd even want me to.

Part of me wishes we'd waited another week before coming together. Then she would be able to make this decision with a clearer head. Or maybe not. If she was as conflicted about us as I was, which I'm pretty sure she was, then she might have had an even harder time. I don't know. I just know that as much as I want her to stay, I know this decision has to be hers and hers alone, and that sucks because I want to share every part of our lives together.

I hear the bell over the door when she comes outside, and I turn to greet her. She looks like an angel illuminated by the lights of the café. Her hair is gathered over one shoulder, and she's flashing her megawatt smile like she's got all the energy in the world, even after working for hours on her feet.

"Hey, babe." The endearment comes so naturally and feels so right, but it still takes me by surprise. I'm surprised that after so many years of being best friends, we've landed here together. I wrap my arms around her and press my lips to hers. It feels like we've been apart for a week instead of a few hours, and I can't imagine what it will be like if she goes to New York.

"I missed you," I say, then press another, softer kiss to her lips.

"God, I missed you, too." She kisses me again, and

my body heats up.

"Should we wait for Brooke?" I glance into the café and see Brooke sitting at a table.

"No. She said Jesse's coming by in a bit."

"Jesse?"

"Yeah." She shrugs. "She said they had to go over some things. I think she does some work for his businesses."

"Cool. Want to take a walk before we go home, or are you too tired?" I drape my arm over her shoulder and walk toward the steps to the beach.

"Our first moonlit walk as boyfriend and girlfriend? I'm totally up for that."

"God, I love you." My feelings for Cassidy no longer surprise me. Giving in to my feelings for her is the best thing I've ever done.

We slip off our shoes and I carry them while Cass cuddles against me as we walk down the beach toward home. I want to ask her about the job offer, but I don't. I know she'll talk about it when she's ready.

"Did you find Tim?"

"Yes." I look away, still wrestling with the pain of telling him I never wanted to see him again, and then I explain to Cassidy what happened when I saw him.

"So he's in rehab?"

"Yeah. And I told him to stay away from the bar, from me, and from Delilah."

"Oh, Wy. That must have been so hard."

I swallow past the thickening in my throat. Nothing hurts as much as losing my parents did, but this feels like lead in my gut.

"I honestly don't know what to think. I don't know

what set him into gambling in the first place, but now he's got a gambling *and* a drinking problem. Or maybe he had a drinking problem first, and it became a gambling problem. I don't know, but I can't chance him stealing from us again. I don't know if it's right to turn him away completely. I know he's not my blood relative, but he's always been here. Always. Since the day we were born he's been *Uncle* Tim. It hurt like hell to fire him, and it hurt just as much to tell him to stay away from us." It's so easy to bare my heart to Cassidy that I tell her everything.

"I wish I could talk to my father again and understand what he thought about the whole situation. I think one of the worst things about my parents dying is all the things I'll never get to say to them."

We sit in the sand, and Cassidy buries her feet. "If they were here, what would you say to them?"

I think about that as I watch the waves roll in. "I don't know. I wish I could have told them that I love them with more feeling. When we said goodbye that last time, they hugged me and told me they loved me, but I was so sidetracked by wanting to get to the party that I said it fast, you know? Like I'd be able to say it a million more times."

"They knew you were just excited." She takes my hand in hers. "They knew you loved them."

I nod, because I know that they knew I loved them, but I still wish I could tell them again. "I wish I could tell my father that I appreciated the way he pushed me."

"You hated how he pushed you."

"True. Every second of it. But after everything I've been through, I understand and appreciate why he did it. It's gotta suck to be a parent. It's like you have to force your kids to do things that they hold against you until they're older. If my parents hadn't died, how long would it have been before I understood why he pushed me so hard?"

Cassidy doesn't answer. She doesn't have to. She knows I'm just emptying my mind, and I love that she understands me enough to let me do it.

"I wish I could tell my mom that she was an amazing mother, despite being strict. She was loving and kind and always there for us. I wish I could tell her that she was beautiful. She was, you know. She was so pretty. That's where Delilah gets it from." I shift my eyes away as they tear up.

"And I wish I could yell at them, too. That's really shitty, but I want to tell them how much they messed up Delilah's self-image. I just don't understand why they were so against same-sex relationships. And how could they not know about Delilah? I'm her brother and I realized it. I can't figure out if they really had no clue and were just too verbal with their opinions, or if they had an inkling about her and thought they could change her. It doesn't matter why, really. They made it so hard for her, and I wish I could talk to them about it. But what I really wish is that I could ask them what I don't know yet."

"What do you mean?" Cassidy scoots closer to me, and our bodies touch from shoulder to hip.

"I don't know. My dad always planned things out for me. *Wyatt*, he'd say, *you're going to be successful in everything you do. You'll get your degree, then you'll get a great job, and one day you'll take over the bar.* And I want to know what else he thought."

"You'll figure it out, Wyatt. I know it's hard for you, because you're so used to living day by day, but you're already finding your way. I have faith in you."

She never fails to surprise me in the way she believes in me.

"Why, Cassidy? Why do you have faith in me?"

Her eyes turn thoughtful and her lips curve up in a sweet smile. "Because your father might have guided you, but he didn't *make* you do things. What you've accomplished—the stellar grades, the athletic accomplishments, the amazing friend you are to me and so many others—that's all *you*, Wyatt. All he did was point you in a direction, but you carried out the things that mattered. And now you're the one taking charge of the issue with Tim. *You* figured out a plan. You were there for me when Kyle cheated. You're the most capable and resourceful man I know. When Jesse went away, you took over the bar without hesitation."

"And immediately screwed up by leaving myself understaffed."

"But don't you see? You called your friends to help that night at the bar instead of freaking out or letting the business go untended. When your parents died, you didn't let it beat you, Wyatt. You took charge of the situation with Delilah and got her out of the house that you knew was too hard for the two of you to deal with. That's what growing up is all about. Turning mistakes into lessons."

"You sound like a parent." I bump her shoulder

with mine.

"Yeah. I just realized that I stole that line from my mom."

"So you don't think I need my father to point me in the right direction for the next thirty years?"

She laughs. "I don't think you need anyone telling you what to do. You have a good head on your shoulders."

"Thanks for having faith in me, Cass."

"I would say that even if we weren't boyfriend and girlfriend." She laughs. "I like to say that. Boyfriend and girlfriend. It feels so good."

"You've had a boyfriend before." I'm teasing, because I know exactly what she means.

"Yeah, but he wasn't you." She puts her hand on my chest. "And you've never had a real girlfriend before, so at least I get to claim a first for something in your life."

"Babe, you claimed so many firsts in my life, I lost count."

"Pleeeease." She lies back and looks up at the stars.

I lie beside her and lace our fingers together. "First girl I have ever loved. First person to read my palm. First girl whose hair I held back while she puked—other than Dee, of course, when she was fifteen."

"I remember that." She laughs.

"First person who means so much to me that I want to be a better man for her."

She turns and searches my eyes, like she can't believe what I've just said. Her lips curve up in the tender smile I love so much.

"First person to teach me about life and love when she never even knew she was doing it."

"How do you mean?"

I prop myself up on my elbow and kiss her softly. "All these years, I've watched you make your way through the world without parents helping to guide you. Since you were young, really young—ten, maybe eleven, I don't know how old exactly—you were always so self-sufficient. You didn't need anyone to show you the way or tell you what to do."

"Oh my God, Wyatt. You're kidding, right?" She blinks up at me with a serious scowl. "My parents have told me what to do my *entire* life. They just do it from afar, and they do it underhandedly."

"They left you for weeks at a time, Cass. Day to day you took care of yourself. Even when you stayed with us, you never needed my mom to tell you to do your homework or wash your clothes, or anything."

"Okay, so I'm self-sufficient, but they have always told me my next step. I went into accounting because they told me I should. Remember after my first year when I said I was bored?"

"Yeah, but you joined all those extracurricular groups, and then you weren't bored anymore."

"Yes, because they told me to join them." She sits up and draws her knees up to her chest. "And you know what? I don't even like accounting very much."

"But you said you liked accounting."

"Yeah, because I didn't ever have anything to compare it to."

"But I asked you a million times if you liked your

major."

She nods and her eyes dampen. "All those times, Wyatt, I must have been trying to convince myself, because I don't enjoy it. And do you want to know the worst part of it all?" She doesn't wait for me to answer. "I thought if I did all those things, they'd spend more time with me or love me more or—"

I pull her into my arms and hold her as she cries. "Babe, they love you." Even as I say the words, I know her parents have never taken care of her the way they should have, like ours did. They are absentee parents at best and neglectful at worst.

She wipes her eyes. "That's why I have to make this decision about my job separate from everyone else. I need to figure out if I love it here so much because of you or because of Harborside, and if I love my work because it's not accounting or because I really love what I'm doing. I won't make this decision based on us, Wyatt. I can't do it, and I know you said you don't want me to, so we're on the same page. It would be like putting my fate in another person's hands. I never want anyone having that power over me again."

"Wow, Cass." I let go of her to give us both some space. "I don't *want* power over your life. I just want to be in it."

She smiles, then drops her eyes. I can see this is as hard for her as it is for me.

"Tell me what I can do to help you with this."

"This is going to sound horrible, but just stay out of it. Completely. That's the only way I can make this decision free and clear of us."

Her words pierce my heart, even though I understand where she's coming from. I never imagined that words could hurt so much, but I don't want her to see the way they slay me. That would only make her feel guilty, even though she hasn't said one thing about *wanting* the job or going to New York. I can't figure out why she's even considering it if she doesn't like accounting, but I respect her need to make the decision on her own.

"Okay. When you're ready to tell me your decision, I'm here. And you know I support anything you want to do."

Her eyes soften, and she cuddles up against me again. "I know," she says just above a whisper, like she's a balloon and all of her air deflated. "I'm sorry, Wy. I didn't even realize I felt all of those things, but I do. I really, really do."

"Today has definitely been a day of revelations for both of us. I get it. You said you didn't want anyone having power over you again, and I hope you know that while I may be a little jealous when it comes to you and other guys, I'm not a control freak."

"Of course I know that. And...you *have* been jealous over me and guys forever." She giggles, and I give her a questioning look. "Come on. You know you found fault in every guy who ever asked me out. Why do you think I didn't go out with most of them?"

"I did not." *Did I?*

"Jon Delleux, eighth grade. Terry Crom, ninth grade. Oh, and let's not forget Clay Morton, when I was a senior. Do you want me to continue?"

"Jesus. They were all douche bags."

Her eyes widen. "They were not. Clay was a linebacker on the football team. You said he was cool until he asked me out, and then you changed your tune."

I tackle her beneath me, and she laughs and struggles to get free. I pin her to the sand with my body weight. "Okay, so I'm jealous. I can't help it. Maybe I was in love with you then and I just hadn't figured it out yet."

She leans up and nips at my chin. "Why do you think I never went on the dates?"

"You told me it was because you didn't want to."

"No, silly. It was because they weren't you. I guess I accepted I'd never have you."

Finally, my beautiful girl is wrong about something. I seal my lips over hers and wrap my arms around her, kissing her until our hips are grinding together and we're swallowing each other's moans of pleasure. When our lips part, I gaze into her eyes and trace her cheek with my finger.

"You didn't really like me like that back then, did you? I never got that vibe from you." I wish I had.

She rolls her eyes. *Aw, man.* I touch my forehead to hers.

"Babe, I had no idea. And you never said a word about the girls I hooked up with. God, Cassidy. Most girls would have given me all sorts of shit or called the girls whores."

"I'm not most girls," she whispered.

"No, you're not." As I gaze into her eyes I know it's more than her just not being like most girls. Her parents really did a job on her, and I never realized how their lack of love had affected her until just now. Did they make her repress her feelings for everything in life, or just people?

"Tell me why you never said anything."

She swallows hard. "At first it was just because I figured you were so popular and so cute, you'd never want someone like me."

"You mean I wouldn't want the prettiest girl in school?"

"I was not. Anyway..."

I cup her cheek against my palm. "You were. You always were, Cassidy, but you were also my best friend. So I never looked at you like that."

She blushes and looks even more beautiful.

"I was so stupid." I smile, and she laughs.

"And in college..."

There's a hint of mischief in her eyes. "In college..."

"I, um. On some level I wanted to be all those girls you hooked up with, but I didn't know how to tell you or if you'd reciprocate, or anything. So I basically spent years trying to ignore that I felt that way, and most of the time it was such a habit to push away the thoughts that I didn't even know I was doing it."

"You know what I think? I think you were so busy trying to do the right thing that you wouldn't have let yourself chance the wrong thing." I pause, because reality creeps in and I don't like it. "And I probably—no, I definitely—would have been the wrong thing."

Her lips curl downward into a frown. "Why?"

"Because I was too wrapped up in me. It took Kyle, or Kyle and my parents dying, to pull me from my selfish place and see what was really going on around me, Cass. I think we're together now for a reason. As wrong and chaotic a time as this is, it's the right time for us."

"And what if I go to New York? Will it still be the right time for us?"

I smile, because as much as I know it will kill me if she leaves, I don't think anything could ever really tear us apart.

"There will never be a time that isn't right for us."

Chapter Twenty-Six

~Wyatt~

CASSIDY MOVED INTO my bedroom the night after we made love for the first time, and I can't believe that it's been only four days since she moved in. I'm already used to waking up with her in my arms and falling asleep with her body nestled against mine. I really don't want her to go to New York, but I'm doing as she asked and not saying a word about it. Last night we had a bonfire on the beach and she took loads of pictures. She's so happy when she's got the camera in her hands. I hope if she does go to New York she makes time for that, too. She sang several songs while Brandon played the guitar, and I heard Tristan tell her that if she moved to New York he'd never hear her beautiful voice and that he'd miss her. I was hoping she'd give some indication of what she was thinking, but she just smiled and told him that if she went, she'd still visit and sing for him. She's obviously still considering the move.

She's working with Brooke today, and a few minutes ago she texted to say that another lady asked her and Brooke to coordinate an event. She sounded pretty excited in the text, considering she added three exclamation points. It's hard not to get my hopes up about her staying. I try to keep my mind busy with other things. I can't completely erase Tim from my thoughts. I wonder how he's doing and what he'll do if he gets clean. I know my father would have had no reason to talk to me about the stuff with Tim, but I wish I'd had some warning.

Jesse's back, but he's pretty busy overseeing the renovations of his restaurant, so he stops in and touches base when he can, which is fine. That's how it should be, I guess. It's strange how I went from being a college kid with no responsibilities to a guy who owns a bar, two houses, two cars, and is head over heels in love. I'm not complaining—well, except about losing my parents. That part sucks big-time. I miss them, and there are times when I expect a text to come through from my dad or when we're sitting on the deck of the house and I expect him to crack a very dry joke. But as each week passes, the hurt becomes less of a gaping wound and more like a paper cut—ever present but not life stopping.

It's late afternoon and Jesse, Delilah, and I are sitting at a table in the bar. Tristan is bartending, and Livi's waiting tables. Cassidy taught me how to use QuickBooks, and I've been putting together a filing system that is organized and easy to navigate as we move forward. Jesse has already reviewed the schedules Delilah made, and now the elephant in the room needs to be dealt with—filling Tim's position. I know we're all thinking about it, because Delilah keeps stealing looks at me and Jesse *isn't* looking at me.

Delilah gets a text, and when she reads it, she smiles. She responds and sets her phone on the table. "How late do you think we'll be?"

She dealt with Tim's gambling well enough. She was shocked and angry, but after a few hours she and I were making plans about what needs to be done now that he's gone for good. She hasn't wanted to talk about our parents much, but I know when she's ready, she will, and I know she's planning on meeting Ashley on the boardwalk tonight. That friendship seems to mean a lot to her, too, and I'm glad Ashley's filled whatever emptiness Delilah feels.

"I'll stay, Dee. You can go."

"You sure you don't mind? I want to run home and shower before I meet Ash."

"Jesse?"

He looks up from the report. "Sure. We're cool. You've got a handle on the inventory and deliveries, and your schedules are meticulous. Even your backup schedules are great, Delilah. I want to talk about Tim, but Wyatt can fill you in later."

"Great. Thanks." She heads to the back room.

Once we're alone I fill Jesse in on what I'm thinking. "We need to hire a bookkeeper, but I don't want to do it yet."

"Why not?" Jesse sets down the reports and crosses his arms.

"I want to rework the filing system and make sure every step of our accounting system is transparent. Then I think we can get away with hiring a part-time accountant. We don't have that many monthly transactions, and they come on a consistent schedule. We'll need more hours at month's end, but I want to keep my eyes on the reports on a weekly basis so we don't fall behind again. I also want to hire an outside accounting firm to audit every six months. We have the money, and it's a good safety net. I'm not sure why my parents never arranged for it."

"Your mom was pretty good about handling those things."

"Except when she was too busy. I want to do this right." From what I can tell, my mother kept good tabs on the books most of the time. She obviously trusted Tim, but I guess she'd been busy with other things the last few months before she died, and that's when Tim fell over the edge and began embezzling. I have no way of knowing if my father told my mother about Tim, but I assume he did. I guess there are some things I'll never fully understand, but in the grand scheme of what we've been through this summer, if she knew or not, what she thought about it, or how she planned to handle it, all seem like small potatoes. I can't change the past. I can only deal with what's happening now and try to safeguard us from the same kind of thing in the future.

Jesse leans on the table. "And what about the money Tim took?"

I shrug. "I'm not pressing charges, and I told him to stay away from the bar and from me and Delilah.

Let's see how he does with rehab and if he pulls himself together. I'm inclined to write off that money. Assuming he cleans up his act, I don't want him to start off with one foot in the hole. He's already going to have to find a new career. It's not like I can recommend him for an accounting position after what he's done."

"Your dad was a hard ass for rules, but he had a soft spot for those he loved. I have a feeling you're a softy like your dad." Jesse smiles.

His words warm me. I'd like to think I'm something like my father. At least the good parts of him. "I'm a realist. Tim fucked up, but hey, I did, too. I could have been thrown in jail for beating up Kyle or the other guy. Sometimes good people do bad things." I shrug as he nods. "Jesse, I probably never thanked you the way I should have. You protected me from being arrested. Thank you. I think my father's soft side rubbed off on you, too."

"Luckily, a lot of your father rubbed off on both of us. He was a good man."

"I know. Thanks."

"You know, Wyatt, you can lean on me anytime. No one expects you to deal with all this stuff on your own right now."

People who don't know Jesse tend to give him a once-over because of his biker image. This is understandable, because most people don't wear jeans, boots, leather, and chains around the beach, but as I meet his empathetic dark eyes, I can't help but think how his image and his sentiments are like a square peg going into a round hole. Then again, maybe we're all square pegs just trying to fit into round holes.

I smile, knowing Jesse is sincere and not caring if he looks like a biker or a baker. I'm just thankful he's in our lives.

"My father would have, and it's not even about that anymore. I want to do this. I want to be part of something he built and believed in. It makes me feel like I didn't lose them for nothing. I know he'd be proud of me and Dee."

"Okay, let's do it. Let me know what I can do to help. I'm going to be pretty busy with the restaurant renovations, but I'll still be around if you need me."

"Just let me know if I do anything that seems way off base. I'm sure there are things that I don't realize I don't know, and that's the trouble zone."

Jesse pats my shoulder. "Your father had nothing but confidence in you, and I can see why. There's nothing you can't do."

~Cassidy~

WHEN I GET off work I walk down to the Taproom to see Wyatt. He's been so good about not asking me about New York. So much is happening so fast that it's exciting and scary at once. Brooke and I have been going over budgets and schedules and trying to figure out if we can really pull off an event-planning business along with the café. The idea of doing more photography is really exciting to me, and I find myself daydreaming about it. Brooke obviously needs the help at the café, and I love working with her. We make a great team, but I'm not sure I'd want to work in a café my whole life, and I am trying to be smart about the decision. I need to have a long-term plan. My father always says that the only way to succeed in life is to plan. I'm trying, but the more I think about leaving Harborside, the more I don't want to, and the more I want to stay in Harborside, the less I want to plan. Maybe I've been planning for way too long and it's time to live on the edge a little.

I try to imagine not having the next step in my life planned out. What would it be like to just be content being with Wyatt, working, and enjoying life a little without a corporate ladder to navigate and plan for?

The idea is tantalizing.

Wyatt and I have breakfast on the deck most mornings. I've taken so many beautiful pictures of the sunrise, and it always leaves me wanting more, just like Wyatt does. I can't get enough of him. I love our walks on the beach, and I am happier than I've ever been. And with Tristan living with us and Brandon sort of living with us, it's like we have our own little family. A family of friends who really care about one another. Everyone helps with keeping the house clean, and when Wyatt's working late, I hang out with Tristan or we go listen to Brandon's band.

Sometimes I sit on the deck, trying to figure out my life, and I wonder if I really *need* to figure it out. I'm finally working at a job I really *want*, and I'm in love with the man I've adored for years—and can finally admit it to myself *and* out loud. It's so freeing, allowing myself to act on feelings I've repressed for so long.

I fill my lungs with the crisp evening air. When I reach the pier I turn toward the ocean and smile as the breeze stings my face. I love that feeling, and I know if

I go to New York it'll be ages before I feel it again. *Ugh.* I hate thinking about it, and I'm not even sure I want to keep considering that job, but I feel like I should.

I continue walking toward the sound of music coming from the bar, remembering that night when the guy wouldn't stop kissing me and the way Wyatt rescued me. I'd like to believe that I don't need rescuing, but I think there are times in all of our lives when we do need to be rescued. Wyatt and Delilah needed rescuing that night they climbed into my bed when their parents were killed, and on some level, I think Wyatt needed rescuing from his own internal torture. He had convinced himself that loving me was too risky, and I think he might have stayed in that lonely place for a long time, just like I would have. But my heart has belonged to Wyatt for too many years to allow that. I don't think I would have let anyone into it the way I let Wyatt.

A few minutes later I walk into the Taproom and see Wyatt standing behind the bar, talking with a blond girl who's wearing the tiniest miniskirt I've ever seen. "Babe!" he calls when he sees me, and waves me over.

My heart skips a beat every time I hear him call me *Babe*, and to hear him say it when there's a hot girl standing in front of him makes me feel even better. I trust Wyatt, and I know that's weird, since he hasn't ever had a long-term girlfriend before, but he's been the most loyal friend to me for seventeen years. That speaks volumes about his character in my book.

When I reach the bar, Wyatt leans across it and kisses me. "Cassidy, this is Samantha. She runs a bridal shop in town, and she said Brooke sent her here to find you. I was just giving her your cell number."

"A bridal shop? Why are you looking for me?"

Samantha smiles and holds out her hand. "Because I saw the pictures you took of that beach wedding and I think I can refer a lot of business to you."

"You saw my pictures?"

"They're all over Pinterest and Facebook, and getting loads of comments." Samantha looks from me to Wyatt. "Haven't you seen them?"

I can hardly believe it. *Loads of comments?* I shake my head.

"Well, you should Google them!" Samantha glances at the stage. "You must be new in town, because I'd never heard of you before, and since I'm in the bridal industry, I make it my business to know all the photographers in Harborside."

"I'm not a real photographer. That was really just a onetime thing to help out."

"Can I at least give you my number? Maybe you'll make it more than a onetime thing."

Wyatt's beaming at me from behind the bar. I can't help but give in to the excitement inside me. "Yes, sure." I take out my phone, and she gives me her phone number.

She touches my arm like we've been friends forever and leans in close. "Your boyfriend said you take the best pictures in all of Harborside."

I wonder how Wyatt would even know. Not that it matters. It's an obvious exaggeration, but I love hearing that he said it.

"Well, I've got to go meet my girlfriends. Thanks, and look up your pictures online. You'll be amazed at the comments." Samantha waves to Wyatt and heads for the door.

My phone vibrates with a call, but I'm still reeling from the conversation, thinking about the pictures I took being seen by so many people. It's exciting and scary at the same time, and I can't wait to find them online. I see my mom's name on my screen and worry because it's past midnight where she is. I answer the call, but I can barely hear, so I go into the back room, where it's quieter. "Hello?"

"Honey, it's Mom. How are you?"

"Mom? Isn't it like one in the morning there? Is something wrong?"

"We're always up late. Dad and I just got in and we thought we'd try to catch you. Can you Skype?"

My mother's voice sounds funny, but I can't place what I hear, and it momentarily throws me off-balance. "Um...I'm not at home, but let me see if this computer has Skype." I search Tim's desktop for Skype, then log on to the application.

As I'm watching the Skype icon spin, I can't help but wonder about my parents wanting to Skype with me. We've Skyped before, but very rarely. They didn't even offer to Skype after Wyatt's parents died, and I'd think that's when parents would want to look into their daughter's eyes and make sure she's okay. Then again, it's not like I have normal parents. I assume they're really excited about my job offer and gung ho to push, push, push me toward accepting it.

"I got you grapefruit oil. I know you'll need all the

energy you can get once you move to New York."

Grapefruit oil? Skype connects, and I move away from the screen because I don't want to see my mother's face right now. I can't believe she bought me something I'm allergic to. *Again.* Aren't mothers supposed to know what their daughters are allergic to? I've only been allergic to grapefruits forever, for God's sake. I try to rein in my disbelief.

"Thanks, Mom, but I can't use grapefruit oil, remember?"

"Huh. Sorry, Cassidy. I guess I'll keep the grapefruit oil for myself. I'll find you something else."

She pauses, and I wonder if she realizes how this makes me feel. Or if she even cares.

"Skype is working. Where are you?" my mother asks.

Wishing I were someplace else. "I'm here."

I end the call and sit in front of the computer so she can see me. It's after midnight there, and my mom is in full makeup and my father's still wearing a dress shirt and tie. I see an open bottle of wine between them on the table where they're sitting, and I wonder what kind of parents wait until after midnight, and after they've obviously had several drinks, to call their kids. Were they out partying too late and just realized they wanted to pressure me a little more to make a decision about New York? Or maybe dangle another carrot? Why can't they be like Wyatt? He respects my need to make a decision without pressure.

"How are you, Cassidy?" my father asks.

"Okay. Really good, actually." I sit down in Tim's chair, and they share a glance that seems uncomfortable.

"Why are you calling so late?" I swear if they start giving me crap about New York or Wyatt, I'm going to blow up.

"Cassidy Lynn." My father pauses, and I realize what he's just called me.

"You only call me that when bad stuff's happening, like when Grandma died. What's wrong?"

"Nothing. Calm down," my mother says.

"Okay, good." I take a few deep breaths, and they share another uncomfortable glance.

"Cassidy Ly—Cassidy, your mother and I are getting divorced."

I blink several times, sure I've misunderstood them. "What? I thought you said you were getting divorced."

"We are." My mother's expression doesn't change. Her eyes are flat, nonplussed, as if she's just told me she lost her shoe. No, then she'd at least look upset.

The air leaves my lungs. "No. No, you're not. You love each other."

"Honey, people grow apart." My mother says this like it's a fact of life, like she's not tearing apart the only family I've ever known and turning my world upside down.

A fleeting thought careens through my head. They're not the only family I've ever known. They're more like the family I have never known. I have everyone here now, too. I push the thought away. It feels like a rationalization for what she's just said. A way to let her off the hook.

"No." My heart races, and I'm breathing so fast I

can't slow it down. "You two love each other too much to fit me in." I don't know where the words are coming from, but they feel as though they're being ripped out of my soul. My body begins to tremble, and my thoughts scatter.

"Honey, calm down. You have lots of friends with divorced parents. It's not that big of a deal, and it's not the end of the world. It just means that your father and I will live in separate houses."

"Oh, is that all it means? Really, Mom?" I push away from the desk as Wyatt appears in the doorway. His smile immediately fades.

"Cassidy. Honey, are you okay?" my father asks.

"Oh, right. Yeah. Fine. Apparently, your life can be ripped to shreds and all it means is...No big deal." I push past Wyatt and run out the back door of the bar and into the night. I sprint down the pier as fast as I can, away from Wyatt's voice calling after me, away from the bar, away from my parents, away from everything and everyone. My feet hit the pavement and I take off across the road. I don't think about where I'm going or why I'm running from Wyatt. I don't think at all, because every time my mind begins to work, I hear my mother's stupid voice telling me their divorce is *no big deal.*

I run onto the grass and through the woods until I hear the trickling of the creek, and I keep on running, right into the creek. The cold water brings my mind back to the terrible, awful moment. I fall to my knees and sink back on my heels as water swirls around me and I sob. I sob for the parents I wish I had and for the parents Wyatt lost. I sob for the little girl I once was, watching my parents and thinking about how they loved each other so much they'd used up all their love and had none left to give me. I sob because New Fucking York is hundreds of miles away from where I really want to be, and I sob because I feel guilty for crying. My parents are alive and Wyatt and Delilah's are gone.

I sob because it's the only thing I *can* do.

I feel his arms around me, hear his words floating far away. I feel myself lifted from the water, and I punch and kick and fight while he tries to soothe me. I smell his masculine scent and I feel him holding me so tight I can't fight. My arms are pinned, and my legs are pressed against him. All I can do is cry, and cry, and cry until my lungs burn and my eyes feel swollen shut. I cry until I can't see and I can't feel, and I cry until everything turns black and my mind goes blank. I cry until I float away into a dark place that feels like heaven, because I know Wyatt is right there with me.

Chapter Twenty-Seven

~Wyatt~

WHEN I FOUND Cassidy in the water, crying and completely zoned out, I didn't know what had happened. I bundled her in my arms and carried her home. I filled a warm bath and climbed in with her, then held her until she stopped shaking and crying. I helped her dress in one of my long-sleeve T-shirts, tucked her into bed, and held her until she drifted off to sleep. Only then did I get up and call Dutch, who went to check what Cassidy had been doing on the computer. He found Skype open and Cassidy logged in. The last call was to her parents. I didn't want to call her parents because they're not exactly my favorite people, but I had to find out why she was so upset, so I called, and they told me what had happened.

Cassidy's been asleep for most of the day. Tristan and Delilah are managing the bar so I can stay with Cassidy. Brooke and Jesse came by, as did Brandon.

Her parents might have abandoned her, but she's surrounded by people who care, and right now I'm so fucking glad she's here with me. I can't imagine her getting that news when she was alone. I guess everyone heard about what happened, and I don't give a shit about anything right now except Cassidy. I'm so worried about her I can barely see straight. She stirs beside me, and I help her sit up and try to get her to drink water, but she turns away. She's so out of it that I'd think she were drugged if I didn't know her as well as I do.

"Cassidy, sweetheart, you need to drink something." I hold the cup to her lips and she takes a tiny sip. I set the glass down and fold her into my arms. She feels fragile and small, and I want to wring her parents' necks.

She leans back against my chest and sighs. "My parents are..." Tears spring from her eyes.

"I know, babe." I wrap my arms around her and press my lips to her temple. "It's okay, Cass. Cry it out." I've never seen her so upset. There have been many times when I wanted to give her parents a piece of my mind for leaving her or treating her badly, but right now, seeing her like this, makes me want to protect her from them. I swear if they called right now I'd probably tell them to never call her again—and that would be a mistake. Even if they're shitty parents, they're her parents, and they're still alive. I have to believe that even though they're cold-hearted, somehow, sometime, they'll see they're losing out on the best part of their lives. But they've made her feel so bad over the years, and to give her this news—

news that knocked her to her knees—over Skype was cold. I can't even begin to process the news itself. They're getting a divorce? Their entire life has been wrapped around each other and having fun while they left their daughter behind. Maybe they *divorced her* long ago. It shouldn't surprise me that they'd do this to her, but it does. I feel like they barely know their daughter at all. They have no idea how sensitive and loving Cassidy is, and they don't deserve her tears.

Cassidy lies down across my lap and rests her cheek against my stomach. "I figured it out." Her voice is thin and quiet.

"What, babe? What did you figure out?" I hate seeing her eyes puffy, with dark crescents beneath them.

"My parents were consumed with filling up all their empty parts by looking for the next-best thing. They must have always been searching for it, like you."

Ice slices through my chest. "Cassidy, I'm not searching for anything."

She nods. "I know. But you were. All those years, you were searching. You were empty, like them."

"I'm not like them, Cass. I know how to love. I love you. I adore you." All those years I was probably running from my feelings for Cassidy, but I don't want to argue with her, not at a time like this.

She shakes her head, and fear rushes through me. "It was all a farce. The love between them. The trips. Everything. You can't trust anything."

"You're wrong, Cass. You can trust me. You're it for me. There is no *next-best thing*."

She laughs, but it's a strangled, painful laugh.

"Apparently, there's always a next-best thing, and when you least expect it, it bites you in the ass." She sits up, and as if she's slipping into protective armor, she shakes her shoulders, then draws them back. "I'm okay. I'm sorry I freaked out."

"It's okay to freak out. Your world was just turned upside down."

She looks away, and I don't know if it's the dark and sad look in her eyes or the way her voice sounds, but I have a bad feeling. I reach for her hand, and it lies limp in my palm.

"Cass?" I bring her hand to my lips and kiss her knuckles. "What can I do to help?"

She shakes her head. "I think I'm just grieving."

I know a little something about grieving. Grieving sucks, but as Livi said, time does heal all wounds, and I want to help her through this.

"Babe, they're just getting divorced. They're still here, still your parents."

She whips her head around. "That's just it, Wyatt. They're not *just* getting divorced. Maybe for anyone else it would be just a divorce, but you've seen them. I can't imagine two people more in love, or at least I couldn't before now. Now I realize that it was all fake."

"You don't know that, Cassidy. They were probably madly in love, and they just...grew apart."

She slides me a deadpan stare. "Any way you cut it, it all means the same thing. It means that all those years when they were acting like I didn't belong with them, like I was an imposition, a third wheel...all those years that I accepted it were for nothing. They're not staying together. And if their love wasn't fake, and they really were so crazy in love that they would treat their own daughter that way, then what does that say about love?"

"Cass, I know the news threw you for a loop, and I know how they treated you sucks, but it doesn't mean that love is that way for everyone."

She shrugs. "I honestly don't know what to think. I guess I'm still in shock."

"That's understandable. Come on. Why don't you shower and we'll go down to the beach for a while, or walk on the boardwalk. We'll get your mind off of it."

She agrees, and I breathe a little easier, but there's no missing the fact that the spark of light that's usually shining in her beautiful eyes is gone, and it's all I can do to try to remain positive and not just bundle her up in my arms and keep her from having to face anything else for as long as she needs. Deep down I know she needs to get out and put some distance between herself and the situation with her parents so she can begin to deal with it. She's too mired down with shock right now. The impact is still too fresh. A distraction will hopefully help.

"It'll be okay, Cass. We'll figure this out." I fold her into my arms again and press a kiss to her lips. "I'll wait downstairs. Take your time."

~Cassidy~

WYATT IS GOOD at distracting me. He's always been able to pick me up when I'm sad, and today's no different. After we left the house, we went down to the boardwalk and walked for a long time. He didn't try to get me to talk about my parents, and I'm glad. My stomach growls, but I don't want to go into the café. I don't want to talk to Brooke about my parents yet. I need to get a handle on it first. I'm still having trouble with the fact that I thought it was okay when they were treating me like I was an accessory rather than a daughter because I thought that they were in love. I feel guilty that I didn't speak up, which is totally messed up, but I do feel that way. I even wonder if it might have saved their marriage if they'd have paid more attention to the fact that we were supposed to be a family. But those are all pipe dreams. They're thoughts from the little girl they left behind too many times, and I'm not that little girl anymore. I'm not *their* little girl anymore. I'm twenty-two years old, on the cusp of some of the most important decisions of my life. Could they have picked a worse time to separate?

We buy burgers from the grill at the far end of the boardwalk, and by the time we head back, the sun is dipping from the sky. We walk down by the water, splashing each other's feet and laughing, and it feels really good to let this happiness in. My mind wanders to my parents again, and I begin to wonder if they were ever happy or if it was all a show. Were they trying to convince themselves they were happy? I fight those thoughts tooth and nail, because Wyatt—wonderful, caring, loving Wyatt—is pulling me back onto the boardwalk and tugging me toward a photo booth.

"Come on, Cass. We haven't done this all summer."

He puts money into the slot in the photo booth, and we step behind the curtain. He pulls me down on his lap and gathers my hair over one shoulder, and then he leans his chin on my other shoulder. Right before the camera flashes, he presses his lips to my cheek. It makes me smile.

"Kiss me," he says.

I turn to him and press my lips to his. Tears well in my eyes, and I close them tight as the camera flashes. Luckily, he can't see that they're damp, and when he deepens the kiss, I get caught up in him. His arms are strong and warm around me, and our mouths fit together so perfectly. Everything about us is familiar, and I feel like an idiot for the tears streaming down my face. I don't even know why I'm crying.

When our lips part, Wyatt's eyes fill with concern. He wipes my tears with his thumb. "Babe? It's going to be okay. I promise."

I nod, because I'm afraid I'll cry harder if I try to talk.

"Is it me?" he asks.

I shake my head.

"Your parents?"

I nod and force myself to answer. I don't want him thinking that it's him. "I bet my parents were happy at first."

"Of course they were, Cass. Maybe you should talk to them about this. Talk it out so you can understand what they're going through, and tell them how you've felt all these years."

"No way. Why would I? So they can make excuses about why they did it? Or worse—deny it?"

"No. So that you can get it out of your system." We step out of the photo booth, and he grabs the strip of pictures. Wyatt doesn't even look at it. He folds me into his arms again and kisses my cheek.

We walk to the boardwalk and sit with our feet dangling over the sand.

"You don't get it, Wyatt. You don't know how this feels. I know it's selfish to worry about how it makes me feel, when their lives are messed up, too, but I can't help it."

"I do get it, Cass. But your parents are still here. You can communicate with them and try to clear the air. I can't do that, and if I could, I would, no matter how much it hurt."

I look out at the water feeling guilty. "I'm sorry. I know this is nothing compared to losing your parents."

Wyatt jumps off the boardwalk and stands in front of me. The boardwalk comes up to his chest. He pulls me forward and lifts me down off the decking and holds me tight. He always holds me tight, and I don't want there to ever be a time when he won't be here for me.

"That's not what I meant. This isn't *nothing*. All I'm saying is that you have a lot of people who love you and are here to support you, and if you ever want to, you can confront your parents and figure it out, or work through it. You have options, even if they seem hard or bad right now."

He sets me down on the sand and takes off our shoes, then he takes my hand and we walk down the beach toward the pier. The sand feels luxurious as it cools with the setting sun. I'm so glad I'm here with Wyatt while I'm dealing with this. What if they'd told me when I was in New York? That would have sucked.

"It's okay to be angry, or sad, or whatever way you feel, but don't let your parents' messed-up relationship be your guide for what can or can't be in our relationship. Look at my parents. They were happy, and they treated all of us like we mattered."

"I know, Wy. Can we talk about something else?"

We walk in silence to the pier, and Wyatt nods at the Taproom. "Want to get a drink?"

"God, yes."

Brandon's band is setting up on the stage. He waves as we grab seats at the bar.

Tristan sets a blue drink in front of me, his eyes full of compassion. He knows how much I love blue margaritas.

"You okay, hon?"

"Better now." I sip the margarita. "This is perfect. Thank you."

"I put a little extra tequila in there to numb the pain. I assume Wyatt's got your back tonight if you decide to overdo." Tristan hands Wyatt a beer and winks.

Wyatt drapes an arm over my shoulder and kisses my cheek. "I've got her back every night."

I down my drink, trying to drown the part of me that winced when Wyatt said that. I know he means it, but the bomb my parents dropped on me makes me wonder how *anyone* can know when love is real.

"You have all night, Cass." Tristan holds up my empty glass and arches a brow.

"Another, please." I feel Wyatt's eyes on me, and I lean my shoulder against him. "Don't worry. I won't puke this time. I just want to be numb."

"There are times in every person's life when they need to drink until they puke. Besides, I'm a good hair holder. Don't worry. I won't leave your side tonight."

He kisses my forehead, and I feel guilty for cringing inside earlier. He's so sure that love is real, and I want so badly to believe that my parents aren't the example of love, but the example of what love shouldn't be. I still feel like my whole life is whirring around my head.

Brandon's band starts playing and we turn to watch them. Brandon lifts his chin in our direction and Wyatt raises his glass in greeting. We listen to a few songs, and when they play a slow one, Wyatt gets up from his stool and reaches for my hand.

"Dance with me?"

I narrow my eyes, wondering what he's up to. I've never seen him dance before, except at parties when he was two sheets to the wind. "You hate to dance."

"I hate to dance with random girls. I *want* to dance with you." He pulls me to my feet and holds me tight as we join the other couples on the dance floor, and I realize that while all the other pieces of my life are spinning and upended, Wyatt is my rock. The one stable person who has always been there. I feel wonderful and safe in his arms.

Our bodies move perfectly together. Everything about being with Wyatt feels right, but I still can't shake the feeling that I'm supposed to learn from my parents' mistake. They married when they were young, and if they couldn't hold it together, then it's even more of a reason for me to make my decision about the job in New York completely separate from my relationship with Wyatt.

I see Jesse and Brooke take a seat at a table by the bar. Delilah comes out of the back room and joins them, and when the song ends, we join them, too.

"Hey, Cassidy. How're things going?" Jesse's leaning on the table, both hands clutching a beer bottle.

"Okay. Thanks for asking," I answer, as Wyatt pulls out a chair for me, then sits beside me and drapes his arm over my shoulder.

"I'm really sorry about your folks, Cass." Jesse glances at Wyatt. "I hope *all* of you guys know if you want to talk, I'm around."

"Thanks, Jesse, but I'm okay. It's just going to take some getting used to."

Tristan brings another margarita. "You tell me when, okay?"

I nod, wondering how I'd handle my parents divorcing if I didn't have our friends to lean on.

"My parents were divorced when I was your age, Cassidy. It's weird at first, but you'll get used to it." Brooke takes a sip of her drink. "It's one of those things that seems like it changes your entire world, and then you realize that it actually changes *your* world very little. You're not living with them full-time, so the times you see them, you may see only one parent, but at least you're not twelve years old, being shuffled from house to house."

My eyes shift to Brandon playing his guitar. I know his parents were divorced when he was young. "Yeah, I think you're probably right. It's just..."

"I understand," Delilah says. "You thought they'd

always be there. Together. Even if you didn't want them or need them to be. You never imagined a time when they wouldn't be together, or when you wouldn't be able to pick up the phone and call them. So it's new, and scary, and it makes you question everything else in your life."

We're all silent for a beat, and I know everyone is thinking the same thing I am, that Delilah just told us how she feels about the loss of her parents. It's the first time she's really said much about it, but since she framed it as being about me, I don't mention that. Sadness washes over Wyatt's eyes, and I wonder if he's sad for Delilah, for me, or for all three of us.

"Yes, it does," I admit. "I know it shouldn't be that big of a deal, and I'm sure in a month I'll look back and feel like it isn't. But right now it feels pretty big."

"That's understandable. Plus, you have so much on your plate right now. Did you decide about going to New York?" Brooke asks.

I feel Wyatt stiffen beside me, and I bristle against the question, too. "Um. I haven't decided."

Jesse shifts his eyes to Wyatt, and it seems like a silent message that I can't read passes between them.

I feel the heat of Wyatt's hand on my thigh, and I think about being in New York and not being able to see him after work, or in the mornings. Or at all, until weekends or vacations. Part of me wishes the job in New York hadn't come through, but another part of me knows I'm *supposed to get out there and be on my own. Make a name for myself. See the big city.* Why are we always pushing ourselves toward bigger and better things? Why is it bad to have aspirations that aren't going to make us a million dollars but are going to make us rich in other ways, ways that matter, like being happy, fulfilled? Loved.

Brooke tucks her dark hair behind her ear. "Cassidy and I are thinking about starting a party-planning business if she stays in town, and I'm really hoping she will." She leans across the table and lowers her voice. "No pressure or anything."

Wyatt threads his fingers into mine.

"Cassidy, you might really go to New York?" Delilah's eyes widen, like she can't imagine that I would go.

I shrug.

"How will you decide? I thought that if you and Wyatt were together..." Delilah looks at Wyatt, and I see a silent message pass between them.

"I don't know. It's a really hard decision," I admit.

"But why would you leave Wyatt after you two just got together?" Delilah asks just above a whisper. She shifts concerned eyes to Wyatt, then back to me.

My pulse kicks up, and I'm not sure if it's driven by my own fear of leaving Wyatt or of explaining myself to my friends, or because the words I'm about to say don't feel right to me, but they feel important.

"I don't want to leave Wyatt, and I don't even know if I will." I look at Wyatt, and his eyes are dark and serious. "I have to make this decision separate from our relationship."

"Why?" Delilah's eyes dart between me and Wyatt. *Please stop asking me questions.* "Because." I pull my shoulders back and draw on what little courage I can muster. "Because, you know, after college you're supposed to build a name for yourself, and New York is a big city. There'll be lots of opportunities."

"New York *is* the land of opportunity." Wyatt kisses my temple. "Let's lay off Cassidy for a while, okay? If she goes to New York, we'll make it work, and if she stays, we'll make it work."

"Sorry, Cass. I just hate the idea of you leaving." Delilah's eyes soften, and she smiles an apologetic smile.

"It's okay. I hate it, too."

Over the next hour Jesse and Wyatt talk shop, and Brooke, Delilah, and I talk and dance. We laugh and drink too much, which only makes us laugh more. Tristan shakes his head at us when we go up to the bar for another drink.

By the time Wyatt and I walk home, we're both pretty tipsy. I lean my head against his shoulder, wishing there was a magic wheel that I could spin that would tell me where Wyatt and I will be in five years, or ten, or fifteen. I believe with all my heart that he's my soul mate and that we're meant to be together, but every time I think about my parents divorcing, fear whispers through my mind. How can I know for sure that we won't end up the same way?

Wyatt leans down and kisses me on the way into the house, and all my worries disappear. I never want the kiss to end. The house is quiet. Brandon and Tristan are still at the bar, and Delilah is still staying at Brooke's. When our lips finally part, the look in Wyatt's eyes is white-hot. We both glance around the empty living room. Wyatt's holding me close, and I can feel how hard he is. He brings his lips to mine but doesn't kiss me. My insides hum with anticipation. He backs me up against the door and laces his fingers in mine, then rocks his hard length against me. His tongue slowly traces my lips—God, I love when he does that—and lust simmers deep within me. My breathing becomes shallow as his tongue glides over my mouth. I crane my neck, trying to kiss him, but he has my hands and hips pinned against the door. When he moves his mouth out of reach, a needful sound slips from my lungs.

"Tell me what you want," he whispers as he brings that talented mouth of his to my neck and sucks until I'm wet, writhing against him.

"You, Wyatt. I want you." My head falls back with a *thunk* against the wall, but I don't care.

He's licking and sucking my neck and driving me out of my freaking mind. He brings both hands over my head and traps them in one of his, then he brushes his thumb over my lower lip, and I try to lick it, needing a taste of him. Any part of him. His thumb stills, and his eyes go nearly black. If I didn't know him, I'd think it was anger I see on his face, but I know this look well. Wyatt likes to tease me, and I recognize the look of restrained desire. All his muscles are corded tight, like a caged tiger, ready to claim his prey. I slick my tongue over his thumb and he groans. I love it when he groans, so I suck his thumb into my mouth and swirl my tongue around it. He pulls it from my lips and crashes his mouth over mine, releasing my hands. I push at his shirt until he finally rips it off, and I go a little crazy, clawing, groping, touching every inch of his hard flesh.

We stumble up the stairs, leaving a trail of shirts behind. On the second floor Wyatt presses me against the wall and takes me in a greedy kiss that weakens my knees. He pushes at my pants, and I wiggle out of them, taking my underwear with them.

"Cassidy." My name sounds like a demand as he drops to his knees and spreads my thighs with his hands.

The first slick of his tongue makes my entire body shiver despite the heat searing between us. I close my eyes as he teases me with his fingers and tongue. His hot breath washes over my wetness, and it's all I can do to remain upright. I claw at the wall and rise up on my toes as he plunges his fingers into me. In the next second he rises to his full height and kisses me while his fingers probe and excite me. He tastes like sex as his tongue thrusts hot and hungrily into my mouth, and it turns me on even more. His fingers tease and his thumb strokes my most sensitive area, stealing my ability to think.

"Wy—"

He captures my plea in his mouth, stroking and probing me and holding me up as my body quakes with a powerful climax.

He kisses the corners of my mouth, my upper lip, sucks my lower lip between his teeth, then seals his lips over mine again. I push his pants down his hips, freeing his erection.

"Condom," he says between heavy breaths, and pulls his wallet from his back pocket. He kicks off his jeans as he fishes out the condom.

"Hurry. Hurry." I can't help it. I am aching to feel

him inside me.

He's sheathed in seconds and—*Oh God*—he pushes into me with one hard thrust. He lifts me easily into his arms and holds my ass as he moves inside me, and I bring my lips to his. I can feel his heart thundering against mine, and I use his arms for leverage, moving in sync with his efforts. When I tear my lips away with the need to regain my balance, he backs me against the wall and claims my mouth again. His tongue moves in tandem to every thrust of his hips. My body feels full and tight, and the familiar sear of anticipation builds inside me until I think I'm going to lose my mind. And, finally, my limbs go hot with the rush of another orgasm. He swallows my cries again, thrusting his tongue deeper as he finds his own release, and I feel his rigid length pulsing inside me, taking me higher, extending my orgasm longer than ever before. We kiss long after we reach our peaks, and we don't stop. Jesus, he's hard again, and I'm ready. So ready.

"Aw, shit. Sorry." Tristan's voice sails upstairs.

My eyes fly open, my mouth still attached to Wyatt's. Without missing a beat, Wyatt deepens the kiss and carries me into the bedroom. He kicks the door closed behind us, and we fall to the bed in a fit of laughter.

"Poor Tristan," I say between laughs. "Oh my God!" I can't believe he saw us...again.

Wyatt kisses me again and looks at me with so much love I can feel it washing through me like a wave.

"Don't worry. He didn't see you. He just got a nice

view of my ass."

I peer over his shoulder. "You have a great ass, so you probably made his night."

Wyatt kisses the tip of my nose and then touches his forehead to mine. "I'm sorry, Cass. I couldn't resist you. I'll make sure we're behind closed doors next time."

I wrap my arms around him and smile. "I'm not. I love how spontaneous you are."

"Good, because you are irresistible, and I'm not sure I'll always be able to wait for a closed door." He kisses me again, and when he lifts his body from mine to go into the bathroom, I feel his absence like a missing limb.

New York may be a lot of things, but without Wyatt, it will only feel lonely.

Chapter Twenty-Eight

~Wyatt~

IT'S BEEN FIVE days since Cassidy got the job offer, and she hasn't given me any indication that she's made a decision. It's ten thirty at night and Cassidy and I just arrived home from work half an hour ago. She's upstairs taking a shower, and I'm sitting on the steps of the deck, thinking about the crazy hours I've been working at the bar. I finally have the accounting system worked out to the point where I should feel comfortable hiring someone to handle the books part-time, but I don't. I'm not ready to give up control yet, and I don't mind working the hours that it takes to run things.

Delilah walks around the side of the house and sits beside me. "Hey, stranger."

I put my arm over her shoulder. "I thought you were going to Brooke's after work."

She shrugs. "I did, but I missed you."

"You just worked eight hours with me."

She bumps me with her shoulder. "You know what I mean. That's work. I miss hanging out with you. Does it bother you that I've been staying with Brooke?"

"Dee, whatever makes you happy is good with me."

"Thanks. I never knew how much you remind me of Dad, but it was so hard to see some of the things you did. I'm sorry, Wyatt. I had to go."

"No worries, but...I remind you of Dad?" I cock my head at that. "Dad and I were so different." Even as I say it, I know we weren't. That day at Tim's apartment made me realize how similar we really were.

"No, you weren't."

"Yeah, we were, at least in the ways that mattered, like supporting you."

"I thought so, too, but you're not. Your mannerisms are similar. The way you lift your eyebrows when you drink, and when you shave, you look so much like him that it's scary."

"I almost never shave." I smile at her, and she laughs.

"True. But you do rub your chin like him. And, oh my gosh, Wy, at the bar you're like a different person."

I gaze out at the water. "Yeah. I've felt different ever since I found out about Tim. It's like the bar is ours now, not Mom and Dad's. And I care about it, you know?"

"I know. I feel the same way."

"I want to make sure the schedules are right, the inventory. I want to be sure Dutch and Charley and the others are all taken care of."

"I like the time-off request forms we came up with." Delilah tucks her hair behind her ear. "That should help alleviate your desire to be the good guy and let everyone off work on the same day." She pokes my ribs.

"Hey!" I laugh.

"Face it, Wy. We're growing up." Her eyes well with tears, and her voice trails off.

I pull her closer. "It's okay, Dee. We're supposed to."

I feel a heavy hand on my shoulder and look up at Tristan.

"Two of my favorite people." Tristan pats Delilah on the head. "Scoot over, sister. I need a little love."

We separate, and Tristan sits between us.

"What's up, Tris? Having Ian regrets?" I hand him the beer I was drinking.

"No regrets about Ian. Just feeling like I haven't spent enough time with you two. I mean, don't get me wrong, getting eyefuls of you and Cassidy is tasty, but..."

I punch him in the arm, even though I know he's just kidding.

"Hey, it's not me who can't keep his clothes on." Tristan laughs.

"That would be me." Brandon comes outside shirtless and barefoot, wearing a pair of low-slung black jeans.

"Have you moved in, too?" Delilah scoots closer to Tristan and pats the step beside her.

Brandon sits down, takes the beer from Tristan, and guzzles it down. "Ahh. I stay here sometimes."

"Yes, well, I *know* that. Where do you actually live these days?" Delilah asked.

Brandon shrugged. "I guess here most of all, but sometimes I stay at Brent's or I go home with a hookup. Why?" He looks at me. "Just tell me if it's a problem, Army. I'll take off. And I'm sorry about the ménage the other night."

"Whatever, dude. Just keep it behind closed doors." I don't care what Brandon does with his sex life, but I don't need to see him in action.

Tristan arches a brow at me. I laugh.

"How about you, hon?" Tristan asks Delilah. "Are you coming home, or what?"

She shrugs. "Right now I'm enjoying staying with Brooke and hanging out with Ash. I'll be back, but the therapist thinks it's a good idea for me to be on my own for a while. Well, not really on my own, but you know what I mean."

I reach across Tristan's lap and squeeze Delilah's hand. "Whatever you need, Dee. Come back when you're ready. This house is as much yours as it is mine, as is the bar and everything else they left us."

"I go in to take a shower and you guys have a party without me?" Cassidy crosses the deck and crouches behind me. "Hey, Delilah."

"Hi, Cassidy. Have you spoken to your parents? Feeling any better?"

I turn and notice Cassidy's eyes become serious.

"Yeah, I spoke to them yesterday morning."

"You did? You never mentioned it."

She looks down and fidgets with her toe ring. "Um, yeah. You were at work. I guess I forgot. We talked, and they didn't really say much more about the divorce. They said they just grew apart, but I'm thinking about taking the job in New York."

The world falls out of focus. "You are?" This isn't something I want to discuss with everyone looking at me like they pity me.

She nods. "Thinking about it. I haven't decided. I'd see my parents more, and they're right about the opportunity. There *would* be lots of career growth. It's a big city."

I rise to my feet, trying to tamp down the hurt and anger warring within me.

"Who are you convincing, Cass? Us or yourself?" It's a dick thing to say, and I regret it the minute I say it.

Tristan touches her foot. "Is that what you want?"

She shrugs. I'm so sick of shrugs I could puke. Is it that hard to answer a damn question? I have to escape before I say something else I shouldn't, like asking Cassidy why she'd believe a word her parents said, or why, if she wants career growth in accounting, she doesn't apply to one of the larger companies here in Harborside.

"I'm tired. I'm heading up to bed." I walk around the deck to the outside steps, ignoring the calls of the others. I'm halfway up the deck stairs to the second floor when I hear Cassidy running after me.

"Wait. Wyatt." She hurries up the stairs and follows me into my bedroom, then pulls the doors closed behind her. "Wyatt."

My entire body feels like it's on fire, and not in a good way. "What, Cass?"

351

Her sorrowful eyes find mine, and I know she sees how angry I am. But it's not just anger that I'm feeling. It's sadness, too, only I'm so sick of being sad that I can't deal with it.

"I didn't make a final decision yet." She hooks her finger in the waist of my pants and looks up at me. I can't stay angry. One look and her eyes pull me under her spell.

"Didn't you?"

"Not really, and besides, you said we could make it work even if I went to New York, so why are you so mad?"

I turn away from her, feeling like a prick for my reaction, but the thought of being away from Cassidy is painful enough. I can't imagine it coming true, not after we just found each other. I want to push the thought of being apart away and kick the shit out of it.

"Wy?" She wraps her arms around me from behind, and I force all of my feelings to remain at bay while I turn to face her.

"I'm sorry. Yes, I said we could make it work, and we will. But I feel like an outsider, Cass. You told me to stay out of your decision. We don't even talk about it, and then you come down and drop that bomb, that you're seriously considering it, when we're with everyone else?"

"I'm sorry. I didn't mean for it to come out like that."

"How did you mean for it to come out?" I hold her stare until she drops her eyes to my chest, then presses her forehead to it and shrugs.

"Stop shrugging." Despite how upset I am, I wrap

her in my arms, because above all else, I want to be with her. I want to protect her and love her, and even though I'm hurt, it doesn't change any of those feelings.

"I'm sorry. I just..."

I press a kiss to the top of her head and hug her against me. "It's okay, Cass. I just want to be part of your life. I don't want to feel like an afterthought."

She looks up at me. "You're anything but an afterthought. This isn't easy for me, either."

"I thought you realized that you didn't like accounting very much anymore." I take her hand, and we sit on the bed together.

"I don't."

My tone softens because I fear she's trying to gain her parents' approval, and it kills me that they still have that hold on her.

"So what are you doing, Cassidy?"

She pulls her hand from mine and fidgets with the blanket. I wish she didn't look so conflicted.

"If you were one hundred percent on board with this job, I'd understand, but you're not, Cassidy. Anyone can see that. So that means you're using it as a way to get away from me, that you're considering it for a reason other than the work."

She gets up, and I take her hand in mine and pull her down on my lap. "I'm a thickheaded guy, remember? You need to clue me in if there's something going on between us that I don't know about."

"There's not. I promise. I love you, Wyatt."

"Then what is it, babe? Is it your parents?"

Her face flushes, and it's all the answer I need.

"Aw, Cass. They've got you under their thumb, babe. You've been down that road before."

"Don't, Wyatt. Just don't go there." She stands and walks to the bedroom door.

My gut clenches. "I can't sit by and watch them do this to you again, Cass. I know you don't want to hear it, but they aren't good to you. You're worth more than the few seconds of attention they give you."

"Gosh, Wyatt. You'll say anything to get me to stay."

I reach for her, but she backs away and into the hall.

"Will I, Cass? Or am I just telling you what you already know but don't want to hear?"

She storms down the hall and I follow her. I can't stop myself.

"They'll hurt you, Cassidy. They won't see you any more than they have for the last twenty years. You know that. You're too smart to get hooked into their bullshit."

~Cassidy~

I STOMP INTO my room, wishing he'd stop talking, because everything he's saying is true. But maybe this time it'll be different. Maybe this time my parents will realize how wrong they've been all this time.

"I'm sorry, Cass." Wyatt's voice is soft and caring, and I know it's killing him to hear that I'm considering going, despite how badly I know he wants to be supportive.

I can't look at him. I fold my arms over my

stomach as tears slip down my cheeks. My mother might be wrong about a lot of things, but she was spot-on when she said that when the right guy came along, I wouldn't be able to breathe without him. "Just give me time to make a final decision, Wyatt. Please." I hardly recognize my own shaky voice.

I can feel the heat of him standing behind me. He brings warmth and comfort, and the rest of my room feels cold and foreign. I haven't slept in this room for so long that it doesn't feel like I ever did. I don't want to sleep in it now. I want to sleep with Wyatt, curled in his arms with his heart beating against my back.

He wraps me in his arms like he knows exactly what I need, and I can't believe I'm lucky enough to be the woman he chose to love. Out of all the women in the world, he's standing here with me, holding me, loving me, when I know no other woman would ever even think about leaving Wyatt. He's everything I could ever hope for in a boyfriend, and yet I'm still torn because of my stupid parents.

He presses his cheek to mine, and for a second I think he's going to try to convince me again that my parents are full of empty, manipulative promises, but he doesn't.

He holds me tighter.

"It's okay, babe. Whatever you decide, we'll figure it out. I'm sorry I lost my cool. Just the thought of you being disappointed again makes me nuts. But I get it. I understand, and we'll make it work." Wyatt kisses my cheek and leaves the room.

I stand there alone for a few minutes, feeling like I don't know who I am anymore. I hate that I'm even thinking about New York and my parents. I hate it so much, and yet I can't turn the thoughts off.

I debate going down the hall and crawling into Wyatt's bed, but I know I'm going to cry a hundred times tonight, and I don't want him to see me so upset. It will only make him dislike my parents even more. So I climb beneath the covers of this bedroom that feels cold and wrong and try to sleep.

An hour later I'm lying in bed watching the minutes tick by on the digital clock when I hear my bedroom door open. I know it's Wyatt without looking. I can feel his presence, and as he lifts the covers and slips beneath, curling his body around mine, a different type of tear slips down my cheek. A happy tear.

I snuggle against him and lace my fingers with his, knowing that no matter how many times I push him away, he's not like my parents. He'll never leave me.

Chapter Twenty-Nine

~Cassidy~

THE SKY IS gray the next morning, but despite the overcast day, Wyatt and I have breakfast on the deck. This is my favorite time of morning, before the rest of the town is shuffling about, when the beach feels serene and our bodies ease gracefully into the new day. I toss pieces of bread to the seagulls. Wyatt laughs when they swoop low, and I startle. I think about what it will be like waking up in New York, to the sounds of car horns and tires on pavement instead of waves breaking and the squawks of seabirds. I wonder how I'll feel putting on a skirt and heels and rushing to catch a train, living with my aunt Aggie, who's weird as pig shit.

"You okay?" Wyatt asks as he reaches for my hand, then kisses the back of it. I love when he does that. It's such a small thing, but I wonder how many twenty-two-year-old guys do that. Certainly none that I know.

"Yeah. Just thinking."

"Sorry I lost it last night." He moves his chair closer so our knees touch. "I was just taken by surprise."

"It's okay. I'm glad you came into my room. I missed you, and I couldn't sleep, but I didn't want you to see me so upset."

He leans forward and kisses me. "Not that I'm an expert on relationships, but if we're only supposed to share the good times, then we won't make it very long. My whole life is up and down. Good and bad."

"When did you get so relationship savvy?"

He smiles that easy smile that melts my heart. "Since I found a woman worth growing up for." His smile fades. "Cass, you told me I had to grow up, and I have. I am. If that's why you're considering leaving, then at least give me credit for what I *have* been able to fix. I handled the situation with Tim, and I'm doing the best I can with Delilah. I may not be my father, or yours, but I'm doing my best."

"It's not that, Wyatt. It's not you at all. I love who you are. I have total faith in you."

"Then what is it? I need to understand. If you leave me for New York, I just want to know why." His soulful eyes make my heart squeeze.

I can't tell him that my parents are pressuring me or that part of my stupid heart hopes they will really spend more time with me. Instead I shrug, which is lame and an unfair reaction, because I know how Wyatt feels about my parents, but it's all I can muster.

"A shrug? That's the explanation you give me?" He shakes his head and leans back in the chair.

"I'm sorry, I—" My phone rings, and my mother's number flashes on the screen.

He kisses me, then rises to his feet. "It's okay, Cass. Talk to your parents."

I watch him leave, and I'm so upset that my hands are shaking when I finally answer the call.

"Hi, Mom. What's up?"

"I wanted to let you know that your father and I have gone through our schedules, and if...*when* you move to New York, we probably won't be able to visit until at least Thanksgiving. Separately, of course. I think we can each stay for two days, and I was thinking that we'd go to dinner and..."

Thanksgiving? Two days? They can't even make time for me for another three months, and then it's only two days? I totally zone out. I don't want to listen to her plans that may or may not come true. I look over my shoulder at Wyatt leaning against the counter. His bare back is facing me. His cargo shorts are army green and remind me of his nickname, which makes me smile, because Wyatt never needed a nickname. His parents could have named him Grace and he'd still be the most rugged, bravest man I know.

I want to see him like this every morning. I want to wake up in his arms and I want to fall asleep beside him, whether I'm happy or sad. He's been there for me for seventeen years. *Seventeen years.* It blows me away. Almost every day for at least as long as I can remember, he's been there for me. When my parents traveled without me and his parents let me stay at his house, it was Wyatt who stayed up late talking me through my loneliness. It was Wyatt who carried me inside when I fell off a skateboard and hurt my knee. It was Wyatt who told me how beautiful I looked at senior prom when he refused to take a real date and took both me and Delilah instead. Wyatt understands when I need to eat a gallon of ice cream and cry over a stupid chick flick, or when I cover my eyes watching scary movies. And it's Wyatt who came into my room last night, when I know I hurt his feelings, and he pushed his own discomfort aside to make me feel better.

I have no idea what my mother's rambling about. Something having to do with sushi, and for once I'm not hanging on to the hope that she'll find room in her life for me, because my life is full. She can't change the past, and holding out for a future that will never happen will crush me. I've given up enough of my emotional energy for parents who probably never should have had a child in the first place. I'm not going to waste another second of my emotional energy on them when I have more love than I could ever dream of right here.

I finally understand what it felt like for Wyatt to risk giving in to his feelings for me. It's my turn. It's our turn. Time for me to take a risk.

"I always thought I was the mature one," I mumble, more to myself than to my mother.

"What?" my mother asks.

I look out at the ocean and pull my shoulders back, and my confidence is reflected in my voice. "I always thought I was the mature one. I thought I was more mature than Wyatt."

"Oh, honey. Wyatt Armstrong? You're far more

mature than him. He'll never grow up."

Her words sting, and my chest tightens. "No, you're wrong, Mom. He's more mature than I am. He's grown up."

"I hardly think that—"

"To be honest, I don't really care if you think he is or not." I can't believe I'm saying this, but I can't stop. I've hidden my feelings for too long. "Do you even remember that his parents died a month ago? Do you realize how much he and Delilah have gone through? Their parents took me in time and time again because you and Dad were jetting off somewhere, and you don't even have the decency to show up for the funeral." I'm screaming, and somewhere in the back of my mind I'm aware of a door opening, but I'm knee-deep in giving my mother shit for the last twenty-two years and not about to stop.

"We were across the country," she explains.

"So what? They were supposedly your friends. They took care of *me. Your* daughter. You know what, Mom?" I don't wait for her to answer. "You and Daddy are selfish. I'm ashamed to have even been thinking of leaving Wyatt with the hopes of seeing you."

"Leaving Wyatt?"

"Yes, Mother. You want the truth?" Tears stream down my cheeks. My body's shaking, and I have no idea how my legs manage to carry me down the steps of the deck and onto the sand, but they do.

"The truth is, I don't want to leave Harborside. I want to be a stupid girl who follows her heart instead of her head. I want to stay because I love Wyatt. I might love my job here, but that isn't the reason I want to stay, and I don't care that you think it makes me weak or pathetic, because I love Wyatt. And it feels good, Mom. He loves me, too."

"Cassidy, slow down. You're just confused."

I walk across the sand feeling empowered and brave, unable to keep the words from tumbling out of my mouth. "No, Mom. I am seeing clearly for the first time in my life. You and Dad need to hear this. I'm staying in Harborside, and if you think that makes me unworthy of what little love you dole out to me, well whoop-de-do, because guess what? I've been unworthy in your eyes since I was a little girl. And you know what else? I'm so fucking worthy, it's sick. I don't want to go to New York and live in some crazy city where I can't see the beautiful ocean or hear the waves at night. Where I can't fall asleep in Wyatt's arms or watch him running on the beach. I don't want to live where I'm afraid to walk around the streets alone. I love it here, and I don't care if you don't agree with my decision." A sudden calm comes over me, like I've been set free from years of oppression, and in a way, I have. I draw in a lungful of sea air and wipe the tears from my eyes.

"Cassidy, what about your plan?" she asks with a thread of anger.

I close my eyes and let the peaceful sounds of the sea drown out my mother's voice and focus on the breeze as it sweeps across my skin. I love it here. I love the smell of the ocean, the feel of the sticky sea air on my skin. I love the seaweed that lines the shore in the mornings and the gulls that call for food. I love my friends, who haven't once abandoned me, and I love

Wyatt. My head has finally caught up to my smart heart. I know I have a stupid grin on my face because I'm too happy not to, and I can hear my mother breathing hard into the phone, waiting for me to tell her my plan. But I can't. I think my father was wrong. Planning is *not* the only way to succeed in life. Following my heart is.

"Cassidy, what has gotten into you?" she asks.

I turn and nearly bump into Wyatt, who is standing wide-eyed behind me, his arms open, waiting to envelop me.

I gaze up at him as a smile spreads across my lips.

"Love, Mom. That's what's gotten into me. Something I'm starting to understand that you and Dad don't know much about."

I end the call and fall into Wyatt's arms. He holds my trembling body tight. His heart is slamming against mine in the same frantic rhythm, as he strokes my back, soothing me with his strong embrace.

"Does staying with you make me weak?" I ask.

I look up at him and see the question in his eyes. If I open my mouth again I know I'm going to cry. Not from sadness, but from knowing that I made the best decision of my life, for freeing myself from the confines of my parents, and for Wyatt and Delilah and their losses. He folds me into his arms and holds me like he's never going to let me go, and that seems like the best plan ever.

"Sweetheart, staying makes you a thousand times stronger than anyone I know."

Chapter Thirty

~Wyatt~

I LOCK THE bar behind me and reach for Cassidy's hand. It's been two weeks since she made her decision to stay with me in Harborside, and I can't remember a time when she seemed more relaxed. She's been working with Brooke, and they're putting together a plan to try to make a go of their party-planning business, which will include Cassidy as the event photographer, and I couldn't be happier for her—or for us. I can't imagine my life without her in it, and I feel like the luckiest guy on the planet that she stayed.

"Are you ready?" She's wearing the same minidress she wore the night she drank too much and slept in my bed, and a sweet smile that hasn't faded once since she made her decision.

"Yeah, more than ready." We walk to the end of the pier, where one of Dane Braden's boats is lit up with decorative white lights.

"Remind me how you know Dane Braden again?" Cassidy asks.

"Dane's older brother Treat, is married to my cousin Max. I hooked up Charley with him in the spring." Dane and his fiancée, Lacy, came into the Taproom last week to talk with me and Delilah about our parents and invited us all on a moonlight boat ride. Lacy and Cassidy hit it off right away.

Music is playing and our friends are already here. I considered having a goodbye ceremony for my parents tonight. I'm finally ready to deal with saying goodbye to them, but Delilah isn't ready, and I want to wait so we can do it together. When she's ready, we'll also deal with all the stuff they left us. For now, a night at sea with our friends is a welcome reprieve.

Jesse reaches down from the boat to help Cassidy up, then pulls her into his arms and kisses her cheek. "You made the right choice, Cass. Army's a good man."

"I think I like it better when you call me Wyatt." I don't mind that Tristan and Brandon still call me Army, but I've shed that college-boy attitude and grown into a responsible bar-owning adult, and Jesse has helped me with that transition. I want him to know that I take it seriously. I pat him on the back as I reach for Cassidy's hand again. I can't get enough of her, and I know by her smile that she feels the same way about me.

"Yeah, well, sometimes I revert to your nickname because I don't want you to forget that although you're a grown-up, you're still a twentysomething kid who deserves to have some fun."

"Not too much fun," Cassidy chimes in.

"Only with you, babe. Only with you." I press my lips to hers and feel a heavy hand on my shoulder.

"You got a license for those lips?" Dane is in his late thirties. He's got a few inches on me, thick dark hair, and eyes as dark as night, like each of his five siblings. He's got one strong arm wrapped around Lacy, and he pulls me into a hug with the other.

Cassidy is looking at me with so much love in her eyes I'm sure everyone else can see it, too. She's easily the most beautiful woman I've ever seen, but even if she were to lose her looks tomorrow, it wouldn't make a difference in how much I adore her. It's her heart that won me over time and time again, and I'll spend my life making sure she knows just how much I love her.

I know there will be ups and downs as she figures out things with her parents, and I'll do what I can to facilitate a friendship between them, but I'll be damned if I'll let anyone hurt her ever again. I think Cassidy was forced to grow up overnight, just as I was, only in a different way. I know that if we can weather the loss of my parents and her coming to grips with how her parents have treated her all this time, we can handle anything. We make a perfect team.

"When are you tying the knot?" I ask Dane. He and Lacy have been engaged for what feels like forever.

Lacy presses her hand to her stomach and sighs dreamily. "Soon. Very, very soon." The wind blows her blond, corkscrew curls across her cheeks.

Dane tucks a wayward strand behind her ear and kisses her cheek. "When Lacy tells me to walk down the aisle, I'll show up, and with the news we just received, hopefully it'll be in the next six months."

"News?" I notice Lacy's hand still resting on her stomach and feel a smile stretch across my cheeks. "Are you...?"

Lacy presses herself closer to Dane as her smile broadens, but she shakes her head.

"Oh, sorry. I just thought..." I get the feeling there's more to her smile than she's letting on.

"Maybe one day there'll be another little shark tagger in the world." Dane draws his shoulders back and kisses Lacy's cheek again.

"Or maybe," Lacy says, "we'll have a girl who hates sharks."

"Babe, I won't care if we have a boy or a girl, a shark lover or a land lover. You know I'll adore our baby." Dane motions to Jesse and Charley, and they begin untethering the boat from the dock, then he turns his attention back to me. "Any notion you had of being in charge of your relationship, Wyatt, you might as well toss it overboard right now. If you're smart, what your woman wants, she gets."

I pull Cassidy against me, and before I can respond, she does.

"I have all I want, and he's right here, right now."

Lacy reaches for Dane's hand. "You guys are so freaking cute."

"So are we." Dane winks at us, then points to the front of the boat, where our friends are gathered.

We join them at the bow, and it's windier than where we boarded. Cassidy's hair whips around her. I gather it in one hand, and her fingers brush mine as she fastens an elastic band around it. As Dane pilots the boat away from shore, the lights of the city fade to mere dots. Dane cuts the engine then, and it's pitch-black, save for the lights of our boat and the misty haze of the moon.

Brandon's sitting on the deck playing his guitar while Cassidy sings. Dane and Lacy are dancing to the slow beat. Ashley's sitting with Brooke and Jesse, talking about the party-planning business, and I'm standing at the railing with Delilah, who's looking out into the darkness. I put my arm around her.

"You okay, sis?"

"Yeah. I was just thinking about how much things have changed since Mom and Dad died, and how much things haven't changed at all."

"What do you mean, haven't changed at all? I feel like my entire world has shifted." I glance at Cassidy, who's singing her heart out and sounds like she's been heaven sent. I blow her a kiss.

"Yeah, yours has." Delilah sounds sad, and I know she's talking about her personal life.

"Dee, what can I do to help?"

She turns around and leans against the railing like I am. "Nothing. I just have to figure out how to navigate my life. We don't have to talk about it, Wy. I'll figure it out."

"It's okay. I want to help."

"I'm not sure you can. I'm not sure anyone can."

I follow her gaze to Ashley. "You and Ashley?" I can't hide the surprise in my voice. I thought Ashley was straight.

Delilah blushes and turns away. "No. No, Wyatt. God."

"What? She's great-looking and really sweet."

"She's also my closest friend right now, not to mention that I think she's straight." She shakes her head. "Besides, even if she's not, I've never been with a woman, so..."

This isn't new information for me. She never wanted to take the chance that our parents would get wind of her sexuality. "But now you can, Dee. No one here will judge you. We love you."

"Can we not talk about it? It's not just that. It's everything."

"The look Mom and Dad gave you?"

She steps back. "Wyatt, please. Let's not ruin tonight. I'll figure it out."

"Okay, but this stuff doesn't wig me out, you know. I might be able to help."

"I know, and I love you for that." She hugs me, then goes to sit beside Ashley.

Ashley leans over and whispers something that makes Delilah laugh, and somehow I know she'll be okay. Even if she has a long road ahead of her, she's surrounded by people who love her.

We're all pretty lucky to have each other. I used to think it was strange that my conservative parents opened a business in such a diverse place. I will never know what drew them here or why they stayed, but I think Dee and I are lucky they did.

I watch as Cassidy takes her camera from her bag and begins snapping pictures. I love the way she concentrates when she's taking pictures and gliding across the deck like she's in a trance. When she turns the camera on me, I smile, and she clicks off at least ten shots, then lowers the camera, and my father's voice comes back to me as strong as if he were standing right beside me. *And when you graduate and get a job and find the one woman who finally stays— who you want to stay—she won't care that there's not a chance in hell you'll ever figure her out.* I wish my father were here right now. I want to tell him that he was right.

"You look pretty cute with that haircut I gave you." She runs her hand along her camera strap.

I swoop her into my arms before she can lift it again. "Maybe I need to start paying you as my barber. I pay with sexual favors."

"Oh, look. You need another haircut."

I take her in a brain-numbing kiss, ignoring the cat calls from Brandon and Tristan. "Are you glad you decided to stay in Harborside?"

"Yes, but it's not Harborside that I stayed for." She slips the camera strap over her shoulder and entwines her arms around my neck. "I stayed for you. I'm Weak-Girl Cassidy, remember?"

"You have that so wrong, Stronger-Than-Anyone-I-Know Cassidy. I'm the luckiest guy on the planet, but I have to clear something up. Remember when I said that I couldn't think about us because I could barely handle myself?"

"Yeah."

"I was wrong. There is no me without you."

Please enjoy a preview of the next
Harborside Nights novel

HARBORSIDE NIGHTS
Book Two

#LGBT

MELISSA FOSTER

HARBORSIDE NIGHTS

Discovering Delilah

New York Times & USA Today Bestselling Author

MELISSA FOSTER

Chapter One

~Delilah~

"COMING OUT OF grief is like coming out of a long, dark tunnel." Meredith Garland folds her hands in her lap. Her feet are crossed at the ankles and tucked primly beneath her chair, one pointed toe touching the carpet. Her warm brown eyes slide around the room, slowing on each of the other four attendees of the grief-counseling session.

I've been coming to a grief-counseling support group for the past month at the YMCA. My friend Brooke Baker brought me to my first session, having attended herself a few years back to get over her own grief. Only she didn't lose her parents to the drunk driver of a tractor trailer like I did. She was merely getting over a bad breakup. Merely, because really. Can anything match the grief of losing your parents at twenty-two, on the evening of your college graduation, when you should be celebrating and making plans for your life?

Meredith is talking about the stages of grief, all of which I know by heart: denial, anger, bargaining, depression, and acceptance. When we first moved here after our parents were killed, my twin brother, Wyatt, was also dealing with his new feelings for our best friend, Cassidy. I, on the other hand, was not dealing with anything. I was thoroughly entrenched in denial. One night a guy forced himself on Cassidy, and Wyatt beat the crap out of him—and scared the daylights out of me. Wyatt went straight to anger, skipping over denial altogether. I couldn't watch Wyatt falling apart, so I moved in with Brooke, who has been a family friend for years. It's been a little more than two months now, and I've finally made it past denial. Now that I'm living at our beach house again, I'm trying really hard to find a way to deal with my grief as well as the personal desires that I've spent a lifetime repressing—and hiding from everyone I know other than Wyatt and Cassidy.

"You must learn to envision a future for yourself without those you have lost." Having lost her husband a few years back, Meredith says this with the confidence of someone who's achieved such a future. "Find ways to turn your memories into something you can live with and celebrate, rather than something that pulls you under."

Meredith smiles at me, but I'm unable to muster one in return because my toes are dipping in the anger pool. I'm not thinking about envisioning a future without grief. Although that would be nice, I'm pretty sure grief will be my partner for a very long time.

Sometimes it hides in the shadows, waiting to swallow me whole, while other times it's front and center, taking a bow for the way it's laid me out flat.

No, it's not grief I'm thinking about coming out of, and I can't return Meredith's smile because my parents left me a legacy of fear and shame. The dark tunnel I'm thinking about coming out of feels even scarier than grief. I steal a glance at the other people in the group and envy the way they know who they are, even if they're a little lost at the moment. I envy the way Michael eyes me and the other girls in the room and how Mark and Cathy hold hands during the entire hour. I try not to look at Janessa, because I can't help but stare, and I know how rude that is. She's a little older than me, and I don't have to look to know that her head is held higher than mine and her cocoa-brown eyes glisten with a surety that I can't even imagine how to possess. She wears shorts and loose shirts that show her cleavage, and if I look at her, I know my eyes will be drawn to the swell of her breasts and the curve of her bare shoulder as her blouse slips down, which it always does.

My attraction to Janessa is not because I want her. It's not the same heart-pounding, palm-sweating, I-can't-breathe attraction that I have to my friend Ashley. It's more of an appreciation of her beauty and her confidence, and for the first time in my life I have no one standing in my way of acting on my feelings toward girls. I am free to look at whomever I please and feel whatever my body wants to feel. I'm free to come out, but thanks to my parents' disapproval, my desires are still tightly encased in shame, so I don't lift my eyes to admire Janessa.

Come out.

Gosh, if that isn't the stupidest phrase in the world, then I don't know what is. Do straight people have to come out and announce they're straight? For that matter, do they even think about their sexuality in terms of caring how others perceive them? I think the whole idea of coming out makes it ten times worse for someone like me, whose parents were ultraconservative and made no bones about their opinions against same-sex relationships. I was both elated and mortified when states began to debate same-sex marriages. Elated because, let's face it, it's a personal decision that others shouldn't have a say in, and mortified because it meant that every time the issue was mentioned in the news, I'd have to sit through my parents' lectures about why same-sex relationships are wrong. And weak little me never wanted to rock the boat, so I hid my attractions. All of them. My whole life. I even went so far as to hook up with a few guys to try to fit in and figure out if I was sure I liked girls. Well, I know I don't get all fluttery inside like I have over the years when I've been attracted to girls, and I definitely don't get wet between my legs over guys, like I do over Ashley. But then again, I've never been intimate with a woman, so my only validation is what I've felt toward women, and more specifically, what I feel when I'm with her.

Ashley.

Ashley. Ashley. Ashley.

I even love her name. It's feminine and confident, just like her.

After our parents died, everything about our Connecticut house, from the conservative neighborhood to the house itself, felt repressive, stifling. When Wyatt suggested that we come to Harborside after the funeral, I practically ran to the car. I met Ashley the first night after we arrived, at a party at our house, and I haven't been able to stop thinking about her since. She came with Brandon, and I remember thinking that she was the prettiest girl I'd ever seen, then immediately pushing that thought away because I felt like, even dead, my parents could read my thoughts. Ashley and I clicked right away. When we decided to do shots, Jesse took everyone's keys so no one would drink and drive. We have seven bedrooms, but that first night the downstairs beds weren't made up yet, so Ashley slept on the futon in my bedroom. I think I spent the whole night staring at her.

I think about her all the time, count down the hours until I'll see her again, and I swear when she's around, gravity doesn't exist. It's really hard to stay grounded and focused around her, because I spend my time admiring her and wanting to touch her. Not even make out with, just touch, like when you sit with someone who's funny and warm and smart and you want to be closer to them. That's me with Ashley—although I also want to make out with her. God, do I want to.

My pulse quickens, and I shift in my seat. I can't even think about her without getting all hot and bothered.

I guess I zoned out because the counseling session

is over and everyone's leaving. It's late summer, and when I step outside, the cool evening air stings my cheeks and clears my head. I head down the concrete steps and start my short walk home to our beach house. When my parents died, my twin brother, Wyatt, and I inherited everything—the house in Connecticut where we grew up, the beach house here in Harborside, Massachusetts, where we've spent summers since we were kids, and the Taproom, the best bar and grill in town. We've been living here and running the bar for a little more than two months, and Wyatt and I finally decided to sell the house in Connecticut this fall. Too many ghosts in that house.

"Wait up." Janessa jogs to catch up. "Are you okay? You seemed down tonight."

"I'm okay, thanks. Just thinking." We walk down the dimly lit residential street toward the lights of the boardwalk. Harborside is small enough to walk most places but still big enough that the outskirts of town are more secluded and less commercialized.

"Yeah, that's kind of what this whole grief-counseling thing is supposed to do to us, right? Make us introspective and force us to deal with our feelings."

I know Janessa lost a family member, but she was already attending the group sessions when I started, and she's never said exactly who it was that she lost. I'm not about to ask. If there's one thing I've learned in group, it's that when people want to talk about their grief, they'll bring it up.

"Yeah, I guess it is."

"Want to grab a cup of coffee at Brooke's Bytes?"

"Brooke's is so crowded at night. How about someplace else?" I try to say it casually, but the truth is, counseling leaves me feeling uneasy, and the last place I want to be is near giddy teenagers in a boardwalk café. Not to mention that my friend Brooke owns the café, and I really just want to be away from people I know while I come down from group.

Janessa's eyes drop from mine, linger around my mouth, then lift to my eyes again. Her scrutiny makes me nervous, but it feels good at the same time, and I'm not sure how to handle it, so I tuck my hair behind my ear to distract myself.

"Sure," she says. "The Sandbar, over on Shab Row?"

The Sandbar is a pub, so I know we won't be drinking coffee. Ashley is working at the surf shop tonight, and my other friends are just hanging out at home, which means I have no plans, and looking at Janessa all night is not a hardship, so I agree.

Shab Row is a quiet street with old-fashioned, bulbous streetlights on tall black poles, brick pavers, and only a handful of shops. Unlike the many commercial streets of Harborside, which boast bright signs and sidewalk displays, Shab Row is more subdued. The signs have muted colors of slate blue, maroon, and earth tones, and the most paraphernalia that I've ever seen outside are holiday lights on the wrought-iron railings lining the steps into the shops and pub.

The bar is dimly lit and nearly empty. We sit at a booth in the back and order drinks from a tall, slim waiter who looks like he wants to be anywhere but here. My phone vibrates and my heart skips a beat when Ashley's name appears on the screen.

It's kind of pathetic that I'm crushing on her so hard that I get excited over seeing her name on my phone.

How was counseling? I smile as I read her text, loving that she cares enough to ask.

"Boyfriend?" Janessa asks as the waiter returns with our drinks.

I shake my head and laugh as I reply to Ashley. Fine. Having a drink with a girl from the session. Still on for sketching sunrise tomorrow? Ashley and I have been meeting at sunrise or sunset a few times each week. She paints landscapes, and I'm teaching her to sketch. It's about the only hobby that I have, but I'm pretty good at it. The only problem is, I'm usually so busy looking at Ashley that I don't get much sketching done when we're together.

"Why did you laugh?" Janessa sips her drink as I read Ashley's confirmation for tomorrow, then set my phone aside.

Ashley's my first real girl crush ever—although it feels like a hell of a lot more than a crush. I have to stop lusting after her. Not knowing if Ash is straight or into girls leaves me longing for someone I'll probably never have. Besides, having absolutely zero intimate experience with girls, I can't even be sure that I'd enjoy the sexy side of being with her if she is into me. When Ashley and I are together, we don't really talk about frivolous stuff like hooking up with people. It's like we're so in sync with each other that nothing else even exists. I guess between learning to run the

Taproom and dealing with moving in and out of the beach house—which I know hurt Wyatt's feelings—and trying to deal with the death of my parents, my focus has pretty much been on survival. And when Ash and I are together, I'm working so hard to ignore my burgeoning feelings for her that I avoid any topics having to do with dating or hooking up.

"Hello? Delilah?" Janessa waves her hand in front of my eyes.

"I'm sorry. I totally zoned out."

"Yeah, I noticed you did that at counseling, too. You sure you're okay?" She tilts her head, and her long dark hair slips over her shoulder. She reminds me of Megan Fox, except Megan's eyes look sharp and catlike, like she's always either on the prowl or ready for the paparazzi. Janessa's are a little larger, slightly rounder, and usually thoughtful or filled with compassion, as they are now.

"Yes." I down half of my drink.

"So, are you going to tell me why you laughed when I asked if you had a boyfriend?" Her lips curl up in a smile, revealing a row of perfect pearly whites beneath.

I run my finger over the rim of my glass to keep her from seeing what's going through my mind. I was always so afraid of my parents finding out that I thought I liked girls that I admitted it only to Wyatt and Cassidy.

"Okay, here's the thing." Janessa reaches across the table and covers my hand with hers. "I know you're grieving for your parents, and my heart goes out to you. It's going to take a really long time to deal with that, but I can see that something else is going through that pretty little mind of yours, and if you want to talk about it, I'm here."

Pretty little mind? She leaves her hand on mine. It's warm and soft and makes my pulse speed up. Did I misread her? Is she into me? Me? Why would she be? Do I look like a lesbian? No woman has ever come onto me before.

"Thanks, Janessa." I finish my drink and move my hand, feeling a little queasy.

She waves the waiter over and orders another round of drinks. "So...was that your girlfriend on the phone?"

My eyes shoot to hers.

"It was just a guess." She holds both hands up in surrender, then leans across the table and lowers her voice. "But your look is very telling."

"She's not my girlfriend." I feel my cheeks heat up, but I can't look away from Janessa as she arches a brow. We've spoken only a handful of times. How can she possibly guess this about me?

"But...you wish she was?" Janessa's phone rings and she holds up her index finger. "Hold that thought." She looks at me as she answers the call, and the attention makes me even more nervous. "Hi, baby. Are you going night-night?"

Night-night? Oh my gosh. I'm thinking she's into me and she's a mom? She's probably married. My radar is totally off. My stomach feels like there's a tornado brewing inside me. I look away, embarrassed that I was so far off base.

"Okay, sweetheart. Have fun with Uncle Dean." She

blows a kiss into the phone, then holds up her finger again. "Hey, Dean. Yeah. She's okay? Great. Okay. I'll be there tomorrow morning." She pauses. "Okay. Love you, too." She ends the call and stuffs her phone into her purse. "I'm sorry. My little girl is staying with my brother for their weekly slumber party."

"You have a daughter?" If I was wrong about how she was looking at me, how will I ever know when someone's really interested?

"Mm-hm. Jackie, she's three. Here, I'll show you a picture of her." She pulls her phone back out and scrolls through pictures, then reaches across the table and shows me a picture of the most adorable little brown-haired girl. Janessa is lying on a bed hugging Jackie, cheek to cheek.

"Aw, she's so cute. She looks just like you, too."

She shows me a bunch more pictures, and in every one she and Jackie are both smiling. Even in the picture of Jackie sleeping on Janessa's shoulder, it looks like the little girl is smiling.

"What does your husband do?"

She puts her phone away. "Oh, I'm not married." She locks eyes with me. "And I'm not straight, either."

"Oh." It comes out as a whisper, and the fact that I can't even answer like a normal human being embarrasses me. I wonder if she adopted Jackie. She must have...No. She could have used artificial insemination. Or maybe Jackie's her girlfriend's child? I'm not curious because I'm interested in her. I've never thought past one day having a girlfriend—which in itself seems like a fantasy. I'm curious about how it all works.

"Delilah, I'm going out on a limb here, so feel free to tell me if I'm off base, but you haven't come out yet, have you?"

I sigh, but this time I don't look away. I have to start somewhere, and I've already admitted more to her verbally and nonverbally than I have to anyone else, so I force myself to answer her.

"I hate that term."

"I hate it, too," she admits. "So, are you out?"

I shake my head.

"Aw, Delilah. I'm sorry. I didn't mean to—"

"It's okay, really. I'm...This is all new to me. My parents were very conservative, so..."

"So, you never told them?" Her brows knit together. "Want to talk about it?"

"I told them right before I walked for graduation, but they weren't very supportive." I feel my eyes tear up and I down my drink in one gulp. When I told my parents that I liked girls, they looked at me like I disgusted them, and it nearly took me to my knees. They never said a word about my confession after graduation, but it was chaotic. There were pictures to deal with and congratulations from friends and my aunt Lara who had come with them to watch me and Wyatt graduate.

I push the memories away and blink several times, trying to repress my tears. "I'm sorry. Can we not talk about my parents?"

"Of course. I'm sorry. I'm being too nosy."

"No, it's not that. Actually, I like talking to you. This is the first time I've had a conversation like this. It feels good to get some of it out in the open."

She smiles. "I like talking to you, too."

"I don't really talk about this stuff with anyone else. My brother, Wyatt, tries to talk to me about it, but it feels weird even though he's supportive."

"Listen, I get it. My parents were surprised to find out that my brother, Dean, and I weren't straight." Her eyes fill with sadness, and just as quickly, that sadness is replaced with something else. Determination? Acceptance? I'm not sure.

"Our parents came around, and they're very supportive, but I've dated women whose families weren't exactly on board with their lifestyles, and I know how hard it can be."

"Even around here? Harborside is so diverse. I still can't figure out why my parents had a summer house here and bought the Taproom."

"Your parents owned the Taproom?"

"Yeah, well, Wyatt and I do now." Knowing that she understands my situation puts me at ease.

"So..." She sips her drink and lifts her chin in the direction of my phone. "Want to tell me about the texter we're not talking about?"

I laugh. "Ashley. I just met her at the beginning of the summer, and she's..." My heart is sprinting in my chest, and I can feel a goofy smile coming on.

"Uh-huh. You have a major crush on Ashley. So, what's the problem?"

"Take your pick. I've never kissed a girl. I have no idea if she's into girls or guys, and oh yeah, did I say I have never even kissed a girl?" I know I'm blushing, but at the same time, it feels so good to get the words out that I can't seem to stop myself.

"Never? Didn't you say in therapy that you just graduated from college?"

I nod, knowing what's coming next.

"And you never explored your sexuality?"

I shake my head.

"You never got drunk and kissed your best friend, or got into a little girl-on-girl action and blamed it on the alcohol?"

I laugh and shake my head again. "That would have been a good idea, if I drank a lot, but I was too afraid of my parents catching wind of it. And believe me, they would not have approved. I have no idea what they would have done, but the idea of them finding out and...I don't know, refusing to pay my college tuition, or just making me feel worse than I already did..." I shrug again, unable to believe how I'm opening up to her. She's so easy to talk to, and I feel oddly safe sitting in this dimly lit corner booth, spilling my heart to her.

"Oh, Delilah. No offense, but your parents did a job on you. At least you're in the right place to figure it all out, and it sounds like your brother is supportive even if you don't want to talk to him. Believe me, support is everything." She finishes her drink and slaps money on the table. "Want to get out of here and walk for a while?"

"Sure. Thanks for the drinks." We grab our stuff, and once we're outside she loops her arm into mine, like a friend who's known me for years.

"I promise you, Delilah. It won't always feel like you're living in a fishbowl. Life has a way of working itself out, and there will come a time when you know you're on the right path, and when that happens, you'll stop worrying about what everyone else thinks."

A fishbowl. That's exactly what I feel like, even though my parents are gone. They drove their beliefs into my head so strongly that I can't get out from under the feeling of being scrutinized. Walking with Janessa is nothing like walking with Ashley, where I'm dissecting every step, every breath, searching for hints that might reveal if she's into me or not. Being with Janessa is different. Then again, no one makes me feel like I do when I'm with Ashley.

When we come to my street, I stop walking. Janessa stops, too, our arms still linked. It feels nice to have another friend.

"This is my street. So I guess I'll see you next week?"

"Yeah, sure." She steps in closer and touches my hip, causing goose bumps to race up my limbs. "Delilah, I know your heart is wrapped around Ashley. I can see that when you talk about her, and that's such a good feeling. But I've also been where you are, with no experience."

Her eyes are warm and her touch is caring, not pushy. Even though I'm crossing into new territory by opening up to her, and even though my stomach is more nervous than a fly on a lily pad, I don't retreat. And I don't feel like she's coming onto me, although there is something in her eyes, her touch, the sensual sound of her voice, that makes my breathing become shallow.

"Every woman deserves to feel safe when she has her first experience and to feel confident when they're with the woman they care about." Her eyes never waver from mine. "If you ever want to...you know...explore that side without the pressure of doing it right or the embarrassment of feeling inexperienced..."

Ohgodohgodohgod.

"I'm here for you, as a nonjudgmental friend. My life now is all about Jackie. I don't have room for anything more than sharing an intimate night. Or a few. Or whatever. I'm not looking for a girlfriend or a quick hookup. I'm offering to help, and trust me, there's a big difference between hooking up with someone and overcoming your fears in a safe environment." She smiles like she hasn't just sucked all the air from the world, and it's all I can do to remain erect.

I can hardly believe she's offering herself up to me, but more than that, I can hardly believe I'm considering it.

(End of Sneak Peek)

To continue reading, be sure to pick up the next Harborside Nights release:

DISCOVERING DELILAH

Please enjoy the first chapter of the first
Love in Bloom novel

Sisters in Love

Snow Sisters, Book One

Love in Bloom Series

Melissa Foster

"A beautiful story about love and self-growth and
finding that balance to happiness. Powerfully written
and riveting from beginning to end."
—*National bestselling author Jane Porter*

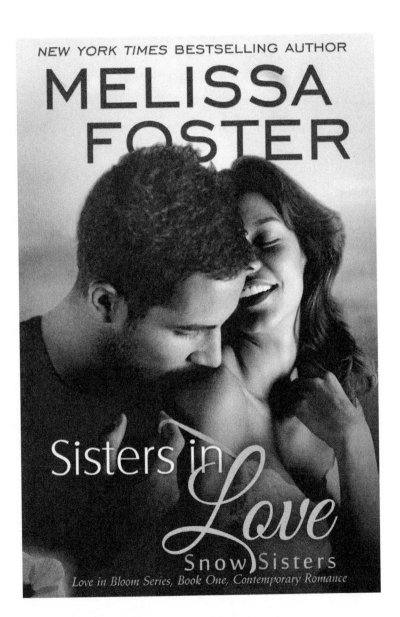

NEW YORK TIMES BESTSELLING AUTHOR

MELISSA FOSTER

Sisters in *Love*

Snow Sisters

Love in Bloom Series, Book One, Contemporary Romance

Chapter One

THE LINE IN the café went all the way to the door. Danica Snow wished she hadn't taken her sister Kaylie's phone call before getting her morning coffee. Living in an overcrowded tourist town could be a major inconvenience, but Danica loved that she could walk from her condo to her office, see a movie, have dinner, or even stop at a bookstore without ever sitting in a car. Every minute counted when you lived in Allure, Colorado, host to an odd mix of hippie and yuppie tourists in equal numbers. The ski slopes brought them in the winter, while art shows drew them in the summer. There was never a break. Every suit and Rasta child in town was standing right in front of her, waiting for their coffee or latte, and the guy ahead of her had shoulders so wide she couldn't easily see around him. Danica tapped the toe of her efficient and comfortable Nine West heels, growing more impatient by the second.

What on earth was taking so long? In seven minutes they'd served only one person. The tables were pushed so close to the people standing in line that she couldn't step to the side to see. She was gridlocked. Danica leaned to the right and peered around the massive shoulder ahead of her just as the owner of that shoulder turned to look out the door. *Whack!* He elbowed her right in the nose, knocking Danica's head back.

Her hand flew to her bloody nose. "Ow! Geez!" She ducked in pain, covering her face and talking through her hands. "I think you broke my nose." Each word sent pain across her nose and below her eyes.

"I'm so sorry. Let me get you a napkin," a deep, worried voice said.

Two patrons rushed over and shoved napkins in her direction.

"Are you okay?" an older woman asked.

Tears sprang from the corners of Danica's closed eyes. *Damn it.* Her entire day would now run late and she probably looked like a red-nosed, crying idiot. "This hurts so bad. Weren't you looking where—" Danica flipped her unruly, brown hair from her face and opened her eyes. Her venom-filled glare locked on the man who had elbowed her—the most beautiful specimen of a human being she had ever seen. *Oh shit.* "I'm...What...?" *Come on, girl. Get it together. He's probably an egomaniac.*

"I'm so sorry." His voice was rich and smooth, laden with concern.

A thin blonde grabbed his arm and shoved a napkin into his hand. "Give this to her," she said, blinking her eyelashes in a come-hither way.

The man held the woman's hand a beat too long.

"Thanks," he said. His eyes trailed down the blonde's blouse.

Really? I'm bleeding over here.

He turned toward Danica and handed her the napkin. His eyes were green and yellow, like field grass. His eyebrows drew together in a serious gaze, and Danica thought that maybe she'd been too quick to judge—until he stole a glance at the blonde as she walked out of the café.

Asshole. She felt the heat of anger spread up her chest and neck, along her cheeks, to the ridge of her high cheekbones. She snagged the napkin from his hand and wiped her throbbing nose. "It's okay. I'm fine," she lied. She could smell the minty freshness of his breath, and she wondered what it might taste like. Danica was not one to swoon—that was Kaylie's job. *Get a grip.*

"Can I at least buy you a coffee?" He ran his hand through his thick, dark hair.

Yes! "No, thank you. It's okay." She had been a therapist long enough to know what kind of guy eyes another girl while she was tending to a bloody nose that he had caused. Danica fumbled for her purse, which she'd dropped when she was hit. She lowered her eyes to avoid looking into his. "I'm fine, really. Just look behind you next time." Not for the first time, Danica wished she had Kaylie's flirting skills and her ability to look past his wandering eyes. She would have had him buying her coffee, a Danish, and breakfast the next morning.

Danica was so confused, she wasn't even sure what she wanted. She chanced another glance up at him. He was looking at her features so intently that she felt as though he were drinking her in, memorizing her. His eyes trailed slowly from hers, lowered to her nose, to her lips, and then settled on the beauty mark that she'd been self-conscious of her entire life. She felt like a Cindy Crawford wannabe. Danica pursed her lips. "Are you done?" she asked.

He blinked with the innocence of a young boy, clueless to her annoyance, which was in stark contrast to his confident, manly presence. He stood almost a foot taller than Danica's impressive five foot seven stature. His chest muscles bulged beneath his way-too-small shirt, dark curls poking through the neckline. *He probably bought it that way on purpose.* She glanced down and tried not to notice his muscular thighs straining against his stonewashed denim jeans. Danica swallowed hard. All the air suddenly left her lungs. He was touching her shoulder, squinting, evaluating her face.

"I'm sorry. I was just making sure it didn't look broken, which it doesn't. I'm sure it's painful."

She couldn't think past the heat of his hand, the breadth of it engulfing her shoulder. "It's okay," she managed, hating herself for being lost in his touch when he was clearly someone who ate women for breakfast. She checked her watch. She had three minutes to get her coffee and get back to her office before her next client showed up. *Belinda. She'd love this guy.*

The line progressed, and Adonis waved as he left the café. Danica reached into her purse to pay for her French vanilla coffee and found herself taking a last glance at him as he passed the front window.

The young barista pushed Danica's money away. "No need, hon. Blake paid for yours." She smiled, lifting her eyebrows.

"He did?" *Blake.*

"Yeah, he's really sweet." The barista leaned over the cash register. "Even if he is a player."

Aha! I knew it. Danica thrust her shoulders back, feeling smart for resisting temptation.

(End of Sneak Peek)

Check online retailers for the Snow Sisters series

SISTERS IN LOVE (Snow Sisters, Book One)

Watch for the complete
Harborside Nights series

Find the complete release schedule at
www.MelissaFoster.com

SIGN UP for MELISSA'S NEWSLETTER to stay up to date with new releases, giveaways, and events

NEWSLETTER:
http://www.melissafoster.com/newsletter

CONNECT WITH MELISSA

TWITTER:
https://twitter.com/Melissa_Foster

FACEBOOK:
https://www.facebook.com/MelissaFosterAuthor

WEBSITE:
http://www.melissafoster.com

STREET TEAM:
http://www.facebook.com/groups/melissafosterfans

Complete LOVE IN BLOOM SERIES

SNOW SISTERS
Sisters in Love
Sisters in Bloom
Sisters in White

THE BRADENS
Lovers at Heart
Destined for Love
Friendship on Fire
Sea of Love
Bursting with Love
Hearts at Play
Taken by Love
Fated for Love
Romancing my Love
Flirting with Love
Dreaming of Love
Crashing into Love
Healed by Love

THE REMINGTONS
Game of Love
Stroke of Love
Flames of Love
Slope of Love
Read, Write, Love

SEASIDE SUMMERS
Seaside Dreams
Seaside Hearts
Seaside Sunsets
Seaside Secrets
Seaside Nights
Seaside Whispers
Seaside Lovers

Seaside Embrace

HARBORSIDE NIGHTS SERIES
Includes characters from
Love in Bloom series

Catching Cassidy
Discovering Delilah
Chasing Charley
Tempting Tristan
Embracing Evan
Reaching Rusty
Loving Livi

More Books by Melissa

Chasing Amanda (mystery/suspense)
Come Back to Me (mystery/suspense)
Have No Shame (historical fiction/romance)
Love, Lies & Mystery (3-book bundle)
Megan's Way (literary fiction)
Traces of Kara (psychological thriller)
Where Petals Fall (suspense)

Acknowledgments

I have been spending summers on Cape Cod since I was a toddler, and those of you who regularly read my work and have enjoyed the Love in Bloom series know that the Cape is truly my favorite place on earth. When I first started to develop the Harborside Nights series, I was going to set the series in Provincetown, Massachusetts, because it's a very diverse community that I adore. I quickly realized that Harborside was quite different from Provincetown. Even though it's an artsy community that is very diverse and accepting, the flavor of the town was very different from any town I had ever visited, and Harborside came to be a fictional world of its own.

I want to share with you the feedback that I received before writing this series. I was warned not to write about gay and lesbian couples unless I wrote under a pen name. I was told it would upset my readership, and upsetting my readership is the last thing I want to do. However, hiding behind a pen name is sending a message I don't believe in. I trust my readers, and because I have such faith in their love of *love* and their enjoyment of my storytelling abilities, I proudly wrote these stories under my own name. For readers who do not wish to read about same-sex relationships, those books have been clearly marked with "LGBT" on the retailer pages, and the covers reveal the nature of the relationships. I can assure that, as always, the stories are written with raw emotions and real issues.

A hearty thank you to my good friend Greg

Cassidy for taking the time to answer my questions about photography. As always, kudos goes to my editorial team: Kristen Weber and Penina Lopez, and my proofreaders: Jenna Bagnini, Juliette Hill, Marlene Engel, and Lynn Mullan, for bringing readers the cleanest read possible. I am indebted to Elizabeth Mackey for my amazing Harborside Nights covers. I can't stop looking at them!

Last but never least, thank you to my supportive husband and family, who make my writing possible.

Melissa Foster is a *New York Times* and *USA Today* bestselling and award-winning author. Her books have been recommended by *USA Today's* book blog, *Hagerstown* magazine, *The Patriot*, and several other print venues. She is the founder of the World Literary Café, and when she's not writing, Melissa helps authors navigate the publishing industry through her author training programs on Fostering Success. Melissa also hosts Aspiring Authors contests for children and has painted and donated several murals to the Hospital for Sick Children in Washington, DC.

Visit Melissa on her website or chat with her on social media. Melissa enjoys discussing her books with book clubs and reader groups and welcomes an invitation to your event.

Melissa's books are available through most online retailers in paperback and digital formats.

CPSIA information can be obtained at www.ICGtesting.com
Printed in the USA
BVOW08s0312010216

434462BV00006B/87/P